Robert Rankin ('The drinking man's H.G. Wells' *Midweek*) describes himself as a 'teller of tales' and his work as 'far fetched fiction'. A seminal writer with a fluid style and a prodigious outflow, when once asked by an inspired talk-show host where he got his ideas from, he muttered something about his dog, made his excuses and left.

Robert Rankin is the author of *Sprout Mask Replica*, *Nostradamus Ate My Hamster*, *A Dog Called Demolition*, *The Garden of Unearthly Delights*, *The Most Amazing Man Who Ever Lived*, *The Greatest Show Off Earth*, *Raiders of the Lost Car Park*, *The Book of Ultimate Truths*, the *Armageddon* trilogy, and the *Brentford* quartet which are all published by Corgi Books. Robert Rankin's latest novel, *The Brentford Chainstore Massacre*, is now available as a Doubleday hardback.

Also by Robert Rankin

THE ANTIPOPE
THE BRENTFORD TRIANGLE
EAST OF EALING
ARMAGEDDON THE MUSICAL
THEY CAME AND ATE US,
ARMAGEDDON II: THE B-MOVIE
THE SUBURBAN BOOK OF THE DEAD,
ARMAGEDDON III: THE REMAKE
THE BOOK OF ULTIMATE TRUTHS
RAIDERS OF THE LOST CAR PARK
THE GREATEST SHOW OFF EARTH
THE GARDEN OF UNEARTHLY DELIGHTS
THE MOST AMAZING MAN WHO EVER LIVED
A DOG CALLED DEMOLITION
NOSTRADAMUS ATE MY HAMSTER
SPROUT MASK REPLICA

and published by Corgi Books

For Mike Petty
With Many Thanks . . .

THE SPROUTS OF WRATH

Robert Rankin

CORGI BOOKS

THE SPROUTS OF WRATH
A CORGI BOOK : 0 552 13844 4

Originally published in Great Britain in Abacus by
Sphere Books Ltd, a division of the Penguin Group

PRINTING HISTORY
Abacus edition published 1988
Corgi edition published 1993
Corgi edition reprinted 1993
Corgi edition reprinted 1995
Corgi edition reprinted 1997
Corgi edition reprinted 1998

Set in 10/11pt Compugraphic Paladium by
Colset Pte Ltd, Singapore

Corgi Books are published by Transworld Publishers Ltd,
61–63 Uxbridge Road, London W5 5SA,
in Australia by Transworld Publishers (Australia) Pty Ltd,
15–25 Helles Avenue, Moorebank, NSW 2170,
and in New Zealand by Transworld Publishers (NZ) Ltd,
3 William Pickering Drive, Albany, Auckland.

Printed and bound in Great Britain by
Cox & Wyman Ltd, Reading, Berkshire

Foreword

Brentford was enjoying another tropical summer.

Although torrents of rain fell unceasingly upon Hounslow, Ealing and Chiswick, and the gardeners of Kew had taken to the wearing of sou'westers and fisherman's waders, the good people of Brentford lazed in their deckchairs and sipped cooling drinks or strolled the historic thoroughfares in shorts and sunhats. Brentford was like that.

To commuters passing daily across the flyover, bound for the great metropolis somewhat east of Ealing, all seemed mundane enough. Lines of slate rooftops sheltering late Victorian houses, a gasometer, a watertower, a row of flatblocks. Nothing unusual here, one might have thought, nothing to inspire wonder, just another West London suburb. A few more acres of urban sprawl. But no. There was something more to Brentford than that. And though it was difficult to put a finger on just what that might be, it was definitely there all right. A very very special something.

Upon a May morning, shortly before the dawn, a long black automobile of advanced design and foreign extraction turned off the Great West Road, crested the railway bridge beside the Mowlems building and cruised soundlessly down towards the streets of Brentford.

Upon reaching the London Road, where the Arts Centre thrust its jagged shadow up towards the night sky, the car halted and a curiously stunted figure, clad in chauffeur's livery, emerged from it map in hand.

Having examined this carefully, by the light of a pentorch, he tapped with caution upon a blackly tinted rear window. The panel of glass slid away with a hiss and the chauffeur momentarily stiffened as an exhalation of stale and stagnant air filled his nostrils. Coughing politely into a scented handkerchief, he proffered the map to the unseen occupant of the rear compartment and said, 'The site lies just beyond the building, sir, upon the island. It is the last of the five. You now possess them all.'

A sigh issued from the rear compartment, a plaintive, yet unearthly sound, followed by an agitated wheezing, as of lungs far gone in chronic decay.

'Then all is as it should be,' hissed a voice, scarcely more than a choked whisper. 'And today the plan will be put into operation.'

The chauffeur dabbed at the cold sweat which had risen to his brow and accepted the return of his map with a trembling hand. Even through his white kid driving gloves he could feel that the paper was now cold and damp. He bowed stiffly, returned to his seat and put the curious vehicle once more in motion.

As the thin line of dawn broadened along the rooftops of Brentford, the car swung away towards Kew Bridge and was presently lost to view within the shadow of the great gasometer.

1

The dawn choristers completed their rowdy ovation to the new day as the *Brentford Mercury*'s driver tossed his first Friday bundle in the general direction of a cornershop doorstep. On high Olympus, the Fates, nodding in agreement across their breakfast ambrosia, declared the day officially begun.

Norman hoisted the bundle of weekly locals on to the worm-eaten countertop, where it struck with an appropriately dull thud and raised a glorious cloud of dust. The shopkeeper sighed with pleasure. Since the departure of his wife with a former editor of the borough's organ he had allowed the business to run magnificently to seed. His dust was the envy of every married man in the neighbourhood and Norman, revelling in each new pleasure afforded to him by his unexpected return to bachelorhood, was living, as he considered it, 'life to the full'. Upstairs last week's underpants lorded it upon the bedside rug; today's sartorial excesses stretched to a pair of odd and undarned socks and the garish Hawaiian shirt his wife had particularly hated. Norman had also recently cultivated a pair of ludicrous mutton-chop whiskers which he considered to be rather dashing.

'It's not a bad old life if you don't weaken,' he constantly informed his customers, adding guardedly that this was of course dependent upon not letting the bastards (whoever they were) grind you down.

Whistling tunelessly, between teeth of his own design and construction, Norman slid the blade of his reproduction Sword of Boda paperknife through the twine bindings and spread away the pink covering to expose the FRONT PAGE NEWS. There was always more than the merest hint of ceremony about this weekly routine. Something vaguely akin to the mystical, although performed subconsciously and without the solemnity generally accorded to ritual. But such was often the way of it in Brentford. Certain customs appeared to have acquired almost magical significance. Professor Slocombe's dawn perambulation of the borough boundaries, for example, or Neville the part-time barman's daily check of the Swan's beer engines. Such things were part of the 'vital stuff' of Brentford and a contributing factor towards the town's separateness from its neighbours. Brentford lacked the cosmopolitanism of Hounslow, the upward mobility of Ealing, the young professionalism of Chiswick and the aloof urbanity of Kew. It should not be surprising therefore to note that the initials of these surrounding territories spell out the word HECK, the nineteenth-century euphemism for hell.

Norman flung the length of knotted twine into an overflowing rubbish box beneath the counter, leant upon the threadbare elbows of his ragged shopcoat and took stock of the week's doings. The headline was not slow to engage his attention: INVISIBLE MYSTIC IN CHURCH HALL RUMPUS ran the generously inked banner headline filling a third of the front page. 'Guru Vanishes With The Takings As Fists Fly!'

Norman chuckled to himself as he read the account of how local warlock and self-styled miracle worker Hugo Rune, having failed to make good his promise to dematerialize before a capacity crowd, had performed an entirely different variety of vanishing act when the dissatisfied punters turned ugly and demanded the return of their money. Fearing possible damage to the Jacobean timbers of the newly restored church hall, Father Moity had telephoned for the police. During the ensuing punch-up there had been twelve arrests and the local constabulary were currently seeking the whereabouts of the perfect master.

Norman shook his head and turned the page.

BIRMINGHAM'S OLYMPIC HOPES GO UP IN SMOKE: 'Stadium Fire Ends Brum's Olympic Dreams'. Of course Norman had heard all this on the wireless set. The grim catalogue of mismanagement, bungling, inefficiency and chaos had been daily news for months. As David Coleman had said, 'The final kiss goodbye has long been on the cards.'

'Shame,' said Norman to no-one but himself, 'I thought I'd have a crack at the javelin.'

On a lower portion of the same page was an item that any other editor might well have considered to be front-page news: GOLD BULLION ROBBERY: 'Thieves Net Largest Ever Haul In Crime Of The Century'. Norman whistled once more through his home-made railings as he read the figure. Even allowing for the exaggeration of the *Mercury*'s cub reporter, Scoop Molloy, there seemed little doubt that this was, as the Sweeney's now legendary 'Guv' would have put it, 'One big blag, George.'

Exactly how the robbery had been carried out was still something of a mystery and Norman marvelled at the ingenuity of the light-fingered gentry who had slipped unseen through the high security cordon to abscond with the many tons of golden booty. Norman counted up the rows of noughts and tried to reconcile them into hundreds, thousands and millions. It didn't bear thinking about.

A quick flip through the remaining pages disclosed pretty much what he had come to expect. The same tired old stuff, although strangely comforting in its tired old sameness. Local fêtes and flowershows. A listing of next week's car boot sales. (Norman never ceased to be amazed by the public's apparent craving for car boots.) A three-page tide table. Next week's demonstration of the art of Levitation called off due to unforeseen circumstances. The council still flogging off portions of wasteland in a vain attempt to make the books balance. Old Sandell, the *Mercury*'s oracle, predicting scandal for the house of Windsor and a one-eyed Puerto Rican to win the Derby. The same old, tired old stuff.

Shaking his head once more – just for the hell of it – Norman dug a biro from his top pocket and began to number up the papers.

'An invisible guru, a gold bullion robbery and aloha to the Brum Olympics,' muttered Norman. 'Worth a bit of chit-chat in the Swan come lunchtime, but hardly likely to change the face of civilization hereabouts.'

In the light of future events, however, Norman might have done well in discarding this particular remark in favour of something completely different . . . possibly one of the less cheerful doom prophecies from the Book of Revelation, or a simple 'The end is drawing nigh'.

But precognition had never been one of Norman's stronger points. For indeed had he possessed this rare gift to even the slightest degree, he would not now have been unnecessarily numbering up papers which he would shortly be delivering himself. For upon this particular morning, as on several past, Zorro the paperboy had chosen to remain in his cosy bed rather than face the rigours of bag, bike and bull terrier.

Thus it was that with a Beefheartian air upon his lips and the dust settling thickly upon his 'mutton-chops', Norman continued with his task, blissfully unaware that he had just glimpsed the beginning of the end. Or if not that, then something that looked very much like it.

2

Not one hundred yards due north of Norman's shop, as fair flies the griffin, there stands a public house which is the very hub of the Brentonian universe. Solidly constructed of old London stocks and fondly embellished with all the Victorian twiddly bits, the Flying Swan gallantly withstood the slings and arrows of outrageous brewery management. Its patrons have never known the horrors of fizzy beer or pub grub that comes 'à-la-basket'.

The Swan had grown old gracefully. The etched glass windows, tinted with nicotine and the exhalations of a million beery breaths, sustained that quality of light exclusive to elderly pubs. The burnished brass of the beer engines shone like old gold and the bar top glowed with a deep patina. The heady perfumes of Brasso and beeswax blended with those of hops and barley, grape and grain to produce an enchanting fragrance all its own. Only a man born without a soul would not pause a moment upon entering the Swan for the first time, breathe in the air, savour the atmosphere and say, 'This *is* a pub.'

But of course, for all its ambience, redolence and Ridley Scottery, a pub is only as good as the beer it serves. And here it must be said that those on offer were of such a toothsome relish, so satisfying in body and flavour as might reasonably elicit bouts of incredulous head-shaking and murmurs of disbelief from the reader.

Nevertheless the eight hand-drawn ales available were of a quality capable of raising eulogies from seasoned drinkers, their bar-side converse long hag-ridden by clichés of how much better beer tasted in the good old days.

So who then was the paragon, the thinking man's

barkeep, this publican amongst publicans, this guru of good alery? The tap-room tenant of this drinking man's Valhalla?

A carpet-slippered foot flaps upon a stair-tread, the hem of a worn silk dressing-gown brushes the gleaming mahogany top of a Britannia pub table. A gaunt shadow falls across the row of twinkling pump handles, as a shaft of sunlight, diamond flecked with floating motes, glistens upon a brilliantined barnet. A slim, almost girlish hand snakes out towards the whisky optic.

Surely we know those monogrammed carpet slippers, recognize the faded dressing-gown, have seen that brilliantined head bowed as in reverence as its owner draws off a shot with that slim yet certain hand?

Yes, there can be no mistake, no doubt can remain. Neville the part-time barman, it is he.

Neville yawned, belched, scratched at his stomach and drew off a large measure of breakfast. Flexing his rounded shoulders and puffing out his pigeon chest he downed the 'gold watch' with a practised wrist-flick and prepared himself to face the day.

Still a-yawning, a-belching and a-scratching, yet now inwardly fortified, Neville sallied forth in search of his weekly newspaper. Knowing Norman's paperboy of old, he did not trouble with the doormat. Last week, the errant rag had gone to earth in one of the hanging geranium baskets, the week before that in the waste-bin. Neville felt no animosity towards young Zorro, rather a deep sympathy, one which had its foundations in the part-time barman's current passion: psychoanalysis.

Every successful barman is something of a natural psychologist, and of late Neville had felt his particular talents leading him into the tortuous labyrinths of the human psyche. And jolly good stuff it all was too.

Young Zorro was a case in point. The rolled newspaper and the open letterbox were quite obviously sexual symbols. Zorro probably had a father fixation or a subconscious desire to return to the womb. Neville also

14

considered that the root cause might lie in Zorro's mother. Perhaps she had been a victim of Brentford's notorious fifties-flasher, whose peccadillo was to ring upon a lady's doorbell and poke his willy through the letterbox. Conversely, his mother might have been frightened by a postman during the moment of his conception. Anything was possible. In the cosy bedroom of Nine Noahs Ark Lane, Zorro slept on.

He was blissfully unaware of his supposed pathological disorder, simply considering that it was far easier to chuck Neville's paper towards the door whilst cycling by, than struggle to ram it through the inadequately sized, although beautifully polished, letterbox.

Neville slipped the bolts upon the saloon bar door and swung it open to the day. As he stood framed magnificently by the famous portal, drawing great draughts of early morning air through his quivering nostrils and exercising what he described as extra-nasal perception to gauge the quality of the hour, he pondered upon where this week's *Mercury* might be cooling its metaphorically wingèd heels.

Like the legendary sleuth of old he knew that when one has eliminated the impossible, then whatever remains, no matter how improbable, must surely be the solution. Such is all well and good of course, but putting theory into practice is quite another thing. The prospect of rooting in dustbins and shinning up drainpipes to examine dubious gutters held little charm. Neville sighed deeply and took a silent vow that he would deal the errant paperboy the thickest of thick ears the next time their paths crossed, fixation or no fixation.

And there perhaps we might have left Neville, scowling and fuming and preparing to make a lone assault upon the east face of the Flying Swan, had not a small – yet in its own way significant – event now occurred. As he took a deep preparatory breath, the part-time barman suddenly became the unwilling recipient of a great gust of unwholesome stench borne to him upon the formerly rose-tinted Brentford breeze.

'By the Gods!' squawked Neville somewhat nasally as the evil wang engulfed him. He clutched despairingly at his nose and gagged into his hand. His tabloid now forgotten, he fanned at the fetid air and stumbled back into the Swan, slamming the door behind him.

With a brief hiss the tinted rear window of a long black automobile parked outside the Swan sealed itself upon the outer world. The vehicle eased away from the kerb and gathered speed along the Ealing Road. Norman, issuing from his corner shop, bulging paperbag upon his shoulder, watched it pass. There wasn't much the wee lad didn't know about cars, his own revolutionary alternative to the internal combustion engine, the Hartnel Harrier, lacking but a few essential parts in the lock-up, but this one fair had him foxed. Not only was it utterly silent, but it also lacked all evidence of exhaust pipes. Norman scratched at his head, raising small clouds of dust. Now how was that done, he wondered? Antimatter drive? Plasma photon ionizers utilizing a cross-polarization of beta particles to bombard an inter-rositor through the medium of a sub-atomic converter? It seemed a most logical probability. Making a hasty note upon the back of a Woodbine packet, Norman hefted his bag and set out upon his paper-round.

3

The elevation of Ms Jennifer Naylor the former local librarian, to the posts, not only of town clerk but also chairperson of the town planning committee, had been met with howls of dismay and much bitter resentment by the predominantly male council.

They had always been prepared to find a place for a token female (as long as she confined herself to the taking of minutes or the brewing of tea) but now it seemed to them that they were paying a high price for their generous liberality. Ms Naylor was proving herself to be a force none of them had reckoned with. Loath as they were to admit that she had gained her positions through intellectual prowess and sheer strength of personality, noses were tapped, knowing nods exchanged and phallacious conclusions drawn. The talk was that she had 'done a turn' upon some mythical council casting couch.

Acutely alert to the distinctive rattle of tiny minds, Ms Naylor remained unperturbed. Her sights were set upon far higher things, which included Parliament and an eventual shot at the premiership amongst them. Confounding her opposition here in Brentford was, she considered, good practice for what lay ahead.

As she showered upon this particular morning, Jennifer's thoughts were upon the coming day. She had been up since dawn making a number of very important phone calls. If the Fates were with her today she would shortly be issuing the borough a kick up the trouser-seat such as it had never known before, and carving for herself a place in history, to boot. And then? One small step at a time.

The needles of water became gentle cascades as they

struck the contours of a body honed to aerobic perfection. Her shower concluded, she patted herself dry with a peach-coloured bath towel, sprayed deodorant to the appropriate quarters, attended to the minutiae of feminine toilette and finally dressed herself in a confection combining sophistication and understated elegance with provocativeness and heaving sexuality. Just so.

Having examined her image in the cheval glass and found it satisfactory, she strode purposefully back to the bedroom, delved amidst the pale satin sheets and withdrew by the ear a certain bit of rough, by name John Omally.

'Thank you, John, and time for the off,' she said, smiling sweetly. Omally, who knew upon which side his particular piece of bread was buttered, dressed hurriedly and without complaint, and made off sans coffee and croissants.

He left as he had entered, with discretion, by the back door, withdrew his bicycle Marchant from Jennifer's garage, mounted up and pedalled away.

She tossed the bed linen into the laundry basket, set the answerphone, swept up Filofax, executive briefcase and Porsche keys and made her departure from the front of the house.

Omally free-wheeled down Moby Dick Terrace towards the Half Acre, his old sit-up-and-beg whirring away beneath him like a good'n. The oil-bathed ball-races of the new Sturmey Archer purred contentedly and the similarly well-oiled saddle springs afforded John's bum the contentment of all but concussion-free cycling. Bike and rider moved in harmonious accord and many was the Buddhist monk, who, recognizing this exhibition of *dharma*, tipped his head towards this perfect union of man and machine. It was a joy to behold. But it had not always been so.

The bike had been with Omally a good many years and for a good many of those years their relationship had been strained and at times positively painful to the both of them. And so it would no doubt have remained had not

18

Chance, if such it was, chosen to intervene. Chance in the person of Professor Slocombe, Brentford's patriarch and resident man of mystery.

Omally had been pedalling with difficulty across the Butts Estate, an elegant Georgian quarter of the borough, when he had found himself discharged from Marchant's saddle to land in an untidy heap before the elder, who was standing at his garden door.

Professor Slocombe observed the 'accident' and the subsequent violent attack Omally visited upon the prone bicycle and chose to intervene. Having calmed the truculent Irishman, he listened with interest to his tale of woe and requested that the bike be left in his care for twenty-four hours. In order to see 'what might be done'. John, whose immediate thought was that the ancient was adding the science of bicycle maintenance to his seemingly endless list of accomplishments, gratefully acceded to his request.

It was therefore much to his surprise when arriving on the morrow he received for his troubles a large piece of parchment upon which was penned thirteen stanzas of archaic English. These read like the prophecies of Nostradamus and to John made precisely the same amount of sense. The Professor told him that, should he follow these requirements to the letter, he would find things very much to his advantage. Omally perused the parchment, his forehead furrowed with doubt. Whilst he was so doing, the Professor added that regular oiling was a necessity as was a change of brake blocks, a realignment of the dynamo and a set of new mudguards. Whenever possible the bicycle was to be left facing west when parked, sunshine being preferable to shade, that it was never to be left alone at night, but always in the company of another wheeled conveyance (or at the very least a lawn mower), that it was to be repainted vermilion and referred to at all future times by the name 'Marchant'.

Omally peered furtively at the old man. This was a wind-up surely, in fact the wind-up to end all wind-ups.

The Professor, who read not only John's aura but also his thoughts, raised a finger, slim as a twig, and said simply, 'Trust me, John.'

Omally left Professor Slocombe's that day leading Marchant thoughtfully by the handlebar. It really didn't seem worth the candle. It would probably be better simply to dump the old bike and acquire another (Omally being one of those who considered an unpadlocked bicycle public property). But his trust in the Professor was implicit, so before he was half-way to the Flying Swan he had resigned himself that he would take up the challenge.

The parchment proved a great attraction to the lunchtime patrons and a distinguished panel of semanticists, Old Pete, Norman and Omally's closest friend Jim Pooley, set about its translation with relish. As the instructions were teased into twentieth-century Brentonian, their curious nature became apparent. Stanza nine, lines three and four, proved of particular interest:

> Ne'er Widdershins must Marchant go
> lest peril and ill luck bestow.

Old Pete, who had recently joined the local coven, picked up on it almost at once. 'It means,' said he, 'that the bike must never be ridden around left-hand corners, on fear of terrible consequence.'

Omally buried his face in his hands. To plan one's route whilst only ever turning to the right was not only ludicrous, it was downright dangerous. Especially upon drunken nights when the gutter led the way home.

But power to the Irishman's elbow, he had persevered, and many a late-night reveller was left to wonder at the madman upon the vermilion cycle crying, 'Homeward Marchant!' as he drove about in ever-decreasing circles, eventually to vanish like the Oozalem bird of ancient myth into his own back passage.

They had been difficult times and no mistake, but now as Omally pedalled effortlessly up the steep incline of Sprite Street, they were no more than memories. He and

Marchant were *en rapport*, as the garlic eaters will have it, and the degree of this was remarkable in the extreme. For, to the trained observer, skilled in such matters as bicycle propulsion, watching the cyclist's easy motion as he crested the hill, one thing would have been readily apparent: As man and bike moved in fluid harmony, one vital something – hitherto considered an essential prerequisite to bicycledom – was missing. The pedals turned, the wheels spinned, but nothing whatever moved between the chainwheel and the Sturmey Archer cog . . . Omally's bicycle Marchant did not have a chain.

4

Ted McCready blew his whistle, waved his flag and watched with absolutely no interest at all as the early train pulled out of Brentford Central. He was precisely sixty-six days from his Gold Watch And Retirement Speech and he no longer gave a monkey's. In fact, like many an old locoman who had gone before him, he had ceased to give a monkey's with the passing of the age of steam. Ted could recall the young boys who clambered on to the footplates of the great locos, or lined the bridge parapets to be bathed in steam as one of the mighty King Class thundered beneath at full throttle, whistle blowing. But that had all gone now. The romance of railways was behind him and with it had gone the pride. No-one could honestly feel for an electric train. It had no personality, no being, no glory. It was just another carriage, but with a motor in it.

Half-heartedly, Ted offered a two-fingered Harvey Smith towards the departing train and shuffled away to his cosy office, his morning cuppa and the next chapter of *Farewell My Window* (a Lazlo Woodbine thriller).

Upon the platform a solitary figure remained, the only passenger to alight from the morning train. He was tall, gaunt and angular in appearance, clad in a Boleskine tweed three-piece. From his right hand hung a heavy pigskin valise, from his left a black Malacca cane with a silver mount. A small white ivory ring pierced the lobe of his left ear and a pair of mirrored pince-nez clung to the bridge of his long aquiline nose. A pelt of snow-white hair turfed his narrow skull. Such was the singular appearance of this solitary traveller and such it was that had put the wind up many a case-hardened veteran of the criminal

22

fraternity. For this was none other than that doyen of detectives, that Nemesis of ne'er-do-wells – *Let evil doers beware, let felons flee and varlets vanish, run the sound, roll the cameras, cue the action* – enter Inspectre Hovis of Scotland Yard.

The man behind the mirrored specs turned his sheltered gaze upon Brentford Central. 'You there!' His voice tore along the platform, striking Ted McCready, who was turning into his sanctum sanctorium, from behind.

'By the love of St Pancras!' The station master clutched at his palpitations and lurched about.

'That's right, I mean you, porter chappy! Up this way at the trot, if you please.' A shaft of sunlight angling down through the ironwork of the footbridge held the great detective to perfection.

'You talking to me?' choked Ted, squinting towards his tormentor.

'That's right, my man, at the double!' Hovis indicated his pigskin valise. 'Let's be having you.'

With bitter words forming between his lips, Ted humped the heavy case down the platform. He'd had a trolley once, but it had rusted away. He'd had a porter once, but he had been cut back. He'd had a hernia once . . . With his free hand Ted felt at his groin. He still had a hernia.

Ahead of him the spare frame of Hovis bobbed along to an easy stride. A voice called back across an angled padded shoulder. 'Pacy pacy, Mr Porter,' it called. 'Tempus fugit.'

Ted McCready stared daggers into the receding back. He was the first man in Brentford to encounter the great detective and by this token, the first man to really hate him. He would by no means be the last.

5

Omally turned right at the traffic lights, right again and
finally right into Ganesha Lane. Marchant rattled over the
uneven cobbles and John spread wide his legs as they
swept down into the alleyway that led past Cider Island
to the weir, the abandoned boatyards and the venerable
Thames.

John dismounted as they reached the weir. Weird and
wonderful Marchant might have been, but he did not
include the climbing of steps as part of his metaphysical
repertoire. Omally shouldered his bike, skipped up the
steps and continued on his way, whistling brightly.

Suddenly, the bright and breezy, devil-may-care
jauntiness of his step vanished, to be replaced by a furtive,
shifty, quite definitely guilt-ridden scuttle. Omally was up
to something.

A slowing of pace, a quick shufti over the shoulder, a
sudden movement. A section of corrugated iron swings
aside and a boy and his bike vanished from the footpath
and were lost to view.

Beyond the iron fencing, the long-abandoned boatyard
slumbered. The pointless walls of the derelict buildings
were decked with festoons of convolvulus, the windows
swagged with cobwebs. Here and there the tragic debris
of the once proud trade showed as tiny islands amidst a
grassy ocean. Here a crane, strung like a fractured gibbet,
there the gears and gubbins, over-ripe with rust. Capstans
and winches, pulleys and blocks, blurred with moss,
weatherworn and worthless. At a quayside beyond, the
dark hulk of an ancient barge wallowed in oily water.

Once the glittering island boatyards, strung like a neck-
let about the borough's throat, had prospered. Here the

barques and pleasure boats, the punts and Thames steamers had taken form from the hand-hewn timbers, fashioned with the care of craftsmen. Now it was no more, here and there a yard survived heavily secured with barbed wire and night-prowling dogs, knocking out plastic dinghies or casting fibre-glass hulls for Arabian moguls. Floating gin palaces for camel jockeys. The life had gone, and that particular form of melancholia which haunts places of bygone commerce washed over the buildings in waves of lavender blue. For blue is the colour of tears and water, sea and sadness.

Omally left Marchant to rest upon a handlebar, the reflected glory of the early sun cupped in his headlamp. Hitching up his trousers, he set out to wade through the waist-deep grass towards the ancient barge.

Upon reaching the edge of the wharf he again paused to assure himself that he remained unobserved. When so assured he dropped down on to the barge and tapped out an elaborate tattoo upon the hull.

A head popped up from the inner depths and a voice, that of Jim Pooley, owner of the head, called out, 'Watchamate John, you're bloody late!' Omally shinned through the hatchway and down into the bowels of the wreck.

The interior presented a most surprising and unexpected appearance. Over a period of many months Pooley and Omally had effected a conversion of a most enterprising nature. The superannuated vessel now housed a distillery, a series of grandiose fish tanks, wherein lazed river fish of prize-winning proportions, a storehouse for 're-routed' goods and a comfortable salon for the entertaining of special guests.

A line of portholes below waterline looked out upon a string of elaborate fish traps set above the distillery cooling tubes. This was the headquarters of what was known to a select few as the 'P and O Line'. There was much of Captain Nemo's 'Nautilus' to the thing, but there was a good deal more of Fagin's kitchen. Although, in evidence for the defence, it must be stated that John and

Jim drew the line before coining, or the manufacture of hard drugs.

Pooley and Omally took their morning coffee in the forward salon. The style was essentially eclectic. A hint of Post-Modernism here, a touch of rococo there, several boxes of video cassettes just behind the door. A pair of blown glass vases, signed by Count Otto Boda himself, adorned a chromium table of the high-tech persuasion. An antique paisley swathed a gaudy sun-lounger, three china ducks flew nowhere.

Omally stuck his feet up on the Le Corbusier chaise and Pooley leant upon the Memphis-style cocktail cabinet dunking a breakfast biscuit.

'Well,' said Jim when he finally tired of the sight of his partner's inane grin. 'Good night, was it?'

Omally's smile resembled that of the legendary Gwynplaine. 'Propriety forbids a disclosure of details,' he said as he dandled his *demi-tasse*, 'but it was magic.'

'I'm so glad.'

The two drank on in silence, Omally mentally replaying selected highlights and Pooley glowering with evident envy. When he could stand no more of that Jim said, 'We got four, they must be five-pounders easily.'

Omally raised his eyebrows and smiled his winning smile. 'Well now, Neville will take one for the Saturday sarnies and another for his freezer, I have no doubt.'

'Wally Woods will take the other two then.'

Omally frowned – briefly, for the effort vexed him. Wally Woods, Brentford's foremost purveyor of wet fish, was a cold and slippery little customer. 'No,' said John. 'We'll do them off in Ealing, at the King's Head or the Fly's Home.'

'As you please.'

Omally finished his coffee and refilled his cup from the snazzy-looking percolator. 'How are the accounts shaping up?' he asked, in a tone of casual enquiry.

Jim raised an eyebrow of his own. He was well aware that the Irishman had logged within his curly head the dismal sum of their current assets. 'If this business was legitimate,' he sighed, 'we would be in for a tax rebate.'

Omally shook his head. 'Sometimes I think that we slave away so hard in our attempts to avoid honest toil that we shall work ourselves into an early grave through the effort.'

'You are not suggesting we . . .' Pooley spoke the dreaded words in a whisper, '*get a job*?'

Omally winked. 'Not a bit of it. We are free men, are we not? And is freedom not the most valuable possession a man can own?'

'Well . . .' said Jim. A sudden image of Jennifer Naylor's Porsche unaccountably filled his mind. 'Well . . .'

'Of course it is,' Omally went on. 'We live life to the full and do you know why we do it?' Pooley thought that he did, but suspected he would not get the opportunity to say so. 'We do it for the crack,' said Omally, confirming Jim's suspicion.

'Ah!' said that man, 'the crack, that lad.'

'That lad indeed and,' said John, who was evidently in loquacious spirits, 'I will tell you something more.'

'I have no doubt of it.'

'At ten o'clock, Jim, you will walk into Bob the bookies.'

'I always do.'

'But today will be different.'

'It always is.'

'Because today you will place a bet which on the face of it will appear so ludicrous that he of the golden gonads will rock to and fro upon his chair doubled up with laughter.'

'He always does,' said Jim.

'You will ask him what odds he will give you,' John continued, 'and between the tears of mirth he will say something like ten thousand to one, possibly even more if he is feeling particularly rash.'

Jim scratched at his head. 'Ten thousand to one?' he queried.

'At the very least, you will bet ten pounds, and pay the tax.'

'Ten pounds?' Pooley clutched at his heart. 'All at once? Ten pounds?'

Omally nodded, 'I myself will wade in with a oncer.'

'A oncer?'

'Certainly, to show that I have the courage of my convictions. *Ex unque leonem*, as the French will have it.' Here he pulled from his pocket the said groat note, which by its appearance was evidently a thing of great sentimental value, and presented it to Pooley.

'Gosh!' said Jim. 'All this and money too.'

'No idle braggart, I.'

'Perish the thought. But do tell me, John, exactly what shall I be betting on?'

'You will be betting on a sure thing.'

'Ah,' said Jim, without conviction, 'one of those lads.'

'One of those very lads. Straight from the horse's mouth this very morning. A little bird whispered it into my ear and I do likewise into yours.'

'You seem to hold considerable sway with the animal kingdom.'

'It is a sure thing.'

'At ten thousand to one?'

'Would you care now that I whisper?'

'What have I to lose, saving the nine pounds?'

Omally leant forwards and poured a stream of whispered words into Pooley's left ear. Jim stood there unblinking. A piece of chewing gum upon his instep attracted the attentions of an ant.

'Ah,' said Jim at length, when Omally had run dry of words.

'Ah,' said John, nodding enthusiastically.

'No,' said Jim. 'The word is no.'

'The word is yes, Jim, the word is yes.'

'No, no, no!' Pooley shook his head in time to his 'nos'. 'Never, and again no.'

John put his arm about his best friend's shoulders. 'Believe in me,' he said. 'Would I steer you on to a wrong'n?' Jim chewed upon his lip in hesitation, and as the old saying goes, 'he who hesitates is banjoed'. 'Then you'll do it, Jim?'

'Why not?' Pooley sighed pathetically. 'I will be the laughing stock of Brentford, the butt of all ribaldry in the Swan for months to come, a veritable byword for buffoonery, what do I have to lose?'

'But think what we might do with our winnings.'

'You cannot be serious, John, you are telling me that . . .'

Omally clapped a hand across his partner's mouth. 'Not even here,' he said, pressing a free finger to his lips. 'Walls have ears.' Jim shrugged and sighed simultaneously. 'Now then,' John continued brightly, 'I suggest you bung a couple of free-rangers into the old non-stick and have a bit of brekky. We have a busy day ahead and I've a couple of phone calls to make.'

Shaking his head in dismay, Pooley dug eggs and sausages from the fridge. The bangers were Walls. They didn't have any ears.

6

At shortly after nine: Norman returned from his paper-round whistling a tuneless melody which may or may not have been 'Dali's car'. Just before he reached his shop, however, he discovered to his chagrin that he still had a single copy of the *Brentford Mercury* in his bag. Being uncertain as to whether he had posted one to Neville when he first set out upon his round he popped it through the Swan's letterbox. Just to be on the safe side.

The part-time barman, who was still recovering from not only his undeserved nasal larruping but also the trauma of discovering the first ever copy of the *Mercury* to arrive on his doormat, looked up in horror at the arrival of the second and quickly reached for his dog-eared copy of Krafft Ebing's *Psychopathia Sexualis*.

At shortly after nine-fifteen: Inspectre Hovis strode into Brentford police station. He awoke the snoozing duty officer with a summary blow to the skull from his silver-topped cane, identified himself and poured forth a torrent of instructions, demands, directives, exactions, mandates, impositions, requisitions and ultimatums. Pausing only to draw breath and savour the bewildered sergeant's look of horror, he asked, 'Are you receiving me?'

'Loud and clear, sir, loud and clear.' Sergeant Gotting's head bobbed up and down between his blue serge shoulders. He was only the second man in Brentford to encounter the great detective, but he was the second to really truly hate his guts.

At shortly after nine-thirty: Jennifer Naylor steered her

Porsche into the council car park. Binding, the scrofulous attendant, lurched from his sentry box and put up his hand. 'Pass?' he demanded.

Jennifer generally let him do this several times before winding down the window to enquire what exactly he wanted. Today, however, she was in a hurry. Regarding him as she might a dollop of poodle-doo on her Gucci instep, she indicated the pass, affixed as ever to her windscreen.

Binding leant forward, his ghastly hands deep at some nefarious activity within his trouser pockets. He examined the pass and what he could of Jennifer's cleavage by turn. At length, evidently satisfied that each was in order, he mumbled, 'I'll guide you in,' and turned to view the all but empty car park with a thoughtful gaze. 'There's one over there in the corner by the bottle bank.' But his words were lost amidst a squeal of expensive rubber as Jennifer spun the Porsche into the nearest parking space. That of Major McFadeyen.

'*You can't park there!*' wailed Binding, withdrawing his terrible hands from their place of business and waving them in the air. 'That's the Major's bay! It's more than my job's . . .' A loud blast from the Porsche's horn drowned out the deadly phrase.

'Thank you,' said Jennifer Naylor, 'this will do nicely.'

At shortly after ten o'clock: Jim Pooley left Bob the Bookie's at the trot, the millionaire's guffaws ringing in his ears. He had got far greater odds than Omally had predicted. In his eagerness to acquire ten pounds from Pooley all at once, Bob had informed him that upon this special occasion the sky was the limit. Jim felt it best to keep this information from John, as the Irishman would only become over-excited if he knew the true extent of the projected winnings. 'Also,' thought Jim, 'as I have taken the greater financial risk then so should I reap the greater reward.'

Pleased with the persuasiveness of this argument he

jingled the last of his small change, winked at the sky and sauntered into Norman's cornershop in the hope of five Woodbine on tick. 'You never know your luck,' thought Jim Pooley. 'You never know.'

At shortly after ten-thirty there was a council meeting.

7

'Lunacy! Madness!' Major McFadeyen struck the council table with two tightly knotted fists. A surprising tangle of veins arrayed themselves upon his neck, lending it the appearance of one of those nasty anatomical models surgeons like to frighten patients with. Something resembling a blue slug pulsed away upon the major's left temple.

'Madness!' Momentarily exhausted by the ferocity of his out-cries, he slumped back into his chair. 'And I'll tell you this . . .' He rose again, supporting himself upon his palms. 'It's . . . it's . . .' A button flew from the top of his waistcoat, tinkled to the table and rolled in a curious geomantic circle before rattling to a standstill. 'It's . . . *lunacy!*' He sat down, puffing and blowing.

Councillor Ffog examined his fingernails and made little embarrassed tutting noises with his mouth.

Philip Cameron chewed his lower lip and rattled coins in his trouser pocket. Sensing his anxiety, Mavis Peake slipped a calming hand on to his thigh and smiled encouragingly.

For their part the brothers Geronimo stared into the middle distance, arms folded, knees together, minds upon the Little Big Horn. Ms Naylor regarded the Major with a mild expression.

'Lunacy, I say.' McFadeyen, now a shade of purple that interior decorators describe as crimson magenta, arose for another blast.

Ms Naylor smiled the sweetest of smiles towards the fuming fogey. 'And might I enquire as to why?'

'Well . . . well . . .' The Major reclenched his fists. '*Dammit, woman!*'

'Yes?' Ms Naylor leant forward as if attentive to the

Major's every word. As she did so, her breasts, constrained within her silken blouse, gently caressed the table top. The calculated eroticism of the act was not lost upon Philip Cameron, who found his loins responding appropriately. The fingernails of Mavis Peake dug in deeply.

'I'm speechless.' Major McFadeyen sank away into his seat, fanning himself with last week's minutes.

'It is all perfectly straightforward.' Ms Naylor rose upon the four-inch heels she had considered suitable for the occasion, and tossed her auburn hair back in delicious waves across her perfect shoulders. 'As you are all no doubt aware, the disastrous fire at Birmingham this week has, on the face of it, ruled out Great Britain's chances of hosting the Olympic games.' Heads nodded, Ms Naylor continued. 'It is my proposal that Brentford rise to the call of its country and host the games. This is the motion that I am forwarding.' She stared deeply into Philip Cameron's eyes. 'Will someone second me?'

Wilting visibly beneath the emerald stare, Councillor Cameron bobbed his head up and down after the fashion of a nodding dog in a Cortina rear window. Mavis Peake gave his left testicle a terrifying tweak which doubled him up in a paroxysm of pain. As his forehead struck the council table with a sickening thump the brothers Geronimo considered his scalp, their hands straying towards the Bowie knives in their trouser pockets.

'Why, thank you, Philip,' said Jennifer Naylor.

The Major, now Ribena-hued and apoplectic, gathered what wits remained to him and prepared to come up fighting. He hadn't blasted buffalo in the Ngora Gora basin, topped tigers in Tibet and walloped the Watusi in God knows where, to be put down by a damned woman. '*Where?*' he spluttered. '*Where?*'

'Right here,' Ms Naylor indicated the immediate vicinity.

Councillor Ffog put up his hand. 'If you will pardon me for asking, who would be expected to foot the bill for this . . . uh . . . venture?'

'I have all the figures to hand. What particular costs were you interested in?'

Councillor Ffog wiggled his fingers foolishly. 'I mean the expense, how much would it cost?'

Ms Naylor snapped open her Filofax. 'To build an Olympic stadium, complete with all facilities, Olympic village, public access roads, etc., etc., etc.'

'Yes?' said Councillor Ffog.

'Around one hundred million pounds.'

Now, there are silences, and there are silences. Some are such that a pin hitting the old fitted Axminster is capable of breaking them. This one, however, was of such a nature that within it the distinctive *futt futt* of brain cells dying within Major McFadeyen's head were clearly discernible.

'We have fifty-one pounds, thirty-four pence in the kitty,' said Mavis Peake, a woman to whom silences were simply moments that people used to draw breath between statements. 'If you can come up with ninety-nine million, nine hundred and ninety-nine thousand, nine hundred and forty-eight pounds sixty-six pence we shall be home and dry. Here,' she continued, with what she considered to be crushing irony, 'I'll throw in my box of matches to light the Olympic flame.'

Councillor Ffog chuckled horribly. Major McFadeyen munched upon a phenobarbitone. The brothers Geronimo made grave faces and nodded towards one another.

Paul said, 'One hundred million heap big wampam, squaw gott'm screw loose in wigwam attic.'

Barry nodded. 'Me agree, noble brother, squaw been bunging too much locoweed down cakehole.'

Ms Naylor drew back her shoulders and smoothed down her blouse. 'I am well aware that Brentford Borough Council cannot be expected to raise such a sum. The money must come from a private backer.'

Councillor Ffog, who considered himself to be, as the French have it, 'somewhat of a *garçon*', enquired as to whether anybody had Bob Geldof's telephone number.

Rising from his seat he said, 'Although one hundred million is a mere dip into Paul McCartney's petty cash box, it might not be readily accessible to the average punter.' Satisfied that he had wrought crushing defeat upon his adversary, Ffog grinned smugly and resumed his seat. Before his bum had hit the cushion, however, he was aware that Ms Naylor was continuing her discourse as if he had never spoken.

'And what if such a backer could be brought forward at this very moment? What then, gentlemen?' Ms Naylor glanced pointedly towards Mavis. 'And lady, of course.'

'*Do so!*' roared the Major. '*Do so, madam!*'

'Macca's petty cash box, eh?' whispered Ffog, winking lewdly and nudging a Geronimo twin about the buckskin ribs. Mavis Peake leant forward in her chair. Any attempt upon her part to indulge in any erotic breast-brushing, however, would have required her to place her chin firmly upon the table. 'If you can find a philanthropist willing to finance a Brentford Olympiad to the tune of one hundred million pounds,' she sneered, 'then we shall all second the motion and declare it carried.'

'Hear, hear,' mumbled a muddy brown Major, drifting into a pharmaceutical haze. A further chorus of hear hears filled the unhealthy atmosphere of the council chamber. Philip Cameron clutched at his testicles and maintained a bitter, clench-toothed silence.

Ms Naylor smiled and nodded her head gently as if in time to some secret melody. 'So be it then,' she said dramatically. 'Consider it done.' She clapped her hands and at the signal the doors of the council chamber opened to reveal a pair of Covent Garden design-studio-executive-types sporting designer sunglasses, clipped beards and Paul Smith suits. They flanked what appeared to be a hospital trolley, its upper regions shrouded beneath folds of white linen.

'Oooh!' said Clyde Ffog, straightening his tie. 'Nice.'

'May we enter?' enquired the taller of the two.

Clyde Ffog nodded enthusiastically. 'Please do,' said he.

'Ladies and gentlemen,' said the smaller of the pair, 'I am Julian Membrane and this is my associate, Lucas Mucus.' Lucas bowed slightly from the waist, anticipating the looks of disbelief which generally greeted his name. 'Of the Membrane, Mucus, Willoby, Turncoat and Gladbetook Partnership, specialists in the conceptualizing of new marketing trends through increased consumer product awareness. Design Consultants. Our card.'

Paul Geronimo eyed the thing suspiciously, 'White brother speak with forked tongue,' he observed. 'Talk load of old buffalo chips,' his brother agreed.

'We should very much like to make for you our presentation,' Membrane continued. 'We are acting upon the part of our client, a great philanthropist who wishes to finance the games here. He is a scientist and something of a recluse and he wishes for us to make this presentation upon his behalf. He chooses anonymity; we honour his wishes.'

'Words spill from white brother's mouth like wheat from chafing dish of careless squaw,' said Paul Geronimo. Barry eyed his brother proudly. He could never think of things like that to say. He went along with Paul's conviction that they were a dual reincarnation of the great Apache chief mostly because he liked dressing up.

'Thus,' said Julian Membrane, 'we offer our conceptual representation for the proposed Brentford Olympiad.' With a flourish, he drew aside the linen cover from the trolley to expose a scale model of Brentford. With a chorus of 'oohs' and 'ahs', those councillors that were able rose from their seats to view the wonder. For wonder it indeed was.

The model's realism was uncanny – the entire borough reduced, as if by magic, to doll's house proportions. The councillors gathered about it, cooing and pointing, anxious to examine their own houses, as well as those of their fellows. Mavis Peake let out a little excited cry. 'Even my bedroom curtains are the right colour!'

'What are those things in your back garden then?' Philip

Cameron asked Clyde Ffog. 'They look like instruments of torture.'

'Rubbish,' spluttered the reddening Ffog. 'They're . . . er . . . bean-frames.'

Philip Cameron was unconvinced. Paul Geronimo whispered loudly to the effect that 'brown-hatted brother heap heap big bondage fan'.

'This is an invasion of privacy!' cried Ffog. 'So where is the bloody stadium then, under the ground?'

Lucas Mucus shook his cropped head. 'On the contrary, very much over the ground, as it happens.'

'Oh, yes!' crowed Ffog. 'And where do you propose to put it?'

Mucus took up a pointer. 'Here, here, here, here and here,' he dipped variously about the borough.

Clyde Ffog looked baffled. Ms Naylor said, 'I think you'd better demonstrate, Lucas.'

'Certainly, madam. If you would be so kind, Julian.'

Julian smiled, nodded and, stooping, withdrew from a compartment in the trolley a glittering object approximately a third of the size of the model village. It had much the look of a flat star which contained at its centre a dancehall mirror-globe. Julian held it out proudly before the assembly. 'The Star Stadium,' he said. If he had been hoping for a round of applause then he was to be sorely disappointed.

'And where would you like to stick that?' asked Ffog pointedly.

'Lucas, if you would be so kind.'

Lucas nodded with politeness and pressed a small button at the side of the model. There was a hiss of hydraulics, and from each of the five locations previously appointed arose a telescopic column. When these had risen to their full extent, Julian stepped forward and placed the 'star' gently upon them, tip upon tip. 'Wallah,' he said.

Lucas made free with his pointer. 'The columns will be five hundred feet high,' he said proudly. 'Traffic will flow into the North and East legs directly from the Great West Road, to rise upon a continuous belt lift to parking bays beneath the stadium. Each area between star tip and sphere houses an Olympic village, the central sphere a stadium seating five hundred thousand, swimming pools, full games complexes, etc., etc., etc.'

'Hold on, hold on,' blustered Clyde Ffog. 'You are seriously proposing to hang this thing above Brentford? Apart from the obvious dangers, it will plunge half the town into permanent darkness.'

'Do you think so?' Julian asked. 'Look closely at the model.'

Clyde Ffog gave the thing a good squinting. To his amazement he realized that the stadium cast no shadow. 'There is no shadow!' he exclaimed.

'That heap big medicine by any reckoning,' declared Barry.

'A scientific breakthrough,' said Lucas. 'The top of the stadium is covered in solar cells, these absorb light and project it through similar cells on the underside. In fact, when the real stadium is completed it will appear literally invisible from below, there will simply be the appearance of a clear sky.'

'If not talking out back of loincloth then that technological miracle of first magnitude,' Barry said, nodding respectfully. 'Nobel prize in that for inventor.'

'That is only one small miracle,' said Lucas. 'You mentioned obvious danger did you not?'

Clyde nodded fiercely, 'What if the whole shebang falls down on Brentford? Don't tell me you can put up a thing like that without something getting dropped, or falling off!'

'Julian,' said Lucas. Julian reached into his trouser pocket and withdrew a flat black disc about the size of an old penny. 'This, ladies and gentlemen, is "Gravitite". A self-buoyant polysilicate which has rather special qualities.' He held the disc between thumb and forefinger and then released it. To general amazement and gasps of disbelief it did not fall to the floor, as one might reasonably expect. Instead it remained where it was, suspended in the air in defiance of all the laws of nature, or some of them at least.

'That not heap big medicine,' said Barry Geronimo. 'That fucking impossible!'

'Not really,' said Julian Membrane. 'You see, it is not actually defying gravity. The disc is falling, but it is falling so slowly that its movement is scarcely perceptible. So you see the stadium is really only moored to the five columns. During the two months or so it is in use it will fall possibly two inches or so.'

Even though he felt sure it would get him nowhere, Clyde Ffog persisted, 'What if someone drops something during the actual assembling? Hammer? Rivets? Someone in Brentford is sure to get killed!'

'No chance of that whatsoever.' Julian's smugness was becoming roundly intolerable. 'Gravitite possesses other qualities. Its molecular structure is such that two pieces need only be touched together for them to weld unbreakably as one. Therefore no rivets, no visible joins, no hammers. The stadium will be constructed elsewhere in sections, towed into place by dirigibles and manoeuvred together at night.'

Councillor Ffog knew when he was licked. (He also enjoyed it very much at times.) The whole thing was utterly fantastic. Pure science fiction.

Philip Cameron's eyes suddenly shone with a strange light. It was the light of realization. Realization that The Moment that only comes to a man once in his lifetime had just arrived. Before him, hanging motionless in the air was an apparently endless row of pound note signs.

'This Gravitite stuff,' he said casually, 'obviously it can be produced pretty cheaply if you intend to build an entire stadium out it.' Julian nodded. 'Then I'm sure you won't object if I have this piece as a souvenir.'

Julian plucked the disc from the air. It turned weightlessly in his hand. 'I'm afraid not,' he said, thrusting it back into his pocket.

'How rude of me,' said Philip, praying despairingly that the cold sweat breaking out on his forehead would remain unnoticed. 'Let me write you out a cheque for your time and trouble.'

'I'm afraid not.'

'Come now,' crooned Cameron, 'you'll take Barclay-card surely, American Express?'

'I'm afraid not.' Julian patted his pocket.

'Oh, come on, please, it's only a tiny piece, you can spare it!' Cameron's voice was cracking and he knew it. So did everyone else.

A suddenly enlightened Barry Geronimo broke in with, 'I'll go cash on it, John, how does a century sound?'

'One hundred and fifty,' said Councillor Ffog, 'no, make it two hundred.'

'Gentlemen, gentlemen!' Julian raised his hand to bring the feverish bidding to a halt. There were knighthoods in this project and he knew it. Also his partnership had been promised the Gravitite account when it went public after the games. 'It is not the money, I assure you,' he lied. 'I cannot sell what is not mine to sell. We have been honoured with the trust of our client. M.M.W.T. and G. never betray the trust of a client.'

Philip Cameron sank away into a chair. He had missed his Moment and would live out the rest of his days a broken man. Mavis Peake put her arm about his shoulder and offered her hanky. 'Have a good blow,' she said.

'Gentlemen, please.' Julian Membrane raised an admonitory palm towards the Geronimo brothers, whose conversation had turned towards the taking of paleface scalps and who were delving into their medicine bags for suitable war-paint. 'Lucas here is a master of Dimac, dead-liest form of martial art known to mankind.'

Paul peered suspiciously over his make-up mirror. 'Sitting Bullshit,' he said, smearing Mary Quant across his right cheek.

'If there are no further questions,' said Lucas, 'we shall not take up any more of your valuable time.'

'I have a couple,' said Clyde Ffog.

'And they are?' The unveiled condescension in Julian's voice grated upon Ffog's soul. She's a prize bitch, this one, he thought to himself.

'Just a couple of small matters I'd like you to put me straight on.'

Julian glanced at the Geronimos. They were momentarily preoccupied with their make-up. 'Yes then?'

'Firstly, who owns the sites on which you plan to erect the leg columns?'

'Ah,' said Julian. 'That is the beauty of the concept. Our client owns all five sites; he purchased them all most recently. From you, the Brentford Council.'

'I see,' said Ffog. 'You seem to have been very thorough indeed.'

Julian smiled broadly and bowed slightly. 'Anything else, was there?'

'Just one thing.' Clyde Ffog stroked at his chin. By a bizarre twist of fate his One Moment was just about to occur and he wanted to savour it. 'I was just wondering,' he said slowly, 'whether you'd got planning permission?'

Julian and Lucas looked at one another. They had not got planning permission. '*Ah*,' said Julian. '*Ah*,' said Lucas. '*Ah*,' said the councillors, although theirs was an entirely different kind of *ah*. '*Ah, indeed*,' said Clyde Ffog, smiling broadly.

If *The Guinness Book of Records* was ever to include a section for 'The Largest Backhander Ever Taken By a District Surveyor' it would appear above the name of Clyde Merridew Ffog, formerly of Brentford and now domiciled in the Seychelles. 'Would you gentlemen care to step into my office?' asked this most exalted amongst men.

Amidst gasps of horror, murmurs of disbelief and the sound of tomahawks being drawn, Clyde Ffog ushered the two young oiks hurriedly from the chamber.

8

At precisely eleven o'clock Neville sheepishly opened the saloon-bar door, upon the safety chain. Lowering his pomander he took a delicate peck at the air. It smelt like fish. 'It smells like fish,' said the puzzled barkeep.

'That's because it is fish.' John Omally grinned through the crack. 'Open up there, Neville.'

'Sorry, John.' The part-time barman slipped the chain and flip-flopped back across the bar. Omally followed him, a bulging bin-liner slung across his shoulder. 'By the saints, Neville,' said he as the barman placed the pomander upon the bar counter and himself behind it, 'you smell like the proverbial tart's handbag!'

'Again, sorry.' Neville held a shining glass beneath the spout of the beer engine and drew off a pint of the very best. He held it to the light. It was clear as an author's conscience. 'The drains must be up,' he tapped at his sensitive nostrils with a free finger, 'or something.'

'I understand.' Omally settled himself on to his favourite stool. He had no intention of being drawn into another discourse on the barman's ENP. 'I've two beauties here,' he said, depositing his load on to the bar counter. 'Fresh river trout,' he explained. He placed his glass to his lips and took the first sip of the day. Neville paused a moment, his day was won or lost upon the outcome of this single sip. 'Magic,' said John, smacking his lips together and taking another draught. 'Magic.'

Neville relaxed. 'Still ten bob a pound, I trust?'

'The very same, a couple of six pounders here.' Neville gave Omally the old fish-eye and took out his pocket scales. 'Well, fives at the very least, hand-fed on hempseed and mealworms.'

43

'Not hand fed upon spanners like those other two you sold me?'

Omally smiled his winning smile and sipped his ale. 'You will have your little joke,' said he between sippings.

'And you yours, but not at my expense.' Neville weighed up the fish, cashed up NO SALE on the publican's piano and drew out five crisp one pound notes. 'Shall I take for your pint now?' he asked.

'That's a bit previous,' said John. 'Jim will be here at any moment.'

Neville offered Omally a sociable smile and hauled the day's catch away to the pub freezer.

Old Pete, Brentford's horticultural elder statesman, entered the Flying Swan, his half-terrier Chips hard as ever upon his down-at-heels.

'Morning, John,' said he, joining Omally at the bar.

'Morning, Pete,' himself replied. 'Morning, Chips.'

The dog sniffed quizzically at the air. His antiquated master did likewise. 'Now there's a thing,' said Old Pete.

Omally plucked a copy of the *Brentford Mercury* from the bar counter and began to fan nonchalantly at the air. 'What's that?' he enquired.

'Funny how a particular smell can stir a particular memory.'

'Oh yes?' How the miasmal cocktail of wet fish and pomander could stir up anything other than acute nausea escaped Omally.

'Her name was Jasmine,' Old Pete recalled wistfully, 'she ran a Bangkok brothel.'

'You disgusting old bastard,' said John Omally, concealing his mirth.

'Of course I could be wrong.' The ancient had another sniff or two and thought to detect the familiar whiff of a large dark rum hovering in the overcharged air. 'It might just be ten pound of freshly poached river salmon,' he announced loudly.

Omally spluttered into what was left of his pint. 'A large dark rum over here, please, Neville,' he said, wiping foam from his nose.

'Why, thank you, John,' said Old Pete, chuckling wickedly, 'most unexpected.' Neville, returning from the freezer, wiping his hands upon his bar apron, drew the old rogue his prize from the bullseye optic.

'Your very good health, John.'

'And yours, Pete.' Omally raised his glass and peered sadly through its now empty bottom.

'Same again, is it?' Neville enquired. 'Care to settle up now, would you?'

As if upon cue Jim Pooley entered the Flying Swan. 'Watchamate all,' said he.

Pete touched his flat cap, Neville inclined his shining pate, Young Chips woofed non-committally and Omally said, 'Good day.'

'Who's in the chair?' Jim enquired.

'Guess?' Omally proffered his empty glass.

'Ah.' Jim patted his pockets. 'I regret that a business transaction has sorely taxed my purse upon this morning,' said he, turning to Omally with what he considered to be a 'significant look'.

'We'll split it then.' Omally pushed his glass across the shining bar top. 'Two pints of Large, please, Neville.'

'And a dark rum,' said Old Pete with a blackmailer's optimism.

'And a small dark rum,' said Omally, 'which will be your last.'

Old Pete grinned toothlessly. He knew better than to kill the fish that laid the golden egg. There was always another Friday. 'Much obliged,' said he.

The honours were done and Omally called to account. John led his partner away to the privacy of a side table where he split the change and tossed Jim another pound note.

Pooley sorrowfully examined the residue of the day's wages. 'I do not appear to be quids in here,' he observed.

'It is impossible to project a specific return upon working capital,' said John informatively. 'For the wheels of commerce to spin freely, their axles must receive constant financial lubrication.'

'You mean paying off that old villian?' Pooley nodded towards Pete, who raised his glass in reply and said 'Cheers!' Young Chips, whose hearing was more than acute, made a mental note to visit Jim's ankle when the occasion arose.

'A mere bagatelle,' said Omally. 'Now what about that other bit of business?'

Pooley supped his ale. 'Your prediction odds-wise was somewhat over-optimistic,' said he, 'but then it is always impossible to project a specific return upon . . .'

'*Touché*,' said Omally, peeling another pound note into Jim's direction. 'I believe I might have short-changed you in error.'

'By another ten shillings, I believe,' replied Pooley.

'Ah, yes.' A ten-shilling note changed hands.

'Thank you, John, but truly, do you honestly believe that this is going to come off?'

Omally nodded. 'It is a sure thing, I am telling you.' He drew his companion closer. 'And Bob went for it?'

'He made a small provision or two, but, yes, well, he went for it.'

'Wonderful,' said Omally. 'Then shortly we will both be very, very rich. Neville!' he called out, 'what is the exact time, do you know?'

The part-time barman eye-balled the battered Guinness clock. 'Do you mean pub time or GMT?'

'GMT.'

'Eleven twenty-two.'

'Thank you, Neville.' Omally turned to Jim and patted him upon the shoulder. 'You honestly have nothing to fear,' said he, 'we can now leave it all to the messenger of the gods.'

'The what?'

'The what and the whom. Mercury, the wing-heeled wonderboy.'

'Oh, that lad.'

'That lad,' said Omally. 'Now drink up, the next is on me.'

'To Mercury.' Jim raised his glass.

46

9

The editor of the *Brentford Mercury* peered up from the
dog-eared reporter's note-book towards the dog-eared
reporter who stood panting breathlessly before his desk,
one Seamus Molloy. 'Scoop' to his friends. 'And this is
actually true?' he asked.

Scoop nodded vigorously. 'I interviewed the councillors who were at the meeting. Those that were still able to
stand, that is. It all ended in a bit of a punch-up. The garda
and all. I ran all the way back.'

The editor scratched at his head with the wrong end of
his magic marker. Scoop watched in silent fascination
as royal blue zig-zags appeared across his employer's
polished cranium.

'You are not pulling my wire, Molloy?' The aforementioned employer squinted towards the desk calendar.
Even allowing for a day or two unturned, it was well
starboard of April the first.

'I swear not.' Molloy crossed his heart. 'See this wet, see
this dry . . .'

'Quite so, but I should take an extremely poor view of
this if it turned out to be another Brentford Griffin
story.'

Molloy hung his head. 'It's as true as I am standing here,
sir,' said he. 'Been following the story for weeks now,' he
lied.

'Then, it's . . . wonderful!' The editor's voice rose an
entire octave. 'Wonderful!' He thrust aside his chair and
clasped Molloy's sweaty mitt, wringing it between his
own. 'Do you realize what this means, Molloy?' he asked.

Scoop's head bounced up and down; he did indeed. 'It
cost me an arm and a leg,' he said guardedly.

'We have it.' The editor clenched a fist towards a damp patch on the ceiling. '*I* have it! *The* story! *The exclusive!*' He turned upon the broth of a boy who stood smiling modestly. '*The exclusive!* And it's all mine!' He flung out a hand towards the internal telephone. 'All mine!' Suddenly he froze. His eyes flashed towards the reporter. His hand hovered over the handset. 'Molloy,' he said slowly, 'Molloy, you have not given this story to anybody else, have you?'

'Anybody else, sir?'

'You know . . . *them* . . .' The hated words stuck in his throat.

'You mean Fleet Street, sir?'

The editor flinched and made the sign of the cross. Molloy genuflected subconsciously.

'You haven't, Molloy?'

'Certainly *not*, sir!'

'Good man! Good man!' Snatching up the receiver the editor dialled six. As his finger described the mystical arc he whispered to himself, as one reciting a catechism, 'Twenty years in this game. Twenty long years of flower shows and boy scout jamborees and now, and now . . .' He paused a moment, a hand across the mouthpiece and stared towards the unspeakable ceiling beyond which, somewhere distant, sat the great proprietor in the sky. 'Thank you, God,' he said. 'Amen.'

'Amen,' echoed Molloy pushing across the desk a petty cash slip which was in its way as great a work of fiction as any that Harold Robbins had ever come up with. 'If I might just have your signature, sir.'

Without even looking, the editor signed away a sizeable chunk of the paper's financial resources. 'All these years,' he continued, 'I've prayed for an opportunity to do this.'

'Sir?' said Molloy.

'Listen,' said the editor.

'Hello,' said a sleepy voice at the other end of the line, 'Print Room.'

'Williams?' said the editor. 'Williams, is that you?'

'Of course it is, who's that speaking?'

'Williams.' The editor took a deep breath and said, 'Williams, hold the front page!'

'Oh, not again, Molloy, said the voice, 'just piss off, will you!' The receiver fell and the line went prrrrrrrr . . .

10

The brothers Paul and Barry Geronimo sat in the police cell, handcuffed together. A more disconsolate pair of renegade redmen it was hard to imagine. With his unmanacled hand Paul nursed the Victoria plum which had ripened upon his left temple. Barry made dismal groaning sounds as he tested his many tender spots for signs of fracture. At great length it was he who was the first to speak. 'Mum is not going to like this,' he said simply.

Paul made as to affect a surly frown which caused him considerable pain. 'This mean warpath for certain,' he muttered. 'Many scalps decorate lodge before teatime.'

Barry glanced sidelong at his bandaged brother. 'Paul,' he said, 'Paul, you really are quite certain about us being the dual reincarnation of Geronimo, aren't you? I mean, there couldn't be any mistake now, could there? I mean, I reckon we're on a hiding to nowhere here . . . I mean . . .' For his outspokenness, brother Barry received a blow much favoured by the now legendary Billy Two Rivers and known as the Tomahawk Chop. 'You bastard, I'm telling Mum.'

'Break it up in there,' a Metropolitan Police voice called through the peephole, 'and get on your feet, you've got a visitor.'

A heavy key turned in the lock, making all those really good noises that jail door locks make in prison movies. The door swung in to reveal a grinning Constable Meek, bearing three teacups and a plate of digestives on a regulation enamel tray. 'Here you go, Tonto,' he smirked. 'Sorry, we're out of firewater.'

'Half hour on red ant's nest with honey pot up back passage wipe smile off your face,' said Paul Geronimo, making an obscene North American gesture.

Barry rubbed at the new bruise on his head. There had to be something to this reincarnation business, civil engineers just did not come out with off the cuff remarks like that. 'Two sugars, please,' he said.

'You've got a visitor,' said the still smirking constable, placing the tray upon the bunk. 'Great white chief come smoke pipe of peace.'

'That will be enough of that, thank you, Constable.' The voice belonged to Inspectre Hovis, who now followed it into the cell. He carried beneath his arm a buff-coloured folder. 'Kindly relock the door behind you, Constable, and await my call.' Constable Meek slunk away, slamming the door dramatically behind him. 'Now,' said the Inspectre, taking a digestive from the plate and seating himself. 'Would you like to tell me all about it?'

Paul Geronimo looked Hovis up and down. 'Under articles of Geneva Convention, we tell you nothing but name, rank and telephone number,' he said. 'So go suck.'

'I see,' said Hovis. 'Then let me tell you something. This is my first day in Brentford.'

'Careful it not your last,' said Barry.

'My first day,' Hovis continued. He delved into his pocket and drew out a small brightly coloured book. 'Do you see this?'

Paul nodded. 'It famous *Guide to Brentford*, written by esteemed local author P.P. Penrose.'

'Author of the Lazlo Woodbine thrillers,' Barry added.

'Quite so,' said Hovis. 'I purchased it this very morning.'

Paul studied the ceiling and made war-drum sounds beneath his breath.

'It is my belief,' said Hovis, 'that a guidebook tells you as much about a town by what it does *not* say as by what it *does*.'

'Esoteric dichotomy alone insufficient basis for theoretical reasoning,' said Paul. 'Brave who always search skyline for enemy smoke ofttimes walk in buffalo shit.'

'Be that as it may,' said Hovis. 'Then I shall confine my observations to what the guide book does say.' He thumbed

51

it open and, between munchings of his biscuit, read aloud. 'The historic Borough of Brentford is notable for, amongst other things, the beauty of its womenfolk, the glories of its architectural heritage and the quality of its fine hand-drawn ales. In the year 49 AD Julius Caeser . . .'

'Beg to interject,' said Paul, 'but noble history of borough well known to us. We born and raised here.'

'All right,' said the Inspectre. 'Then, to be succinct, it is this. In one thousand years of recorded history Brentford has never known a race riot. Not until today, when you incited one.'

'We done what?' queried Barry.

'Incited a race riot.' Inspectre Hovis took a signed statement from his file and glanced it up and down. 'Did you or did you not refer to Councillor Clyde Merridew Ffog as "Mangy white cur fit only for roasting over a slow fire"?'

'Well, er,' said Paul.

'And a Mr Julian Membrane, who is recovering, I am pleased to say, from the tomahawk wound, records in his statement that you made the inflammatory remark, "Yellow blood of palefaces belong painted on toilet walls".'

'We true victims of racial harassment,' cried Paul Geronimo, rising from his bunk and dragging his brother with him. 'Long-nosed white dog twist truth like snake twist . . .'

'There you go again,' said Hovis. 'This is not going to look very good on my report now, is it? Inflammatory remarks of a racial nature, damage to council property, disturbing the peace, inciting riot, grievous bodily harm, assault with a deadly weapon, resisting arrest, insulting behaviour, need I go on? You'll get five years for this lot, I shouldn't wonder.' He gestured towards Paul's blackly dyed and magnificently braided barnet and made scissor snips with his fingers. 'At Her Majesty's barber shop.'

Paul fingered his hair; it had taken three years to grow. Brother Barry's grazed chin sank on to his buckskin chest. 'We up shit creek in barbed wire canoe,' he observed.

'How aptly put,' said Inspectre Hovis. 'Now what do you

suppose we should do about it?'

Paul peered dubiously towards the gaunt vulture, hovering upon the opposite bunk. 'What exactly are you suggesting?' he asked.

Hovis folded his mirrored pince-nez into an elegant tortoise-shell case and slid this into his top pocket. He reached forward for another biscuit and fixed Paul Geronimo with a penetrating gaze. The brave wilted visibly. 'Well?' said Inspectre Hovis.

'Er . . . um,' said Paul Geronimo.

'Squaw who dance too long round cooking pot praising cook find that meal grown too cold to eat, if you get my meaning.'

'I do,' said Paul, 'I mean I think I do.'

'Well, what say we smoke pipe of peace and parley just a little?'

'I can dig it,' said Paul Geronimo.

Forty-five minutes later, the final cell door having closed upon his departure, Inspectre Hovis strode into the newly painted office that was now his own, placed his bum upon the chair and his heels upon the desk. All in all it had been a most satisfactory day. By skilful manipulation he now had half the town council virtually in his pocket. He had spared the borough the embarrassment their prosecution would have brought upon it and himself the ensuing notoriety for having arrested them in the first place. He had become blood brother to the dual reincarnation of Geronimo and been invited out to dinner by one of the most attractive women it had ever been his privilege to interrogate. All in all it had been a *most* satisfactory first day.

Reaching for his cane, Hovis flipped open the silver top and withdrew a pinch of ground black Moroccan snuff. He offered this to an eager nostril and drew deeply upon it. But there was little time for self-congratulation. He was here upon a mission, one upon which the fate of his entire career could be said to rest. Like Dick Whittington and the Count of St Germaine, Inspectre Hovis had come to Brentford with only one thought in his mind. The search for gold.

53

11

From its eyrie atop the tower, the Memorial Library clock proclaimed the hour of six. Soft breaths of late spring honeysuckle shared the air with other smells of early evening. Smells which mingled to become that special sub-urban smell which is the sum of its parts. Smells of frying fish, of Scotch whisky, of cheap cigar smoke, of exclusive perfume and of other smells, strange and haunting and unfathomable.

Of frying fish. Old Pete turned the large salmon steak (an unexpected gift from Neville) in his cankerous frying pan and whistled 'When the Boat Comes In'. Young Chips barked an off-key counterpoint. It hadn't been a bad old day all in all and there was still the evening to come.

Of Scotch whisky. In the allotment shed John Omally poured two large glasses of ten-year-old malt and handed one to Scoop Molloy.

'Cheers,' said the star reporter, passing John a brown envelope containing several bank-notes of high denomi-nation. 'And thanks for the tip-off.'

'My pleasure,' said himself. 'I suggest that we drink to further scoops of an exclusive nature.'

'Your health.'

'And yours.'

Of cheap cigar smoke. The editor of the *Brentford Mercury* paced the floor of the print room, enveloped in a thick blue haze. Through this, Williams, the languid typesetter, peered up at intervals from the vast cryptic crossword he was composing to catch the latest philippic directed towards a certain newly arrived police inspectre.

Beneath the editor's pacing feet and torn asunder lay the trampled remnants which were some of the greatest headlines never to see the light of day: BRAVES PASTE POOF IN BRIBERY SCANDAL SENSATION. This and no less than twenty-seven permutations of equal literary worth had been done to death that very afternoon when Hovis had unexpectedly arrived at the office, slapped a D-notice on the whole thing, declared it *sub judice* and paraphrased the famous Fleet Street axiom with the words, 'Publish and be nicked.'

The editor puffed and paced, effed and blinded and did such other things as ruing the day and damning the eye of. Williams squinted through the blue fug towards his wristlet watch. He'd soon be on double time. He would wait until that time before he suggested that they could always use BRENTFORD TO HOST NEXT OLYMPICS! which was probably the greatest headline the *Mercury* was ever likely to get – without fear of prosecution. In the meantime, he was having a problem finding a word to fit forty-seven across. He had something 'A', something something 'A', something 'D'.

'Bastard!' shouted the now invisible editor.

'Ideal,' said Williams. 'BA-STAR-D, astronomical graduate likes a cuppa, or something like that.'

Of exclusive perfume. Jennifer Naylor arrayed herself upon a chromium bar-stool before the faux-marble counter of Punter's Wine Bar, sipping a cocktail and considering the doings of her day. A wry smile played about her delicate lips and her equally delicate fingers played about a ludicrous miniature sunshade which shish-kebabbed a Morello cherry and a slice of canned pineapple.

To the sounds of a drum-roll and stupendous applause (heard only to himself), the establishment's proprietor, one Robert Tucker, known and hated locally as Bob the Bookie, swaggered through the reproduction art deco doorway.

Tonight he was a vision in white. A Japanese silk jacket hung upon his shoulders at 'Full Zorro'. Sleeves dangling like those of a double amputee. The inevitable Raybans were strung about his neck and the two-inch Cuban heels raised everything except his credibility. This was amply catered for by the Rolls-Royce key-ring which swung from a belt loop above his padded crotch, and a wallet containing a secret contrivance, designed for him by Norman, which could project his American Express Gold Card into the lap of a likely-looking female at the touch of a secret button.

Feigning nonchalance at the singular lack of 'punters' this Happy Hour, he flexed his shoulders, stooped to retrieve his jacket and sauntered over to his single patroness.

'Hi, Jen baby,' he crooned, clambering on to the next bar stool. 'What's happening?'

'Simply enjoying the tranquillity of your wine bar,' Jennifer explained. 'All the others get so crowded around this time.'

Bob leant forward to bring Jennifer within the killing range of his aftershave. 'Punter's is . . . er . . . somewhat exclusive. Say, is that your new Porsche outside?'

Jennifer nodded. 'Like it?'

'Not half. Got one on order myself. The new reg. of course. Electric blue, drinks tray on the back, holophonic sound system, the lot.'

'Electric blue?' Jennifer sighed wearily, took up the minuscule umbrella and bit purposefully through the shining cherry. Bob crossed his legs and winced painfully. 'I like my cars as I like my men,' said Jennifer Naylor, 'big and black.' Bob sank from his stool and made his way behind the counter. Here, as if by magic, he became some four inches taller. 'Mind you don't fall,' said Jennifer, who had seen the platform installed.

'Where's Eric?'

'Picking his nose over the quiche the last time I saw him.'

56

'Eric!'

'Watchawant?' The voice drifted from the kitchen where the cocktail barman stood combing his dandruff into a bowl of green salad.

'There's customers out here want serving.'

'Chance would be a fine thing.' Eric slouched into view adjusting his bow-tie and stroking stray flecks from his waistcoat shoulders. 'Same again, dear?' he asked Jennifer.

'Same again for the lady,' said Bob, settling himself in behind the bar, 'And I'll have a Raging Stonker.' He winked lewdly towards Jennifer. He'd come up with all the suggestive names for the cocktails himself, after a holiday in Benidorm. It seemed to go down a bundle over there and Bob was at a loss to understand why the Brentford glitterati had not taken to it.

'How would you like your Raging Stonker?' Eric asked. 'Shaken or stirred?'

Bob stared some daggers at the barman and smiled one of those you-can't-get-the-staff-nowadays kinds of smiles towards Jennifer.

'Stirred,' he said from between gritted teeth. Eric went off about his business worrying at his scalp with a cocktail stirrer.

'What do you think of this?' Bob bared his left wrist towards Jennifer, exposing something that resembled a broad gold band and swiftly changing the subject.

'A bracelet, how sweet.'

'Not a bracelet,' said Bob. 'It's the very latest innovation in wrist-watches from Piaget. The dial encircles the wrist, see, and this little light inside travels round once every twenty-four hours, telling you the time. Clever, eh? Press this button—' Bob did so, 'and all the digits shift, so you can tell the time anywhere in the world. Waterproof and shockproof and very exclusive.'

'Paid for by the punters, no doubt.'

'You're not kidding.' Bob leant forward smirking. 'If you knew just how eager some of them are to give their money away.'

'Really?'

'Really. You'll never guess what one of them came in to place a bet on today.'

'Won't I?'

Bob shook his head and guffawed. 'Jim Pooley only came into my shop and bet ten pounds that the next Olympic games would be held in Brentford.' Bob collapsed in paroxysms of laughter, tears filled his eyes and ran down his cheeks, streaking his suntan. 'Can you imagine?' he croaked between spasms. 'Can you imagine?'

'And you took the bet?'

'Oh yes, I gave him a million to one on it.'

Eric returned with a Split Beaver and a Raging Stonker.

'Did you say your watch was shockproof, Bob?' Jennifer asked.

'Why yes, I think so.' Bob dabbed a tear from his eye. 'Why do you ask?'

'Let me whisper, just to be on the safe side,' said Jennifer Naylor, drawing the likely lad into the aura of her exclusive perfume.

The sun, slanting away beyond Royal Kew, laid its trail of shadows and turned the gasometer, the flatblocks, the Arts Centre and the ancient island oaks into frail theatrical props.

From the black shadow of the gasometer, a car of still deeper black emerged, as if drawn from a dark wall of water. A small quizzical face was scarcely visible, peering through the steering wheel. A chauffeur's cap perched upon the dwarfish head and tiny gloved hands guided the silent vehicle towards the Ealing Road. At intervals the car shuddered violently and the chauffeur flinched. Within the rear compartment something fearful was occurring.

Blows rained upon the dividing glass screen and a series of great thumps, as of something heavy being tossed to and fro, sent shivers through the weird black automobile. The chauffeur pressed his foot to the floor.

'Be still,' he whispered. 'Please be still.' A sharp little tooth penetrated his lower lip and a slim line of blood divided his up-turned chin. A strangled, death-rattle cry arose from the crippled throat of the unseen occupant and a curious smell penetrated the driver's cab. A smell, strange and haunting and unfathomable.

12

Those soothsayers, weather-watchers, old-wife-tale-tellers and local shepherds who, having taken delight in the red sky of the previous night, felt confident to predict a great day on the morrow, awoke upon a Saturday morning that was to be a turning point, nay a veritable watershed in the borough's history. For today, the eyes of the world would turn upon Brentford.

Some, of course, knew it was coming. Bob the Bookie, for instance, who had watched the dawn rise and who even now sat alone in his betting shop weeping bitterly into his gin glass.

And Jennifer Naylor, who enjoyed a most pleasant evening at the 'Comfy Canard', dining upon oysters in Armagnac and fricasséed quail with pâté de foie gras. All at the expense of Inspectre Hovis. Much to Jennifer's surprise, the detective had turned out not only to be a witty and skilful conversationalist, but a gourmet of the first magnitude.

And then there were the brothers Geronimo who had been despatched upon a sacred mission. One which, as Hovis had put it, required the cunning of the native coyote, the eye of the mountain eagle, the heart of the black bear, the ears of the pampas jack rabbit and the sagacity of the ring-tailed possum.

But for most, the unexpected arrival of the *Brentford Mercury*'s Special Olympic Souvenir Edition came more as a terminal shock than as a pleasant surprise. Jaws descended, eyes popped, pyjama tops were biblically 'rent asunder' and phonelines jammed as the first murmurs of what is euphemistically referred to as Public Unrest rumbled ominously across the borough.

Some, like internationally famed journalist Gary Jenkins, smelt griffin and returned to their sleeping partners. Others, and this must certainly include the likes of John Omally within their avaricious ranks, could only smell the green and folding stuff.

By ten o'clock the *Mercury*'s office was under seige. The crowd spilled from the pavement and blocked both sides of the high street. Traffic ground to a halt. Horns were honked, hooters hooted, blasphemies exchanged and invective given its full head. From his open window on high the editor, already in a state of high delirium, raved at the crowd who answered his words with cat-calls, hoots of derision and the waving of improvised banners. For the most part his words were lost amidst the ferment below and lovers of mime were similarly lost in admiration for the dramatic, although often enigmatic, nature of his gestures.

The *Mercury* office, being less than one hundred yards from Brentford Police Station, the arrival of the boys in blue seemed very much on the cards. And so it was that – their official coffee-break completed – the gallant lads climbed into their squad cars, set the sirens a-wailing and the beacons a-flashing and sat eagerly in the car-park waiting for the traffic to clear.

At a little after ten-thirty Inspectre Hovis appeared on the scene. He entered the *Mercury*'s office by the rear door, thrust the gibbering editor away from the window and addressed the crowd through an amplified loud-hailer.

His speech was brief and to the point. He informed the crowd that a model of the Olympic stadium complete with full plans and specifications could be seen that very afternoon at the town hall from two o'clock onwards. He made some mention of riot shields and extendible truncheons, tear-gas canisters, rubber bullets and policemen on horseback. And went on to offer his own feelings about the severity of sentences currently being meted out to rioters and those engaged in unlawful assembly. Finally, for good measure, he read the riot act.

All in all it proved quite successful upon this particular

occasion. The plucky Brentonians, who were strangers to such matters, hung on his every word, digested the intelligence to be found therein, perused the lines of SPG officers who had lately materialized on every side and finally drifted away with talk of pressing engagements at Tesco's and Safeway's.

Inspectre Hovis joined the editor in a glass of Fleet Street Comfort. 'I am going to be keeping a watchful eye on you in the future,' he told the gibbering wreck. 'And I shall take a very poor view of it if I see any headlines such as TRIGGER HAPPY COPS SAVAGE SATURDAY SHOPPERS.'

The editor tossed a triple down his throat. 'I was thinking more along the line of GALLANT INSPECTOR QUELLS MOB.'

'Inspectre,' said Hovis. 'It is so much more enigmatic, don't you think. You'll want a photograph of me for the front page. I'll have an officer drop you round a couple of ten by eight glossies.'

'Thanks very much,' said the editor of the *Brentford Mercury*.

13

Jim Pooley sat upon his favourite bench before the Memorial Library. Hands clasped behind his head, legs outstretched, Special Olympic Souvenir Edition aproning his knees. Jim appeared to be whistling, 'Money Makes the World Go Round' – that or an ancient Abba hit, but the air was constantly disjointed by contented sighs and deep chuckles. Once in a while Jim would stretch out his arms and punch at the sky, much after the fashion of a Wembley Cup tie striker who had just hammered the winning goal into the back of the net. The sun was certainly in Jim's heaven and all seemed very much all right with the world.

Pooley was, however, finding some difficulty in coming to terms with his good fortune. Within the span of twenty-four short hours he had risen from the ranks of 'no-mark' to those of potential millionaire. In a strange way he had almost come to resent it. Basically because it was not of his own doing. He'd been betting away for years, with scheme after scheme and system after system. Then along comes Omally who, to Jim's knowledge, had never laid a bet in his life and the next thing you know – *Eureka! Shazam! Bingo!* – things of that nature. And it wasn't just that. There was also Omally's remarkable and uncharacteristic altruism in allowing him to place the bet in his own name, even though he knew it was a sure thing. That was most puzzling.

And so there sat Jim, torn between moments of rare joy and others of brooding bafflement, although it must be fairly stated that the rare joy was winning the uneven struggle.

From the corner of his eye, Pooley noticed a scruffy-looking individual approaching. Normally he would not have given a stranger a second glance, but there was something furtive and suspicious in the way that he moved which set Jim almost instantly upon the alert. A small red warning light flashed on the dashboard of his brain. In the light of future events, those of a mystical nature might incline to the belief that our old friend, the sixth sense was at work again. Those of a more cynical disposition might well suggest that it was nothing more than a clichéd literary device aimed at holding the reader's wandering attention. Whatever the case, Jim, recalling a night at the Flying Swan when he'd watched a drunk who claimed to be ex-SAS roll an ordinary newspaper into a sharpened point and, to Neville's horror, drive it a full inch into the bar top, began to twist his copy of the *Mercury* into a clumsy sausage which might possibly have put the wind up a poodle.

The furtive figure crept closer and hovered a few yards from Pooley's bench. Jim, nerves taut as fiddle strings and sagacity possibly rivalling that of the ring-tailed possum, turned upon him. 'Good morning to you,' said Jim. 'Can I be of some help or what?' Taking full stock of the stranger, Pooley was not all that taken with what he saw. From shiny suede chukka boots to frayed corduroys, the observer's eye led over an expanse of shabby raincoat to a grizzled face, unshaven of chin, dark of eye and topped by a greasy fedora. Here, thought Jim, is a man whose flirtation with hygiene never led to a lasting relationship.

'Jim Pooley?'

Jim nervously rolled his newspaper. This man was definitely not Eamonn Andrews proffering the big red book, neither was he Chalkie White or one of the Page Three lovelies offering to exchange a five spot for the answer to a simple question. 'You just missed him,' said Pooley. 'He teaches unarmed combat down at the church hall on Saturday mornings. I expect you'll find him there.'

'This is it,' said the shabby man, withdrawing from his pocket something that looked for all the world to be none

64

other than the legendary 'Judge Colt'. 'Your luck just ran out.'

Jim's brain struggled to encompass this sudden shift in fortunes, a no-mark, a potential millionaire and a coffin case all within the same twenty-four hours. It took some getting used to. 'I don't think I quite understand,' said Jim, staring into what looked like the muzzle of a howitzer.

'It is perfectly straightforward,' explained the shabby man. 'I am going to kill you, do you want it here or elsewhere?'

'Oh, definitely elsewhere, name the place, I'll meet you there.'

'Get moving.' The shabby man returned his peacemaker to his pocket and gestured with the bulge of the hidden barrel.

I wonder where all the nice policemen are, wondered Jim. It's funny how there's never one around when you need him.

'This way.'

Jim found himself being prodded down a side alley, which he knew led to a break in the allotment fence. 'You'll kick yourself when you read tomorrow's paper,' said Jim, 'you've got the wrong man, you know.'

'Get moving.'

'I am but a poor man but you can have all that I own.'

'I shall anyway.'

'What have I done to deserve this?' wailed Jim. 'I haven't harmed no-one.'

'Over here.'

Pooley hung his head and moved on over. The two threaded their way through the shanty town of corrugated iron huts, between well-tended plots and pastures wild. There was not a tenant to be seen.

'Stop.'

'Must I?'

The shabby man drew out his pistol and pressed the cold steel against the nape of Pooley's neck. 'Recommend yourself to your deity.'

Jim spun round. His terror was absolute but his nerve had not absolutely deserted him. 'Now see here,' he said, 'a dying man is entitled to a last request. Everybody knows that.'

'So what is it?'

Jim fell to his knees. 'Don't kill me,' he begged.

'Request denied.' The pistol rose and levelled at a point midway between Pooley's eyes.

'Look out! Behind you!' cried Jim. It had always worked in the movies, well, a couple of times anyway.

'Do me a favour.' Jim could see the black crescent of finger-nail as it drew back upon the trigger. There was a very loud bang and then things went very black indeed.

John Omally stood above the fallen twosome, spade in hand.

'Wake up, Jim,' he called. 'It's opening time.'

Pooley stirred from his nightmare and found himself still staring into his would-be assassin's face: stubble, spots, halitosis and all. 'Aaagh!' went Jim, rolling smartly in a swift sideways direction, 'and help!'

'You're lucky I saw you coming past my hut,' said John, reaching down to take up the fallen revolver. 'This bugger would have done for you.'

Pooley climbed shakily to his feet. 'What's all this about?' he mumbled, feeling himself all over for bullet holes. 'I didn't do anything to anybody.'

'I don't think Bob would agree with you.'

'You what?' Pooley was swamped by sudden realization. 'So that's why you let *me* place the bet! You knew he'd try something like this.'

'Come, come, Jim, you cannot blame me for your lack of foresight. You are the victim of your own avarice. I saved your life, did I not?'

'You put it in jeopardy first.'

'I would not have let any harm come to you.'

'I've got a weak heart.' Pooley indicated the wrong side of his chest. 'Such a shock could have done for me.'

'You'll survive.'

'Give me that gun. I will deal with Bob directly.'

'As you please.' Omally handed the weapon to his companion. 'But it will do you no good.'

Pooley spun the gun upon his finger, anger and a lust for vengeance leant him an unexpected dexterity. He sought out a short cigar from his top pocket and wondered how he might appropriate a poncho and a cowboy hat at short notice. 'And why will it do me no good?' he asked.

'Because,' said John, 'the gun is a replica, it's not real.'

'What?'

'It was meant to frighten you, to make you give up the betting slip. Bob hasn't got the bottle to hire a hit-man, this is Brentford, not Chicago in the roaring twenties.'

'I'm not so sure. Bob, as we all know, is a very sore loser.'

'Where am I?' groaned a shabby fallen figure.

'He's not quite dead,' said Jim. 'At least I might give him a slight kicking to aid him upon his way.'

'If you feel it necessary,' said John, 'although I do not believe it to be in your nature.'

Pooley tossed the gun into a nearby waterbutt. As an afterthought he pulled off the shabby man's chukka boots and did likewise with them. 'It's not,' said Jim.

'Lets get down to the Swan,' said John Omally, 'I'll buy you a pint.'

'Now that,' said Jim, 'is an excellent idea.'

14

The Flying Swan was unusually crowded for the time of day. John and Jim elbowed their way towards the bar and cried out for attention. Neville detached himself from a noisy throng at the counter and came over to do the honours.

'It's busy,' John observed.

Neville tapped at his slender nose. 'Whitehall,' he whispered hoarsely, 'there's all sorts in from Westminster, and on a Saturday too. It seems you can't just say you're hosting the Olympic games without getting some kind of official say-so. All seems a little fussy to me. Something to do with red tape.'

'So you mean that there might be some doubt.' Pooley clutched at his breast pocket, wherein rested his key to the potential millions.

'Your guess is as good as mine,' said Neville, presenting the pints. 'Still, it's all good for business isn't it?'

'Oh yes,' said Jim, 'yes indeed.' He had paid for the drinks before he recalled that they were Omally's treat.

'Cheers,' said John.

'I don't like the sound of this coloured tape,' said Jim. 'This could cost us.'

'I suggest we listen in.' Omally nodded towards a nearby conclave and Pooley followed him in the direction of the nod.

The Whitehall types were clustered about one 'Badger' Beaumont, the *Mercury*'s inebriate theatre critic. In the absence of Scoop Molloy, who was recovering from the effects of a night without shame, he was acting as official Olympic correspondent.

John and Jim pondered long upon the Whitehallinesians.

They were of a species new to the borough. Omally's eye for a well-tailored suit recognized that rare variety that is measured for in inches without laughter and paid for in guineas without complaint. Their faces had that scrubbed and plucked quality only found elsewhere upon Madame Tussaud's dummies and oven-ready chickens. Noses inked in by suffused veins found favour and weak chins were all the rage. There was an even half dozen of them, and from right to left, in terms of position rather than political persuasion, they were: ministers for Sport and Recreation, Development, Housing, Trade and Industry, Foreign Affairs and Finance. There were also under-ministers, under-secretaries, press secretaries, advisers, chauffeurs, masseurs, minders and minions. Omally also spied out several of those young ladies that are trained in the arts which amuse men.

All were arrayed about the Swan in their social groupings, clucking and chatting, laughing and nodding. And doing it all very loudly.

Pooley and Omally listened carefully to the ministers as they conversed.

'I am perplexed,' said Jim.

'You and me both,' said John.

Neville swept by with a platter of salmon sandwiches. 'Everything to your liking, gentlemen?' he asked, his good eye all awink. He appeared to be sporting his bestest suit, the weddings, funerals and special lodge meetings number. 'Quality punters, eh?'

Omally watched in dumb disbelief as Neville fawned over a group of pin-striped 'Hoorays' and their females, who were nonchalantly sipping halves of bitter and flicking cigarette ash into the *jardinières*. 'Who would have thought it,' said John, 'Neville sucking up to these cretins.'

'It will end in tears,' said Jim philosophically. 'But see, here comes Bob. Will you hold him whilst I do the hitting or likeways about?'

'Let us hear his story first, there might well be free drinks in it.'

Bob waded bravely through the crowd, fifteen hundred pounds' worth of dental crowns beaming from his face. 'Hello, lads,' he said, 'hoped I'd find you here, how's tricks?'

'Never better,' said Jim. 'And yourself?'

'Oh, fine, fine.'

'That is good to hear,' said Pooley, 'that is very good.'

'It is good,' Omally agreed.

'Listen,' said Bob. 'No hard feelings, eh?'

'Hard feelings?' Jim looked mystified. 'About what?'

'You know.' Bob made a gun from his right hand and clicked it towards Pooley's head. 'All a misunderstanding, no offence meant.'

'Oh, that.' Pooley put his forefinger to his temple and cocked his thumb. 'No offence meant? None taken, I assure you.'

'Oh, good, good, it's just, well, joke over, eh, Jim?'

'Joke?'

'The bet.'

'The bet?'

'Come on now, Jim, the one million to one.'

'One million!' Omally's eyebrows rose towards his curly crown. He could not restrain his hands from rubbing together.

'Good joke,' said Bob, 'but let's call it off now, eh? Tell you what, I'll buy back the betting slip, what shall we say, twenty-five pounds?' Pooley looked at Omally. 'Fifty then?' Omally looked at Pooley. 'All right,' said Bob. 'Never let it be said that I am not a good sport. Seventy-five pounds and that's my final offer.'

'I'll hold,' said John. 'You hit.'

'Good morning, gentlemen.' The voice belonged to Jennifer Naylor.

'Let me buy you a drink,' said Bob, grinning up at his angel of deliverance and detaching himself from John's grip.

'Later, I'm rather tied up at the moment.' Jennifer indicated Philip Cameron and Mavis Peake who had entered in her wake, freighting large bundles of xeroxed paper. 'This way!'

Pooley flinched. 'This way' would forever now hold only bitter memories for him.

Jennifer approached the Hoorays' table, considering it suitable to her needs, then ushered the entire bunch away with a simple, 'I hope you don't mind if I sit here, thank you.'

John watched in admiration. 'Jim,' said he, 'now that *is* a woman. If ever I was to marry.'

Jim turned to his friend in surprise. 'Marry?' said he. 'Whatever do you mean?'

'It comes to all men, or at least to most.'

'But not to you, John.' Pooley straightened an imaginary tie. 'A man would have to be worth a lot of scratch to get a woman like that for a wife. A veritable millionaire at the very least.'

'My glass is empty,' said John. 'Whose round is it?'

'Yours, John, without a shadow of a doubt.'

'Itineraries, ladies and gentlemen,' said Jennifer Naylor as Mavis and Philip moved amongst the throng, distributing the xeroxed sheets. 'You will see that everything has been laid on for your convenience. If there are any problems, I will be happy to help out wherever I can.'

Neville, returning to the bar, found an itinerary pushed into his hand. Somewhat flattered, he thrust out his chest, grinned broadly and examined the thing with keen interest.

'A coach will pick us up from here at twelve noon,' Jennifer continued.

'Twelve noon?' The grin fell from Neville's face. He gazed up in horror towards the Guinness clock. It was already eleven forty-five. 'Hang on,' he cried. 'What's the hurry?'

'There will be a reception at the town hall,' said Jennifer, ignoring the barman's protests. 'Full buffet, choice of wines, etc., etc.'

Neville found a large platter of salmon sandwiches being thrust back into his hands. 'Sorry, old chap,' said one of the Hoorays, 'and could you cancel those bottles of vino.'

'Then there will be a private viewing of the Olympic model at one o'clock where you will have the opportunity to pose questions to Messrs Membrane and Mucus, the design consultants. A tour of the local brewery and a later wine tasting at Punter's Wine Bar will lead us through nicely to the Mayoral banquet at seven-thirty. Do please keep your itineraries with you as they will serve as security passes to the various functions.'

John Omally hastily availed himself of two copies. 'This sounds like our kind of day out,' he told Jim, who nodded enthusiastically.

'Same again?' Neville asked, spying out Pooley's empty glass.

'Ah, no thanks, Neville, I think we've had enough for now.'

The barman turned away in fury to view more plates of salmon sandwiches being pushed back across the bar counter. 'Bastards!' was all he had to say.

Pooley and Omally were the first to board the coach. Although Jim wanted to sit next to the driver, Omally counselled subtlety and the keeping of the now legendary low profile and thrust him towards a rear seat.

'Not over the wheel,' said Jim. 'It makes me travel sick.'

Omally shook his head. 'You're so childish,' he said.

The ministers and team climbed on board, talking loudly, all white collars, blue ties and red faces. After a brief kerfuffle over who got to sit next to the driver, a pecking order was established and they lowered their Gieves and Hawkes and prepared for the off.

Jennifer Naylor climbed aboard, with the unnecessary assistance of Philip Cameron, and took up the microphone. 'If you are all sitting comfortably,' she said, 'then off we go.' And off they jolly well went.

15

The town hall's hospitality suite was no stranger to events
and receptions. The West London Wandering Bishops, the
Chiswick Decorative Egg Society and the Association of
Invisible Aryans each held their annual meetings there.
It had not, however, seen a spread like this since the
Brentford Blow-Out Club had dined themselves to collec-
tive oblivion there five years previously with a marathon
eat-in. Today's spread was of that rare and almost
unknown variety that combined quality with quantity.

'You know,' said Jim Pooley as he pushed an exquisite
sweetmeat into his face and held out his glass for a top up,
'this is the life.'

'I was thinking something of the sort myself,' Omally
replied, as he decanted another measure of chilled French
wine into his own glass.

'Do you think it's always like this for politicians, John?'
Omally perused the congregation. Those present looked
very much at ease and pretty much at home. 'Can one still
buy one's way into Parliament?' Jim asked. 'Seems like a
decent enough job for a married man.'

'Definitely not!' The image of Pooley giving forth across
the floor of 'The House' whilst Jennifer Naylor laced
herself into the French maid's outfit and plumped up the
pillows of the marital bed, had Omally cringing.

As if at a psychic summons the future Mrs Pooley
approached them through the crowd. 'I shall turn a blind
eye to your presence if you remain sober. But any trouble
and out you go.'

Omally raised his glass and smiled his winning smile.
'This is all very impressive,' he said. 'You have a flair
for organization, to have arranged all this so quickly.

Remarkable. The Olympic games in Brentford – who would have thought it?'

Jennifer Naylor glanced from John to Jim and back again. 'The odds against it must be something in the nature of a million to one, wouldn't you say?'

'I am not a betting man,' said Omally, in all truth.

Jennifer Naylor smiled. 'You have so few vices, Mr Omally.'

John offered the beautiful woman a canapé. 'This is a glorious spread,' said he. 'A *nouvelle cuisine* belly-buster, no less.' He turned the bottle of wine in his hand and marvelled at the vintage. 'And I thought that the council was down to its last few bob.'

'It is,' said Jennifer, dabbing her lips with a napkin. 'This function has been privately funded.'

'Indeed, and might I ask by whom?'

'I really wish I knew.' The wistful tone in Jennifer's voice and the faraway look in her eyes were not lost upon John, who felt a sudden pang of jealousy.

'Miss Naylor,' interrupted Mavis Peake, 'sorry to tear you away from your friends, but the Minister for Trade and Industry would like a word.'

Jennifer Naylor smiled down between her cleavage to her frustrated associate. 'Why, thank you, dear,' she said, steering her breasts close by Mavis's nose. 'If you will excuse me, gentlemen.'

'Your servant, ma'am,' said Jim Pooley. 'It is all a bit lavish though, isn't it?' he said, thrusting something of an exotic nature into his mouth. 'Who do you think is paying for it all?'

Omally shrugged. 'I haven't the faintest idea, but it's big money, big out-borough money. I suggest we mingle, Jim. Keep our eyes and ears open.'

'And our mouths,' said Jim. 'What do you suppose that is?'

'An asparagus tip, you buffoon,' said John Omally. 'Somewhat *al dente* for my palate, but nevertheless quite passable.'

*   *   *

Neville thrust a sullen salmon sandwich into his mouth
and munched. The bar was all but empty. In a corner Bob
the Bookie engaged in heated conspiratorial chit-chat with
a shabby-looking man with a bandaged head and bare
feet. Other regulars had, upon discovering the bar to be so
crowded, taken themselves elsewhere for their lunchtime
repasts. Neville had lost out all the way round.

Old Pete entered the bar. 'You're quiet today, Neville, a
dark rum if you please.' The ancient surveyed the loaves
and fishes. 'Jesus been in then?' he asked.

Neville was not amused. 'Members of Parliament as it
happens,' he said. It sounded equally far-fetched. 'Heads
of State. Have a sandwich.'

'Thank you.' Old Pete took two. 'Heads of State, eh?'

'Truly,' said Neville, handing Old Pete his rum and
accepting the exact price in pennies and halfpennies.

'So I suppose that would be the pundit Nehru himself
over there, chatting with Bob.' Old Pete applied himself to
the salmon sandwich. 'Any ketchup?' he asked.

Neville thrust the official itinerary towards Old Pete.
'Doubting Thomas,' he murmured. The elder statesman
cocked a wise'n over the schedule. 'It reads like a piss
artist's day out in paradise. How much are the tickets?'

'Free,' said Neville, turning away to replenish the bottle
on the rum optic. 'If you have the itinerary you get in free.
Privileged bastards, unto those that have it shall be given
and unto those that have not . . .' He turned back just in
time to see Old Pete hobbling at speed out through the
door and off down the street. '. . . Even that which they
have shall be taken away from them.'

The exhibition hall had undergone a dramatic facelift.
Gone were the nicotine paintwork and fusty curtains,
gone too the clapped-out benches and several hundred
excruciating water-colours, the work of budding local
artists, which had graced the walls for a twelve-month.
What had previously been a grim foreboding edifice was

75

now bright, vital, a visual symphony of Post-Modernist primaries and soft pastels. The Victorian marble floor, previously capable of turning a whisper into a public broadcast and a footstep into a thunderclap, was lost beneath tiles of new audio-soluble polysilicate which effectively swallowed up the sounds of foot-falls, harmonized the acoustics and offered cushioned comfort to the visitor's feet.

In the centre of the floor stood the model town of Brentford, with its great five-pointed companion hovering above. It looked very much the way Bethlehem must have looked upon that first Christmas, although slightly less up-market. Lines of VDUs, literally overflowing with 'user-friendliness', displayed the minutiae of detail, specifications, stress factors, variables, co-efficients of linear expansion, quantum mechanics.

On the far wall, the borough's roll of honour was lost behind an enormous video screen upon which, portrayed in advanced computer graphics of a three-dimensional kind, the projected stadium assembled and disassembled itself again and again and again. Below this, and flanked by two ex-sumo wrestlers ladled into security guards' uniforms, stood a tall transparent cylinder, and within this floated the slim disc of Gravitite. In front of this a large red sign put the security-conscious visitor's mind at rest. For, should a would-be felon succeed in overpowering the guards, dynamiting his way through the two-inch plexiglass, setting off the numerous alarms and bringing down the steel portcullises, he would still have the laser beams and the poison gas to deal with.

The double doors from the hospitality suite swung open and the Whitehall chappies, now in various stages of inebriation, entered in a rowdy concourse. In their wake strolled Pooley and Omally.

'Holy mackerel,' said Jim. 'This is all a bit sudden. I was down here a week ago and there was no talk then of redecoration.'

Omally just whistled and shook his head.

The Whitehall types, several clinging amorously to their female assistants and all with equal passion to their glasses – swarmed amongst the exhibits, cooing and ooh-ahing. Finally, at a command from Jennifer Naylor, they assembled about the model town.

'Now, ladies and gentlemen,' she said, 'I will hand you over to Messrs Membrane and Mucus who will explain to you all aspects of the proposed stadium and answer whatever questions you might care to ask. Sirs.'

Lucas and Julian entered somewhat sheepishly, in the close company of two plain-clothed minders. Lucas sported a selection of cuts and abrasions and Julian had apparently taken up Sikhism. In the bruised face of yesterday's Indian uprising, they were taking no chances. The minders flexed and made menacing gestures. The Geronimo twins were nowhere to be seen.

Once more, Mucus and Membrane ran through their polished double act. If anything it had become even more polished, and by the time they had concluded and were preparing themselves to meet the bombardment of questions from the excited ministers, Omally for one was convinced that the battle had been won. Julian and Lucas knew this to be a fact. They had spent the morning at the Ministry of Defence demonstrating the wonders of Gravitite. Contracts had already been signed to the effect that in exchange for the formula, the government would give the games the go-ahead and defray all costs that the transfer from Birmingham to Brentford would involve. This meeting was nothing more than a formality.

'How long will construction take?'

'Something less than a month.'

'Who is going to pay for the actual stadium?'

'Our client.'

'When might we meet him?'

'Regretfully, never. Our client is a millionaire recluse and seeks no publicity.'

'The sites where the legs are to be erected, has planning permission been granted?'

Lucas and Julian looked painfully at one another. 'It has now.'

'Do you think you could run through the locations of the sites just once more for the record?'

'Certainly. Now as I have said, these were unwanted parcels of land sold off by the council to our client. When the games finish they will be returned to the borough. Such is the nature of our client's philanthropy.'

'And the sites are . . .?'

Julian outlined the proposed sites: 'West Point: Area of wasteland beside car park in Butts Estate. North-West Point: Disused works car park in Brook Lane North. North-East Point: Area of wasteland in corner of park, Clayponds Lane. East Point: Foreshore area to east of Griffin Island. South Point: Abandoned boatyard next to undeveloped area known as Cider Island.'

Abandoned boatyard next to undeveloped area known as Cider Island. The words took a moment or two to sink in before Pooley and Omally started in simultaneous horror. Thrusting their way through the crowd they gaped at the model town. There, sure as sure, the southern leg of the great stadium reached down and pierced a half-sunken barge in the abandoned boatyard. The half sunken barge which was the headquarters of the 'P & O Line'.

'Excavations will begin on Monday,' said Lucas Mucus. 'The legs will be up by the following weekend.'

16

If there is one thing that can be said in favour of council buildings, it is that they inevitably possess a wealth of corridors which seem to have been expressly designed so that the distraught and despairing might pace back and forwards along them swearing and muttering, yet secure in the knowledge that no-one will ever pay them the slightest attention.

Within moments of Lucas's terrible disclosure, John and Jim had found one of these aforementioned corridors that was ideal for their present needs. John did the pacing whilst Jim leant upon a wall smoking a cigarette. But the more John paced and worried, the more did Pooley become calmly philosophical about the whole thing. Presently, he said, 'John, we may be losing a headquarters, but we will be gaining ten million pounds.'

Omally gazed at him, the boy was clearly a fool. 'Jim,' said he, 'Jim, we will not simply be losing a headquarters, we will be gaining a prolonged period of incarceration at the pleasure of her Majesty the Queen. God bless her.'

Jim raised his glass, 'You what?'

'Prison, Jim. When the local garda get aboard that barge, as they are certain to do once the site foreman or somesuch gets a look inside, then we are marked men. It may just be a video recorder here and a bit of potheen there to us, but to the boys in blue it will be a chance to clean up every outstanding case they've got on their books.'

'We shall deny it all of course,' said Jim defiantly.

'Jim, the barge is full of stolen property, it is covered in our fingerprints, personal possessions, articles of clothing, why, you've even got your holiday snaps up on the salon wall.'

'I thought they made the place more homely.'

'We'll get five years at the very least.'

Jim's hands began to quiver. At times of great stress it had always been his habit to flap his hands wildly and spin about in small circles. Exactly where this had its genesis is hard to say, though no doubt Neville might have offered a suggestion or two. 'Hang on,' said Jim in mid-flap. 'We could always do a runner.'

'Do a runner?'

'Certainly, off to Rio de Janeiro! We could get Bob to post our winnings when the games start.'

'And perhaps he'll advance us the air fare if we ask him nicely.' Omally's voice had what they call an 'edge' to it.

'Do you think so?'

'No, Jim, I do *not* think so. Nor do I think that doing a runner would be of the slightest use. Unless you happen to have the necessary fake passports, know the underworld safe houses, and hold sway with bribable officials. And as to the matter of Bob bunging ten million pounds in an airmail envelope and posting it on, Jim, you are a double buffoon!'

Pooley flapped his hands wildly and spun about in small circles. 'All is lost,' he wailed, 'o doom and gloom!'

'Get a grip of yourself, man.'

'The ball and chains,' moaned Pooley, 'the manacles, that tent of blue the prisoner calls the sky.'

'Very prosaic, Jim, now do hush, will you?'

'I'll go stir crazy, a Pooley in the pokey, the shame, the terrible shame.'

'Pooley, cease this foolishness or I will give you a smack!'

'We'll have to clear it all out,' said Jim, 'all the evidence, get it away, round into your house for instance.'

'Oh no,' said John, 'not *my* house, absolutely not!'

'Then think of something else then.'

'I am trying.'

'Slammed up in the slammer,' mumbled Jim, 'bunged in chokey, banged up in the nick.'

'That's it!' said Omally, plunging his right fist into his left palm.

'What, give ourselves up?'

'No, banged up. That's it, Jim. Bang. Up.'

'Strangely,' said Jim, 'I fail to understand.'

'Bang,' said Omally, 'as in bombs go bang. We shall blow up the barge.'

'Blow up the barge.' Jim took in this intelligence and mulled it over in his mind. 'Be seeing you,' said Jim Pooley in a manner not altogether unknown to *The Prisoner* of the now legendary television series.

The unmarked coach bearing the well-breeched, well-fed, well-pissed and well-and-truly-out-of-it workers of Whitehall on the next leg of the Brentford day-trip, left discreetly from the rear car-park at two o'clock as the front doors of the town hall opened to admit the hoi polloi.

The crowd flooded the exhibition hall with murmurs of dissension and disapproval turning slowly to gasps of wonder and disbelief at the miracles upon display. For miracles are fearsome and fear provokes a grudging respect. It was therefore a somewhat hushed and attentive audience that watched and listened as Membrane and Mucus went through yet another polished presentation.

But this one differed, containing many subtle nuances designed to provoke thought alone. Adolf Hitler, of evil memory, believed that a crowd was only capable of grasping a single idea at any one time and this had to be drummed into it again and again. Here Membrane and Mucus amalgamated two simple concepts, honour for the borough and prosperity for its denizens, into a winning combination. This simple device afforded the avaricious an opportunity to disguise their deadly sin beneath a display of fealty to their town.

Great emphasis was placed upon the safety aspects of Gravitite and the temporary nature of the stadium. But the final line of Membrane's speech sold it completely. 'Of course,' said he, 'every Brentonian will receive a free pass valid for the entire games.'

An ever so tiny silence preceded the tumultuous applause that even the audio-soluble polysilicate floor-tiles were hard pressed to swallow. Choruses of 'For Whoever-he-is Is a Jolly Good Fellow' were chorused and hats cast willy-nilly towards the newly painted ceiling. Messrs Membrane and Mucus wrung each other's hands and flashed expensive smiles. Their minders grinned lop-sidedly and feigned comprehension.

As the crowds conga-lined away to celebrate their good fortune in the nearby taverns and spread the word to those who might have missed it, the great hall returned once more to stillness and silence. The VDUs hummed softly and the giant images upon the wall video continued their endless rote. No-one noticed the elderly gentleman whose slim frail hands rested upon the ivory handle of his black Malacca cane, as he peered down at the model town and its glittering star-shaped companion. His ice-blue eyes glowed with a fierce vitality beneath their snow-lashed lids and his mane of pure white hair flowed over the astrakhan collar of the long black coat he wore, despite the clemency of the season. The tip of his cane traced the outlines of the stadium before tapping out a brisk yet muffled tattoo upon the tiled floor.

Shaking his head in doubt, Professor Slocombe turned upon his heel and strode from the hall.

17

Pooley and Omally did not attend the brewery trip, nor
the wine-tasting at Punter's. They even missed the
mayoral banquet, which was probably a good thing as it
turned out to be a somewhat crowded and boisterous
affair. It was complicated by the arrival of a charabanc
load of pensioners, smelling strongly of brilliantine and
mothballs and clad in Sunday suits of a style which was
currently enjoying a renaissance in fashionable circles.
They sported rainbows of medal ribbons and each clutched
an official itinerary.

Old Pete had long harboured an especial hatred for the
town council over several prosecutions dealt out to him by
the public health inspector. Young Chips was a prolific
footpath fouler. Having left Neville that lunchtime, Pete
had wasted little time in getting down to the library's
photocopier. Thirty bootlegged itineraries soon found
their way into the eager wrinkled hands of his trench-
footed cronies at the British Legion. These veterans,
known and feared by the local Meals on Wheels as the
Passchendaele Piranhas, now arrayed themselves at
the mayoral table, tucked their napkins into their cellu-
loid collars and prepared to do battle.

Jennifer Naylor shook her head in noble defeat and
smiled bravely towards the Mayor who was frantically
leafing through the pages of his appointments diary and
wondering where he had gone wrong.

The representatives of Her Majesty's Government were
now somewhat thin on the ground. Despite Jennifer's
attempts to foil their many escape bids, the afternoon
had seen them drifting away in ones and twos, mostly in
twos. Those that remained had now reached that stage of

alcoholic enlightenment so often granted to those in public office. Talk had turned naturally enough to the reinstitution of hanging, the return of the Empire and Hugo Rune's proposition to feed the world's starving by eating the unemployed. The fogeys called for fodder and broke wind.

Jennifer Naylor raised her glass towards the Mayor and said, 'Cheers.'

'Cheers!' said John Omally, 'Cheers and good luck!'

Pooley raised the glass of ten-year-old malt to his nose and sniffed. 'How did you come by this?' he asked.

Omally gave his own nose a significant tap. 'Services rendered, Jim,' he replied. 'And so to business. You got everything?'

'Ah yes.' Pooley had spent the balance of the afternoon in Hounslow High Street, shopping. Omally had issued him a list of requirements and although each seemed innocent and unrelated, their sum was evidently something more. This was confirmed by John's order that if Jim was taken he must 'eat the list'. 'It's all there,' said Pooley, nodding towards several bulging carrier bags. 'I shall have red rings around my ringers for a week humping that lot.'

Omally ignored this complaint and emptied the bags on to his work bench. He examined the boxes of washing soda, the bags of white sugar, the cans of weedkiller, the drum of red oxide and the range of other sundry items. 'This will serve admirably,' he told Jim. 'Now I think it would be better if you were not here. Why not go down to headquarters and clear your desk out.'

'You mean remove incriminating evidence?'

'I mean take what personal items you hold dear, for come midnight they will have no tomorrow. Cut along now, Jim, I'll meet you in the Swan in an hour or so.' He cast an eye towards the rapidly retreating form of Jim Pooley. 'And open up the fish pens, salmon deserve a better fate than this.' The door slammed shut upon Pooley and Omally drummed his fingers upon the work bench.

The words of an old rebel song sprung unexpectedly to his lips.

Five minutes later a furtive Pooley crept through the long grass towards the rusting hulk of the not-so-abandoned barge. There was a chill in the air which caused the lad to turn up his jacket collar as he trod the path of his own knowing. High above, a bloated moon swam upstream through ribbons of scudding cloud. Herons rustled mysteriously in their skyline roosts and a distant owl made personal enquiries. Suddenly a salmon went plop and Pooley's heart momentarily lost count.

Jim's wide eyes glowed whitely in the moonlight. The abandoned boatyard had a certain charm in the daytime, but at night it lost all appeal and Pooley's over-fertile imagination was already getting the better of him. All those whispered tales of the headless bargee and the smiling smuggler came flooding back. In his immediate condition Jim neglected to remember that it was he and John who had started them off in the first place. And there was always the Brentford Griffin. Jim shivered. It could be out there somewhere even now, licking its beak at the prospect of Pooley in a basket. 'No,' Jim shook his head firmly. It was only a story, only a hoax invented by those nancy boys at the Arts Centre for a bit of prime-time publicity. Nevertheless, you couldn't be sure. The salmon went plop again and Jim scuttled on towards the ancient barge.

Once inside, with the door closed and the lights on, things didn't seem quite so bad, even though they indeed were. Jim perused the familiar trappings, the furniture, the fripperies, the odds and sods. All were now alien, all now had big neon lights flashing the words, 'Damning Evidence' again and again.

Pooley sat down on the Le Corbusier. Where to start? What to take? What mattered? He sighed and scratched his head and his eyes strayed towards the cocktail cabinet.

Jim perked up. He sauntered over to the bottle of Dom Perignon 1807 which stood perpetually on ice in the electric ice bucket, awaiting its Moment. Jim spent little time in arriving at the conclusion that its Moment had now arrived. The bottle was cold and bulky, it would be far easier to carry the contents if they were in fact inside him. To leave it was to waste it and Jim abhorred waste. He would toast the end of an era in vintage shampoo whilst gathering up his goods and chattels. Out with the old and in with the new. Pleased as ever with the power of his reasoning, Jim applied pressure with his thumb and popped the cork.

The Memorial Library clock struck ten as John Omally entered the Flying Swan. Saturday evening here was, as ever, a loud and raucous affair, but tonight more colour had been added by the addition of strings of bunting and large photographs of Daley Thompson and Sebastian Coe pinned up behind the bar. Neville greeted him without enthusiasm and John ordered a pint of the very best, declining the 'Olympic Toasty' which Neville recommended as an ideal complement to his porter.

'This is all very jolly,' said John. 'If it is a taste of things to come then we are in for merry months ahead.'

'As long as the brewery keep their hands to themselves,' said Neville, 'then there might be the prospect of a few pennies to be had.'

'The javelin.' Norman's voice arose amidst the general hubbub to catch Omally's ear. John received his pint, paid for same and sought out the shopkeeper. 'Oh yes, John,' said Norman, 'the javelin.' He made the appropriate movements. Omally sipped delicately at his ale, draining the pint glass by a third. Norman's skills with the feathered flight were legend hereabouts. He was captain of the Swan's team, a team unbeaten these ten long years. The thought of the paunchy shopman taking on the world's finest athletes, however, did not seem to gel.

'You are in training, then?' John asked.

Norman grinned wolfishly. 'It's all on paper,' said he.

'Ah!' Omally joined Norman in an enlightened smile. 'You are designing your own javelin then?' A look passed between the two men which was of that rare sort that can only pass between old and trusted friends, or at least between those who know what each other are up to. 'Then bravo,' said John. 'I will have Jim put a pound or two on the home team.'

'Best I do it,' said Norman. 'The jungle drums tell me that Pooley's face does not exactly fit in Bob's establishment at the present time.'

'Good man.' Omally called out for two refills. 'Has Jim been in?' he asked Neville.

'Haven't seen him tonight. Did you want anything to eat with those?'

'No,' said Omally, 'I do not, I wonder what might have happened to Jim.'

'Surely he is still enjoying his free meal on the council,' said the barman, taking up a glass to polish. 'No doubt you have just done the same.'

'I have not,'

'Then you must be famished, have an Olympic Toasty.'

'Neville,' said John, 'the events of this lunchtime were not of my doing.'

'Events?'

'I am thinking of your sudden loss of clientèle which resulted in the surfeit of salmon sandwiches you are now attempting to pass off as Olympic Toasties.'

Neville took himself off in a huff to serve an impatient customer. 'Bar snacks, anyone?' he was heard to enquire.

'Tell me, Norman,' said Omally as he passed the shopkeeper his pint. 'As a man of science, what do you make of this stadium business?'

'In what way, John?'

'Well, is it feasible? You know, solar panels? Gravitite, all that stuff?'

'It is feasible,' said Norman, a trace of bitterness entering his voice, 'although I cannot as yet say how it is to be done.'

Omally nodded thoughtfully. 'It is all a bit sudden though.'

'Sudden is not the word. The news hits us today and construction appears scheduled to begin come Monday. That is speed beyond human capability. No, Gravitite alone must have taken years to develop. There is a good deal more to all this than meets the eye.'

'So what do you think?'

'Computers,' said Norman. 'Computers and a single brain. And one more fearsome than that of the legendary Albert E. himself.'

'So who is your man?'

'The Lord alone knows. A scientific genius and one of considerable wealth. The paper says, "an anonymous philanthropist who desires anonymity", and if that is his desire then no doubt such a man is quite capable of realizing same. But why do you ask, John? We shall all make something out of this. The stadium will come, the stadium will go. Life will continue. Let us enjoy it as we will.'

Omally finished his latest pint. 'You are no doubt right,' he agreed. 'So whose round is it?'

18

Jim Pooley lazed in the Le Corbusier. Dom Perignon lazed
in Jim Pooley. It is a curious thing how the simple transfer
of a body of liquid from one location to another can alter
so many things. Or at least appear to. The furtive, worried
Pooley of the hour past had now vanished, to be replaced
by a mellow, crisis-what-crisis?-God-is-in-His-Heaven-
and-all's-right-with-the-world kind of body.

Jim tinkered with the remote controller and the twenty-
five inch screen of a 're-routed' television set filled with
Sergio Leone's classic western, *For a Few Dollars More*.
Jim greatly preferred the video (which he had viewed on
many previous occasions) with the sound on, but he had
never achieved full mastery of the controller and did not
feel up to making the stroll over for a manual turn-up.

'It's not a bad old life.' Jim shifted his roll-up to the
corner of his mouth. 'I really cannot see what all the fuss
is about,' he informed the silent set, as the 'Man With No
Name' drew upon Red 'Baby' Kavanagh and sent the out-
law to a two-thousand-dollar grave.

Old Pete rose unsteadily to address the assembled company. 'My lords, ladies and gentlemen, most honoured
guests, friends, Romans and countrymen.' His cronies
enjoined in hearty hand-claps. Jennifer Naylor chewed
upon her lower lip. The Mayor said nothing. 'Unaccus-
tomed as I am to public speaking—' beneath the table
Young Chips gnawed upon a chicken-leg and broke wind
meaningfully— 'I should just like to offer a word of thanks
to all those who have made this evening possible. And to
say that, on behalf of myself and the senior citizens of
Brentford, how very much we have enjoyed the splendid

repast and how very much we look forward to the brandy and cigars which must now bring it to a successful conclusion.' Old Pete reseated himself amidst tumultuous geriatric applause, a line or two of 'Tipperary' and a further barrage of flatulence from his dog. 'I thank you.'

Jennifer Naylor stood up, this single action playing havoc with two dozen formerly defunct libidos, and putting as many pace-makers under considerable strain. A whistle of feedback, as the ancients turned their deaf-aids up full volume, piped her aboard.

'My Lord Mayor, Government Ministers, ladies and gentlemen—' she paused and nodded towards the old contemptibles '—members of the Olympic committee.' A score of turtle necks inclined in response to this unexpected elevation in status. 'Today is a day that shall be writ big in the annals of Brentford. For today, official confirmation has been made that we are indeed to host the coming Olympiad.' She put up her hand to subdue the applause that wasn't coming anyway. 'It is my great pleasure to hand you over to our honoured guest, his worship the Mayor, to give the speech of acceptance.' She primly reseated herself.

The honoured guest rose to the occasion, arranged a sheaf of papers before him on the table and his reading glasses upon his nose. He smiled down the expanse of table towards the rows of ancient faces which regarded him with but a single expression. It was not one of solicitude.

'Dear friends,' he began, 'my dear, dear friends.'

John Omally finished his pint and looked up towards the battered Guinness clock. Nearly eleven o'clock, Neville was calling last orders and Pooley was nowhere to be seen.

This was not how he had planned things at all. In a perfect world Pooley would have been there an hour ago; leaving their drinks unfinished, the two of them would have slipped away from the Swan, picked up the explosives from the allotment, set the charges on the barge and been back in time to finish their pints and comment upon the possible causes of the loud explosion coming from the direction of the river. Surrounded by friends, they might even have taken a stroll down to see what all the hulla-balloo was about. But this was not a perfect world and Jim Pooley was nowhere to be seen. Omally slid his empty glass across the bar counter. What was the lad up to? What had become of him? A sudden grim expression forced its way across John's normally cheerful countenance. Jim had done a runner!

Pooley ran the video forward to the chiming watch gun-fight sequence at the end, his favourite bit. Without the sound, however, the tension lost much of its impact. Jim rose unsteadily and rooted about amongst the rack of video tapes. He had some crackers here and no mistake: *They Saved Hitler's Brain, Plan Nine from Outer Space, Mars Needs Women*. Every one a classic, you couldn't blow these up. There had to be another way.

Pooley almost scratched at his head, it was a close thing. 'Perhaps we can refloat the barge,' he said drunkenly. 'Drift downstream for a bit, that would be the business.' He rattled the neck of the champagne bottle into a Georgian rummer. Empty. 'Time for a top-up,' said the lad, swaying over to the cocktail cabinet. 'Now, eenie, meenie, my knee . . .' There was a wide range of drinks on offer, but most were of the 'brought-home-from-holiday-because-we-liked-the-colour' variety, which seemed a good idea at the time when drunk, but inevitably led to severe brain damage the next morning.

'Banana Liquor,' said Jim. 'That seems like a good idea.' Twisting away a plastic stopper the shape of Carmen Miranda's hat, he decanted a large slug of the yellow liquid into his glass. 'Anchors away,' said Jim.

There was a loud thump upon the hull of the barge. Pooley stiffened. John, already. He hiccupped foolishly. 'You'll have to hang on a minute,' he giggled. 'I've not quite got everything.' There was another thump and the sound of something metallic being drawn down the side of the barge. 'Now what's he up to?' queried Jim. 'Setting the charges, you buffoon,' he answered himself. 'So get a move on.' Pooley took a hasty look around. Most of it was out of focus and none of it really seemed to matter much. He took a deep unsteady breath. He'd be a million-aire soon, who cared about a barge load of booty? This was a new beginning. A new honest beginning. He stumbled over to a nearby porthole and drew aside the blinds.

Peering out, Pooley found himself staring directly into the face of death itself! The face was big and bloated, hideously swollen, a mass of folds and pouches. The skin looked dead and white, the skin of a corpse. But the eyes were alive, round and black with white pupils. Jim drew back in horror, and then in anger. It was the head of a scarecrow, or a somesuch. John was winding him up, and him with a weak heart and everything. And then the eyes blinked, the horrible eyes blinked and a mouth like a gash amongst the folds and flaps of skin opened. It opened to reveal a hideous maw, a gaping black cavern devoid of teeth and gums. And a sound, a voice, a cry . . . Jim thrust back the blind and lurched back in terror. Turning to make his getaway he caught his foot in the TV cable, wrenched the improvised socket from the wall, fused the lights, plunged the salon into darkness, tripped, fell, struck his head on the cocktail cabinet and knocked him-self unconscious.

John Omally climbed down through the open hatchway, clutching a bulging holdall and peered into the darkness. He flicked the light switch. 'Damn it,' said he. 'Jim, are you in there?'

All was silent, except for the gentle lap of water against the hull. Even the plopping salmon had turned in for the night.

'Jim?' There was no reply. Pooley had evidently done a runner. 'Poltroon,' muttered Omally. 'I shall have words to say to that lad when I catch up with him. Buggers the electrics, leaves the door open to all and sundry.' He stood up in the hatchway and placed the holdall upon the deck before him. He didn't need much light for this, it was all down to a single flick of a switch to set the five-minute egg-timer, the work of but a moment.

Omally unzipped the holdall, flipped the switch, rezipped the holdall and received a violent blow to the forehead which sent him tumbling backwards into the blackness of the salon. 'What the . . . who?' Omally sprawled in the dark, cursing and spitting oaths. He drew a deep breath and prepared to come up fighting. The lozange of moonlight visible through the open hatchway was momentarily blotted out as a dark shape dropped down into the barge after him. 'Who is this?' John demanded. 'What's your game?' Something bowled across the floor and struck him in the shins with a sickening crack. Omally screamed in anguish and not a little fury, and doubled up clutching his legs. He fell in an untidy heap on top of an unconscious Jim Pooley.

'Oh, ouch, what's going on here?' mumbled a bleary drunken voice.

'Pooley, is that you?'

'John? Get off there.' This was the second time in one day that Jim had woken up to find a man on top of him. 'John, unhand me . . . my God, I've gone blind.'

'Shut up, man.'

'What's going on? Get off me, I say!'

'Pooley, be quiet.' Omally sought to stifle Jim's cries with one hand whilst seeking out his lighter with the other. 'There's someone in here.' John felt Pooley shudder. The terrible memory of whatever he'd seen through the port-hole suddenly resobered his drunken brain.

'John, there's a thing, a mons . . .'

'Shut up!' Omally struck fire to his Zippo and held it above him. Pooley did what he could to focus his eyes.

'You've got a nose bleed,' he observed.

'And I'll not be the only one.' Omally addressed his unseen assailant. 'Fight like a man, come out!' The slim flame burned and fluttered, the shadows danced. Within the cocoon of light Omally helped his companion to his feet, wincing at the pain of his own battered legs. 'Come on out, you coward, show yourself!'

There was a sudden rush of movement. Something leapt before them. Leapt up. Omally held high his lighter and ducked away as it loomed above them. A terrific figure, gross, unnatural. It clung impossibly, upside down upon the ceiling.

Pooley stood frozen with horror. John thrust him out of the way and dived for cover as the thing scuttled across the ceiling like a great black beetle and vanished through the open hatchway. And the moonlight vanished with it as the hatch swung shut with an almighty crash. John leapt to his feet in the darkness and flung himself towards the hatchway. Above him the bolt slid home, the padlock clicked. They were trapped.

Omally beat at the hatch. 'Let us out!' he yelled. 'Let us out!'

Pooley's voice came from the darkness, 'Don't do that, John. It's on the outside and we're on the in, for God's sake. At least we're safe.'

'*Safe?*' Omally's voice rose to a pitch that was new to Jim's hearing. '*Jim, you bloody fool, I armed the bomb! It's out there. We've got about two minutes left and then . . .*'

'*Let us out!*' screamed Jim at the top of his voice. '*Let us out!*'

'Light, we must get some light.' Omally floundered about the salon. 'Where's the torch? Where's anything?' Unseen, even to himself, Jim's hands began to flap. 'Don't do it,' warned Omally. 'Where's the torch? Where is it?'

'On the hook! On the hook!'

'Where's the hook?'

'By the door!'

'Where's the door?'

'Over there . . . or is it over . . .?'

'It's here.' Omally flicked on the torch. It actually worked. He shone it into the idiot face of Jim Pooley.

'Help,' said Jim in a small foolish voice. 'Help.'

'There must be some way out.'

'If the hatch is locked we can't squeeze through a porthole.'

The torchlight glanced off a glass panel in the floor. 'The fish pens,' said Omally.

'Ah,' said Jim. 'I forgot to open them.'

'It doesn't matter, it's the only way out, come on.'

'We'll drown.'

'We won't.' Omally tore up the glass-panelled trap-door that covered the fish pens and jumped down into the water. It was very cold and very black and sadly lacking in promise. Between his wounded knees, a great trout moved ominously. 'Come on, Jim, we can punch our way through the wire netting and swim out underneath.'

'We'll drown.'

'Come on!' Omally shone the torch up at Jim, grabbed him by the ankle and dragged him down into the water.

'The fish will eat us.'

'Get going, there's no time left, take a deep breath now.'

Jim had time to take about a half of one before Omally thrust his head under the water and propelled him forwards through the wire netting of the fish pen wall. All about him the great fish plunged, as eager as he for freedom. Jim was only beneath the surface for a few brief seconds, but his past life flashed before him several times nevertheless. Then, with a great gasp, he broke water, ten or so feet out from the barge. He coughed and spluttered and spat out Thames.

Above him came sudden movement, sound. Jim turned his terrified eyes towards the barge. On deck, ghastly beneath the moonlight, the thing paced to and fro. It looked almost like a man, yet it walked upon all fours. Its head pivoted about as it sighted Pooley and a low howl escaped from its black throat.

Jim floundered in the water, the undercurrent was strong and he was no swimmer. He was rapidly being dragged downstream and down generally. 'John, help . . .

John!' Pooley's voice faded as the blackness of the river engulfed him.

And then a deafening explosion tore the Brentford night into a million fragments. A great torrent of flame mushroomed up from the ancient barge, billowing into the sky. Shards of burning splinters rained down upon the river and the surrounding area. And amidst that maelstrom of fire and tearing fury something perished that was neither man nor beast, gave vent to a shriek of fury and defiance and became no more.

What had been for most denizens of Brentford a night of jollity and celebration was suddenly a chaos of ambulances, police cars and fire engines. Bells jangled, sirens screamed, beacons flashed. The town hall disgorged a band of martial pensioners wielding wine bottles and walking sticks. Neville buried his face in his hands as the pub cleared for the second time in one day. So much for the 'takeaway Toasties', he thought.

It was some time before the fire brigade were able to batter down enough corrugated iron fencing to gain entry and bring the raging inferno under control. By the time they had accomplished this, the headquarters of the P & O Line was nothing but a blackened shell.

It was some time later still that Inspectre Hovis arrived on the scene. He addressed his inquiries to the leading fireman. 'God alone knows,' that man replied. 'Chemicals is my guess, there's any amount of the stuff lying around here. All this should have been knocked down years ago. A build-up of gases in the barge is my bet, although it could be any of a number of things. We'll give it a thorough going-over in the morning, when it's all cooled down a bit.'

Hovis drew snuff from his cane and pinched it meaningfully to his nose.

19

Professor Slocombe decanted a large Scotch into a crystal tumbler and placed it between the quivering outstretched hands of John Omally. 'Monsters?' he asked.

'Monster,' mumbled the Irishman as he cowered before the Professor's roaring log fire, a blanket about his shoulders and his bare feet in a warming bowl of rose-scented water. 'J . . . just th . . . the one.'

'One, I think, is surely sufficient.' The elder left the decanter within John's easy reach, returned to his study desk and reseated himself. 'Might I trouble you to reiterate?'

Omally huddled nearer to the flames. 'I've told you all I know. It was fast and it was . . .' he lifted a trouser bottom to survey a painful yellow bruised shin, '. . . hard. And it just went up, up and over us, like some great spider.'

'An insect, then?'

'Not an insect, Professor, it was as big as a man.'

'A large river bird then, or an animal, perhaps.'

'It wore clothes, Professor.' Omally finished his Scotch. He refilled his glass.

'A showman's ape?'

Omally shook his head, his teeth rattling like castanets. 'Not an ape.'

'Think carefully,' said the old man. 'The thing struck you, it played with you and then it fled.'

'It ran across the ceiling.'

'Did it? You were in a state of shock when you observed this, you had received a blow to the forehead, you were confused, disorientated.'

'Yes, but . . .'

'The entire event occurred within a few short seconds

under conditions of next to no light. If an ape had swung across the ceiling, from the light fittings perhaps?'

'No, Professor.'

The old man leant back in his chair and tapped his long fingers upon the desk top. 'Upon your own admission, you had been drinking.'

'I was not drunk.'

'John, you have been in the river, you have witnessed an explosion at close quarters, you have crept across Brentford, down back alley-ways and through people's gardens to get here. You are drinking now as we speak. What value is to be placed upon your testimony?'

'You are suggesting now that I am not in full command of my senses?'

'I am suggesting that it is reasonable to assume that, under the circumstances, your judgement might be temporarily impaired.'

'I know what I saw, I just don't know what I saw, I mean.'

'I know what you mean.'

'There's nothing wrong with my judgement.' Sullen and shaking, John refilled his glass.

'All right.' Professor Slocombe rose from his chair and took himself over to the cowering Celt. 'Close your eyes, John.'

'For what?'

'Please, humour me.' Omally closed his eyes. 'Now from memory, what am I wearing?'

'That's easy: white shirt, pale blue cravat, silk dressing-gown, grey trousers, carpet slippers.'

'Very good,' said Professor Slocombe. 'Nothing wrong with your judgement.'

Omally opened his eyes. His host was clad in a three-piece suit of green Donegal tweed, a grey shirt with a bow-tie and brown brogues. 'Be damned,' said John Omally.

'Would you care for a second try?'

'Need I bother?'

Professor Slocombe inclined his old white head. 'The quickness of the mind deceives the eye,' he said enigmatically. By the time the ancient had reseated himself he was clad once more in his former attire. Omally never saw how he did it. 'An illusion, John. A parlour trick – nothing more. I trust the point is well taken.'

'It wasn't an ape.'

'Well, if it perished in the explosion then we shall never know.'

'That is something, I suppose.' Omally's hand was once more about the neck of the decanter.

'Something?' The Professor leant forward across his crowded desk and fixed Omally with a glittering eye. 'I don't think you realize the gravity of the situation, John, the enormity of what you have done in your efforts to save your miserable skin.'

'I don't think I . . .'

'To destroy the evidence of your unlawful activities, you construct a bomb and walk with it through the streets of Brentford. Without care for who you might injure or what damage you might wreak upon private property, you explode same, killing at the very least some animal that will probably prove to be a showman's exhibit or treasured pet.'

'Yes, but . . .'

'John, by bombing one of the sites scheduled for the Olympic construction you have committed an act of international terrorism. If this is not bad enough you have also been directly responsible for the possible manslaughter of your closest friend. Is this the "something" of which you speak?' Omally hid his face from that of his accuser. 'And then you come here,' the old man continued, 'to take advantage of our long-standing friendship, by making me an accessory after the fact of your horrendous crimes. What have you to say for yourself before I telephone the police?'

Omally stared up bitterly, his eyes were moist and his lips quivered. 'I came to you because you are the only man

I could trust, the only man I respect. I told you everything, I made no secret.'

'So, what do you wish, that I wave a magic wand, absolve you of your sins, three Hail Mary's and Our Father, perhaps?'

'I came to you for help.'

'Then this is my help. Go to the police, tell them everything.'

Omally broke into a plaintive sobbing. 'Yes,' he croaked. 'All right, you are right, you are always right! If I have killed Jim, then I have nothing to live for, you are right.'

The whisky decanter was suddenly upon the Professor's desk, he refilled his glass and also another. 'Well, the decision must be yours then. You can go to the police now and make a clean breast of it. Or perhaps you would prefer to wait until they drag Jim's body from the Thames.'

'No,' said Omally, rising to his feet. 'Anything but that. I know what I have done. I am damned beyond redemption.'

'No man is beyond redemption.'

'This one is. My life has been nothing but greed and self-ishness. I see all that now. I know what I have done.'

'And so?'

'I will make amends, I will do the right thing, the honest thing.'

'Good, John, good.'

'I shall give myself up and serve my time,' said Omally, 'and then I will enter a monastery, forswear my former existence, forswear the pleasures of the flesh. I shall be a sinner saved.'

'A sinner saved?' The Professor, who was no stranger to duplicity in any of its myriad guises, stared long and hard at the broken man standing before him. A golden aura surrounded him. 'Blessed be,' said Professor Slocombe.

'The phone,' said John. 'I will do it now.'

The Professor's hand reached out towards the instrument. Suddenly he paused. 'Wait,' he said, stiffening visibly. 'Listen.'

'Listen? To what?'

The old man's eyes darted towards the french windows. 'Something . . .' From without there came a slow unearthly dragging of footsteps. A hideous squelching as of some monstrous mollusc.

'Oh no,' said Omally. 'What is it?'

'By the pricking of my thumbs.' The Professor reached into the desk drawer and withdrew an amulet of powerful potency. Omally shuddered in his footbath; even sitting close to the roaring fire he felt a graveyard chill run through his bones. The footfalls drew ever nearer, ghastly, unnatural. The Professor clutched the amulet to his heart, Omally's eyes glazed, a cold sweat formed upon his brow. 'Professor . . .' The slow footfalls crashed in his head, closer, closer. And then it was upon them. Something dark and awesome lurched into view. An evil smell filled the air as the creature pressed forward. Thick slime hung about the discoloured visage, a dripping claw-like hand rose, a mouth opened and from the horrible maw a voice came.

'Watchamate, John,' it said.

'Jim?' gasped Omally in a cracked and broken voice. 'Jim, is that you?' The apparition stepped into the room and nodded its weed-clung head. 'Jim, you're alive!' Omally toppled out of his footbath and fell to his knees before him. 'You're alive, Jim!'

'It was a close run race.'

'Then did you . . .? Did you?'

'Did I bloody what?'

'Did you save the betting slip?'

Professor Slocombe buried his face in his hands and groaned dismally.

20

A thin yet insistent drizzle, of the type one generally associates with bank holidays and state occasions, fell upon a borough that was suffering a severe case of that 'morning after' feeling.

A hazy mist arose from the embers of last night's holocaust as Inspectre Hovis delved here and there with the tip of his cane, seeking a why or a wherefore. Several constables, hands deep in their blue serge pockets, shuffled their feet, hunched their shoulders and shared wistful thoughts of poached eggs and kippers.

Hovis rooted with a will. His four short hours of sleep had been anything but restful. He had tossed to and fro in his bed whilst terrible dreams assailed him from every side. Headlines sprang up before his eyes: TERRORISTS SABOTAGE BRENTFORD OLYMPICS! POLICE HELPLESS AS GAMES BOMBED! BUNGLING INSPECTRE GIVEN THE ELBOW!!!

He'd only been in the borough for forty-eight hours and already he'd banged up half the town council, read the riot act and become embroiled in an international terrorist bomb plot. This sleepy west London suburb was proving to be about as sleepy as Beirut, Afghanistan, Libya and the Falls Road all rolled into one. And amidst all this confusion and distraction here was he, desperately seeking to save his tattered reputation and redeem himself in the eyes of his superiors and the world. He didn't need all this, what a carve-up.

At the end of his cane something colourful twinkled. Hovis stooped to pick it up, wiping away the ash. Although somewhat charred about the edges, the photograph, for such it was, shone out at him like a little Kodak-colour jewel.

Hovis examined it with interest. It was a holiday snap, a foolish red-faced tourist in a sombrero drinking wine from a Spanish *pouron*. The Inspectre's eyes swiftly became hooded slits. This was it. A clue, a mug-shot, God-given. Many people would have seen many things in that snapshot, well, not that many, but a few at least. But Hovis saw only one, the face of a born killer, a revolutionary of Pancho Villa proportions. The face of Public Enemy Number One.

'Inspectre.' The voice belonged to Constable Meek. 'What do you make of this, sir?'

Hovis picked his way through the sodden ash to join the young constable. 'What is it?'

'Look, sir.' Meek pointed up towards the wall of a gutted warehouse, which had taken, by its appearance, the full force of the blast. 'It's like a shadow, sir.' Hovis cocked his head upon one side and stared up at the wall. Clearly outlined upon the charred concrete was a curious image. 'What do you think, sir? A man crouching, or a dog perhaps?'

Hovis flicked open his cane and applied snuff to his nose. The image was disproportionate, exaggerated. It glowed with a dull effulgence and struck an odd chord of recognition. Hovis was, however, unable to name that tune in one. 'Get the forensic lads to take some photos before the rain washes it off. It may be significant, it may not.'

'Yes, sir!'

Hovis drew a tentative finger gently across the image, being careful not to disturb the outline. He examined his finger with interest. 'Now what does that look like to you, Constable?'

Meek peered at the Inspectre's fingertip. 'Gold paint, sir, or gold leaf.'

'Or gold dust. Full marks for observation, Constable. Well done.'

Meek puffed out his chest. 'Thank you, sir.'

'Now get on to forensic, get the photos and get them on to my desk by lunchtime and no later.'

Meek's chest sank away. You bastard, he thought. 'Yes, sir,' he said.

Jennifer Naylor tilted the cafetière towards the exquisite china coffee cup and poured a measure of decaffeinated.

She freighted the delicate cup into the living room, where an occasional table rose to meet almost any occasion upon legs of faux-grained maple. Its sun-golden top bore the weight of several Sunday newspapers which lay in a casual composition. Jennifer perused a random headline and sipped her coffee. The project thus far had certainly met with the least line of resistance. Things were moving on apace. The public imagination, that fickle beast whose existence is only denied by those who seek to capture it, had been hunted down, snared and thrust into a cage of its own construction. And now she was one of its keepers and her duties were to keep it cosy and warm and above all safe. And upon this point she knew, as did all others directly concerned with the project, exactly what she was dealing with. The humanization of technology. Technology, friend and servant of man, rather than technology, fearsome tyrant to the uninformed. Maintaining government and 'vox-pop' approval for the project was top priority. Every aspect of every aspect had to be handled with the utmost delicacy. The construction was to be the eighth wonder of the world, a technocratic monument to an unknown genius, but for all its awesomeness it had to be *human*. Above all human, that was the brief.

Jennifer scanned a newspaper column or two and nodded in complete approval. Fleet Street was already in a hot flush of patriotic fervour. The disasters of Birmingham were already forgotten. Tomorrow belonged to Brentford.

Amongst the papers lay a large metallic foil envelope which had arrived by special delivery that very morning. Jennifer placed her coffee cup amongst the Sundays and opened it. It contained a sheaf of computer print-outs and a cheque raised in her name to a sum amply sufficient to her current needs. Jennifer examined the signature with keen interest but she could make nothing of it; it was more like a runic symbol. The designer of the great stadium, inventor of Gravitite and financier of the Brentford Olympics was still as much a mystery to her as to everyone else.

Hers not to reason why. Jennifer consulted the print-out. It was a schedule of her duties for the coming week, listing meetings to be arranged, statements to be given, to whom and at when. The names of certain luminaries in the fields of art, literature, the sciences and the media appeared. Their support, considered essential to the overall success of the project, was to be enlisted. And the wherewithal by which this might be achieved was all there, printed in slim computer-type.

Anticipating possible difficulties with local ecologists, traditionalists, reactionaries and other spoilsports, it was considered prudent to bring forward the schedule of works by a day. Work on the five sites would begin at once.

Jennifer shook her beautiful head, lost in admiration for the mysterious organizer. The insight and perception displayed held her in fascination. Ever since her first involvement with the project she had felt a dull pain gnawing away at her insides, a hunger pang which could only be satisfied by one thing. Somehow, someway, she *had* to meet this person whose genius obsessed her. Somehow, someway, their paths *must* be made to cross. And then we should see what we should see.

Reverently she turned the page of the print-out and noted to her further wonder a list entitled: DISSENTERS: CLASS A SECURITY RISKS. Below this encircled in red, were only two names, yet two she knew almost as surely as she knew her own: James Arbuthnot Pooley and John Vincent Omally.

The two dissenters were enjoying a hearty breakfast. They had bathed, slept soundly and now sat in their newly laundered clothes enjoying a magnificent spread in the Professor's dining room.

Gammon, the Professor's elderly retainer, removed the silver dome from the crumpet dish and asked, 'Is everything to your satisfaction, gentlemen?'

'Oh, indeed yes.' Pooley wiped a napkin across his mouth and prepared himself for an assault upon the crumpets.

Omally sipped coffee and watched the Professor from the corner of his eye. Something was coming, that was for sure. All this ill-deserved hospitality, what was the old man up to?

'And now,' said the Professor, as if in answer to John's unasked question, 'I am going to tell you both exactly how you can repay my hospitality.' Omally turned his coffee cup between his fingers, Jim kept right on eating. 'You are both going to change your ways,' said the Professor. 'Dishonesty and duplicity are now but regretful chapters in your dual history. Altruism is now your watchword. Good works will be the standard by which others shall judge you. Honest toil your daily lot.'

'Your colloquy is as ever eloquent,' replied John. 'The points are both well made and well taken, we shall watch our ps and qs from now on.'

'You will,' said the Professor. 'Your behaviour will be exemplary.'

'Be sure of that,' said Jim, 'you betcha.'

'Good. This knowledge affords me a basic security which I place in high esteem. Thus the act I am about to perform becomes nothing more than a symbolic gesture.'

'Oh, yes?' said John, doubtfully.

'Yes.' Professor Slocombe took from his dressing-gown pocket Pooley's tobacco tin.

'Ah, thanks,' said Jim, rising to his feet.

'No, Jim, I shall mind this.' Pooley's pained expression was not lost upon Omally.

'Am I to take it that the tin contains something more than just baccy and papers?'

Jim slumped in his chair. 'Baccy, papers and a betting slip.'

'Exactly.' Professor Slocombe passed the tin several times between his hands. Neither of his breakfast guests saw it vanish, but it did so nevertheless. 'A symbolic gesture, nothing more,' said the magician. 'The slip will remain in my custody the few short weeks until the games begin. During this period I shall watch with interest the manner in which you conduct yourselves.'

'You want us to . . . work?' The full horror of this proposition had not quite hit Pooley, hence he was still able to form the sentence.

'Indeed I do, Jim.'

'Such rectitude is laudable,' said Omally, 'and I applaud your principles. However, it is not often the case that what might appear to be a good idea in principle is inevitably a bad one in practice. Professor, the pursuance of virtue and the turning of the now legendary honest buck are all well and good, but . . .'

'But me no buts, John.'

'Come now,' said Omally, 'you will have your little joke and the humour is not lost upon us.' Pooley groaned in sickly agreement. 'Return the betting slip, put your trust in us, we will not disappoint you.'

'But I do trust you, John. The slip will be safe with me.'

Pooley bit his lip, 'But what, sir, if, and perish the thought, some ill were to befall you?'

'Happily I am in the best of health, Jim.'

'You are not a young man, Professor,' said John.

'You are as young as you think,' declared the ancient, 'which is also a happy circumstance, because my affairs, being somewhat complicated, may well take several years to put in order, should some tragedy befall me. But let us not dwell upon such dismal matters. If one is to believe only half of what one is told, then Brentford stands poised upon the threshold of a veritable Golden Age. If, surrounded by such rich and fertile pastures, two stalwarts such as yourselves are unable to gain honest employment, then one can

107

only lament your lack of enterprise. Backs to the plough, noses to the grindstone, shoulders to the wheel.'

'Professor.' Pooley raised his hand to speak.

'No more,' said the elder. 'The conversation is at an end. I am confident that all aspects have now been covered. Repetition does not enforce a point, it merely belabours it.'

'I wished merely to enquire whether you still require the services of a gardener?'

'You are hired, Jim.'

Pooley smiled broadly. 'My thanks, Professor. What of you, John?'

Omally buttered his crumpet. 'I am cogitating,' he said in a sullen tone.

At a little after nine a.m. a helicopter swooped across Brentford. It circled the borough several times before departing towards the west. Those who saw it remarked upon two things, the advanced design of the thing, which resembled a slim silver fish, and the unusual fact that it made absolutely no sound whatsoever.

At a little after ten a.m. work began on the five Olympic sites. No-one observed the arrival of the engineers, technicians, construction supervisors, operatives and navigators. But at the time no-one thought much about it. There was a charity match on at the football ground between Brentford's First Division glory boys and the Lords Taverners Eleven. Those who weren't at the match were either still in bed, brewing tea in their allotment sheds or sticking the Sunday joint in. And there was little enough of interest to be seen at the sites anyway. For within half an hour, tall impenetrable screens had been erected to shield the operations in progress. And these operations, whatever they might have been, were taking place in absolute silence.

21

Neville drew the bolts upon the saloon bar door but did not bother to take the air. Drizzle depressed him. His carpet-slippered feet flip-flopped across the knackered Axminster and carried him over to the whisky optic and the large buff-coloured envelope that had arrived by hand this very morning.

Neville drew a double and tossed it down his throat. His right forefinger traced the parameters of the envelope and came to rest upon the brewery's coat of arms. A cockatrice rampant above the motto 'Ecce Cerevisia' – 'Behold the Beer'. Neville chewed upon his bottom lip and made nervous sniffing sounds with his sensitive nostrils. Those possessed of the 'third eye' would have noticed that the part-time barman's aura was surmounted by a small black cloud on which the words 'Gloom and Desolation' were written in Gothic type. Neville lived in dread of these missives which were inevitably the work of the brewery owner's beloved son, whose entire being seemed solely dedicated to making life miserable for the part-time barman.

Those envelopes which arrived through the post, Neville instantly destroyed and denied all knowledge of, but young Master Robert, as the little parvenu described himself, had got wise to this and now they came by hand, to be signed for. Neville tapped at the envelope; he was going to have to open it, no matter what. With a dismal resignation he took up the wicked messenger and tore it apart. He emptied the contents on to the bar counter and prodded them disdainfully. There were a set of plans, a number of crude felt-tip drawings (or visualizations as the Young Master called them), several pages of typing, some samples of material and a beer mat.

'Oh dear,' said Neville the part-time barman. This had the look of what the legendary Busby Berkeley would have referred to as 'A Big Production Number'. He picked up the beer mat and turned it on his palm. On the one side was the ubiquitous brewery coat of arms and on the other the Olympic rings etched in gold above the words . . . THE PENTATHLON BAR (formerly the Flying Swan). 'Oh no,' said Neville, 'oh no, *no*, *no!*'

He was still oh-noing a full half-hour later when a rain-sodden Pooley and Omally entered the bar.

'Watchamate, Neville,' said Jim.

'God save all here,' said John.

Neville nodded a thin greeting and drew off two pints of Large.

'Problems, Neville?' Omally enquired as he accepted his pint.

'The brewery.'

'Oh, those lads. And what is it this time, another cowboy night or more video-games machines?'

Neville laughed. It was a ghastly hollow sound and it quite put the wind up the soggy pair. He displayed the beer mat.

'Blessed be,' said Jim.

'Holy Mother,' said John.

'Exactly,' said the part-time barman. 'The little bastard wants to do a full conversion on the whole pub. Do it up like a bloody gymnasium or somesuch.'

'Iconoclast,' Omally declared. 'We shall storm the brewery.'

'Burn him at the stake,' Pooley said.

'An *auto-da-fé*,' Omally suggested.

'Yes,' agreed Jim. 'We'll burn his car too.'

'That's the stuff,' said Neville, 'we'll show him, eh?'

'We will,' said Omally, 'although not right at this moment as Jim and I have a rather pressing bit of business to discuss.'

'A man of words and not of deeds,' said the part-time barman, 'is like a garden full of weeds.'

'As to that I have no doubt,' said Omally, steering Jim away towards a side table, 'no doubt at all.'

'And so?' said Pooley, once the two were seated. 'And so?'

'And so, Jim, I have been giving this matter some careful thought and it is my considered opinion that if you alone perform these few short weeks of labour then the Professor will be under a moral obligation to return your betting slip. It is in your name alone after all.'

Jim shook his head. 'Such has already occurred to him, he mentioned to me upon leaving that he considers the betting slip, as in fact you do, joint property. If needs be, he said, he would return my half alone.'

Omally glowered into his beer. 'Bob will not pay out on a torn ticket, this much is well known. I can see nothing for it, there is only one solution.'

'You will take honest work then?'

Omally crossed himself. 'How can I be expected to work if I am incapacitated?'

'You are ill then, John?'

'Not yet, but suppose I had an accident. Say I tripped over a garden fork that you had carelessly discarded during the course of an enjoyable day in the Professor's garden. Why, I might be laid up for weeks, months even. Remember *The Man Who Came to Dinner*?'

'A bit before my time, John, but you would be bound to be discovered. The Professor would know.'

'How would he?'

'Because I would tell him, John, that is how.'

'A fine friend you are,' sighed Omally, 'it was only a thought.'

'And not one of your better ones. But see, John, a few weeks of hard work is not going to kill us. Considering the life of luxury and ease we are going to enjoy once we pick up our winnings, a bit of exercise will probably do us the world of good.'

Omally pulled at his pint. 'Perhaps,' said he. 'But I feel that there is a lot more to all this than meets the eye.'

'How so?'

'Well, as you know I greatly admire the old man. His whole being is dedicated to the higher truths. Lesser truths and the lack of them generally trouble him but little. Do you not therefore find his present attitude puzzling?'

'The work ethic, you mean?'

'More so the business of what we saw on the barge.'

'Hm.' Pooley had said little about that, it was something he wished only to forget. 'It certainly wasn't an ape and that's for sure.'

'Indeed it was not. Now you and I know that and I think the Professor does too. And I think he knows a good deal more than he's letting on to.'

'He generally does.' A lace garter of ale-foam slid seductively down Jim's glass.

'He knows our transactions have never been one hundred per cent honest, but it's never bothered him before. Something's going on, Jim.'

'I have no doubt of that, but if you will take my advice, John, stay out of it, find yourself a job, nose to the cartwheel, elbow to the sprocket-set, things of that nature.'

'I'll give the matter some thought,' said John, 'I'll give it some close thought.'

Jim Pooley shook his head. 'Whose round is it?' he asked.

The Swan was filling with post-match celebrants, out to toast the charity of the home team in letting the Lords Taverners off with a mere sixteen-nil walloping. Neville was going great guns behind the pump but the grim expression had not left his face.

Omally elbowed his way to the bar. 'Two of similar,' he said. Neville took the glasses. He drew off a pint of the very best and passed it to Omally. John took a thoughtful sip. 'I shall miss this,' he said.

'Why, are you going away then?'

'No, I mean that with all the coming changes, the beer will be the first thing to suffer.'

'It will not,' said Neville whose pride was his beer.

'Come now.' Omally held up his glass and examined its contents. 'We'll be seeing some strange faces behind this bar counter I shouldn't wonder.'

'You what?' exclaimed Neville.

'Well, if the brewery are in for changes, then they'll be supplying new bar personnel I would have thought.'

Neville halted in mid-pull of Pooley's pint. 'By the gods,' said he, 'do you think so?'

'Well, you haven't had a full complement since Croughton left.'

'Left?' said Neville. 'He's now serving eighteen months, his hand was in my till up to the elbow!'

'Young Master Bobsmuck will want one or two of his lady friends in here I shouldn't wonder.' Neville's face contorted into a mask of horror, his good eye started in its socket. He was not by nature a misogynist, but he did not believe there was a woman alive who could pull a decent pint. 'I'd cover yourself now,' continued Omally, 'just to be on the safe side.'

'Yes . . . yes.' Neville dragged at the pump handle, filling Jim's glass with foam. 'Yes, I must.'

'There must be someone locally who knows the trade,' said John, 'someone who understands good ale, respects the brewer's art, someone who would uphold the high standards of this noble edifice, someone trustworthy, someone . . .'

'Someone like yourself perhaps?' said Neville.

'Me?' Omally made deprecating gestures. 'Why, I've never . . .'

Neville turned the full force of his good eye upon Omally. The two men gazed at one another in silence. Along the bar dissatisfied patrons beat upon the counter with empty glasses and expressed doubts over Neville's parentage.

'I pay a basic wage,' said Neville. 'If it is acceptable to the applicant and I consider the applicant suitable to the post, all well to the good. If, however, my choice proves erroneous and the applicant chooses to rob me, then that is a matter for the magistrates' court.'

'I seek only honest employment,' said John. 'My reasons are my own. My word is my bond, I shall not rob you. I can start tomorrow.'

'All right,' said Neville, 'then you are hired. Give me no cause to regret my decision, we have known one another a long time.'

'I shall not,' said Omally. 'Let us consider these two pints a clincher to the deal. My thanks.'

'No,' said Neville, 'we shall consider these two pints to be a physical illustration of an ever-popular maxim, and one that you will come to know and understand when you work for me. Namely, that you only get out of life what you put into it. Cough up.'

Omally coughed up. The mob closed in about Neville.

'You were a long time at the bar,' Pooley observed. 'The service here is not what it used to be.'

'No,' said Omally, 'but it soon will be again. For I now work here.'

22

The days passed into a week and work upon the five
Olympic sites pressed on relentlessly. The stadium 'legs',
elegant columns of chromium and glass, some forty feet
each in diameter, rose higher with the passing of each
single hour. Finally there stood five slim towers, their
lofty pinnacles dwindled by perspective into needle points
five hundred feet above Brentford. The raising of these
towers to such perfection in so short a length of time
was in itself a marvel of engineering, but it was nothing when held up before the face of what was yet to
come.

Early on the evening of the second Wednesday, the first
dirigible appeared in the darkening sky. The gentle drone
of drazy hoops announced its coming as it appeared from
out of the setting sun, a flattened disc of black, lit below by
many twinkling lights, and trailing in its wake the first
segment of the great Star Stadium. The borough's curious
thronged the byways to view the spectacle, *oohing* and
aahing like sprogs at a firework display.

Old Pete leant upon his Penang lawyer and squinted
disapprovingly through a pair of ex-army field glasses.
'Remember the R101,' he told Young Chips. His canine
companion grinned up at him, lifted his furry leg up
against Marchant's front wheel and followed Pete into the
Flying Swan.

The saloon bar was already crowded. Gentlemen of the
press filled the air with rowdy conversation and cheap
cigar smoke and Old Pete was forced to make free with his
cane to clear a path to the bar. 'Terribly sorry, guvnor,'
he apologized to a newly maimed photographer as he
shuffled by. 'No damage done, I hope.' The pressman

glared daggers at the retreating reprobate and nursed his shattered kneecap.

'Evening, Pete.' The voice belonged to John Omally, the cleanly shaven and neatly turned-out barman in the white shirt and clip-on dicky. 'What will it be then?'

'That's very kind of you, John.'

Omally shook his head and applied a finishing touch to a dazzling pint pot. 'Sorry,' he said. 'More than my job's worth.'

Pete grumbled to himself. 'I'll never get used to you being that side of the counter,' said he. 'A light ale if you will, and not a warm one.'

'Certainly, sir.'

Neville watched his Celtic barman from the corner of his good eye. Omally's behaviour, thus far, had been exemplary. His manner was courteous and his skill at the pump handle a pleasure to behold. Neville had hardly to say a word, Omally was always one jump ahead, quick to replenish an optic or replace a failing barrel. His dedication even stretched to the escorting home of young ladies who had imbibed too freely. He was almost too good to be true, which was proving a little difficult for Neville, a man from whom trust had long departed.

In truth Omally, who had spent his formative years as a lounge boy in Clancy's, was thoroughly enjoying himself and had now decided that when he got his share of Pooley's winnings he was going to open a pub.

Jim Pooley now entered the bar and elbowed his way through the crush.

'Did you wipe your boots?' Omally enquired. Neville tittered foolishly and went off about his end of the business.

'Watchamate John, Pete,' said Jim, nodding to the elder and ignoring the Irishman's remark. 'A pint of Large, please.'

'A rough day on the herbaceous border?' asked Pete as John pulled the pint of Jim's preference.

'I fear the Professor is taking liberties with me.' Jim took

116

out his baccy and rolled a cigarette. 'Each time I dig a hole I look around to find the earth unturned. Each spadeful of leaves seems to weigh a hundredweight.'

Old Pete chuckled. 'His good self the Professor wishes to make a man of you,' he suggested. 'He pays a fair daily wage though, I bet. Cash up front, didn't you say?'

Pooley, who was learning always to keep at least two sentences ahead when conversing with Old Pete, dismissed the remark. 'Scarcely enough to make ends meet, and none whatever to permit a largess.' He accepted his pint and passed the exact amount in pennies and half-pennies into Omally's outstretched palm. 'Great stuff all this, eh, Pete?' Jim gestured upwards and outwards. 'Great days for Brentford.'

Old Pete made a contemptuous face. 'Fol de rol,' he muttered. 'Now don't get me wrong, I'd like to see it, I saw the last one over here when it was on at the White City. But this lark, fairy castles in the sky, it can't hold water.'

'It will keep the rain off Brentford.'

'Yes and bugger the allotment crops.'

'Free ringside seats though, think of that.'

'You'll not get me up there.' Pete waggled his cane in the air, causing nearby pressmen to fall back in distress. 'I shall sell my ticket and take a few weeks in Eastbourne till it's over.'

Pooley looked thoughtful. 'I wonder what they will do with the stadium once it's taken down.'

'They should stick it up on Sydenham Hill like they did with the Crystal Palace. Mind you, they haven't got it up yet.'

'I can't see anything stopping them,' said Jim.

'Oh, can't you now.' Old Pete drew Pooley closer and spoke in a conspiratorial whisper. 'Not everyone is as keen as you two to have this thing built. Some think the whole thing is an abomination. There is a small group of people who call themselves "Action by Informed Individuals against a Positive Threat".'

'Oh, yes?' said John.

'Oh, yes, and they are thinking of engaging themselves in a little, shall we say . . .'

'Not sabotage?' The perilous quaver in Jim's voice was not lost upon the elder. 'What are you talking about?'

Old Pete finished his light ale and peered into the empty bottom of the glass, possibly searching for a reply that might be written there upon.

Pooley dug deeply into his trouser pocket. 'A dark rum?' he asked with resignation.

'My thanks,' said Pete. Omally did the business and at Pooley's insistence hovered near at hand to catch what was said. 'They're not local nutters, this lot, in fact they are out-borough.' Old Pete used the all-inclusive and not underogatory term, which was applied by Brentonians to all who lived beyond the borders of the Brentford Triangle. 'Ecologists, Earth Mysteries Investigators, call them what you will. A little coven of them there is. They reckon that the stadium buggers up some kind of ley line configuration that runs through the borough.'

'Are you taking the piss?' John asked. His outspokenness cost him a dark rum, which Neville, ever watchful, observed Omally pay for out of his own pocket.

'My thanks, John. Now as I was saying, these boys consider themselves to be upon some kind of divine mission. They intend to form a circle about each of the stadium legs and chant some kind of exorcism.'

Pooley shrugged. 'That can't do any harm I suppose.'

'Possibly not, except I overheard them saying that it was to be a "fire ceremony".' Old Pete raised his glass and took rum. Pooley and Omally exchanged worried looks.

'You didn't happen to overhear when, by any chance?' Omally asked.

Old Pete perused his glass. 'My memory is not what it was,' said he.

'Your conversation, although of passing interest, incurs too great an expense upon my person,' said John, turning away to serve a customer. 'I must away to my work.'

Old Pete shrugged and turned towards Pooley. 'I am

two to the credit and have no wish to put undue strain upon our friendship. Tonight it is, and midnight, on Griffin Island. For your information, that's them over there.' Pete nodded through the crowd to a small conclave, clad in duffle coats and wellington boots. They sat at a side table whispering seriously over their fruit juices.

'Thanks,' said Jim, 'thanks very much. Whose round is it?'

'Yours, I think,' said Old Pete.

23

Griffin Island had until the great flap of '84 been known as the Brentford Ait; a picturesque parcel of land about one hundred yards in length standing about another fifty out from the Brentford shoreline of the River Thames. To its rear the glorious gardens of Kew, and before it the New Arts Centre, which it faced with apparent lack of concern. Prior to the Hitlerian war it had supported one of the last great boatyards nearabouts, but now the dry-dock was choked with weeds beneath the iron skeleton of the old glass roof. It was very much a wildlife sanctuary, given over to nesting herons, cormorants and black-necked geese. At the island's heart was a natural grove of thirteen cedars wherein, local legend held, certain rites were performed in the days of yore, by wizards of the day. Now it was the haven of courting couples who, armed with wellington boots and a tide-table, performed their own tantric rituals, with one eye open to the rising Thames.

At eleven-thirty upon this particular evening, a tiny coracle, built in the traditional manner from willow and hide, and one of several that Omally maintained at well-hidden moorings, slipped out silently from a dilapidated quayside and drifted downstream upon the night-time river. Pooley steered the circular craft with the single oar and John sat before, gazing out into the darkness.

Ahead, at the western tip of the island, the glass and chromium tower rose from the foreshore to lose itself in darkness. Above, the stars came and went at irregular intervals as airships drifted to and fro about their extraordinary business. The dull hum of their engines had an almost somnambulant quality and the light mist, hovering upon the water, added the final touch to what seemed a dream landscape. The beauty and feeling of it was not lost upon the two boatmen.

'There is a little bay upon the north shore,' Omally whispered, 'we'll beach there.' Pooley swivelled the oar and the current bore the little craft onward without effort.

They had not as yet formed a definite plan of campaign. So far, they were down to watching and listening and only to actually intervening should things look as if they were actually getting out of control. As to exactly what form their intervention might take, or what exactly might constitute 'out of control', these were matters as yet undecided upon.

The craft beached soundlessly and Omally drew it up beyond the tide mark, turned it over and secured it to a tree. On furtive feet, the two men slipped into the undergrowth, moving towards the grove. If ceremonies were to be performed, it seemed to them likely that it was there they would be done.

Ahead, through the darkness, Pooley espied a flicker of firelight. He placed his hand upon Omally's arm and pointed. With a sobriety which was unnatural to them, the two crept nearer until they reached a suitable vantage point.

Five figures could be clearly seen, seated in a ring about a small fire of driftwood. In their duffle coats it was impossible to discern the sexes of the campfire sitters, but earlier observation suggested that they were the same five as seen in the Swan. Two young men and three women, each in their late teens or early twenties.

Omally uncorked his hip flask and pressed it to his lips. He took a slug. 'Seems harmless enough so far,' he whispered. 'A bit of a ging-gang-goolie.'

Jim accepted the proffered flask and drew upon it. 'If the sausages on sticks come out then I suggest we join them.'

In the distance the Memorial Library clock did its duty, and struck the midnight hour. As its last chime faded into silence, the five figures climbed slowly to their feet and removed their duffle coats. The skulking duo pressed their faces forward in rapt attention. As the duffle coats dropped to the ground it was revealed that all five wore nothing whatever beneath. They were stark naked.

'Would you look at that?' said John Omally.

'Just try and stop me.'

The celebrants now kicked off their wellington boots, linked hands and began a slow, clockwise perambulation about the fire, chanting softly.

'This has definitely got the edge on the boy scouts,' said Jim in a hushed voice. 'I wonder how you join.'

The vigour of the dance increased, the chanting became more audible. Words reached the two voyeurs, words they neither knew nor understood: 'SHADDAI EL CHAI ARARITA ADONAI TETRAGRAMMATON, SHADDAI EL CHAI ARARITA ADONAI TETRAGRAMMATON.' The words had a hypnotic quality and Pooley soon found his head bobbing to the rhythm as the naked bodies cavorted in the glow of the twinkling firelight. It was as if he had flown back through the ages and was witnessing some ancient fertility rite at a time when the earth was young and men and the elements were but a single body.

Omally, however, was made of sterner stuff. 'This may not be too clever,' he croaked into Pooley's mobile ear.

'Ssssh!' said Jim. 'It's just a singalong. Good clean fun.'

'It's witchcraft,' said John, 'witchcraft.'

'Really?' Jim looked on with renewed interest. 'Orgies, do you mean?'

'We will have to stop it.'

'Are you mad? You don't get this stuff on the telly.'

'We will have to stop it, Jim.' Omally rose to his feet, he made as if to cry out but the words, whatever they might have been, never left his throat.

With a sudden rush something swept down from above. It was large, dark and ferocious and it dropped directly into the fire with a great shriek, scattering the dancers to every side.

As the two men looked on in horrified fascination the thing drove down amidst the flames, extinguishing them.

And now the light was uncertain and the terror could only be glimpsed. Cries and screams rose in the darkness, above them horrible roars as of some jungle beast. Great wings buffeted the air and Omally saw a gigantic head, like an eagle's, though grossly magnified, rise and fall, driving its cruel beak amongst the writhing bodies that tumbled and fled before it. Yet the thing was not altogether bird – it moved upon four feet and a hellish barbed tail whipped and dived.

Pooley and Omally, numb and speechless, fell back as a naked female plunged by them into the darkness beyond, crying and screaming. They saw a man lifted from his feet and wished to see no more. Turning tail they ran. The cove glowed silver-white in the moonlight, the naked woman was nowhere to be seen. In blind panic, knowing not what could or should be done, numb with fear and horror, they tore the coracle from its mooring, thrust it into the Thames and rowed away.

24

The french windows of Professor Slocombe's study were, as ever, open. John and Jim tumbled through them, panting and wheezing. The old man sat at his desk, before him a galleried silver tray held three glasses and the inevitable whisky decanter.

The Professor raised his ice-blue eyes from his books as the two white-faced survivors blinked at him. Laying aside an ivory-handled magnifying glass, his gaze left his uninvited guests and came to rest upon the decanter. John did not require a verbal invitation. Grasping the thing by the neck he splashed Scotch into the three glasses. 'No ape,' said he, 'no ape, Professor.'

'No,' said the sage, 'no ape. Now if you are able, contain your feelings and tell me what you have seen.'

With tumblers clutched in whitened knuckles the two took up fireside chairs. At Pooley's prompting Omally recounted their tale of terror.

At length the Professor raised a slim forefinger. 'This time I must telephone for the police,' he said. 'You have no guilty secrets to hide and therefore nothing to fear. If people have died upon the island then it is a matter for the civil authorities. I will telephone at once.' Pooley and Omally shared wary glances, hunched over their drinks and said no more. The Professor made his call. 'Is there anything else you haven't told me?' he asked as he replaced the receiver.

'Nothing,' said Jim. 'We've done nothing wrong, Professor, we've stuck to our side of the deal, as you are no doubt well aware.'

'I can find no fault in your behaviour, Jim.'

'So what was it?' Omally demanded. 'And don't give us "performing monkey".'

Professor Slocombe placed his thumbs and forefingers together and pressed the former to his brow. 'It would appear to be witchcraft as you surmised. Those that choose to practise the dread art forever risk the consequences.'

'But I understood that this particular bunch were "white".'

'The dividing line has a tendency to waver. Do you recall any of the words of their incantation?'

John scratched his curly head. 'Adonai,' said he, 'and tetra-something, gramaphone, I think.'

'Grammaton,' said Professor Slocombe. 'Tetragrammaton. The four syllables that represent the unknowable and unpronounceable name of the Judaic god. The most powerful of all names of power. These children were, as you say, "white".'

'So what attacked them?' Omally's voice was scarcely to be heard. 'And killed them?'

'They were attempting to raise a cone of power, of protection, if you like. But to do so one must be well versed and well protected psychically. Such is the product of years of training. These youths had not the wherewithal to protect themselves. The man that dares consult the dead expects in return to hear the truth. He that would conjure with the gods dares amply enough by any reckoning, he needs must seek protection.'

'From what?'

'From primal forces, elementals, old evil that can be conjured but rarely contained. That which is sought is not, by experience, always that which is found.'

'It was the griffin,' said Jim, 'the Brentford Griffin, they found.'

'In as many words, yes, it was. Whether the griffin exists in flesh and blood reality is debatable, but in occult terms, in folk memory, in the subjective, the common consciousness, the imagination which is at the heart of all magic, then yes. It was called into objective existence. It is primal, uncontrollable.' The Professor rose suddenly to his feet. 'And in all probability it is still out there.'

'O misery,' said Jim burying his head.

'We must get over to the island at once,' said Professor Slocombe.

'You speak for yourself.' Pooley sought invisibility behind his glass.

The island was ablaze with lights. Several River Police launches were moored along the Brentford side, beacons flashing. Teams of constables and officers moved to and fro with torches and flares.

The Professor, accompanied by two most dissenting dissenters, arrived in the scholar's skiff. Here they were greeted by Inspectre Hovis, who helped the old gentleman from the boat and wrung his hand. 'Professor,' he said, 'I alerted the force at once. I fear this is a bad business.'

Professor Slocombe greeted the policeman as an old friend, which didn't surprise Pooley or Omally in the least, as John secured the Professor's slim craft to the branch of a tree. 'I am a little miffed that you did not contact me upon your arrival to the borough, Sherringford.'

Sherringford? thought Pooley.

'Professional pride,' the detective explained. 'I had of course the wish to renew our acquaintanceship, but under happier circumstances than those I find myself in at the present.'

'You are here upon a case then?'

'The most important of my career. Such vexations as this I frankly have no need of.'

'So what have you found?' Professor Slocombe strolled off up the beach, arm in arm with the detective, and their conversation went beyond Pooley and Omally.

'I might say that there was safety in numbers,' John patted his pockets in search of tobacco. 'But to be surrounded by such a force of the English Garda frankly affords me anything but security.'

There was at least an ounce of optimism left in Jim, so he

said, 'Look on the bright side, the Professor spoke the truth, we are guilty of no crime.'

John shook his head doubtfully. 'I do not share your blind faith, Jim, give us a roll-up, will you?' Jim passed Omally his tin, John rolled a fat fag. 'I suppose we'd better follow,' said he, pocketing Jim's tin. Without any great enthusiasm the two men followed in the Professor's wake, Omally humping a heavy calfskin case that the elder had packed specially for the occasion.

Near the grove they halted. The place was now floodlit and thick with the fuzz. Characters in white coats took measurements and photographs. Constables stared blankly, shared illicit cigarettes and spoke in Neanderthal tones.

Inspectre Hovis led the Professor to the centre of the grove. 'I can surmise to a reasonable degree of exactitude what events occurred, though there are of course certain grey areas.'

'Then what do you have?'

'I have a dance of some sort and by the evidence of the discarded clothing, a naked dance.'

'How many?'

'Five, two men and three women, young and energetic. There has been an attack of some kind, there is blood, but no bodies.'

'I see. Have any of your officers observed anything strange in the vicinity?'

'Such as?'

'Then no matter. What do you suppose attacked these people?'

'That is one of the grey areas, Professor, whatever it was came down from above, there are . . .' Hovis hesitated.

'There are . . .' prompted the Professor.

'There are other footprints, very large, not human. I am having casts made.'

'I would appreciate a set, if possible. I am currently following a line of research which might lead to interesting conclusions.'

Hovis stroked his chin. 'If you are prepared to confide your findings then, certainly, this is all a bit out of my line.'

'You have my word on it. Now I would ask you a very great favour. Request that your men make haste with their operations and vacate the island as quickly as possible.'

'You ask the impossible, Professor.'

'Sherringford, I would most strongly recommend you to do as I say.'

Hovis stared long and hard at the ancient scholar, sufficiently long in fact for Professor Slocombe to implant the concept of 'immediate withdrawal for the sake of safety' firmly in his mind.

'We will withdraw immediately,' said Sherringford Hovis. 'I will speak to you later this morning, an answer or two in return would be greatly appreciated.'

'Then so be it.' Hovis pressed his hand into that of Professor Slocombe's, the handshake was unconventional but significant.

John and Jim were sharing the remains of the hip flask and a single fag. They watched in no small wonder as at the Professor's request the lads of the force withdrew from the island, mounted up their launches and motored away into the darkness.

'Such power,' said John respectfully, 'and he wastes it upon honest dealings.'

'I heard that,' said Professor Slocombe. 'The case, John, if you please.'

Pooley peered around at the now all but deserted island. 'Professor,' said he, 'I was thinking to have a go at your rose-bed first thing, an immediate sojourn to my own might prove favourable.'

'The tide is up, Jim, you'd best stay.'

'But my work! Late nights do not agree with me.'

'You are excused duties for tomorrow. John, the case.'

Omally hefted the case. 'Where do you want it?' he asked.

'Here, where the fire has been.'

'All aboard,' said John Omally.

'Kindly lay out the contents.'

Omally applied himself to the locks but they would not budge.

'My apologies.' The Professor made a profound movement with his fingers above the case. The catches sprang.

'I think,' said Omally, 'that Jim and I had best away. Leave you to your work.'

The Professor did not dignify the remark with a reply. He flipped down the sides of the case, exposing a cluster of mysterious accoutrements, bottles, flasks, crystals, strange indefinable objects. Blowing on to his fingers, he withdrew something that resembled a folded table-cloth. This he shook out before him. The thing was dark, characterized by a circle enclosing a pentagram, the whole wrought with cabalistic symbols. The Professor laid the cloth before him and stroked out its creases, mouthing certain words and phrases. He stepped into the circle, which was only of sufficient size to enclose himself alone. 'Hand me the case, John, do not cross the line of the circle.' Omally did so. 'And now withdraw.' Pooley and Omally did so, at the hurry-up. They retreated to what they considered a safe distance and squatted amongst the bushes. An owl asked who, but Jim did not reply. 'And now . . .' Professor Slocombe delved into the case and laid about him a strange collection of articles: a lamp, which he lighted, a rock of a colour yet uncatalogued, a silver dish into which he decanted a dark liquid which solidified on the instant of contact, an emerald sphere and certain small caskets which seemed to tremble, as if containing living forms.

John drew Pooley back into the darkness, powerful magic was at work here. 'I can't be having with this,' whispered Jim, 'it is all most unfair.'

And now the Professor stood up in the circle and raised his arms to the four cardinal points. For the second time in a single night the two men heard the words of power called forth: 'SHADDAI EL CHAI ARARITA ADONAI TETRAGRAMMATON.' About the Professor the lamplight seemed contained, it ceased to reach beyond the boundaries of the circle, all else was lost in darkness.

Omally crossed himself and began the Hail Mary. Jim crossed his fingers and said, 'Feinites.'

The ancient magician exhorted the ancient gods, those who were at one with the elements. The words flew from his mouth in rapid, well-practised succession, never faltering, each falling upon the last as part of a stream of consciousness, of understanding.

It was old magic, old and tried and proven beyond the possibility of error or doubt. And the two men who looked on in wonderment knew, knew that those things the Professor understood, that the world he inhabited, was not their own.

Many things passeth understanding and knowledge is given only unto the few.

'OMNE AUM AMEN AMOUN.' Professor Slocombe slumped into the circle, worn, wasted and silent.

John and Jim rushed immediately to his assistance. John cradled the old white head and pressed his hip flask to the parched lips. 'Professor,' he said, 'are you all right? Speak, speak.' The old eyes opened, the lips moved, John withdrew his flask and drained away the final measure.

'There is nothing more,' said Professor Slocombe, his voice coming as from a great distance. 'Nothing, it is gone, we are safe.'

25

'I have called this meeting,' said Jennifer Naylor, 'to clarify procedure, assuage doubts and re-establish co-ordination.' The council members received her words without conviction, each in their own manner, each with their own assimilation of 'the facts' as they saw them. 'Rumour runs rife, truth is as ever its victim.'

'How prettily said.' The words belonged to Mavis Peake. 'Concern, however, exists regarding the bomb attack upon one of the sites and the talk of mass murder upon another.'

'Mass murder indeed,' Jennifer laughed. 'You are letting your imagination run riot, dear.'

'Don't patronize me.' Mavis smoothed down her vertical blouse. 'My brother is a constable on the Brentford force, he told me that he spent half the night on Griffin Island, a blood bath he said.'

Jennifer Naylor made a note in her Filofax. 'And your brother is prepared to swear this in court?'

'He isn't going to get the opportunity, there is a cover-up, a conspiracy of silence, this new inspector . . .'

'A conspiracy,' said Jennifer. 'The masons, is it, or the illuminati?'

'I will not be held to ridicule, I know what I know.'

'You know nothing but hearsay. There was a small chemical fire upon the Cider Island Site. As to mass murder, who were the victims? Where are the bodies?'

Mavis sat down, speechless with rage. Major Mac-Fadeyen lurched up from his seat. 'Madam,' said he, 'the facts of the case are evidently being suppressed, but do not think to pull the wool over our eyes. Brentford is a small borough, one man sneezes and we all catch a cold.'

'How colourfully put,' said Jennifer.

131

'Since the outset of this . . . this business,' the Major fumed on, 'you, madam, have been in possession of facts otherwise denied to us. Things are going on here and by God I will get to the bottom of them!' He sat down, life-readings fluttering into the red.

'Does anyone have anything factual to recount?' Jennifer asked. 'Hearsay and conjecture have yet to prove themselves a reliable basis for informed opinion.'

Paul Geronimo raised his 'howing' palm. 'Squaw utter brave words, but bravery alone insufficient to carry battle when greatly outnumbered by enemy.'

Barry nodded in agreement. 'Buffalo bullshit not always baffle brains,' said he.

'You may scoff at speculation,' said Philip Cameron, 'but it exists none the less. Factions are forming, the rule of the mob becomes imminent. Doubts are being expressed. If you cannot quell ours to any satisfaction what chance do you have with the plebs?'

'That is exactly why I have called this meeting. We do not want dissenters, violence and uproar in the streets. We have been given the opportunity to host the next Olympic games. Do you not realize our responsibility, the importance of all this?'

'That is all well and good,' said Philip. 'We are all well aware of the benefits to the borough. But incidents have occurred. If you do not choose to confide in us then you must bear the full responsibility.' Jennifer turned her devastating gaze upon him, but for the first time it failed to devastate to any visible extent. 'Listen,' Philip continued, 'you believe absolutely in this project, we would be happy to, but anomalies exist. If you can clear these up to any satisfaction, perhaps we could share your optimism also.'

Jennifer seated herself. 'I will answer whatever questions I can.'

Philip gazed about at his associates, their faces egged him on. 'All right,' said he. 'Firstly, who is financing the games?'

Jennifer shook her head. 'In truth, I do not know.'

'Then I have no further questions to ask. It is clear from the outset that you are not prepared to furnish answers.'

'I hold that this meeting is in disorder,' quoth Major MacFadeyen. 'In fact, I press for an extraordinary general meeting to re-elect governing bodies and re-establish a respectable colloquium.'

'I second this motion,' said Mavis Peake.

'Gentlemen and lady,' said Jennifer. 'There is nothing to be gained from such indecorum. As chairperson I reject the motion proposed. I have on my agenda several new proposals that I wish to have resolved. If I am opposed then I shall declare this meeting out of order and may possibly be forced to call each of its members before a board of my own choosing to discuss whether they be deemed suitable to continue in their offices or whether their replacement be considered necessary.' Amidst general uproar she raised her hand. 'Anyone who feels that I am over-exceeding my authority has but to consult council doctrine. Under section five, subsection fifteen, paragraph seven, "the chairperson is empowered, during times of special circumstance to call for re-election any member of the council who performs an act or acts which are considered by he or she, in the body of the chairperson, detrimental to the public good, or welfare, inasmuch that . . ."'

Philip Cameron shook his fist. 'What you are saying is that if we don't agree with what you're saying you can sack us and get somebody else in!'

'I am only quoting from textual doctrine, I hope that the need will not arise.'

'Well, let me spare you the requisite paperwork. I quit.'

'I also,' said Mavis. 'Goodbye and good riddance.'

The Geronimo brothers exchanged knowing glances. 'Brave who see buffalo upon plain,' said Paul, 'care not for buffalo's thoughts, only for how many cooking pots be filled. White squaw care only fill own belly, buffalo die yet other braves starve.'

Profound, thought his brother, dead profound. 'Does this mean we quit too?' he asked.

'It does,' said Paul Geronimo. 'When waterhole dry, no good complain to desert, best seek river elsewhere.'

'You're all bloody mad,' said Major MacFadeyen. 'I leave you to it, madam, but you haven't heard the last of me.' With that parting shot he tucked his riding crop beneath his tweedy armpit and limped from the chamber.

Jennifer Naylor surveyed the now empty room with evident satisfaction and turned her attention towards the computer print-out which lay before her upon the table. Everything had now run exactly to the letter outlined to her. Inclining her beautiful head towards the direction of the door she smiled sweetly and made her own departure.

26

Inspectre Sherringford Hovis paced the floor of the Professor's study. 'No,' he said, shaking his head fervently, 'no, I will not be having with this.'

Professor Slocombe offered a passive smile to the great detective. 'Nevertheless I have no doubt that it occurred very much in the manner that I have stated.'

Hovis sank into a fireside chair and spread out his long legs before him. 'You are suggesting that these young people invoked some kind of spirit, in the form of a mythical griffin no less, and that it turned upon them?'

'Not exactly, it is far more complicated than that.'

'More complicated? Such a concept alone is surely enough?'

'Do you have another theory then?'

Hovis shook his head once more. 'None immediately springs to mind. But my superiors will not buy "griffin", Professor. They have little truck with the supernatural and even less with me at present.'

'You have the plastercasts, you have the blood samples, I offer you the explanation, you must do with it what you will.'

Hovis rose from his seat and resumed his pacing. 'But it won't do.' He worried at the knot of his tweedy tie and sought other things to do with his hands. 'I can't make a case of this. My superiors will fall on me from an impossible height. And what of the games? MYTHICAL BEAST STALKS OLYMPICS, FIVE DEAD SO FAR. This won't do. It is disaster, spell it as you will.'

'You have two witnesses,' suggested the Professor.

'Ah yes, the nocturnal "bird watchers" who just happened to be on the island.'

Professor Slocombe flinched inwardly; Omally had been bound to come up with some explanation other than the truth for their being there. 'Well, they would testify to what they saw, they have nothing to hide.'

'Indeed?' Hovis took from his pocket a morocco wallet and from this a charred photograph. 'And what do you make of this, Professor?'

The sage examined the photograph. 'It would appear to be a drunken holidaymaker in a foolish hat,' said he.

'It would appear to be your Mr Pooley.' Hovis returned the snapshot to his wallet. 'Well then?'

Professor Slocombe shrugged. 'Whatever can you mean?'

'I discovered this photograph amongst the debris of the Cider Island explosion. A rare coincidence, do you not think?'

'The science of coincidence has never been fully explained, formularized and understood. I have made a study of it for some years now. My conclusions, however, still remain open to personal interpretation.'

'Be that as it may, I feel that an in-depth interview with Mr Pooley down at the station might yield interesting facts.'

'A little uncharitable, don't you think? He came forward upon his own volition to report this incident.'

'You phoned it in, I so recall.'

'At his prompting.'

'Hm.' Hovis took snuff from the tip of his cane. 'If he has nothing to hide then he has nothing to fear.'

'Hm,' said Professor Slocombe. 'History teaches us that this is not always the case. More sherry?'

'Yes indeed.' Hovis found his discarded glass and the Professor refilled it. 'Something very odd is going on in Brentford,' he said, 'and I am the man who will get to the bottom of it.'

'Of that I have no doubt, but tell me, Sherringford, what exactly brings you to the borough?'

'I am here following the course of my inquiries.'

'What else? But would you care to enlarge?'

Hovis pressed shut the french windows and leant upon them; he stared about the Professor's study, the walls of books, the stuffed beasts, the thaumaturgical objects, the domed wax fruit and antique furniture. 'It is a queer business,' said he, 'and one which has cost me no small embarrassment.'

'I have no wish to pry.'

'I know this, but no matter. It is gold that has brought me here. The airport gold bullion robbery.'

'Yes, I read of it, a curious business. I had no idea that you were personally involved.'

'My name has stayed thankfully out of the papers, but I was responsible for the security of the entire operation. I was to supervise the loading of the gold at the Bank of England and then its unloading for freight at the airport.'

'And so what went wrong?'

'Herein lies the mystery. The bullion was loaded. I supervised this myself. Unmarked lorries delivered it to the airport. These were sealed into the high security compound for the night. When they were opened the next morning, again under my personal supervision, they were empty.'

'Ah,' said Professor Slocombe. 'Of course a thousand questions spring immediately to mind.'

'And not without due cause. My head is on the block over this entire affair, I am being made the scapegoat. If I do not recover the gold then it is farewell Inspectre Hovis. The best I can hope for is to sell my memoirs to the Sunday press and retire with the loot to a bit of beekeeping on the Sussex downs.'

'It won't be the first time, but it would be an ignominious end to a fine career. So tell me, Hovis, as I am sure you shall, what led you here to Brentford?'

'Logic, Professor, what else? The gold went on to the lorries and the gold was not upon them when they were reopened. I have examined all possibilities. The gold could not have been removed whilst the lorries were in the airport compound. The sheer mechanics of such an operation preclude it. To penetrate the security, unload the bullion, move it out, such is an impossibility.'

'Not an impossibility, but I follow your reasoning.'

'Then follow it to the logical conclusion, if the gold was not removed at the airport then it must have been done so somewhere along the way.'

'The thought had already crossed my mind. So did the lorries make an unscheduled stop en route?'

'They did,' said Hovis, 'right here in Brentford. I will not go into the details, the thing has been an almighty balls-up, the lorries were left unattended for more than an hour.'

'Oh dear,' said the Professor. 'But surely, even if this was the case you would have no reason to believe that the gold is still here. It could be anywhere.'

'Oh, it's here all right, Professor, I know it.'

'And how do you know? Intuition? The reliability of this faculty, if faculty it proves to be, remains uncertain.'

'I hear whispers.' Inspectre Hovis tapped at his nose in a significant fashion. 'The gold is here all right, the entire invidious operation stemmed from here, the heart of it all is here. It is here and I shall find it.'

'As indeed you must. You have your constables scouring the area day and night, I trust.'

Hovis shook his head. 'Perish the thought. There is sufficient going on here without complicating matters further. A hoard of flat-footed bobbies turning out every lock-up garage in the area or giving the local padre the dawn call is the last thing I want. No, I've got them all on traffic duty and litter patrol. I will go this one alone.'

'But you are out-borough,' said Professor Slocombe. 'I mean, well, you will find it hard going on your own.'

'I have enlisted the help of several locals, who, shall we say, owe me a favour or two. I am not completely on my own. Thus, I regret that for now, last night's incident must be left to hang in the files. Should further evidence, in the shape of bodies, appear, then the matter will be dealt with accordingly. Other than for that I have no further wish to know what is going on around here.' Hovis held up his hand towards the Professor, whose face now expressed outrage. 'I am sorry, but there it is. I have spoken to you in confidence and I trust that you will respect same. The matter is for now closed. There will be no further word of it spoken. Do I make myself clear?'

'You are making a very grave mistake, Hovis.'

'Be that as it may, I have leads to be followed, a skein to be untangled, I must be gone. Goodbye.'

'Goodbye,' said the Professor, 'and good luck, for you will surely need it.'

27

Further days did as one might expect them to and the weeks began to pass. The media were playing something of a waiting game. Regular reports were issued as to the progress of the stadium's construction, and certainly the sheer scale of the operation and its unique nature made everything newsworthy. But the Birmingham débâcle and the sheer eccentricity of the Brentford project had the newsmen hedging their bets.

The work progressed nightly and more and more pre-constructed sections were pressed into place, but the greatest wonder of all was that none of the stadium was actually visible come morning. A thin and hazy line delineated its expanding borders but the solar cells and the ingenious system of sub-stadia optics projected daylight on to the borough and laid an all but perfect camouflage. But the eyes of the world were upon it, or at least upon what little they could see of it. Reporters prowled the borough seeking a twist or a turn that might be moulded into an exclusive. But they got little in return for their pains. Through motives entirely unconnected both Ms Jennifer Naylor and Inspectre Sherringford Hovis saw to that.

At a little before ten-thirty on a particular Thursday morning John Omally strolled into the Flying Swan. The terrors of the night on Griffin Island were pressed far to the back of his mercurial mind; his thoughts were now, as ever, fixed upon the main chance. As such he was singularly unprepared for the horror which now met his naked gaze.

At the end of the bar-counter Neville stood glowering, his teeth and hands painfully clenched and the cause of his consternation all too apparent. In the centre of the saloon bar perched upon a bar stool sat Young Master Robert, demon spawn of the master brewer. About him moved his evil catspaws, coldly and efficiently tearing the living heart from the grand old watering hole.

Omally caught at his breath, his head swam and his eyes bulged painfully from their sockets. He had known many shocks and traumas during the course of his eventful life, but this, this was torment to the very soul. Nightmare become reality.

'Away,' quoth the Young Master, gesturing to the line of Britannia pub tables, which, it had been previously assumed, nothing less than the long awaited nuclear holocaust event would have been capable of shifting. 'Out with the old and in with the new.' A menial dragged away one of the antique tables exposing four bright discs of carpet which hadn't seen daylight for one hundred years. 'To the dump, to the dump, to the dump, dump, dump,' sang the boy wonder in a ghastly parody of the Lone Ranger's famous theme.

Omally staggered over to Neville. The part-time barman stared through him, his good eye ticcing violently. 'Neville,' gasped Omally, 'Neville, *do* something!'

The part-time barman's eye finally focused upon a friend. 'John,' he whispered, 'John, *do* something.'

'Bin the chairs,' cried Young Master Robert unfolding an enormous set of plans across his bony knees. 'I want a line of chrome bar-stools over there. Where are the video machines?'

'Video machines?' Neville gripped the bar-counter for support. He was fast approaching 'wipe-out'.

Omally glanced about in desperation, searching his brain for a solution. Kill them all, said his cerebellum, spare not even their children lest the evil persist. 'Shotgun,' ordered Omally, 'where is the shooter, Neville?'

'No guns,' stuttered the banjoed barman, 'no killing in my pub, John, anything else, do something, *anything*.'

'Get the dartboard down,' crowed the young vandal, 'Bin it.'

'*Kill them all!*' shouted Neville. '*Spare not even their children lest the evil persist!*'

There were five brewery menials, big fellows to a man. John considered that he could bring down at least two of them, possibly three if luck was on his side, but as a long-term solution to any problem, violence had only so much going for it and no more. There had to be another way and one that did not endanger life and limb. 'Leave this to me,' said Omally, straightening his dicky bow.

'What are you going to do?'

Omally looked long and hard into the face of Neville. It was a face he had known for nearly twenty years, through long and short and thick and thin, but it had never looked like this before. The barman's expression spelt defeat. His face said 'beaten'. John patted the good man upon the shoulder. 'Chin up,' he said, 'Just leave it to me, I'll sort it out.'

The barman's mouth said 'thank you' but no words came from it.

Omally straightened his shoulders and strode across the bar towards the Young Master. He owed Neville, every regular in the Swan owed Neville. In Brentford Neville was respected and in a manner which had no side to it he was loved also. No-one, no matter for the what, which or why, should be allowed to do this to him.

Omally strode across the bar this day a titan, an avenging angel, a Knight Templar. He didn't have an idea in his head.

'What do you want?' asked the Young Master, when John was near enough to make his presence felt.

'I . . . er, whatchadoing?' asked Omally.

'I would have thought that was clear enough.'

John looked about, as if seeing the carnage for the first time. 'Oh,' said he, 'redecorating, is it?'

Young Master Robert ignored him and returned to his plan. Yokel, he thought.

'Perhaps I can be of some assistance,' said John Omally, holding up a corner of the plan. 'You've got it upside down,' he added helpfully.

'I know what I'm doing, kindly clear off.'

John thrust his unwanted hands into his pockets. 'It's a brilliant concept, ideas-wise,' he said thoughtfully.

The Young Master eyed him over the plan. 'You approve?' he said with suspicion.

'Oh yes,' lied Omally, peering at the plan with a knowing eye and convincing enthusiasm. 'I see that the wall-bars are going to divide the saloon bar from the public; where do you propose to put the Nautilus machine?'

'Right here.' The Young Master pointed appropriately, watching for Omally's response.

'Across the entrance to the gents, shrewd,' said John, 'very shrewd.'

'You think so?'

'Indeed yes, the punters will literally have to work out on the machine to get to the gents, work up a thirst, eh?'

'That's what I thought,' said Young Master Robert, though he hadn't until now.

'This kind of theme bar is definitely the bar of tomorrow,' John continued. 'I was only chatting with Lucas about it the other day.'

'Lucas?' queried the Young Master.

'Lucas Mucus,' said John, 'of Membrane, Mucus, Willoby, Turncoat and Gladbetook. Covent Garden,' he tapped his nose, 'one of the big five, need I say more?'

'Oh, *that* Lucas . . .'

'Which other? Surely you know him?'

'Slightly,' said Young Master Robert. 'You know him well then?'

'Like a brother. We did visual design, marketing management, advanced concept realization, audio and televisual of course . . .'

'Oh, of course.' Robert's head nodded foolishly.

'Consumer response-objectivity and mass-media inter-inductional transmogrification at the Slade.' Omally studied the Young Master's face for signs that he had been rumbled.

'Go on?' said the buffoon, very much impressed.

John did so, with growing confidence. 'Surely I see the hand of Lucas at work here?' he said, gesturing grandiloquently.

143

'No, no, this is all my own work.'

'Brilliant,' said John, 'I am very impressed. So how did you get wind of it then, a bit of industrial espionage, eh?' He pulled at his lower eyelid in a lewd manner.

'Sorry?' said Young Master Robert. 'I don't think I follow you.'

Omally nudged the hoodlum confidentially in the rib area. 'Come on,' said he, 'you're not telling me this is a coincidence?'

'Coincidence? What are you talking about?' John studied his toecaps. Without the Young Master's prompting, work in the Swan had ceased and the menials were standing about like run-down clockwork automatons. So far so good, thought Omally. 'Out with it,' demanded the Young Master. 'What are you talking about?'

Omally beckoned conspiratorially and put his arm about the brat's rounded shoulder. 'All this,' said he, 'you sly dog, you got wind, eh?' He tapped his nose with his free hand.

'Got wind?'

'Certainly, got wind that the brewery's rivals were about to convert all their pubs into theme bars of a similar ilk.'

'They what?' Young Master Robert toppled backwards from his stool. Omally considered stopping him, but the thought passed on almost as soon as it had been born. He helped the boy up from the floor.

'Now don't come the innocent,' he said. 'Lucas told me that his company were engaged in converting the Four Horsemen, the North Star, the Jolly Alchemist, the Hands of Orloff, the Shrunken Head, the . . .'

'I . . . stop! Wait!' Young Master Robert flapped his hands at the menials who were doing nothing anyway. 'All the other pubs?' he asked Omally. 'All of them?'

'Every other local,' said that man, crossing his heart and hoping not to die in the process.

'Shit,' said Young Master Robert. 'Oh shit, shit, shit!'

'Oh no,' said Omally, striking his forehead, 'now I see it all.'

'You do? You do?'

'Of course, what a fool I am!'

'You are?'

'I am,' said Omally, who was anything but. 'They've stolen the idea from you, of course, it all makes sense now. One of them was in here a few nights back. Neville must have let the cat out of the bag.'

'You bastard.' The boy turned upon the part-time barman, who stood alone in silent prayer.

'Pardon?' said Neville. 'I what?'

'No, no,' said John, 'it's not his fault, he was only blowing the brewery's trumpet. You never told him it was a secret. Professional pride got the better of him. That man worships you.'

Robert looked from Omally to the part-time barman and back again. For one terrible moment John thought the game was up. 'He does what?'

'Not a man to show his feelings,' said John hurriedly. 'There's a way out of this though, I'm sure there is.'

'Think, man, think.'

Omally sought inspiration amongst the bumblies upon the Swan's nicotined ceiling. 'I have a plan,' said he, suddenly. 'It is an old trick but it might just work.'

'Tell me . . . tell me.'

Half an hour later Neville stood alone in the Flying Swan, it was just as it had ever been, same threadbare carpet, same tables, same chairs, same dartboard, same everything.

Omally stood in the doorway waving goodbye. 'Don't mention it,' he called, 'any time.' The door swung shut upon the sound of Young Master Robert's departing BMW.

'How?' said the part-time barman. 'How did you do it?'

Omally turned to his esteemed employer, the look upon Neville's face was one John would forever cherish. 'Psychology,' said the great man of Eire, 'and a small white lie or two.'

'Have a drink,' said Neville, making for the whisky optic, 'have two, have three if you like.'

'Not when I'm working, sir,' said John in a voice of mock sincerity.

Neville drew off a couple of large stiff ones. 'Sit down and tell me,' he said. 'Every last little bit.'

'There's not much to it,' said John sipping Scotch. 'I simply told him that to my knowledge the rival brewery were converting all their pubs into Olympic theme bars and that to really clean up, with the big influx of Yanks, the best thing to do was to retain the Swan's "Olde Worlde" atmosphere. An island of unspoilt old England in a sea of pseudo-Americana was the phrase I used. Quite a nice one I thought. Seemed to do the trick rather well.'

'You are a genius,' said Neville. 'But what when he finds out that it's all lies, when the other pubs don't do the conversions?'

'I took the liberty of telling him that the other pubs were not going to be converted until the day before the games begin, so when he does find out it will be too late anyway.'

Neville looked thoughtful. 'But when he does find out . . .' His voiced trailed off.

'When he does find out then I will tell him that it is yet more industrial espionage. That the rival breweries have all followed his lead. But of course it will be too late for them because our sign will already be up.'

'Our sign, what sign?'

Omally put on a brave face. 'The new pub sign,' he said in a whisper.

'What?' roared Neville. 'Are we still to be the Pentathlon Bar?'

'No, no.' John shook his head. 'In fact I got away with only a letter or twos' change.'

'All right, let's have it.'

'Well,' said Omally, flinching from the part-time barman, 'the new sign will say: YE FLYING SWAN INN, OLDEST AND MOST AUTHENTIC PUB IN BRENTFORD, WELCOMES ITS AMERICAN COUSINS.'

'Ye Flying Swan Inn,' said Neville. 'Ye Gods!'

28

At around four that afternoon, Omally was to be found cycling unsteadily down Cagliostro Crescent. He and Neville had enjoyed several 'afters' of the triple persuasion to celebrate John's triumph in saving the Swan from a fate which, if not actually worse than death itself, amounted to very much the same thing. Neville had waxed sentimental, as was often his way when in his cups, and been effusive in his praises.

'You have performed a service to the Flying Swan,' he told the grinning Irishman, 'of such magnitude that any financial reward would be pitifully inadequate as an expression of its worth, and thus to offer it would be tardy and churlish. Instead I give you my sincerest thanks, offer you my deepest respect and promise you my continued good fellowship. Such things you will agree are beyond price.'

John had no reply to make, although several sprang immediately to mind, but he was pleased beyond measure that Neville was his old self again. He had accepted a bottle of Scotch from the barman's private stock and the evening off as tangible appreciation for his noble deed.

Omally turned right into Moby Dick Terrace and brought Marchant to a sudden, unexpected and wheel-shuddering halt. Parked outside his house was a long black car of advanced design and uncertain extraction. 'The Garda,' said John, hastily steering Marchant up the kerb and into an alleyway. Parking up, he dismounted and peered around the corner to see just what was what. A figure issued from his front doorway. It was not a police-man, as he had feared, but a dwarf in chauffeur's livery. The creature hobbled around to the driver's door and entered the vehicle which at once drew away, slowly and soundlessly. John cowered back as it passed him by and strained to get a further glimpse of the car's occupants, but the windows were blacked out and it was impossible.

'Curious,' said John, as he crept out of his concealment and led Marchant home. 'Mrs King is keeping strange company these days.'

As he pressed his key towards the lock, the door receded before it and there in the passageway stood that very woman, John's landlady. She was dressed for the 'out', cashmere coat, knitted hat and string shopper. 'Oh, it's you,' she said, which would have left most people lost for a reply.

'Your servant, ma'am,' said himself.

'You've had a visitor.'

'Did they leave cash or a cheque?' Omally asked. 'I am expecting several such callers this week.'

'And so you should be, you owe a month's back rent.'

'Where did they leave the money?' John enquired. 'I will pay you at once.'

'He didn't leave any money as far as I know, just a parcel.'

'Oh yes?' Omally certainly didn't recall ordering anything.

'He said that you and that Jim Pooley had won prizes. He didn't have your mate's address so I gave it to him.'

'Prizes, eh? Well, I did enter a competition in hope of winning you a microwave oven, perhaps that's it.' Omally often amazed himself by the ease with which words of untruth sprang to his lips. 'Shall we open it together?'

'I haven't got time for that, I must get out before the shops close. I've left it on your kitchen table. And that kitchen wants cleaning, Mr Omally, it's a health hazard.'

'I came home at this time expressly to deal with that.' Omally eased himself past the woolly-hatted harridan.

'Just see that you do.' The front door slammed shut upon her words in blessed relief.

John bested the twenty-three stairs which led to his

chambers and pushed open the door. Things were very much as he had left them, no good-housekeeping fairy had descended from the lands of the blessed during his absence to flick the much-needed duster or make free with the vacuum cleaner. Although he was a stickler for personal hygiene, John's rooms left very much to be desired, tidiness-wise.

Omally took off his jacket and tossed it on to his unmade bed. Turning back his shirt cuffs he entered the kitchenette to examine the package lying on the oilcloth covered table. It was a brightly coloured affair, bound in twine and scaled with sealing wax in a quaint old-fashioned manner. There was, however, no accompanying card expressing congratulations or ill-founded birthday greetings.

'Further curiousness,' said the Irishman, lifting it and weighing it in his hands. It was approximately twelve inches to the side and of no particular weight. Omally shook it, something within thumped to one side and so he replaced it upon the table lest he damage its contents. 'It's not a microwave oven,' he said, searching for a clean knife to slit the bindings. As none was readily available he wandered back to his jacket to fetch his Swiss army knife. Selecting a blade suitable to the task he returned to confront the package.

Upon his return he observed a curious phenomenon. The package appeared slightly larger than before. He lifted it. Slightly heavier also. John shook his curly head. Neville's private stock evidently had somewhat special qualities. He would save the gift bottle for a worthy occasion.

John sliced through the bindings and laid aside the wrapping paper which came away in bright folds. He delved in to gain his prize but, to his surprise and annoyance, he found himself confronted by a further set of wrappings. John flung away the former and reconsidered the remaining parcel. It was no longer a cube, rather a tetrahedron. And . . . it was bigger!

Omally scratched his head. That was a good trick. He lifted the parcel. It was heavier yet again. A very good trick. With renewed vigour he fell upon the thing, slicing at strings, tearing away paper. They fell away with ease, almost springing from the parcel. The shape which now came to light was distinctly pyramidal, well wrapped and at least twice the size of the original cube. John was beginning to work up a healthy sweat. He folded his knife and tore at the parcel with his bare hands. Paper swept away in great sheets and he flung it to every direction. The revealed cylinder filled most of the kitchen table and Omally found himself standing knee-deep in wrapping paper. He found the parcel now impossible to lift. 'Perhaps it's an AGA?' he said, wiping sweat from his eyes. 'We'll soon see.' Ripping at the paper as one possessed, he revealed shape after shape, growing all the time. Suddenly, with an almighty crack, the kitchen table gave at its wormy legs and Omally tumbled aside into the confusion of multi-coloured wrapping paper as the now enormous package struck the floor with a deafening thump.

It was at about this time that he felt cause to question the wisdom of his actions. The hulking parcel now effectively blocked the door from the kitchenette. John arose from his colourful nest, puffing and blowing for all he was worth, and attempted to shift the obstacle. But to no avail. All he succeeded in doing was tearing away several more layers of paper. The parcel burst asunder, now visibly growing in size, to the accompaniment of loud ripping and tearing sounds.

John flattened himself against a wall. He was trapped and not only that, he was in dire peril. The door was now completely blocked, the kitchenette window too small to permit squeezing through, and a further series of ominous sounds informed him that the parcel was far from finished with its untoward quest for further expansion. With a sharp snap the thick length of rope which had restrained the Pandora's box severed, whipping Omally painfully across the face. Spitting blood, the indefatigable Irishman sought escape. 'Take your Pick' this wasn't, and he had no further wish to 'open the box'.

The parcel bulged menacingly about its lower regions and a huge appendage sprang out from it, splintering the remnants of the dilapidated kitchen table and pummelling against the wall. Omally leapt up on to it and clung on for dear life. Crockery crashed down from the dresser shelves and the elderly porcelain sink crumbled from its mountings and was gone in a cloud of whitened splinters. John scrambled across the seething parcel which was unfolding into every direction with unrestrained force, destroying all that lay before it and rapidly filling the room. The thing pulsed with life and John could feel a hideous strength moving beneath him. Suddenly he was in darkness.

The window was blocked and he was now being driven upwards into the ceiling. It was not going to be a pleasant way to go. John lay on his back across the swelling mass of homicidal packaging, his hands pressed against the polystyrene ceiling tiles he had known and always hated. The smell of a generation's nicotine, much of it his own, filled his nostrils, his ears popped from the pressure and his breath came in short pants. He was surely done for.

The spreading parcel of death rumbled beneath him wreaking further destruction, pulverizing furniture and fitments, horrendous, unstoppable. Omally's nose edged closer to the ceiling, he fought to reach his knife, but his hands were trapped at his sides, he was powerless to resist the irresistible, relentless force which bore up underneath him.

'Holy Mary, Mother of God,' said John Omally, 'put a good word in at some speed for this unworthy son.' There was a bone-sickening crunch and Omally was no more. Omally was no more in the kitchenette, he was now in the loft.

John opened his eyes; if this was Heaven, then it didn't look all that heavenly. Dust and dirt and pigeon shit weren't much of a happy ever after. Perhaps he'd gone to the bad place. So hell was an eternity of loft space. John sought to escape before the rolls of insulation arrived, his for the perpetual laying. What torment!

He leapt to his feet, striking his head on a roof timber and squinting about in what light the missing slates admitted. He was still alive, or at least he thought he was. Nursing a multiplicity of cuts and abrasions he climbed across the joists seeking the hatch which opened above the stairwell. Beneath him the sounds of groaning timbers and cracking plasterwork were not exactly music to his ears. The unstoppable package was filling the entire house. It had to be now or never.

John found his way around the unlagged water-tanks and dug his fingernails about the flap of the loft hatch, tearing it away. Without a thought for safety he leapt down through the opening and crashed in a heap on the landing. Cracks were racing across the walls of his room, furniture splintering, glass shattering. Ignoring the pain in his ankles, John dived headlong down the stairway, tore open the front door and rolled into the street. He picked himself up, hands upon knees, and bent gasping for breath, a terrific figure besmutted with plaster, roof dust, soot, blood and pigeon shit. Not a pretty sight.

'Afternoon, John,' said Old Pete. 'Decorating, is it? A job for a professional, that.'

John climbed painfully on to Marchant, cocked the pedal and cycled away with as much haste as he could muster.

Old Pete watched him go, before angling his deaf aid towards the sounds of destruction issuing from Omally's house. 'Structural alterations,' the ancient told his dog. 'I hope he's got planning permission.' Young Chips woofed noncommittally and addressed his nasal attentions to a nearby lamp post.

Pooley stood in his bath-towel skirt perusing the brightly coloured parcel which rested upon a tablecloth of equal vulgarity to Omally's. The Professor had granted him an early finish to the day and he had just been running the bath water when the package had arrived. 'I don't remember entering any competition,' said he, unfolding his pocket knife. 'Still, never look a gift parcel in the wrappings.'

Omally turned right into Abbadon Street and then left, much against Marchant's wishes, into Mafeking Avenue. 'We have to get to Jim's,' he told his complaining bike, 'he's in danger, I'll make it up to you later.'

Jim seated himself before his free gift and turned his knife between his fingers. 'Gently does it,' he said. 'Don't want to damage the contents.'

Omally mounted the pavement and rattled along over uneven slabs.

Jim applied his blade to the twine bindings. There was an almighty crash and he toppled from his chair to land in an indecent exposed heap upon the floor.

'Don't do it!' Omally stood in the doorway. Jim's door dangled uneasily from its hinges before slamming to the floor with a great bang.

'Don't do it, Jim!'

Pooley looked up fearfully from beneath the table at the besmutted apparition standing shakily in his doorway.

'Watchamate, John,' he said in a voice of no small surprise. 'This is all a bit drastic, is my doorbell broken or what?'

29

Professor Slocombe examined the multi-coloured parcel which lay before him on his desk.

'Don't open it,' said John Omally. 'Don't even think about it.'

The hastily re-clad Jim nodded in agreement. 'John had one too, it's had his house down by the sound of it.'

The Professor laid Pooley's parcel gently aside. 'It is safe until opened, then?' he asked.

'So I believe.' John indicated the roaring fire. 'That would be the best place for it. We brought it to you as . . .'

'As evidence? Yes, you did the right thing. You have been drawn into a horror not entirely of your own making.'

'Someone is out to kill us,' said John, 'that is for certain. As to the who and the why, these escape me for the present.'

'It is Bob,' said Jim. 'I'll fix his wagon for this, see if I won't.'

'No,' replied the Professor, 'it isn't your bookmaker, although I believe these matters are not entirely unconnected.'

Pooley took to the maintenance of a seething silence. 'Bastard,' was his last spoken word on the subject.

'What is going on?' Omally asked. 'I think we deserve to be told.'

Professor Slocombe refreshed his visitors' glasses. 'You cost me a small fortune in Scotch,' he told them, 'but no matter, you are alive and well and that is cause for celebration. In answer to your question, I fear that something deadly is going on here in the borough. I have no absolute proof and I do not value speculation, but I suggest that this attempt has been made upon your lives because some person or persons consider that you have seen too much.'

'On the island?' whispered Pooley.

'Yes, and on the barge.'

'The ape?' said John sarcastically.

'It was no ape,' the old man replied. 'Of that I am now quite convinced.'

'Then what?'

The Professor raised his old wrinkled palms. 'I cannot say for certain. I have my suspicions.'

'Which you evidently choose not to confide in us.'

'All in good time, I must be sure.'

'You can be sure of that,' said Jim pointing to the parcel. 'That leaves little to the imagination.'

'It does mine,' said Omally. 'It is not your everyday murder attempt, now is it? I mean, guns I can understand, or old Mark Three Jags mounting the pavement when you're stooping to tie your shoelace, but parcels which grow when you open them and smash your house down, this is a new innovation, is it not?'

'Yes,' said Jim, 'you can at least try to explain that surely?'

The Professor looked thoughtful. 'From what you have told me,' he said, 'my thoughts are that it contains a multi-cellular polysilicate with an unstable atomic base which expands uncontrollably upon contact with the air through close proximity with the radiation of body heat.'

'Ah, one of those lads,' said Jim. 'Then all is clear, my thanks.'

Omally was doubtful, but to save himself the spectacle of one of Pooley's flapping and spinning displays he said, 'Chemical warfare, Jim, a sophisticated anti-personnel device.'

'Something of the sort,' said the Professor. 'I suspect that when expansion reaches an optimum point the polysilicate evaporates, leaving little or no trace of its existence. A devilish weapon, and the product of a dark and sardonic humour.'

'The joke is certainly lost on me,' said Omally, in an appalled voice. 'Attempts upon my life rarely cause me to smile.'

'A cruel irony, John, your inquisitiveness was to prove your ruination.'

'Your understanding of such things is a tribute to your learning,' said John, 'but your detachment sometimes verges upon the inhumane.'

'Quite so, I apologize.'

'We should take this thing to the police,' said Pooley.

Professor Slocombe joined John in some vigorous head-shaking. 'I feel that might complicate matters even further. Inspectre Hovis is already quite keen to interview you. I should recommend strongly to the contrary on this issue.'

'Ah,' said Jim. 'In that case, if irony is the name of the game, then let us readdress this parcel back to its sender.'

'The prospect has a certain charm, but we have yet to identify him. John, what do you know about the patron who has put up the money for the games?'

'As much as you, Professor, probably less, a scientific genius with money to burn and a desire for anonymity. Oh, I see, then you think . . .'

'I do not know, but there is much I would like to find out. Events suggest a link, both incidents occurred at sites directly connected with the construction of the stadium.'

'The thought had crossed my mind.'

'So do you think you might make some enquiries, employ your silken tongue, ask about, subtly of course.'

'But of course.' Omally scratched plaster dust from his blackened barnet. 'It might prove difficult, but not impossible.'

'Good. Then it is my suggestion that you both lodge with me for a while, at a rent found mutually agreeable, of course. I have several spare bedrooms, you will find the accommodation suitable, I trust. Go about your daily business, keep your eyes open and your shoelaces well tied. That is my suggestion.'

Pooley nodded thoughtfully; this was evidently a serious matter. John said, 'What about Mrs King? She'll call the police when she sees what has become of that bug hutch she calls a rooming house.'

'I will deal with that directly,' said the Professor. 'You can owe me out of your winnings.' Pooley reached for the whisky decanter. 'And I will have a bar tariff typed out,' said Professor Slocombe, smiling sweetly.

30

The days continued to pass and the stadium neared completion. Beneath, the borough was changing, the light which now fell upon it was unnatural and laid queer textures on to the familiar landscape. The time-softened edges of the old buildings seemed to sharpen, perspectives became clearer. More startling than this was the sudden fall of night. Gone were the long dreamy summer evenings, when the Swan's patrons took the pleasure of their porter in the warm night air. Now at sunset the solar cells withdrew into the upper canopy and for a brief moment the great umbrella of the stadium was etched clearly against the sky.

Muttering doubtfully the patrons turned up their collars to the sudden chill and shuffled back to the comfort of the saloon bar. Old Pete raised two fingers and Young Chips peed defiantly skyward.

Pooley leant upon the Professor's spade and mopped his brow with an oversized red gingham handkerchief. The recent doings had all but done for him. Had it not been for the thought of his coming wealth and his agreement with the Professor, he would no doubt have taken to his bed for an indefinite period.

Norman laboured away long into the nights upon a project of his own formulation; but for the occasional muted explosion or fluctuation in the neighbourhood electricity supply, his neighbours had little cause to complain and so left him to it.

Jennifer Naylor now received daily instructions and followed them as best she could. Her inquisitiveness towards the identity of the borough's Big Mr X grew with each day to become her waking obsession.

Omally sat outside his allotment hut. Being on the boundaries of the borough the allotments continued to enjoy a natural sunset and a soft afterglow. Thus in the doorways of similar sheds, which formed a picturesque shanty town leading down the natural arc of land towards the Thames, other Brentonian males sat in similar postures, puffing upon their pipes and supping their home brew.

Omally scratched in the dust with his dibber and considered his lot. He had taxed his considerable ingenuity to the very limits in attempting to track down the enigmatic organizer of the games, who might or might not be his would-be assassin. But he had achieved very little in return for his pains. He had inveigled his way into the town hall registrar's office and consulted the land register to discover who had purchased each of the Olympic sites. Each purchaser had told him the same story: they had been commissioned to purchase the land on behalf of a third party who had more than adequately compensated them for their time and trouble. Employing a deviousness previously unexploited, he had teased from each the name of the secretive buyer. The name was always the same: THE KALETON ORGANIZATION.

Sensing victory John sped off to Companies House, but to no avail. The Kaleton Organization was not registered, it was not a research organization nor a charitable institution, nor a trading body of any persuasion, it was not listed in any directory, public or private. It was a bank account alone and nothing more. It was a dead end.

John turned his dibber in the soil. Anyone with resource enough could have got as far as he had, which after all was nowhere at all. He was almost on the point of giving up when a sudden thought crossed his mind. It was such a pleasant thought and so ripe with engaging possibilities that he gave himself a mental boot in the backside for not thinking of it sooner. Leaping to his feet with a wild cry of exaltation, which raised eyebrows from the nearby hut-sitters, he mounted up Marchant and rode away at speed.

He caught Alison's Floral Fripperies in the High Street just as the big girl was closing for the night and charmed her out of a bunch of Day Lilies. At a little after seven, having bathed his body to fragrant cleanliness in the Professor's marble bath, dressed himself in Pooley's best suit and shaved his chin to a manly blue, he set out once more upon Marchant bound for Jennifer Naylor's.

As John rode out he sang softly to himself a lilting ballad rich in the pathos of the hard times of Holy Ireland. That he had never known these hard times himself, being Dublin born and Brentford bred, was beside the point. For when the soul of the Gael is stirred to song, then that song will as like as not be one of lament, heavy with sentiment and stirring memories of Erin's tragic history, and the bitter-sweet times that all but were. 'The night that O'Rafferty's pig ran away,' sang John Vincent Omally. John turned right into Aiwass Avenue and suddenly applied the anchors. Marchant slewed violently and spilled lilies from his saddlebag. Muttering beneath his breath John dragged his bike into the concealment of a parked car and scooped up the fallen flowers before ducking away out of sight.

Parked in front of Jennifer's semi was the long black car which had delivered the all but deadly package to his door. Now what could this mean? Omally's brain turned somersaults. Was Jennifer in for the chop too and if so why? If the car belonged to the Kaleton Organization, and the Kaleton Organization were responsible for the games and if what and if is and, and . . .

At this moment the liveried dwarf shuffled out of Jennifer's porch and entered the long black vehicle. John chewed upon his knuckles. Now was a time for the finding out, an opportunity to learn the whereabouts of the mystery Mr X, but what to do? If Jennifer had received a parcel then he had to warn her. Omally dithered, the car cruised slowly away up the avenue. Think, man, think. His decision was however made for him on the instant he saw Jennifer's Porsche slide out of her garage and turn up the avenue after the receding black car.

'Well, now,' said John, and, much after the fashion of the late and legendary, 'the game is afoot.' He climbed aboard Marchant and set off in hot pursuit. The sheer nonsense of a sit-up-and-beg-bike pursuing a Porsche did not even enter his head; he applied foot to pedal and made out for the off.

At the top of Aiwass Avenue Jennifer turned right. Pleased with this at least, Omally followed. He could see the long black car in the middle distance turning left towards the football ground and spoke honeyed words of bribery to Marchant. Promises of a new back light and aluminium pump were duly made. The bike was evidently satisfied, as when Jennifer's Porsche turned left it permitted Omally to follow without complaint. As a token gesture, signalling disapproval, it did, however, let John do all the work and by the time he passed Griffin Park he was already working up a healthy sweat.

Across Brentford went the little convoy, Omally riding drag in a fervour of pressing pedals. Left at the traffic lights and up the Kew Road towards the Chiswick round-about. As John applied his best feet forward, the thought that the Kaleton Organization's headquarters might well lie somewhere to the East of London, in Penge, or some other far-flung outpost of the civilized world, took the opportunity to cross his mind. Such matters did not bear thinking about so he plodded on. The black car took yet another left turn and entered the new estate to the rear of the great gasometer.

Omally pulled up at the corner and took a breather, rolled and lit a cigarette. To his knowledge there was no other road in or out of there, but then where was the black car heading? Delivering another bomb?

In the distance the Memorial Library clock struck the half hour. Above, a drone of engines announced the arrival of further sections to the nearly complete Star Stadium.

Omally took a final drag and flicked his butt-end into the road. He had two choices: stay where he was, or go looking. He cocked a pedal; hanging about on the off chance had never been his way. Plough on.

John entered the new estate. He knew little about this area now, although it had been his home when a lad. The streets of Victorian houses had gone the way of all flesh, beneath the bulldozer's plough and in their place up went the gaunt flatblocks, built by folk who cared little, to house strangers who cared even less. The place was now a wasteland. Poorly designed and indiffererently constructed, the dwellings were already beginning to sag and crumble and the Brentford council feared daily a disaster of Babel Tower proportions.

It is fitting, if not satisfying, to note that residences similar to those demolished were now commanding huge sums in nearby Chiswick and Ealing. But is it not written in *The Book of Ultimate Truths*, that those who can predict the future rarely work for the town planning department?

Omally pushed foot upon pedal and entered the Twilight Zone. It was seedy and fly-blown and haunted. Graffiti covered each and every wall in indecipherable hieroglyphics, ruined cars stood upon stacked bricks and in the crepuscular glow of a single street lamp, a knot of ne'er-do-wells, clad in the style of Post-Holocaust chic, eyed him with evident hostility. Omally hunched his shoulders, shivered and cycled on, oppressed and depressed. This wasn't Brentford; he might as well be on the moon.

John's thoughts now turned solely to the welfare of Jennifer Naylor. What had become of her? He swung in clockwise circles about the flatblocks, weaving through the dereliction and waste, but there was no sign of her Porsche, or of the long black car which had preceded it into this hinterland of urban decay.

John halted beside the high wire fence which guarded the perimeters of the gasometer. He would have to check the underground car parks next and he did not relish the thought. Even the now legendary Mad Max himself might have his doubts in that neck of the woods.

Suddenly John heard a cry. A woman's scream? He strained his hearing, tense and alert. Another cry and it came from beyond the fence, somewhere near the great gasometer. He leapt from his bike and thrust it against the fence, thinking to shin up from it and over. There was a crackle of blue fire and he found himself upon the ground intimately entangled in his bicycle frame. John disengaged himself and struggled to his feet, cursing, spitting and nursing his singed fingertips. His ears rang and blood pounded in his temples. There was a strange metallic taste in his mouth. The fence was electrified.

Blowing on his fingers, John mounted up and cycled on seeking an entrance. He had not travelled one hundred yards before he espied Jennifer's Porsche through the wire, parked up close to the gasometer. The driver's door hung open, Jennifer was nowhere to be seen.

Omally became frantic, he pedalled on and on, around and around. The fence was endless, there was no entrance to be found. Within a few brief minutes he was back where he started. 'Now that,' said John Omally, 'I do not like one little bit.' He cocked an ear but the night was now silent, now dark, black and silent. Logic and reason presented him with a united front. If the Porsche got in, then there had to be an entrance. That, however, was as far as logic and reason were prepared to go on the matter. 'Damn,' said John. 'Damn and blast.'

Now there is more than one way to skin a cat – not that John had ever seen any technique demonstrated to pleasing effect – yet it followed, somehow, that there must be more than one way to best an electrical fence some fifteen feet in height. Omally set immediately about the formulation of a plan so wildly unfeasible and unlikely to succeed that the very telling of it would tax the reader's credibility to impossible limits. Thus, to spare the reader's sensitivities, Omally's method of besting the fence must remain unrecorded.

Omally dropped down inside the fence brandishing his

bicycle pump. In a manner much beloved of the SAS he scuttled forward from vantage point to vantage point, cover to cover. He crept up behind Jennifer's Porsche. It was abandoned. He skirted the outbuildings, prying into windows, keyhole peering. There was nothing. Upon numb legs he approached the great gasometer. The vast cylinder of Victorian iron, which was the borough's most famous landmark, spread before him. John had never been so close to it before and had never realized just how large it really was. The thing was enormous. An iron stairway led up towards the catwalks and gantries which encircled it and John could think of nothing better to do than climb to a suitable height and see what might be seen. He grasped the hand-rail and learned almost at once the error of his decision. If the fence was hot, then this was cold, and impossibly cold to boot. Omally recoiled with a pained gasp, breathing warmth on to his now sub-zero palm. He knew that gas under pressure drops in temperature but this was ridiculous. Something very wrong was going on around here, and he was up to his neck in it.

Chancing that the cold might take some time to penetrate the patent air-soles of his Doctor Marten's he thrust his hands into his pockets and stepped lightly up the staircase. He gained the first catwalk and skipped nimbly along it, surveying the landscape below and keeping a weather-eye open for trouble. All was silent, dark, unfathomable. He approached the second stairway, breathing heavily. Suddenly, without warning (for isn't it always?) there was a rumbling sound beneath him, a grinding of gears, noises of iron in motion.

Omally flattened himself against the iron wall, cursing as the back of his head made contact with arctic metal. Below a heavy section of gasometer slid aside and a sharp white light floodlit an area of wasteland before it, spreading out in a broad fan. Omally craned forward to look, leaving a tuft of his hair fastened to the frozen iron, like an Indian trophy. Below him a figure left the iron fortress and strode into view. It was Jennifer Naylor.

Omally watched her as she walked to her car, tall, erect, magnificent. She seated herself, slammed shut the door, keyed the engine and roared away. Before her, a section of the fence momentarily dissolved as the car passed through it, to reform almost on the instant. Gears ground, metal moved and the light snapped away, leaving John in shivering darkness.

He had seen enough, much more than enough. Without a second thought he dashed back along the catwalk, down the staircase, across the compound and left the area by the same improbable method by which he had entered.

31

In a white room with white curtains there was a chair, a table and a bed, none of which merit any further mention. Upon a white wall, however, there was a great chart and before this stood Inspectre Sherringford Hovis.

The chart was a complicated affair resembling, at first glance, an underground railway map designed by an infant. At second glance it didn't look a lot better either. The overall design was that of an uncapped pyramid, the base line crowded with newspaper cuttings, photographs, mysterious 'samples' in plastic bags, numbers listed upon shop receipts, odds and bods. Red lines running variously from odd to bod traced intricate networks which occasionally converged. The pyramid was two-thirds covered by such plottings; the apex was bare but for a few pencil lines and a large black question mark which crowned the whole.

Inspectre Hovis cupped his left elbow in his right palm and dug his left forefinger into his right nostril. He sucked air through his teeth, withdrew his rooting digit and tapped at the enigmatic wall decoration. The object of his particular attention was a single charred photograph into which a great number of red lines converged, giving it the appearance of a terminus in the manic metro-system. Hovis leant forward and stared, eye to bleary eye, with the photographic image of James Arbuthnot Pooley. 'I will have you, laddy,' he said, giving the red face a summary tap upon the cheek. So saying, he turned his attention towards a branch line and traced the route to a single stop. Here were what viewers of the now legendary *Untouchables* lovingly refer to as 'mug shots'. These displayed front-face and profiles of two twins with braided hair and folded brows. Beneath were the names Paul and Barry Geronimo. Inspectre Hovis hooked a finger into his watch-chain and drew out his 'Regal Chimer', the very chiming pocket-watch featured in Pooley's favourite Western. But shoot-outs with Mad Indio were not in the forefront of the great detective's mind, as he perused the dial and said the single word, 'Late.' As if in answer there came a rhythmic knocking at his chamber door. Hovis draped a bed sheet over his chart. 'Enter,' said he.

The two braves entered. 'We bring greetings from the tribes of the North,' said Paul. 'We travel with speed of prairie wind to answer call of great white brother.'

'Hot moccasin,' Barry agreed, 'we kid you not.'

'Quite so, gentlemen. Kindly be seated.' Espying the only chair, which was now occupied by Hovis, Paul and Barry lowered themselves cross-legged to the lino.

'We smoke many pipes, tell many tales,' said Paul hopefully. 'Got plenty firewater in medicine bag.' He patted his designer briefcase with the buckskin fringes.

Inspectre Hovis shook his head firmly. 'Smoke many pipes later, but for now, what news?'

'Much news.' Paul made expansive gestures. 'Many wonders in Heavens and upon lands of the white-eyes. In Chiswick, they say, squaw give birth to papoose in shape of fish. Stars fall on Alabama, blue moon seen over Kentucky, famous TV personality named in "gay sex for sale" scandal. Only last night, brother Barry see many strange things at sister's "Ann Summers" party. All portents show times of great tribulation ahead. Old Sandell predict . . .'

'Yes,' said Hovis, 'such news troubles the heart of great white brother.' He tapped at his chest. 'But is it not written that brave who beat about cactus and try pull buffalo hide over policeman's eyes get banged up in the cells with much time to muse upon error of ways?'

'Point taken,' said Paul.

'So what news?'

'Much news,' Paul continued, 'lorries you enquire about

held up for an hour by traffic jam. Traffic jam caused by road-works in High Street. Road-works fracture gas main, all vehicles have to be abandoned while gas mains fixed for fear of explosion.'

'Yes,' said Hovis, 'I know as much.'

'Ah,' said Paul, 'but not know that it not Gas Board van that come out to fix leak.'

Hovis nodded thoughtfully. 'Tell me more.'

'Look like Gas Board van,' Paul continued, 'ID of driver seem genuine, driver spend much time chatting with policeman on duty at site while work done. But Gas Board deny all knowledge of either gas leak or call-out.'

Hovis nodded once more. 'Very clever,' said he, 'very clever, indeed.'

'Criminals cunning as desert dingo, but not too cunning for braves.'

'Go on then.'

'And how,' said Paul. 'Now come clever bit that earn braves big kudos. We follow great white brother's method and have pow-wow with constable who on duty at road-works. Tell him perhaps he make a big mistake and you wear his wedding tackle on watch-chain when you find out. Him eager to oblige and tell us all he know.'

'Very good indeed, go on.'

Paul grinned. 'Constable tell us that he actually escort Gas Board van through traffic jam from High Street on his bike. See van enter grounds of great gasometer, driver even bung him price of drink for his trouble.'

The Inspectre's face fell. 'Then it was a real Gas Board van after all!' he cried.

Paul shook his head, smirking mightily. 'Nothing of sort,' said he. 'Braves think things not add up so check with Gas Board again. Gas Board tells us they not own gasometer in Brentford, deny all knowledge. In fact, they tell us they never own gasometer in Brentford. There is no gasometer in Brentford.'

'What?' Inspectre Hovis scratched at his snowy pelt of hair. 'But it's there for all the world to see!'

'All world may see it, but it not bloody gasometer, that for certain.'

'Then what?'

'Braves suggest it headquarters of international crime syndicate.'

Inspectre Hovis wiped away the goodly amount of perspiration that now clung to his noble brow. 'We get stuck into firewater now,' he said.

32

Omally was in a state of near exhaustion. Both mental and physical. He leant Marchant against Jennifer's front fence and made what efforts he could to straighten his necktie and slick down his hair over the bald spot at the back. He shook the wrinkles from his trousers and gathered up what serviceable lilies remained into a pleasing composition. With unconvincing nonchalance, he pushed open the front gate, walked up the short path and rapped upon the front door. All looked the very picture of normality. Porsche in the garage, downstairs lights on. Presently, in response to his knockings, sounds issued from within, footsteps upon the parquet floor, bolts being drawn.

The front door opened on the chain and Jennifer looked out, cool, sophisticated, composed. 'John Omally,' she said in a toneless voice, 'I was expecting you.'

Indeed, thought John, as she dropped the chain and reopened the door. 'I've brought you some flowers.'

Jennifer took the lilies and stared down at them with a face of pity. 'They are dying,' she said, 'how sad.' This was an unusual feminine response to a present of flowers and one quite new to Omally's experience. 'You'd best come in.' Omally did so, closing the front door behind him. 'You would care for a drink I believe.' Jennifer laid the flowers carefully upon the hall table and led John towards the living-room.

He followed with some trepidation, giving the place a thorough scrutiny. Happily, of homicidal packages it was the nursery cupboard of Lafayette Ron's mother. But it gave him little peace of mind. Something was wrong, although he couldn't put a name to quite what.

'Do sit down.' Omally sat down. He watched Jennifer from the corner of his eye. She appeared to be having some difficulty locating the drink. She opened the doors of the television cabinet and shook her beautiful head.

'Is everything all right?' John asked. 'Can I help at all?'

Jennifer turned upon him with unnatural speed. 'Everything is just as it should be,' she said in an icy voice.

'You seem a little, well, lost.'

Jennifer Naylor smiled broadly, but it was a smile equally lacking in warmth. 'I am just a little tired, perhaps you would . . .?'

'But of course, how ungallant of me.' Omally took himself over to the drinks cupboard, and extracted bottle and glasses with slow deliberation. Jennifer stood like a statue in the middle of the room, staring into space. John did not like the look of her one bit. It was more than possible that she was in a state of shock. Whatever she had seen in the gasometer had unhinged that brilliant mind. He would have to tread a very wary path. He decanted two professional Scotches and topped them up with ice. 'Here you go then,' he said, approaching cautiously, 'gold ones on the rocks.'

Jennifer took her glass and stared into it, rattling the ice cubes. 'What do you want here?' she asked.

'A social call,' John lied, 'nothing more. It's a while since I've seen you. Here, come and sit with me on the sofa.' He took Jennifer gently by the arm, but she resisted and remained firmly rooted to the spot.

'As you please then.' John sat down before her and sipped his Scotch.

'Do you believe in God?' asked Jennifer Naylor.

Omally glanced over his glass. The emerald eyes fixed him in their stare. 'I am a Catholic by birth,' he said slowly.

'You were nothing by birth other than man. Please answer the question.'

John took another sip of Scotch. 'Why do you ask?'

'Because I wish to know.'

'Then in all candour I must confess to uncertainty.'

'Uncertainty as to a Divine Creator?'

'There are many doctrines, each claiming to be true, each at odds with the other. I was brought up to recognize one, to follow it without question. I asked questions but no-one furnished me with satisfactory answers. I do not know.'

'You lack knowledge.'

'As do we all, I fear. I exist, of that I am reasonably sure. You exist, what senses I possess inform me of the fact. Above and beyond are realms that greater minds than mine have floundered when seeking to explore.'

'The minds of men,' said Jennifer Naylor. 'Pitifully limited.'

'They are all we have, we can only make the best of them.'

'Then you never wish to seek a Higher Truth?'

Omally finished his drink. In his experience, such discussions as this rarely led to a satisfactory conclusion, and when held with attractive women, almost never in the direction of the bedroom. 'I have no evidence to suggest that Higher Truth exists,' he said, rising to refill his glass. 'In my small experience I consider it better to appreciate that which you have, than to vainly seek that which you will never find.' With that banal homily out of the way, he splashed further Scotch into his glass.

'And that is your philosophy of life?'

John sighed inwardly; all this was quite exasperating. He was getting nowhere. 'I am sorry if I cannot furnish you with satisfactory answers,' he said, at length. 'If you wish an in-depth theological discussion, then I suggest that Professor Slocombe would be your man. He is one who has dedicated his life to the search for these Higher Truths. In fact if the mood is on you, why do we not go and visit him now? I am sure he'd be very pleased to see you.'

'No!' said Jennifer Naylor. 'I have no wish to speak to him!'

'Then I'm sorry, because I can't tell you what you obviously wish to know.'

'No,' said Jennifer, 'you cannot.' With that, she raised her glass to her lips and, to Omally's amazement, poured the entire drink, ice cubes and all, straight down her throat.

'Here, steady on!' croaked John. 'You'll make yourself sick.'

'Omally,' said Jennifer, 'exactly what are you good for?'

John grinned crookedly. 'I wouldn't have thought you needed to ask.'

The terrible smile once more spread across the woman's face. 'Would you like some sex?' she asked.

'Well,' said John, 'now that you ask . . .'

33

The grounds surrounding the house of Professor Slocombe had long been protected by an ancient spell which afforded the sage advance warning of all who entered there. Upon this night, as upon countless others past, he sat at his study desk, deep in thought. Before him was spread Ordnance Survey map TQ 17 NE, and upon this cartographical representation of the borough, the lines of the great Star Stadium were etched in green ink within the blued boundaries of the Brentford Triangle. The Professor worked tirelessly with compass and protractor as a long black automobile of advanced design and uncertain nationality drew to a silent halt beyond the walls of his domain. The liveried chauffeur stepped from the cab and opened the rear door, a handkerchief clasped across his face.

Professor Slocombe reached towards the tantalus and poured a single dry sherry. A slight tingling at the nape of his neck set his head on one side, but he shrugged it off and continued with his work. The unbearable stench which then soured his nostrils and the cold chill which swept up his backbone, set him bolt upright in his chair.

'Professor Slocombe,' came a harsh whisper, 'am I not to be invited in?' The old man swung about with a gasp of surprise. 'You appear startled,' said the figure who now stood in the french windows.

Professor Slocombe regained his composure with some difficulty. The fact that someone had actually slipped unfelt into his presence was sufficient to rattle him considerably. But the appearance of his uninvited guest was one to inspire horror.

He was of medium height, clad in a suit of dark stuff,

but of his actual physiognomy, what could be seen was at all odds with all normality. The upper part of the head was covered by what appeared to be a plastic film, strung tightly to contain a mass of ugly folds and bulges. Across the eyes a complicated contraption served as an optical aid, with artificial eyelids which opened and closed at measured intervals. The mouth was hardly visible beneath a bulbous shapeless nose. 'Calm yourself, Professor,' whispered the apparition. 'I must apologize for my intrusion and also for my appearance. I am not pleasant to gaze upon, I know. Might I sit down, I have little strength?'

Professor Slocombe nodded, 'Please do so, can I offer you anything?'

'No, no, do not trouble yourself, I have learned to . . . to live with my infirmity.' The intruder moved awkwardly, his legs seemed to bend in the wrong places, low at the ankles, high at the misshapen thighs. Whatever was contained within the folds of the dark suit was a human form far gone in disfiguring malady.

Professor Slocombe winced as the cripple lowered himself into a fireside chair; his every movement appeared to cause him excruciating pain. 'You are in evident discomfort,' said the Professor. 'Might I ask the nature of your illness? I have some skills in healing.'

'No, no,' the intruder raised a gloved hand, 'you will not find it listed in any *Encyclopedia Pharmacia*, nor in any one of your extraordinary books.' He made an inclusive gesture towards the Professor's vast collection of Thaumaturgical librams. 'I am a scientist and a victim of my own experimentation.' Professor Slocombe raised an eyebrow; the invalid had much the look of one who had tampered with occult forces and become subject to the three-fold law of return, whereby an evil sending rebounds upon the magician thrice powerfully. 'That, I can assure you, is not the case,' whispered the intruder, breaking in upon the thoughts of his unwilling host.

Professor Slocombe lowered a mental shield and watched in fascination as a shiver ran through the body of his guest.

'As you now understand, my infirmity has brought with it some compensations. They say that when one sense is lost the others become heightened. In my case I have lost almost all my senses. I now possess others that most men would fail to understand.'

'You are an unusual man, to say the very least.'

'I might well say the same about you.'

The Professor composed the fingers of his right hand into a curious grouping. 'And now that we have exchanged these pleasantries, I suggest that you outline the purpose of your visit.'

'Quite so. But I surmise that during the brief moments of our acquaintanceship you have already surmised who I am, and suspect why I am here.'

'I believe that you are the organizer of the games, the designer of the stadium and the inventor of the improbable Gravitite.'

'Do I detect a note of chagrin in your pronunciation of the word "improbable"?'

'Who are you and what do you want?'

'My name is not important. For the sake of commerce, I am called Kaleton. Do not waste yourself trying to read into it, it was chosen at random. I am here upon what you might call a diplomatic mission to engender a peaceful co-existence between us.'

' "As a thief in the night",' said the Professor, quoting Scripture.

Ignoring this, Kaleton said simply, 'I am dying.'

'You seek my help.'

'On the contrary, I seek only that you do not hinder me.'

'In dying?'

Kaleton's mouth became a perfect 'O' and an exhalation of rancid air escaped from it. Professor Slocombe, who had switched off his olfactory sense upon Kaleton's entrance, sat back in his chair, fearing the spread of disease.

'The games,' said Kaleton, 'the stadium and the games are to be my epitaph. I may not live to see them, but through them I will live for ever.'

'Posthumous fame for one who will not reveal his true name to the public, how can this be?'

'By their deeds shall you know them.'

'But at what expense?'

'Expense?'

'Deaths have already occurred, I believe you must answer for them.'

Sounds came from Kaleton's mouth, sounds of coarse mocking laughter, 'No one has died, Professor,' he crowed. 'Are you too so easily fooled?'

'Not as easily as you might believe.'

'The creation of holographic images as a security system, guard dogs without teeth, without substance, conjured from the Ids of the trespassers. Effective, do you not think?'

'The chimera on the barge and the island griffin?'

'Advanced optical trickery, nothing more.'

'I think not, Kaleton.' Professor Slocombe reached beneath his desk and brought out Pooley's present. 'And this?'

'All right,' said Kaleton. 'The creation of the stadium is too important to risk interruption from meddling ne'er-do-wells.'

'Quite simply, you are prepared to kill in order to protect your interests, your immortality.'

'Men die daily, men without vision, without worth. My genius will benefit generations to come.'

'Monomania. You are sick not only in body, but also in mind.'

'If you are not for me, then you are against me!'

'Then I am against you, in body and soul. I do not fully comprehend your true motives, but I suspect them to be anything other than beneficial to mankind. I request that you leave immediately.'

Kaleton climbed with difficulty to his feet and stood with his back to the Professor. 'You are an annoyance,' said he, 'I think perhaps I should be rid of you.'

'That might prove more difficult than you imagine.'

'You say that, knowing how simply I voided the spell of protection which surrounded your house.'

'You will not invade my privacy with such ease in the future, I can assure you.'

Kaleton's head revolved slowly until it reached a point midway between his malformed shoulder-blades. 'You have no future,' he said, in a voice which might have been one, or a chorus of many. 'You are finished.'

'Leave now while you are still able.'

'I think not.' Kaleton's mouth widened, became a gaping maw, devoid of teeth, gums or tongue. A torrent of icy wind swept from it, striking the Professor from his chair and blasting him against the wall. But the effect was momentary for the sage rose from behind his desk and stared defiantly at his attacker, words of an ancient formula upon his lips.

Above the study Jim Pooley reclined in rose-scented bath-water, a copy of the Lazlo Woodbine thriller *Farewell my Window* propped before him upon the bath-rack. 'That Laz,' said Jim, 'he slays me.'

In a house, not so very far away, John Omally lazed upon silken sheets, clad only in his boxer shorts. Before him, humming gently to herself, Jennifer Naylor shed her outer garments.

Kaleton raised a crooked hand to fend off the tongue of darting fire which leapt towards him. The flames froze into glassy splinters tinkling on to the Persian carpet to dissolve into nothingness. A look of perplexity crossed Professor Slocombe's face as he summoned the powers that greater words commanded. Kaleton made a single gesture and the world which was the Professor's study vanished, became a darkened sphere enclosing only himself and the magus. 'There is no future,' whispered the crippled man, 'not for you or any of your cohorts.'

Jennifer Naylor's brassière fell to the floor, exposing a pair of breasts most men could only dream of witnessing, first hand. Omally felt the mark of his manhood rising to meet the occasion as the rare beauty slipped her thumbs into her silken camiknickers and dropped them to her feet.

'Only you and I,' said Kaleton.

'Only you and I,' echoed Jennifer Naylor.

Professor Slocombe made a series of lightning passes with his old frail hands. Before him a wall of white chitin composed itself and behind the light returned, as a small opening, through which he stepped backwards with some alacrity. He was once more at his desk, but from within the dark sphere the wall of protection crumbled away and the image of Kaleton swam into view swelling ever larger. The black mouth spread encompassing all before it. 'And so die,' came the chorus of a thousand voices which were also only one.

'And so die,' said Jennifer Naylor. Her left hand slid up behind her back, rose to the nape of her neck where it took hold of something which might have been a zip fastener. She drew it down the length of her naked spine.

Kaleton's image bulged and grew, the mouth was a great black hole, all-consuming. A bottomless pit, into which all must surely fall. The Professor folded his arms across his chest and uttered the syllables of his final spell.

A great shock wave passed through the ether of human-kind.

The outer shell, which had been the skin of the bogus Jennifer Naylor, dropped to the floor, a crumpled empty husk. Before Omally stood a group of elemental horrors supported one upon another in a writhing mass, which momentarily retained Jennifer's shape before tumbling towards the boy in the boxer shorts.

'Hell's teeth!' said John Omally, which was a close approximation.

The things swept towards him in a heaving, crying cacophony. Great bloated maggots with the heads of babies, beasts all spine and scorpion stings, bladders and entrails. Eyeless heads with one mouth set beneath another. A gross and fetid stench burned the air like fumes of acid. Omally flattened himself against the bedhead as the whirling, screaming nightmare engulfed him.

'Up and begone!' Professor Slocombe raised his arms and exerted the final issue of his strength, spoke the final syllable of the great spell. The black image wavered in intensity, crumpled in upon itself with a deafening explosion, re-gathered in a cluster of spinning fragments and finally flew upwards through the ceiling, an icy maelstrom of escaping energy.

'*Aaaaaaagh!*' Jim Pooley howled in anguish as his bath-water froze into a solid block of ice.

In a room of unutterable blackness, Professor Slocombe collapsed unconscious to the floor.

In the bedroom of a house not so very far away, a thick green slime dripped down a silken sheet to mingle in a pool of human blood.

'Oh, help,' wailed a living iceberg in a marble bath. 'Oh, bloody hell, *help!*'

34

The police cordon parted as the Inspectre's car tore
through it at speed. As it slewed to a halt amidst the
confusion of police cars, ambulances and fire-engines,
Hovis leapt from the cab and followed a wildly gesticu-
lating constable towards the house of Professor Slocombe.
In the rear seats of the car, Paul leant over and whispered
into his brother's ear, 'More big shit going down here, best
we bugger off pronto.' With all the tenacity of the four-
toed civet the two braves eased open the offside rear door
and melted into the night.

'Stand aside if you please.' Hovis elbowed his way
through the crush before the Professor's gateway and
into the magical garden. 'Is he alive?' the Inspectre
demanded. The constable's head bobbed up and down.
'Only just, sir. Constable Meek was on beat duty here
when the whole place went up. He pulled the old man
out and gave him mouth to mouth. He was nearly gone.
They're treating him in the ambulance, sir. Sir, he's frost-
bitten, in a terrible state!'

'Where is Meek?'

'He's inside, sir, but sir, frost-bitten, it's nearly mid-
summer!'

'Clear everyone out and that means now!'

'Yes, sir.'

Hovis thrust his way up the garden path and between
the shattered French windows, which lay driven from
their hinges. 'God, what's that terrible smell? Something
dead in here, is there?'

'Could be, sir, place is in a terrible mess.' Within the
study, flash-bulbs popped and the lads from forensic took
readings and measurements, made educated guesses and

sipped coffee from Thermos flasks. Several constables, whose sole function appeared to consist of getting in everybody's way, went about their duties with a will. The room was devastated, the precious tomes scattered, antique furniture upturned, priceless artifacts smashed beyond repair.

'Good God!' said Hovis. 'He lived through this?'

'Just about, sir.'

Hovis turned upon the lookers and loafers. 'Out!' he ordered. 'Clear the room! Where is Meek?'

The constable was stoking up the fire, beside which sat Jim Pooley, swathed in towels and blankets, blue of face and bitter of eye. 'Here, sir,' said Meek.

Hovis glared down at the kneeling constable. 'This is a balls-up of the first magnitude, Meek,' he roared. 'What have you to say for yourself?'

'Sir?'

'Meek, I ordered a twenty-four-hour watch put on this house, where were you when this occurred?'

'Right here, sir, I . . .'

'You what? What happened here? Who did this?'

'Well, sir . . .' the constable hung his head, 'I can't rightly remember, there was this car . . .'

'*Car*, lad?'

'A long black car, I've never seen one like it before.'

A loud and plaintive groan issued from the fireside blanket man.

'Ah,' said Hovis, raising a quizzical eyebrow, 'and what do we have here?'

'Chap was upstairs in the bath, sir, frozen into a block of ice. The firemen had to cut him out with their axes.' Meek stifled a titter. 'You should have heard him howl, sir.'

As Jim stared daggers at the young policeman, Inspectre Hovis stared hard at Jim. 'Mr Pooley, is it not?'

Jim cowered nearer to the fire and did drum rolls with his teeth. 'James Arbuthnot Pooley, born 27th July nineteen forty-nine, Parsons Green Maternity Hospital. No previous convictions.'

'No previous, eh?' said the Inspectre. 'And what is your part in all this?'

'An innocent bystander, caught in the cosmic crossfire,' Jim declared. 'One minute I'm having a bath and the next thing *bejam*! I'm a bloody fish-finger!'

'I think we'll get you down to the nice warm interview room before any more misfortune befalls you,' said Hovis.

'I'm fine here, thank you.'

'Meek, kindly escort Mr Pooley to the station. Presently I will speak to you both.'

'You can't do this to me,' Jim complained. 'I've done nothing, it's a frame-up whatever it is. Is there no justice, answer me someone?' Constable Meek took Jim firmly by the elbow. 'Police brutality!' howled the innocent man. 'I'm not without influence, you see if I'm not.'

'Take him out, Constable.'

Amid further protestations of innocence, cries of outrage, and pleas for mercy, Jim was led away. By the time he had reached the squad car, martyrdom was very much in the forefront of his mind. 'Cossacks!' he cried, as the car door slammed upon him. 'Wield your rubber truncheons, stick your electrodes up my bottom, I'll never talk, the present-day Pooley refuses to die!'

Hovis surveyed the tragic room. 'I wonder,' said he.

'And what do you wonder, Sherringford?'

The Inspectre's face broke into a smile. 'I wonder how you did that, Professor,' he said, turning to confront that very man, who was standing with his back to the now blazing fire.

'An extremely complicated transperambulation,' the magus replied, by way of explanation. 'I should not wish to repeat it, nor expound upon its intricacies. Frankly, I am somewhat spent.' He looked about at his study. 'Oh dear,' he said, 'this is something of a shambles. Allow me to set it to rights.'

Hovis held up his hand, 'Before you demonstrate the impossible yet again, I should care for a few words.'

'As you will.' The Professor crossed the room, stepping carefully through the debris, swept fallen papers from the chair by his desk and settled into it. Hovis scratched his head and wondered where to begin. 'Begin at the beginning,' the old man suggested.

'Then, what happened here?'

'I was subject to a visitation.'

'Evidently, but by whom?'

'By whom – or by what?'

'You have lost me already.'

Professor Slocombe dug amongst the chaos of his desk top and unearthed the sherry decanter and two glasses. 'I am not certain that I was visited by a "whom". I spent twenty years in the Potala, Tibet, studying under the Dalai Lama. I can read men's auras, which gives me a certain edge, shall we say. I can often tell what questions they are likely to ask, or what moves they might make, shortly in advance of them doing so. My "visitor" had no aura, Inspectre, none whatsoever. This can mean only one of two things, either that he was dead, which I consider unlikely, or that he was not human.' He poured sherry and handed the baffled detective a slim glass.

'Not human?' said Hovis. 'Kindly continue.'

'It was possessed of enormous power, certainly more than a mere man could contain. There was a great rage there, something primordial, atavistic, inhuman, subhuman, protohuman, call it what you will, but not human.'

'You are telling me that some "thing" is abroad on the streets of Brentford?'

'It has been for several weeks now.'

'And you have destroyed this thing, whatever it might be?'

'I fear not; temporarily disabled it, perhaps. I countered its attack with "calling of disassociation", of confusion. I preconceived what was about to occur and created a "tulpa" or "doppelgänger" of myself upon which I allowed it to spend its energy, before I struck back at it.'

'Then the you in the ambulance is not the you that is here, or is it . . .'

'I was in Penge during the attack, but I will not add to your confusion.'

'My thanks,' said Hovis. 'But what was this creature, the devil is it, or some monster from outer space? Come now, Professor.'

'Not outer space. This thing was impossibly strong, it was almost as if it drew its power from the planet itself, from the Earth.'

'Is this connected with the business on the island?'

'Almost definitely, and by the by, I never got to see those plastercasts.'

Hovis looked shamefaced. 'Yet another balls-up,' he said. 'The casts were mysteriously broken. By the time they got around to taking more, rain had washed the original prints away.'

'I see,' said the Professor, in a tone which suggested that he did. 'And how goes the great quest?'

'Great quest?'

'The search for gold.'

'Ah now,' said the Inspectre, 'I believe the popular expression is, that police are expecting to make an early arrest.'

'Bravo, then you evidently have made significant progress.'

'I believe I know where the loot is stashed. The dawn swoop is imminent.'

'Then the case is all but wrapped up.'

'All but,' said Hovis proudly.

'Good, then I would appreciate the immediate release of my gardener.'

'Ah!' said Hovis. 'The holidaymaker.'

'Yes, Sherringford. Rather unsporting of you I thought, you may use my telephone if you wish.'

'I would rather not, but I suppose . . .' Hovis was

interrupted by the sudden arrival of two white-faced ambulance men.

'He's . . . gone . . .' said one.

'It's all right,' the Inspectre replied, 'he's here.' Turning towards the Professor's desk he was surprised to discover that the old man was not. 'A man of many talents,' said Inspectre Hovis. 'None of which I understand.'

35

A beaming face beamed out across the nation. 'This is the London Olympics.'

'London Olympics?' muttered Neville. 'What happened to the Brentford Olympics?'

'Sssssh!' went the patrons gathered about the large television set, which had been supplied by the brewery and bolted firmly to the bar counter 'for the sake of security'.

'A miracle of modern technology, a wonder of the age, the great Star Stadium straddles an anonymous West London borough.'

'I think we'll have this off now,' said Neville.

'Ssssssh!' went the patrons.

The camera dipped low over the seemingly endless spread of the stadium, a mind-boggling panorama. It swivelled about, following the running tracks, the jumps and throwing areas and then swept down into the subterranean world beneath the arena. Here it found the squash courts, rifle ranges, swimming pools and further a myriad of sports complexes. Then out it went towards the five star points which housed the Olympic villages, each like a five star hotel, rising towards the heavens. 'The world of tomorrow today.' Throughout the camera's wondrous journey the announcer's voice-over continued to pour forth a never-ending stream of minutiae, seating capacities, dimensions, miracles, miracles, miracles.

'Oooooh!' and 'Aahhh!' went the patrons, well hooked.

Old Pete entered the portal of the newly named Ye Flying Swan Inn. 'The whole bloody lot will be down about our ears, you mark my words,' muttered the old reprobate shuffling up to the bar counter, his dog Chips as ever upon his down-at-heels. Neville nodded in profound agreement

187

and drew the kindred spirit a freeman's from the rum optic. 'Your very good health.' said the ancient. 'I see that idiot sign is up outside, but a small price to pay, I suppose. No signs of any wall bars creeping in here, I'm pleased to say.'

Neville smoothed down the folds of his apron and straightened his bow-tie. 'That has been dealt with for good, I hope. Although I see no sign of Omally creeping in here either.'

'Lying in his drunken pit I should think.'

Neville made a thoughtful face. 'If he doesn't show up by twelve, I may be forced to "let him go", if you will pardon the euphemism.'

'I will pardon almost anything of the man who buys me a drink. A man's religious persuasions are his own affair.'

Neville slicked down his brilliantined scalp, he'd need some time to work that one out. But where was Omally? His work record so far was flawless. Neville had tried every trick in the publican's book to catch him out, but his behaviour was above reproach. His timekeeping was impeccable, his helpfulness a legend, his politeness in the face of drunken insult another legend, his honesty a thing to fear. So now why suddenly go and ruin it all by taking time off and not calling in with an excuse, however lame? It was very strange indeed. A terrible thought crossed Neville's mind: perhaps there had been an accident, perhaps Omally was lying ill in his bed? The part-time barman felt suddenly wretched, how shallow he was, how pitifully shallow, and him a budding psychologist. What did he really know of human nature, sweet bugger all, that was what. Neville hung his head. He'd go round to Omally's come closing-time and see how he was. 'At times I think that this profession has ruined me,' Neville told Old Pete. 'I have become an uncompromising, untrusting, single-minded pedagogue.'

'There's no shame in that,' said the old one. 'Many of my best pals lost a limb or two back in the first lot. A man with one leg can hop as easily as a man with two.'

'And the lion never roars until after he's eaten,' Norman chimed in as he jogged up to the bar. 'What's to do then, Pete?'

'Neville has joined a religious order and has had one of his legs amputated,' the other replied. 'What *do* you look like, Norman?'

'Good, eh?' said the shopkeeper, giving a twirl. 'Designed it myself, pretty natty, eh?'

Old Pete scrutinized the shopkeeper's apparel and Neville leant forward across the bar counter to get a better look. Norman was sporting, and that was definitely the word, a confection which, even given his penchant for eccentricity, was extreme to say the very least. Ancient plimsolls dyed a dayglo orange, football socks in the Brentford colours, knee-length shorts cut from mattress ticking and a baggy T-shirt with the Olympic rings and the legend 'Hartnell Goes For Gold' emblazoned across the chest in felt-tip pen. A pink towelling headband and matching wristlets completed the ensemble to a pleasing effect. 'The official Brentford Olympic kit,' said Norman proudly. 'I designed it and Father Moity is fitting out the whole team.'

'The whole team?' queried Neville.

'Secret training sessions.' The shopkeeper tapped his nose. 'Seems fitting that the home team take most of the gold medals.'

'Norman,' said Neville, 'surely there is an official British team. Haven't I heard such names as Daley Thompson and Sebastian Coe being bandied about?'

'They won't let you in,' said Old Pete scornfully, 'it's the Olympic games not the bloody Notting Hill Carnival.' Chips stifled a titter.

'A prophet is without honour in his own land,' quoted Norman. 'Just you wait and see.'

'And what's your event then?' Old Pete asked. 'Or are you just the frigging mascot?'

'Javelin.' Norman mimed a mighty throw. 'Up and away and Hartnell takes the world record.'

'Sssssh!' went the patrons at the counter's end.

'A pint of Large, please, Neville,' said Norman.

'Not while you're in training, surely?'

'My . . . er . . . technique requires the minimum physical effort, a pint will be fine.'

'He means to cheat,' said Old Pete. 'Some electronic hocus-pocus, I shouldn't wonder.'

'Ssssh!' went Norman. 'There's nothing wrong with having the edge on the foreigners. That has always been the British way, hasn't it?'

Neville pulled the gold medallist a pint of Large. 'So how is it done?' he asked.

Norman accepted his pint, tapped once more at his nose and drew the two listeners close. 'Gravitite,' he whispered.

'Gravitite? You mean you've nicked a bit of it?'

'Nothing of the sort. I concede that the idea is not my own, but I perfected the formula unaided. Took me almost two weeks to get it right; you see, the old chemistry set is a bit limited and I was right out of copper sulphate and pink litmus paper.'

'Are you confident that it will work?'

'Just watch this.' From a pocket in his voluminous shorts Norman withdrew a single dart. He rested it upon the palm of his hand and lined up at the dartboard, a good twenty feet beyond. With a casual flick of a right forefinger he sent the missile winging upon its way. It struck home in the double twenty with a resounding whack. 'Double top,' said Norman, smiling proudly.

Neville shook his head in wonder. 'My hat, if I wore one, would now be off to you,' he said. 'The pint is on the house. May I hang your medal behind the bar for the world to gaze at?'

'Mine and all the rest. The applications are limitless, pole vault poles, plimsolls for the high jump, the shot-put, and one or two others I've got up my sleeve. "If gravity is holding tight, it's just the job for 'Normanite'." Little jingle there, I'm already working on the advertising campaign. Save that until after the medals have been given out though, I think.'

'Bloody unsporting,' said Old Pete. 'Cheats never prosper.' Norman and Neville stared at him in disbelief. 'Sorry,' said Old Pete, 'don't know what came over me, just slipped out.'

'I should think so too,' said Neville. 'Cheats never prosper indeed.'

'Well, it will be good for a laugh, whatever,' said Norman. 'Worth it just to see the looks on the Yanks' faces alone.'

'It certainly will,' Neville agreed. 'Serve the buggers right, all the inconvenience. A Brentford team whopping the world's finest, what a hoot. It is an inspired plan and one which I feel deserves yet another on the house.'

'Thanks,' said Norman, 'I haven't finished this one yet.'

Old Pete considered the empty bottom of his own glass. 'Be all right as long as no one gets wind of it in advance,' he said meaningfully.

'Another for yourself?' Neville asked. 'As an old Brentonian, you will no doubt wish to toast Norman's bid to gain glory for the borough.'

'Indeed,' said Old Pete. 'Nothing less than a double would be sufficient, don't you agree?'

'It is all you will get.'

'My lips are sealed,' said Old Pete. 'To the honour of the borough.'

'The honour of the borough.'

'Ssssssh!' went the patrons.

'Oh, bugger off,' said Neville the part-time barman.

36

In the teepee at the bottom of the garden Paul and Barry
Geronimo sat cross-legged sharing a long pipe.

'The time draws near,' said Paul solemnly. 'As the great
spirit moves upon the face of the waters, the sky darkens,
the birds fly upside-down and the crickets call with the
tongues of men.'

Barry sucked at the pipe stem. He considered the dope-
taking one of the finer aspects of Red Indian day-to-day
life. Grudgingly, he passed the pipe back to his brother.
'This a good toke in here,' he said, grinning lopsidedly,
'dealer not stitch you up on this occasion.'

'To become one with the Manitou,' said his brother, 'to
understand the ways of the elk, to soar with the eagle,
to feel the pulse, the universal note of which all things, all
matter, all men, are each but component parts. Each but
single elements, yet one and the same. To do this, one has
to get a little high once in a while. If you get my meaning.'

'Not exactly,' said Barry, 'but I get the drift.'

'Barry,' said Paul, 'Brother Barry, as a "human being",
you are a bit of a failure.'

'Oh, thanks very much, you haven't exactly excelled
yourself, have you?'

'That is not what I mean.'

'Well, it's what I mean.'

'Barry, when first, in many moons past, I told you of
my great revelation, your heart was troubled. You had
no belief. Have I not schooled you in the ways of our
fathers, taught you the skills of bow and tomahawk, made
you knowledgeable with the wisdom of the people and
now . . .'

'And now we're both on the dole,' said his brother,

snatching back the pipe.' A fine lot of use it's all been.'

'You are not a "human being", Barry, you are a white man.'

'We are both white men, for crying out loud!'

'No, Barry, I divine the great purpose, the infinite meaning. Our trials have not been in vain. The scorn and ridicule we have suffered mean nothing to me. I am above all that, I see the golden light.'

'You are stoned, I'm keeping this pipe.'

'Barry, now is the time of the great awakening. The earth moves and shudders. It has grown weary of the ways of men. Those few who understand may yet survive the reckoning, by becoming at one with nature, as it was in the times of the elder ones. Those who lack wisdom will be lost amidst the tongues of leaping flame. Such it is so written and such it will be.'

Barry sucked ruefully upon the long pipe. 'You really believe all this, don't you?'

His brother nodded sagely. 'I have numerous A-levels and an honours degree. Do you think I would act as I do if I did not have the conviction that I am right?'

'You just might be bonkers.'

'Barry, the soul of the great chief now dwells within me, and you also. This makes us aloof to the jibes of lesser men. I shun them all, I am led by a guiding star and by the glorious golden light.'

'So what do you propose we do, o learned brother?'

'We will act as the spirit dictates, open our minds to its instruction, we will smoke many pipes and speak of many things.' He opened a bag of Peyote buttons. 'Here,' he said, 'chew upon these awhile and I will tell you of the dreams I have dreamed. Then we will act together, as one.'

'In for a penny then,' said Barry. 'Bung them over.'

'There is a big evil abroad amongst the fields of the white man. It overshadows us, darkens the sky, I sense it, we must combat it.'

'All right,' said Barry, 'but I'll hang on to the pipe for now, in case these magic mushrooms turn out to be the ten-bob-a-pound variety from Tesco's.'

Inspectre Hovis paced the floor of the briefing room. He was not alone. The seated ranks of the Brentford constabulary watched without comment. Presently, the great detective halted and turned to face them. 'One hundred million pounds in gold bullion,' his voice echoed about the room, 'and it is all right here.'

The beat-plodding bobbies jerked upright in their seats. Their crime-consciousness extended little beyond the bounds of the occasional collar-feel for petty pilfering. There was mass murmuring in the ranks.

'One hundred million,' Hovis reiterated. 'Right here and I want it back.' He peered about the sea of faces, seeking a little island of intelligence. 'Not keen, gentlemen? A little out of our league, is it?'

Constable Meek raised a tremulous hand. 'Sir?'

'Meek?'

'Is this the proceeds from the Heathrow robbery, sir?'

'Oh, very good, Meek, been watching *Police Five*, have we? Good lad.' Meek grinned foolishly. 'Of course it is the Heathrow robbery!' thundered Hovis. 'How many more hundreds of millions in gold are knocking about?' Meek's mouth opened. 'The question was rhetorical,' said Hovis, 'if you have an answer I do not wish to know it.'

'But the gold is really in Brentford, sir?'

'Right here.'

'Gosh, sir.'

'Officer.' Inspectre Hovis gestured towards a constable who stood to his rear before a large draped easel. The constable drew away the drape with a flourish and a chorus of *oohs* and *ahhhs* filled the metropolitan air.

Exposed to the mass gaze was none other than old TQ 17 NE, the Ordnance Survey map of the borough. As on the Professor's copy, this had Brentford's triangular boundaries blued in, the great Star Stadium superimposed in red, but unlike the Professor's version, this had a thick black ring in the lower right hand section. A ring drawn about the location of the great gasometer.

'Now for all you lovers of geometry,' said Hovis, 'this will prove a disappointment. This is not the square on the hypotenuse, nor any other Pythagorean tongue-twister. Here,' he tapped with his cane, 'the Brentford Triangle, here,' another tap, 'the Star Stadium and here,' multiple tapping and a firm face towards the troops, 'here, the Brentford gasometer containing, unless I am very much mistaken, one hundred million in gold bullion.'

There was a moment of silence during which many glances, which meant many things, were exchanged.

'Inside the gasometer, sir?' Whatever tones of sarcasm existed in Meek's voice they were concealed with consider-able skill.

'As cunning a concealment as any I have yet experienced.'

'Who's in there then, Doctor No or Goldfinger?'

'Who said that?' Silence reigned supreme. Hovis cast his eagle eye over the congregation. 'It is the headquarters of an international crime syndicate and we, gentlemen, that is all of us, are going to nick the blighters. All leave is cancelled, all other investigations shelved, I am about to outline to you our plan of campaign and by God I want no balls-up this time. Do I make myself understood?' A roomful of heads bobbed up and down in unison. 'This, gentlemen, is the big one.'

'Fuck me,' said Constable Meek.

Gammon brought the Professor a tray of light lunch, con-sisting of exotic tropical fruits, a few nuts and raisins and a glass of water. 'As you ordered, sir.'

Professor Slocombe smiled up at his elderly retainer. 'Thank you, Gammon. Just place it upon the small table.'

'Certainly, sir.'

'And how is Mr Pooley, Gammon?'

'He is recovering, sir. I have just topped up his hot water bottles.'

'And Mr Omally?'

'Still no news, sir. I have followed up the few slim leads we have. I fear for the worst, sir.'

'I also, Gammon. Mr Omally is, I think, beyond our help now.'

'That is very sad, sir, shall I inform Mr Pooley?'

'No, Gammon, I will do so, all in good time.'

'Very good, sir.'

'Thank you, Gammon.'

'Thank you, sir.'

37

It was to be a day to remember and one to be inscribed in the very bestest copperplate lettering upon a nice clean page of the annals of Brentford. The arrival of the athletes from the globe's four corners, the official ribbon-cut and stadium opening. Brass bands were to play, morris dancers to dance, the biggest parade in the borough's checkered history. Streamers and spangles, balloons and bangles, flowers and fripperies. An unparalleled extravaganza.

Minions of the town council, all hearts of oak and double time, had been at work half the night, festooning the lamp posts with bunting and flower garlands. The Boy Scouts and Girl Guides had been rehearsing their marching for weeks. The hot-dog hucksters, souvenir programme-sellers, ice-cream vendors, Union Jack wallahs and general wide-boys were already on their pitches. The good people of Brentford had declared the day an unofficial bank holiday and were preparing to line the streets. The mayoral limousine stood polished and waiting before the town hall, upon its gleaming bonnet, the borough flag fluttering in the gentle breeze. The Brentford Olympic squad were bending their knees in the Memorial Park to the rallying cries of Father Moity, and the sun was shining bravely in a sky that was rich and blue and cloudless. This was the big one, the biggest one that ever was.

Jim Pooley sat up in bed supported by several comfy pillows, perusing the latest batch of holiday brochures which had arrived with the morning post. Gammon cleared away the few sparse remnants of Jim's morning fry-up.

197

'Will sir be requiring any coffee?' he asked.

'Certainly,' said Jim, 'cream and sugar.'

'Then sir knows where the kettle is and can make his own,' said the Professor's retainer, taking up the tray. 'And before sir says anything, the Professor suggests that sir gets on with weeding the west lawn.'

'But,' said Jim, 'but . . . but . . .'

'The Professor says that sir is swinging the lead,' Gammon continued. 'He says that he values my time at ten pounds a minute and begs to enquire whether sir will be requiring my services any further this day.'

'Come on, Gammon, old buddy,' crooned Jim, 'I'm not up to any work just yet, I'm still in shock.'

Gammon took out his pocket watch and watched the second hand sweeping the face. 'Will there be anything else, sir? Time is money, you know.'

'Certainly not, Gammon, you are dismissed, depart in haste now, I should not want to keep you from your work.'

'Very good, sir.' Gammon left without bothering to close the bedroom door, his undisguised chuckles echoing down the hallway.

'Weed the west lawn,' moaned Jim, 'what a carve-up.' He tossed aside the holiday brochures and climbed gingerly from his cosy bed. Here he was just days away from millionairedom and he was expected to weed lawns, it seemed hardly fair. The Professor was definitely having a pop at him. No doubt because Omally had legged it. Jim sought his shirt amongst the untidy pile of clothing which lay at the bedside. It was just typical of Omally to leave him holding the baby. The Irishman would come swanning back all smiles and excuses once Jim picked up his winnings, that was for sure.

But that, Jim considered, was the lot of the millionaire. There was always some 'Johnny-come-lately' out to get a share of the booty. The world was full of avarice. Sad times, everybody wanted to cop the pot of gold. This cosmic truth set the lad a-thinking. Now, the Professor was actually paying him to do the gardening, so perhaps a deal could be struck. A thousand or two out of the winnings wasn't going to hurt the bank balance very much. He could write out an IOU and put his feet up for a couple of weeks. A bit of 'tax free' for the old boy and an easy life for himself. Gammon's services came a mite expensive, he would engage his own servant, an au pair girl perhaps, or one of those Filipino beauties one reads about, or even two.

Smiling and whistling at the same time, Jim unearthed his trousers and a jumper and slipped them on over his pyjamas. 'No sense in going the whole hog,' he told himself. 'If the Professor agrees, I can be back in bed in ten minutes.'

Professor Slocombe worked at his study desk. He did not look up as Jim entered the room. 'Nice to see you up and about,' he said, as Jim dithered in the doorway. 'You'll be a bit hot working with your pyjamas still on, I would have thought.'

Jim chewed at his bottom lip. 'I've been thinking,' said he.

'Good, then your time has not been altogether wasted. I trust that the conclusions reached during this period of cogitation will be put to practical use in the garden?'

'Might I have a cup of coffee?' Jim asked, spying the turkish pot bubbling at the fireside.

'But of course, Jim. Kindly pour one for me if you will.'

Pooley did so. 'About this lawn weeding business,' he said as he placed the Professor's cup upon his desk, 'under the circumstances, I think we might dispense with it.'

'My feelings exactly,' said Professor Slocombe, much to Jim's surprise and momentary relief. 'Under the circumstances.'

'Oh good, that is pleasing to my ears.'

'Yes, we must place lawn weeding as one of the least of our priorities.'

'That's the stuff,' said Jim.

'Yes, we must channel every ounce of our energy and resources into a matter of a far more pressing and urgent nature.'

'We must?' Already Jim didn't like the sound of it.

'Sit down, Jim. You will not like what I have to tell you.'

Taking the Professor, as ever, at his word, Pooley settled into a fireside chair. 'What do you see here, Jim?' Professor Slocombe rose from his desk and displayed his map of Brentford. Jim perused it with less than passing interest.

'Am I looking for anything in particular?' he asked.

'This.' The sage tapped at the outline of the Star Stadium.

'The stadium?'

'Yes, but what do you see?'

Jim was as ever puzzled. 'I see a big star, what else should I see?'

'A five-pointed star.'

'Well, of course I see that.'

The Professor took up his quill and joined the five star points. 'Now what do you see?'

'A thingamegig, pentathing.'

'Pentagram, Jim, an inverted pentagram.'

'Ah!' said Pooley. He didn't know much about the occult, but anybody knew this much. 'That's not good, is it?'

'No, it is anything but. The inverted pentagram is the symbol of diabolism, the symbol of negative energy, negative force, all that is evil.'

Jim was unconvinced. 'You see an inverted pentagram, Professor, the world sees an Olympic stadium.'

'I think there is a great deal more to it than that.'

'No,' said Jim, 'put such dark thoughts from your mind. The thing is the proverbial work of genius. Eighth wonder of the world. Today the athletes are coming – in fact I thought I'd take a stroll down to join in the festivities myself, why don't you come too?'

'Does nothing about this stadium strike you as mysterious, Jim?'

Pooley blew out his cheeks. 'Well, of course it does, but the world is full of mysteries, what is one more or less to me? We do live in quite extraordinary times, by any account.'

Professor Slocombe rolled the map and flung it down on his desk. 'The Birmingham stadium meets with disaster after disaster, culminating in a fire which destroys it completely. Within a single day – a *single day* – mark you, a substitute is proposed here. It is instantly accepted and construction begins almost at once. A few short weeks later it is completed and the athletes arrive. What does this say to you?'

'Fast thinking?' Pooley suggested. 'That is the way of the world today.'

'It is impossibly fast, Jim. It is frankly impossible from beginning to bitter end. If this stadium was preconstructed by any normal means, it would be the work of years. But it springs up here in days. Where was it constructed? How could it be ready for erection precisely when it was required? How did the land on which the legs rest come to be available at exactly the right time? Where did the money come from? How could such a vast project be conducted in utter secrecy? How was it all done, Jim?'

'You've got me, but it certainly was, you can trust the evidence of your own eyes.'

'I have learned, through bitter experience, never to trust that alone.'

'Oh, be fair, Professor, you are a man of the old school, your knowledge is this here.' Pooley indicated the antique library and for the first time realized that the Professor's study had been completely restored as if the destruction wrought upon it had never occurred. 'This, er, old stuff,' Jim continued. 'But the world is changing. It's all computer whizz-kids and micro-technology, silicon chips, things like that. Who can say how it's all done? Not me for one. You read mysticism into everything.'

'And that is your considered opinion?'

'Well, sort of. I admit that I only know what I read in the newspapers or see on the television. But that is the only information most of us have to go on. If it is incorrect or biased or even downright lies, how can we be expected to know? We can only believe what we are told. We have to believe in something.'

'Why, why believe what you are told?'

'Well. Well, you kind of learn it from childhood. Someone tells you that two and two make four and you believe it. It does make four, doesn't it?'

'Most of the time, yes.'

'Well then.'

'Well then, and you have already made most of my arguments for me, I am telling you that something totally at odds with all you have been told is occurring, so where does that leave you?'

'It doesn't leave me anywhere, you have told me nothing, you have only asked me questions I cannot answer.'

'Then I will tell you this. The stadium is not simply a stadium. It was built by a man who is not simply a man, if he is even a man at all, which I doubt. And this man who is not a man has . . .' The Professor halted in his words and stared at Pooley with a look of deepest compassion.

'Yes,' said Jim slowly, 'has what?'

'Has murdered your dearest friend.'

Jim's jaw dropped. 'Has what?' he said in a voice hardly audible. 'Murdered John? What are you saying?'

'I regret to say it, I would have given anything in my world not to say it, but yes, Jim. John Omally is dead.'

Jim rose to his feet, there were tears in his eyes. '*No*,' he said, 'John is not dead. If he was dead, somehow I would know it. It cannot be true, why are you saying this?'

'Jim, there is a dark power behind this stadium, a malevolent power which must be destroyed. I have stared it face to face right here. You have seen its work at the barge and on Griffin Island, it froze you into your bath, it killed your closest friend.'

'John,' said Pooley, his voice toneless and numb. 'God, I love that man as I love myself, we have been friends since . . . we have always been friends. No, it cannot be.'

'It can and it is and that is why you must fight with me.'

'I understand nothing of this, Professor. Up there is just a bloody stadium. Who killed John, and why? Why?'

'Because you had seen things that you should not have. You were a threat, hence the parcels.'

'Bombs. It was Bob, that. Bob has killed John.'

'No, no, Jim, you must pull yourself together. The world as we know it may shortly be coming to an end, if something is not done fast.'

'Then let it. If John is dead, then I no longer care, I will collect my money and take my grief elsewhere and I will enjoy it for John and his memory, bugger Brentford, bugger the stadium and bugger you.'

'Then leave,' said Professor Slocombe, 'leave if you can.' He took the tobacco tin containing Pooley's betting slip from his pocket and tossed it into the mourner's hand. 'Make your getaway, collect your winnings, if you get the chance, desert the sinking ship. When this comes you will have nowhere to run to.'

'What do you mean?'

'I mean leave if you can.'

'Then I shall.' Jim strode to the french windows. 'I don't know what all this is about,' he said, turning, 'I never have. If you know about all this then maybe you should have saved John. I'm done here, I'm away.' He turned once more towards the outside world and flattened himself upon an invisible barrier which sealed the Professor's study from escape. 'Let me go!' howled Pooley, rising from the carpet and nursing his bruised nose. 'Let me out!'

'I cannot,' said Professor Slocombe. 'That is why the lawn weeding has had to be postponed.'

Outside, the crowds were gathering. The Swan had

opened somewhat earlier than is prescribed by law and the patrons jostled on the pavement. Croughton, the pot-bellied potman, fresh from Strangeways where he had learned the error of his ways, had been re-employed by Neville in desperation, after he had failed to track down Omally. Now he was dispensing drinks and failing to fill his pockets in the process.

'Where are they then?' asked Old Pete, as the bands played, the Boy Scouts drilled, the morris dancers danced and the accordians and penny whistles did their bit to add to the general confusion.

'Here comes the Mayor!' shouted someone and the crowd parted to admit the arrival of a big shining car. The Mayor, clad in full regalia of office, clambered out. 'Where are they?' he asked Old Pete.

'Buggered if I know, your Lordship,' said the ancient as his dog took a well-aimed pee at a mayoral mudguard.

'Hot-dogs! Get your Olympic hot-dogs while they're hot!' Shouts rang out amongst the joyful throng, watches were being perused and doubts expressed. Perhaps they're not coming. Perhaps it's the wrong day. Perhaps, perhaps.

Young Master Robert entered the Flying Swan and approached the bar counter. 'Where's that Irish barman?' he demanded.

Neville did some pretty nifty thinking. 'I sacked him,' he said, 'a spy from the rival brewery he was, saw through him in no time. Why do you ask?'

'Quick,' came a chorus of voices, 'they're coming!'

Neville put the towels up. 'I'll speak to you later,' he said to the fuming brewery boy.

A dull hum filled the air above Brentford, the flapping of copter blades, the whirr of drazy hoops. From the direction of Heathrow a fleet of helicopters and dirigibles was approaching. A cheer went up from the assembled multitude beneath, a cheer which faded almost as quickly as it had begun. The crowds watched in silence as the flying machines drew nearer, passed overhead and vanished into nothingness as they came in to land at the stadium far above. 'They came in by air,' said someone, and the carnival world that had been Brentford suddenly came apart at the seams. There was to be no golden jubilee, no big march past, no big welcome, no jamboree, no bloody nothing. They came in by air. The borough had been betrayed.

The crowds stood in embarrassed silence and then melted away as if they had never been. The drinking men took themselves off to the pubs, the womenfolk to their unenlightened kitchens, the children, who had at least got a day off school, to joyful street corners. The Mayor climbed back into his car and waved the chauffeur homeward.

The copperplate letterist, poised over the Brentford annals, stuck his pen back in his pocket, drew up his invoice for waiting-time in ball-point pen and buggered off back home. The bunting hung limp and meaningless, the hot-dog sellers and all their dire ilk slunk away and that, for all it was worth, was very much that.

38

'Let me out!' yelled Jim Pooley with renewed vigour. Outside, in the Professor's magical garden, bees buzzed amongst the heavy blossoms and dragonflies hung in the air, their wings a blur of rainbow colours. Beyond the gate several members of the Brentford Olympic squad trudged by wearing grim expressions. The lads' heads were down, Brian. 'I think it's beginning to give,' Jim panted, 'lend a hand there.'

'Jim, it is not beginning to give, you will bruise your knuckles.'

Pooley ceased his fruitless beating and examined his skinned fists. 'Do something,' he implored, 'you are the big magician.'

'Sit down and rest yourself, there is time enough to act.'

Jim slouched over to the fireside chair and dropped into it. 'This won't do for me, Professor, this is no good at all.'

'I have a plan,' said the old man, 'if you are interested in hearing it.'

Pooley regarded the ancient with no small degree of bitterness. 'I don't seem to have much else on today.'

'You won't like it.'

'Now that I do find surprising, as I have loved every minute so far.'

'Jim, there is nothing I can offer you other than my deepest sympathy for your loss. I do not expect you to get over it for some considerable time to come, should you ever truly get over it. However, if you wish to save yourself then I suggest you work with me rather than against me.'

'Save myself from what? I don't even know what we are supposed to be fighting against anyway.'

'I will tell you all that I know. And tonight we shall put the missing pieces of the puzzle together.'

'Tonight?' and 'We?' said Jim, doubtfully.

'Tonight I shall perform a conjuration. It will be a complicated procedure and I shall require your assistance. I mean to conjure our enemy into our presence, constrain him by magic and compel him to furnish us with the necessary wherewithal by which to destroy him.'

'Just like that?'

'Anything but "just like that", it will be extremely dangerous. I doubt that he will come willingly. Alone I may not be able to contain him, will you help me?'

'Do I have any choice?'

'Not really.'

'Then I shall be pleased to. In the meanwhile, how about me telephoning for a couple of strong lads to knock us a hole in the wall? It wouldn't hurt to have a bit of fresh air, now, would it?'

Jim rose to take up the telephone but the Professor drew it beyond his reach. 'I understand that this is something of an unofficial holiday today,' he said. 'It would prove difficult to get someone at such short notice.'

'I know lots of likely lads,' said Jim brightly, 'and I have nothing else to do. Hand me the telephone, it will be the work of but a minute.'

'I think not, Jim. This is a grade two listed building, we can't just have holes knocked in it, willy-nilly, now can we?'

'Hm,' said Jim. 'It is an emergency after all, perhaps a 999 call then?'

Professor Slocombe shook his head. 'Definitely not,' said he. 'That is the last thing we want. In fact I have gone to some lengths to see that we shall not be bothered by Inspectre Hovis and his boys in blue.'

'Oh yes?' said Jim, without enthusiasm. 'And how is this?'

'A certain chess-playing chum of mine. A Mr Rune.'

'Oh,' said Jim, looking about, 'I like a game of chess,

I didn't know you had a board.'

'I don't.'

'Then you play at your friend's house?'

'No.' The Professor tapped at his forehead. 'Mental chess, Jim, telepathic.'

'But of course,' said Jim Pooley, 'how silly of me, now about the phone . . .'

'No,' said Professor Slocombe.

The constables sat in the briefing room. They'd had a rotten day what with all the disappointment and everything, and if that wasn't enough, now Hovis had called yet another meeting. They had all slunk away from the last one wondering how they could avoid any further involvement. Fearing, not without good cause, that in such situations as the arrest of gold bullion robbers, 'shooters' were likely to be wielded. And the likely wielders would be trigger-happy police officers.

Before them, Hovis perched upon the table, a gaunt bird of prey. 'Are we sitting comfortably?' he asked. 'Then I'll begin.'

'Sir?' said Constable Meek.

'Yes, Meek?'

'Sir, about this gasometer business, the lads and I were wondering.'

'Yes, Meek?'

'About the way in, sir? Into the gasometer.'

Hovis took out his 'Regal Chimer' and flipped open the cover. 'I am expecting a visitor,' said he, 'who is going to put you straight on all the details. In fact at any moment now.'

The door of the briefing room swung open to admit the entrance of a curious-looking man. He was well over six feet in height, bald of head, heavy of brow and jowl and somewhat wild of eye. His ample frame was encased in a flowing black robe constrained about the portly waist by a scarlet cummerbund.

'Gentlemen, allow me to introduce Mr Hugo Rune.' The

self-styled Perfect Master and Logos of the Aeon bowed towards his doubtful audience.

Constable Meek leapt immediately to his feet. 'Hugo Rune, I arrest you in the name of the law. You are not obliged to say anything but anything you do say will be taken down and may be used in evidence.'

'Not now, Meek,' said Inspectre Hovis.

'But, sir, this man is wanted in connection with numerous offences in breach of the Fraudulent Mediums Act, the Witchcraft Act of 1307, the . . . the . . .'

'Not now, Meek.'

'Sir, it is my bounden duty to arrest this man, he is a charlatan and a con-man.'

'Not now.'

'Sir, we have a file on him a yard wide.'

'Meek, sit down.'

'But, sir . . .'

'Sit down. Mr Rune has agreed to help us in this most sensitive matter. I have offered him immunity from prosecution in return.'

'A supergrass!' said Meek. 'So that's his game now, is it?'

'Sit down and shut up, Meek.'

'But, sir . . .'

Rune took a step forward, and stood towering over the young officer. 'I can seal your mouth with a single word,' said he, 'and you will be forced to sup tea through your nostril.'

'Threatening behaviour. I'll add that to the charge sheet.'

'Sit down, Meek, Mr Rune is helping us with our inquiries. During this period, he is under my protection.'

'And afterwards?'

Hovis looked at Rune. 'We will see.'

'Oh, will we?' said Rune. 'And I the only man who can get you into the gasometer!'

'That remains to be seen.'

Hugo Rune drew himself up to his full improbable height. 'I am Rune,' quoth he, 'Rune whose eye is darkness,

Rune whose brain fathoms the impossible conundra, Rune whose soul seeks ever the light of infinite knowledge.'

'That also remains to be seen.'

'Then be it as it will, I shall take my leave now and my chances as they present themselves. Goodbye.' Rune turned upon his heel.

'Not so fast. If you succeed, I will waive any other charges.'

'But, sir!'

'Do shut up, Meek. Rune, kindly tell us what you have to say.'

'Mr Rune,' said Mr Rune.

'Mr Rune then, if you will.'

'All right, you may find it difficult to comprehend, but I will do my best to simplify matters for you.'

Hovis made an exasperated face. 'Then kindly do so, we have little enough time to waste.'

'So be it.' Rune clapped his enormous hands together and a shaven-headed acolyte in shabby robes of a saffron hue, entered the room, burdened by the weight of several ancient tomes. He had a small red R tatooed on his forehead. 'Master,' he said.

'Place them on the table, Rizla.'

'Yes, Master.' Rizla did as he was bid and departed, bowing to the floor.

'The neophyte Rizla,' Rune explained. 'And so to the facts in the case.'

Hovis jostled away a constable and settled into a front-row seat, resigned to the ridiculous. 'Go ahead then.'

'Thank you, Inspectre.' Rune leafed through a leather-bound volume until he found the page he sought. 'The great gasometer, or gasholder, call it what you will. According to the county records, constructed in eighteen-eighty-five by the West London Coal Gas Company. The surrounding gasworks were demolished in nineteen-sixty-two and the site is now occupied by that bastion of ethnic "entertainment" and mis-spent local government funding, the Arts Centre.'

'Easy on the personal prejudice,' said Hovis. 'It is well known that their Board of Directors refused your repeated demands to be made Magus in Residence.'

'Quite so, but be that as it may. The gasometer. A local landmark, used by RAF Northolt during the Hitlerian War as a ground-marker. A symbol of the borough. It is not a gasometer, never has been a gasometer, never will be a gasometer. It is something else entirely.'

There was a murmuring and a mumbling amongst the constables.

'I know that,' said Hovis, 'it is no revelation. So what is it, Rune?'

'I will not bore you with the intricacies of my research, the difficulties encountered, the countless hours of fruitful meditation.'

'Good, then do not.'

'Then I will tell you this. It has existed throughout at least eight centuries of recorded history. Local legend speaks of the two kings of Brentford, warlords in the time of King Arthur, one dwelt in a tower of stone and one in a tower of iron, such the old rhyme tells us. I cannot speak for the tower of stone, perhaps it has long become dust, but the tower of iron is here for all to see. It is the gasometer. Possibly it has not always appeared as it does now, but the deception it creates has existed in one form or another down the centuries.'

'*Ooooh!*' and '*ahhhh!*' went the constables.

'Go on,' said Inspectre Hovis.

'I quote the words of Samuel Johnson on his trip to the Brentford Bull Fayre: "I entered the town of Brentford by the river road, passing beneath the old iron tower, a fortress of great age, which still survives, although weed-grown and hung with ivy, striking in its presence." Johnson visited the fayre and actually witnessed a live griffin in a showman's booth. All this is recorded in his memoirs, for anyone to check.'

'Curious,' said Hovis. 'Continue.'

'A record of land charters, granted in fourteen-seventy-two, states that, "One Able John Rimmer tills land to the North and West of the iron tower. His land extends to the North Road for Ealing, up against Ye Flying Swan Inn and bordering upon the dell of Chiswick, wherewhich the pasture grounds of our Lord the King abound for twenty leagues." I have sought even further back, but it is all the same, the gasometer is old beyond the point of memory. And where memory and the written word become myth and legend still it is there. It has been there for perhaps one thousand years.'

'And now it is a den of thieves,' said Hovis.

'You are dealing with no ordinary thieves,' Rune warned. 'I can offer you many quotations to prove that you are dealing with a legacy of evil which has existed for a millennium unrealized.'

The constables shifted uneasily in their seats. This was all beginning to sound distinctly iffy.

'So,' said Hovis, 'can you guide us in, that we might beard the evil lion in his den?'

'Of course,' said Rune, 'am I not Rune the all-knowing, Rune the cosmic warrior, Rune the . . .'

'Yes, yes, we all know that.'

'It will be no easy venture,' said Hugo Rune.

'That which is done with ease is done without conviction.'

Rune raised an eyebrow, twisted into a waxed spike. 'Please spare me the homilies, I shall require payment for my services.'

'What? I offer to absolve you of your crimes and you demand payment to boot?'

'The reward for the recovery of the gold is one per cent. As an arbiter of justice you must respect my entitlement. Under the circumstances I consider the sum barely sufficient, nevertheless . . .'

'Nevertheless, you will have it over my carcass.'

'Inspectre, you can huff and puff for all you are worth, but without me you will not blow this house down.'

'Then I will call in the SAS.'

Rune closed the book with a resounding thump. 'If you no longer require my services, I shall depart. I have stuck to my side of the bargain, our tally is now even. I leave with a clean slate.'

'Hold hard, Rune. Why do you think that we will not be able to enter the gasometer without your help?'

'Because a wall of force surrounds it. It is a powerful force and one that cannot be breached by ordinary means. If you bluster in you will lose men. Death will be the reward of folly.'

The constables shrank in their seats. 'Hear him out,' said somebody.

'This is supposed to be the age of reason and logic,' Rune declared, 'of advancement, of knowledge. Take what I say to be superstitious nonsense if you please, but you will pay for your lack of foresight. There is an old evil here that cannot be dealt with by any means you understand. It is my territory and not yours, Inspectre. Without me you will not enter the iron tower.' Hovis chewed ruefully upon his lip and tapped his cane upon the floor. The constables were growing restless. 'If I lead you in,' Rune continued, 'then I demand the reward. If not, then you can do as you please, put me up as public enemy number one if you wish.'

'How do I know that I can trust you?'

'What do you have to lose?'

'All right,' said Hovis. 'Then we go in tonight.'

'All right,' said Hugo Rune. 'So be it.'

'Hip, hip, hoorah!' went the constables, and then wondered why.

At a little after three Neville had cashed up. Despite the débâcle, Ye Flying Swan had done a most profitable lunchtime's trade. If Croughton's hands had wandered, Neville had not observed them. Now the part-time barman sat in a lounge chair sipping Scotch and musing upon the peculiarities of the present times. His Open University course in Psychology had gone right out of the window.

What did psychologists know about life? he asked himself. About as much as the legendary late and learned pig, he concluded. Psychology was as history had been to Henry Ford, bunk. The barman sipped his Scotch and thought all the things that drunken men always think. Why wars, why profiteering, why religion, why racial intolerance, it was a lot of whys. Mankind was an enigma, an impalpable mystery and for all the why-are-we-here's and where-are-we-going's that had ever been asked, we were no-nearer-to-learning-the-truth.

Neville's good eye wandered about the confines of his world. The Swan had seen him fine for twenty years. He was barlord, confidant, guru, bouncer, jovial mine host to patrons he neither knew nor understood. He watched them turn from likeable personalities to unlikeable drunks nightly, but he didn't 'know' them. He liked them, perhaps he even loved them, but he didn't know them. They were basically good people, a little misguided perhaps, but then who wasn't these days? Who was there to guide them? The words of self-obsessed politicians, media personalities, newspaper magnates and half-mad clerics? Who could reason sensibly when supplied with all the wrong information for all the wrong reasons? Neville sank down in his seat, he was really pissed off.

And this business today? The games? It was evident that the people of Brentford were not to be any part of it. The promised free tickets had yet to materialize. Brentonians didn't matter, they were nobody. It all took a lot of thinking about. Neville took a pull at his Scotch. Was there any truth in drink? Experience had taught him to doubt that one. Was there any truth in anything? The barman was forced to conclude once more that he just didn't know. Where had it all gone? Those grand thoughts and dreams of his youth had become trivialized by uneven memory and present-day responsibility, and such it was with all of them. He recalled the high-jinx of Pooley and Omally. He had watched them mellow down, lose their edge, although he still admired them for their freedom.

About the only patron who never changed was Old Pete, but he was hardly any example.

'Where did all the good times go?' Neville asked bitterly. 'If only we had known how fragile they were, would we have treated them with such indifference?' He finished his Scotch and forbore another. Life had to go on, he had to open up in the evening, the game had to be played out. Where it was all leading, he didn't have a clue. The world was changing, and one had to change with it or get left behind. That the planet seemed to be going down the sewer to him did not mean that it actually was. There was always the young, there was always hope for the future.

Neville twirled his glass upon his finger and began to whistle. 'I think I'll have a root in the attic for the old record collection. Dig out some Leonard Cohen and cheer myself up.'

Down in the teepee Paul and Barry Geronimo swayed back and forth chanting softly. In the Professor's study, Pooley paced likewise, a tumbler of Scotch in his hand. In the briefing room Hugo Rune pointed variously about a map of Brentford, whilst constables made jottings in regulation police note-books. And on high in the Star Stadium, athletes trained and practised within a self-contained and air-conditioned environment. While deep within the great gasometer a power beyond any human reckoning seethed and thrashed against the iron walls.

39

In the near distance the Memorial Library clock chimed twelve, midnight.

In the study of Professor Slocombe, Jim Pooley pulled back the Persian carpet to expose the bare oak floorboards. 'What now?' he asked.

'And now we begin,' said Professor Slocombe. The sage was dressed in a white seamless robe which reached to his naked feet. About his neck hung a small leather satchel, in his right hand, a length of chalk. He stood in the centre of the room and bowed to the four cardinal points. 'And now about me I scribe the circle, confining good within good, constraining evil with evil.' He knelt and swung about, transcribing a perfect white chalk circle. 'Step within, Jim, you would fare badly without.'

Pooley skipped into the circle, whisky decanter and glass at the ready. 'This all looks extremely serious, Professor.'

The sage eyed Pooley's weaponry. 'A clear head is required,' he said.

'Dutch courage,' Jim declared. 'I do not share your fearlessness.'

'I would tell you that you have nothing to fear except fear itself, but it would be an untruth.'

In each corner of the room stood a brass censer supported upon a wrought iron stand. The Professor gestured to each in turn and each obligingly sprang into flame. Within minutes the air was heavy with the smell of incense. The old man stooped and laboured about the floor with his chalk, scribing pentagrams, cabalistic symbols, the names of power. Adonai, Balberith, Tetragrammaton, and all the rest. Aleph, the number

216

which is always one and those others which correspond to the elements and the seven most powerful planets.

Pooley tossed Scotch down his throat and considered his reflection in the large concave mirror which the Professor had erected upon his desk. It didn't look all that promising.

'And now, Jim,' said the old man, rising to his feet, 'you will do all that I tell you without question and upon the instant. I have no need to impress upon you the importance of this.'

'None whatever,' said Jim.

'Good, then we shall begin.' The Professor placed his hands across his chest and joined Pooley in the circle. 'The invocation was formulated by the magician John Dee. Distilled from Enochian, Goetic, Gnostic and Tantric sources. The potency of the words lies to some extent in their unfathomability, causing, as they do, an elevation of the magician's mind which unseals his consciousness allowing the release of the "Ka". Do you follow me?'

'Yes, indubitably.'

'ZODACARE, ECA, OD ZODOMERANU! ODO KIKALE QAA! ZODORJE, LAPE ZODIREPO NOCO MADA, HOATHATE IAIDA!'

Pooley shivered and turned up his shirt-collar, the room was becoming impossibly cold. The fire was dying in the grate and the Professor was swaying upon his heels, staring into space.

'ZODACARE, ECA, OD ZODOMERANU! ODO KIKALE QAA! ZODORJE, LAPE ZODIREPO NOCO MADA, HOATHATE IAIDA!'

Pooley's thumbs were now definitely on the prickle.

'He resists us,' said the Professor. 'That is to be expected, but we shall have him.' He returned once more to his invocation, repeating it again and again, each time with greater force. The words seemed to grow from his lips and fly as living things into the ether of space, where they spread and expanded, became charged, alive.

The air trembled and wavered, became soupy. It was

difficult to draw breath, the incense hung, a heavy impenetrable cloud. Pooley felt as if he was drowning, he clawed at his throat, 'Air,' he gasped.

The Professor stooped, drew up his hands, formed the cone of power. Fresh air returned. 'He is coming . . . he approaches.' The room began to tremble, to vibrate, books toppled from the shelves, ornaments keeled over. One of the censers crashed to the floor, spilling smouldering incense in every direction, though none fell into the sacred circle. 'He comes . . .'

Above the mantelpiece, the plaster of the wall was beginning to crack and bulge. A priceless painting snapped from its hook and broke in the fireplace beneath. The wall-lights buckled and shattered. The wall lurched forward. Pooley ducked for cover.

'Do not leave the circle,' the Professor commanded. 'On the pain of your life, remain.' Pooley froze, one foot hovering in the air.

The wall contorted, warped, stretched. A face appeared, formed in the plasterwork. A great grinning face, the face of Kaleton. Jim Pooley was a born-again Christian.

Unrestrained by its plastic sheathing and artificial optics, the face leered down from the wall. It was the face of a tribal god, a pagan deity. The mouth opened and a black tongue lolled out, dripping foul saliva, the lashless eyelids opened to reveal dull white orbs. 'You!' The voice was that of a chorus, a thousand voices yet only one. 'You dare to summon me here?'

'I summon you by a single name and a single image, you are constrained and ordered to obey me.'

The mouth spread into a vast grin and gales of hideous mocking laughter broke from it. Pooley covered his nose and crossed his legs, such things as this were not good for his constitution.

'By the names of power which are those of the elements,' the Professor made the signs with his arms, 'by SET, by SHU, by AURAMOTH, by THOUM-AESH-NEITH, so I constrain you, that you will answer my questions.' The mouth closed, the eyes blinked shut, showing only ghastly whites. 'Spawn of darkness,' cried Professor Slocombe, 'what order of demon are you?'

'Demon?' The eyes flashed fire, black teeth showed in the lipless mouth. 'I am no demon, I am anything other than that!'

'Then what? Angel, perhaps? I think not.'

'You know who I am, you know what I am!'

Professor Slocombe spun about, suddenly distracted. Pooley glanced over his shoulder and felt very sick indeed. Two creatures were approaching from behind, tall and naked, their skin a lustreless black. The bodies were lithe and muscular, their heads featureless ebony spheres. Professor Slocombe uttered a single unpronounceable word. Blue flame leapt from his fingertips, struck the creatures, dissolved them into nothingness.

'Enough of this foolishness.' The Professor turned once more to confront the face, but it had vanished. 'How tiresome,' said the old man to his wet-trousered companion. 'This is going to take a lot longer than I might have hoped. We shall have to begin again.'

A convoy of police vehicles moved up the Kew Road towards the gasometer. In the lead car sat Inspectre Hovis, dressed in battle fatigues, his face boot-blacked. Across his knees lay a sub-machine gun.

Constable Meek crouched across the wheel. 'Are you sure we're going about this the right way?' he asked.

'Onward, Meek,' said the Inspectre. 'You might well earn yourself a promotion tonight, lad. Off the beat and into the cars, you'd like that, eh?'

'Well, sir . . .' Meek wrinkled his boyish nose.

'Well, sir, what?'

'Him, sir. How can we trust him?' The constable nodded over his shoulder towards the back seat where Rune perched, his fat legs tortured into a full lotus, his eyes closed in meditation.

'I know a spell,' said the Logos of the Aeon, 'which can transpose the organ of smell with that of reproduction to great comic effect. Would you care for me to demonstrate upon you?'

'No I wouldn't.' Meek crossed himself with his gear-changing hand.

'Pull up here, constable.' Inspectre Hovis studied his map. 'I am expecting the arrival of a bulldozer.'

'Bulldozer!' spluttered Rune. 'By Crom!'

Hovis consulted his watch and took up a walkie-talkie. 'To your positions, men, and radio blackout until you hear from me.'

In the Professor's study the sage mopped the sweat from his brow and seated himself in the circle.

'What now?' asked Jim, taking the opportunity to refill his glass.

'We begin again. The process is tedious, I regret, but there is nothing for it.'

'He seems to be causing a terrible amount of damage, if you don't mind me saying.'

The Professor nodded in sombre agreement. 'This time we will see to it that he materializes in a more manageable form.' He leafed through his book of spells. 'Ah yes, a formula used by the magicians of Atlantis for hypnotizing captives and transforming them into cattle during times of famine.'

'You are going to turn him into a cow?'

'Hardly, Jim, the image of a man will be quite enough. Now I want you to do something for me. Take this phial.' He handed Jim a silver flask engraved with runic symbols and capped by a cork stopper. 'No, do not open it now, only when I give you the word and then as quickly as you can. Understand?'

Pooley nodded. 'If my brain holds out, which I doubt.'

'Stout fellow, Jim. Then we begin again.'

The bulldozer rumbled towards the police convoy. Some

surprise attack this is going to be, thought Constable Meek. Hovis leapt from the car, loudhailer in one hand and sub-machine gun in the other.

Jungle John, itinerant local builder and now a big name in the demolition game, nudged his hirsute brother who sat as ever at his side, munching sandwiches and swigging beer. 'Look at this, Dave. It's Sergeant Rock and his Howling Commandos.'

Hairy Dave peered down at the approaching detective. 'He's got a bleeding machine gun,' he observed.

'All right, men!' Hovis cried up at them through his loudhailer. 'Timing is everything, have that fence down!'

'That's gas board property,' said John. 'We can't do that.'

Hovis cocked his gun. 'Now!' he commanded.

John looked at his brother. 'He's a bloody loon.'

Dave sank low in his seat. 'Have the fence down and let's get off home.'

'As you please.' John jiggled the joy-stick, revved the engine, spun the tracks and trundled towards the high wire fence which encircled the grounds of the gasometer. 'Tally ho!' he cried.

The Professor raised his arms. 'By the names of power, by Yetzirah, by Briah, by Atziluth, by Assiah. RAPHAEL GABRIEL MICHAEL AURIEL in the form so prescribed I summon you.'

There was a cry of pain, a terrible groaning, as of one in the exquisite agonies of death. The human form of Kaleton became focused in one of the fireside chairs. He swayed, his gloved hands upon his deformed knees. 'You injure me greatly,' he gasped, turning his twisted visage towards his tormentor.

'I will injure you further if you do not answer my questions.'

Pooley stared at the creature. If this was the man, the thing that had killed his friend, then better the Professor slay it now than waste time with questions.

'Your thirst for knowledge is likely to be your undoing. Such inquisitiveness will . . .'

'Answer my questions,' the Professor commanded, 'or I will stretch your neck.'

Kaleton's breath rasped and rattled in his throat, his chest rose unevenly. 'Have you no mercy?' he croaked.

'And why should I? You have none.'

'But mine is the true cause,' whispered Kaleton. 'I bear the pain of centuries. My retribution is just.'

'Explain yourself.'

Kaleton rose to face the Professor. 'You still do not know who I am? You with your books and your learning. Surely you have long expected me.'

Pooley glanced at the Professor. The old man looked frail beyond imagination. The confrontation was draining every last ounce of his energy. 'Expected you? What do you mean?'

'And I thought you a man of understanding, if the word is not anathema to man.'

'Speak now, or I reverse your skin.'

'That's the stuff,' urged Pooley.

Kaleton raised his head and glared at his enemies. His body quivered. 'I am the one and the many,' he declared, 'I am the history of the planet. A planet raped, looted and despoiled by mankind. Your race have pillaged and destroyed. Poisoned the atmosphere, polluted the rivers and the seas. Razed the grasslands. Now is the time of the coming, the time of retribution. Who am I, Professor? I am the "Spiritus Mundus", I am the World Soul, I am the spirit of the earth made flesh!'

'No,' said the Professor, 'no, you lie!'

'Why should I lie? Mankind is now done. You are powerless to resist, powerless to intercede in a plan which has taken centuries to form. Above you a dark star fills the heavens, two feet upon the water and three upon the land. The prophecies fulfil. The time of the reckoning, the time of the great gathering.'

The Professor was noticeably trembling. 'Why, why do you do this?'

Kaleton laughed. It was not the tinkling of fairy bells. 'Why? Man's history has been brief, but the destruction, the wanton waste, the needless horrors . . . the planet will stand no more. The world turns back upon you. A new beginning, Professor, a free world. A world free of men.'

'Madness! How can you think to accomplish this?'

'You have aided in your own destruction. Down the centuries you have built great temples, great cathedrals, seats of learning, but each to a divine formula. My formula. It is all in the stones, the power lies in the stones. From the Henge to the stadium, the power is with us, with me. At the signal the great old buildings will live, the stadium will become charged with power, it will walk, it will reap.'

The Professor's eyes glittered. 'Signal, what signal?'

'You will feel it when it comes. A great shot will ring out across the universe. The earth will tremble, the stadium will live, the great old buildings will live, they will rise and crush you, clean you from the face, sweep you away, like the insects that you are. We will smash you down!' Kaleton raised his crooked hands high above his head. *'Smash you down!'*

'Smash it down!' Hovis shouted as the bulldozer strained against the wire fence. The tracks slewed upon the pavement, tearing up the flagstones, unable to grip.

Jungle John hunched low over the controls. 'This is bloody funny,' he said through gritted teeth. 'Something is holding us back.'

'Give it revs!' shouted Hairy Dave. 'Give it revs!'

'I'm doing it, for Chrissakes! What's going on here?'

Hugo Rune placed a hand upon the Inspectre's shoulder, 'You won't get in this way, I'm telling you.'

'Leave the fence to me,' said Hovis, shrugging off the podgy fingers. 'I'll get us into the compound, you open the gasometer.'

'Please yourself then.'

The bulldozer struck the fence once more and this time a

charge of electricity crackled through the vehicle, scrambling the ignition system and setting the driver's crowning glory ablaze. The erstwhile demolition team leapt from the cab, howling and fanning at themselves. The bulldozer began to turn in circles, its digger rising and falling.

Meek wound down his window. 'Back up!' he shouted towards the goggle-eyed policemen in the convoy behind. His words were of course lost in the noise of the screaming engine. The bulldozer struck the bonnet of the lead car. Meek threw himself out of the vehicle as it upended to fall upon the car behind. Hovis leapt up and down shouting through his loudhailer and brandishing his gun. Meek watched in horror as the bulldozer minced the line of police cars into unrecognizable scrap. Rune turned upon his heel and strode off up the road whistling a tune of his own making.

'Now, Jim!' cried Professor Slocombe. Jim fumbled with the phial and dropped it beyond the reach of the circle.

'Your little diversion has come to nothing. Goodbye, Professor!' cried the Soul of the World.

Jim flung himself towards the silver bottle. As he left the circle, darkness closed about him, the world came to an end.

Pooley clambered to his feet, brushing away the strands of long coarse grass which clung to his clothing. The land about him was flat endless tundra, relieved only by the occasional gnarled black tree. Somewhere near by a river ran, but Jim was unable to see it. Shielding his eyes against the curious magenta glare of the sky, he sought a habitation, a hostelry perhaps? There was nothing. But then there was something.

Borne upon a wind, so light as to scarcely stir the grass, he heard the faint sounds of chanting. And then the jingling of bells, the rattle of harnessing, the tread of the heavy horses. The creak of the wagon wheels. A procession wound towards him, those at the van swung censers, and intoned the chant. Their garments were of rough brown cloth, soiled through much hard travel, their feet unshod, their faces grave. These men and women were exhausted, they had travelled many miles without rest, they stumbled, staggered, but they marched on.

Pooley watched them sadly as they passed. The heads of the great horses were down, their flanks ran wet. The wagon wheels turned in faulty circles, their unequal spokes wrought with the signs of a former zodiac. And Jim watched those who rode the high-sided wagons, the witch-faced women with their bearded chins and tattooed brows. And he glimpsed the treasures which they guarded. Sprawling upon the cushions of hay were infants, swollen and grotesque, the size of oxen. The children of the great folk. The last of their line. They gurgled and croaked, their naked skins grey, their eyes without lustre. Now behind them, in the far distance, the thunder rolled and broke. The sky seethed angrily and muttered threats.

Pooley heard the cry, in a language he knew not, yet understood. 'Onward, onward to the Iron Tower. Onward to the sanctuary.'

The witch-women drove hard upon the faltering horses and those that maintained the endless chant marched on upon wooden legs. And Jim limped after them across the plain and now the wind grew and howled and drove him onward. And there upon the horizon he saw the tower, stark and black, a distant needle piercing the sky. And the cry went up from the marchers and the women drove ever harder upon the dying horses. 'Onward, onward, King Bran is coming.'

And from the heart of the dark and rolling clouds, lightning broke and scoured the land, and the thunder was now the hooves of an approaching army. 'Make haste to the sanctuary.'

And of a sudden the tower filled the sky, and a drawbridge fell like the hand of benediction. The marchers broke into a run. A horse floundered and dropped dead in the shafts of the lead wagon. Men and women tore it away, rolled the body aside, dragged and heaved at the wagon, swarmed towards the drawbridge. 'Make haste, make haste.'

Jim limped after them. A wagon overturned, spilling its ghastly load. The witch-women deserted it, ran screaming. The horsemen thundered nearer. The horsemen of King Bran. And Jim ran, as though the devil was at his heels. And now two called out to him, called through the crashing elements, the terror, the lightning and the pounding hooves of the approaching warriors. A man and a woman, braced against the driving winds, crying through the maelstrom, 'Hurry, Jim, this way!'

Pooley shielded his eyes. 'John,' he gasped, 'Jennifer, I'm coming.'

Then hands grasped him, pulled him back, back from the drawbridge, the threshold of the sanctuary. 'Stop, do not enter, you must not enter.'

'Take the bottle,' cried Paul Geronimo, 'uncork the bottle!'

'Do it now!' his brother urged. 'Only you can!'

Jim's brain reeled, torn with doubt, indecision and fear.

Paul thrust the silver bottle into his hand. 'For the Professor, do it now, open the bottle!'

Pooley stared towards Omally; he was stepping back into the iron tower. Only one wagon had entered, the others were abandoned, people screamed, fled, the winds tore. The horsemen of King Bran bore down upon him. The drawbridge began to rise. Pooley ripped the stopper from the bottle.

40

A beaming face beamed out across the nation. 'This is the London Olympics.'

Old Pete switched off the television set. 'It's not the same without Anne Diamond,' he complained bitterly. The sound of his letter-flap creaking on its rusty spring drew his attention. 'Hello,' said Old Pete, 'it's not Giroday.'

Upon the unwelcoming mat lay a silver-foil envelope. YOUR PERSONAL INVITATION TO THE BRENTFORD OLYMPICS. 'Gold dust,' said Old Pete, pressing it to his lips. 'Thirty-carat gold dust.'

'Gold dust,' said Inspectre Hovis. 'At each of the sites where disturbances occurred, and last night it was in the air, on my clothes.'

Rune sat over a bowl of Tibetan muesli. The mess-room of the Brentford nick was crowded with bandaged officers hunched over their breakfasts. 'The alchemist's quest,' said Rune. 'Pure gold. It is a powerful instrument in any hands.'

'Whoever is at the bottom of this is taking the piss,' said Hovis, applying himself to his cornflakes. 'Having a pop at me personally.'

'I don't like to say I told you so,' said Hugo Rune. 'Well, actually I do, as it happens.'

'A bulldozer,' spluttered Hovis, spraying the magus with half-masticated flakes of golden corn. 'A bulldozer wouldn't go through the wire. I've got six police vehicles smashed to a pulp, a dozen officers banged up in the Cottage Hospital, my reputation, for what it was, is in tatters. My job will be on the line for this.'

'To offer you my sympathy would be as futile as it would be fallacious. You wasted your opportunity.' Rune brushed cornflakes from his shoulders. 'Your man was distracted, I could sense it. It will be more difficult now.'

'Don't even think about raising your fee,' said Hovis.

'You must do it my way, Inspectre. It will take a few days. Keep the gasometer under constant surveillance, arrest anyone who attempts to leave it. Other than for that, bide your time and wait for me to give you the word.'

Hovis pushed his breakfast bowl aside and took to the contents of his cane, pecking a hearty blend of Moroccan Black cut with cocaine in his left nostril. 'If you cross me, Rune,' he said, 'I will have your wedding tackle for cufflinks.'

'I am Hugo Rune,' said Hugo Rune. 'Lord of the seven spheres. Master of the cosmic consciousness, Laird of Cockpen and hereditary heir to the Grand Mastership of the Golden Dawn. I think therefore I'm right.'

'You'd better be.' Hovis looked up towards the magus, but the chair was empty. Hugo Rune had gone.

Professor Slocombe nudged the sleeper on his *chaise-longue* with a slippered toe. 'Wake up, Jim, I want you to look at something.'

Pooley rubbed at his eyes and creaked upright. 'I don't remember dropping off,' said he, stretching his arms and yawning hugely. Suddenly he jerked into realization. 'Blimey,' he gasped. 'Last night. All that.' He gaped at the study. It was as it ever had been, confusing, but in order. 'Did I dream it, what happened?'

'You saved our lives, Jim.'

'Really? But I wasn't here, something happened, I was somewhere else.'

'I know, and now I begin to understand.'

'Has he gone?' Jim stared about fearfully. 'Is he – is it – dead?'

'Not yet, I regret.'

'Oh God,' said Pooley. 'Then we can expect more of the same.'

'Or worse, I suspect. But come, I want to show you something.' The Professor led Jim to his desk where a beautiful Victorian brass microscope stood. 'Have a look in here.' He indicated the eye-piece.

Jim took a peep. 'Bloody hell!' he swore, leaping back. 'It's alive in there.'

'Indeed, very much so. What did you see?'

'Little things, buzzing about like crazy, they looked . . .'

'Yes?'

'Angry,' said Jim, 'very angry.'

'And so they are. They are the very stuff of our friend Kaleton.'

'Friend?'

'My apologies, the word is most inappropriate. They are, if you like, a portion of his very essence. The silver flask drew in a quantity of his substance. He left in some confusion before it could take more, but what we have is sufficient.'

'So what does it mean?'

'It means that the non-man Kaleton is a "Grex". A large body of separate organisms which when grouped together form the semblance of something else, either for camouflage or defence. Certain bacteria have the ability to do this when faced with starvation. They pass a message through a chain of single cells, amalgamate into a larger form and refunction in a different manner. They lose their individuality in the cause of mass survival.'

'It's a bit early for me,' said Jim.

'Then look upon it as a microcosm of human society. A single naked individual could not survive, but in harmony, in rapport with the whole, protected and fed by the whole, he or she is able to function, to exist. Kinship, harmony, team spirit, that is loosely how society maintains its equilibrium. As a single body.'

'Hm,' said Jim. 'It's not the same. We may be part of the whole *en masse*, but we are each individuals, not one big homogenous blob. It doesn't compute.'

'Oh, it does. It may be impossible to predict what a single

individual will do, but one can predict with absolute accuracy what, say, a million people will do at any given time. They will get up at a certain hour, go to work at a certain hour, take lunch at a certain hour.'

'Yes, I get the picture,' said Jim, 'although I don't like it. Every man is an island, I am not a number, I am a free man, that kind of stuff.'

'No-one could ever doubt that *you* are an individual, Jim.'

Pooley chewed upon the Professor's words that might have been a compliment. If it was, he meant to savour it, he didn't get them that often. 'What about this Soul of the World stuff?' he said presently.

'It is an ancient belief,' said Professor Slocombe, 'universal as the Flood legend. The Buddhists believe in Rigdenjypo, king of the world, who dwells at the very centre of the planet in Shamballa, capital city of earth. All religions, past and present, have recognized a single Divine Creator, a God of the gods. Kaleton does not claim to be the universal deity, he claims to be the very spirit of this planet. Soul of the World made flesh.'

'And do you believe his claims?'

'No,' said the Professor, 'I cannot. I dare not. His case is well argued, mankind has much to answer for, but there are too many contradictions. To quote an old chess-playing chum, and putting it crudely, "If the earth seeks to lose man, it has merely to fart." '

'Well, whoever, or whatever he is, he means business.'

'Perk up, Jim, we're not beaten yet.'

Pooley stroked his jaw. 'Something he said struck a chord, I'm trying to think what it was.' Professor Slocombe jiggled Pooley's brain cells with an unspoken word. 'Ah yes,' said Jim, 'I remember. About the stadium, two feet in the water and three upon the land.'

'Yes?'

'It's the old rhyme, "The Ballad of the Two Kings of Brentford", you remember?'

'Tell me.'

' "There live two kings of Brentford
Who fought for a single throne.
One lives in a tower of iron
and one in a tower of stone." '

'Go on.'
'There's a verse that goes,

"And a black star rose above them
A sword in every hand.
Two feet upon the water
And three upon the land."
That's it.'

'There's more,' said the Professor, 'can you recall?'

'No,' said Jim, 'my brain is gone. Something about a final battle and a "heart of burning gold", but I can't remember it.'

'Never mind, you have done very well. Two feet in the water and three on the land, the black star, that is clear enough.'

'I'm starving,' said Jim.

'Then I shall ring for breakfast.'

'Is it on the tariff or on the house?' asked Jim who, despite evidence to the contrary, was still nobody's fool.

'On the house,' said the Professor. 'You have certainly earned it.' He rang a small brass bell and Gammon appeared almost upon the instant, tray in hand. 'You know what this means?' the Professor asked as Pooley set about the morning's fry-up.

'Go on,' said Pooley, between munchings.

'It means that we must enter the stadium, the heart of it all lies right up there.'

'It will be a long hard climb.'

'An impossible climb, defended at every inch, I shouldn't wonder, but you'll find a way.'

'*Me?*' Pooley choked upon his toast.

'Oh yes,' said the Professor. 'I am confident that you will come up with something.' Then you are a fool to yourself, thought Jim. 'Oh no I'm not,' said Professor Slocombe.

231

41

At a little after eleven, Pooley stood in the Professor's garden, breathing fresh air and pointedly ignoring the weeds which sprouted on the west lawn. The invisible barrier was down, which seemed a hopeful sign, and the sky was blue. At least Jim assumed it to be blue, for looking up, he remembered that what he was actually seeing was the image projected by the underside of the great stadium. The black star which rose above them. Jim shrugged away the chill which crept up his back, put his best foot forward and strode down to the Swan. 'The condemned man enjoyed a hearty pint' being the order of the day.

To Jim's amazement, the bar was already quite crowded, the piano was playing and Neville was going hell for leather behind the pump. The part-time barman spied Pooley's approach as did a shabby-looking man in a greasy brown trilby, who cowered behind his newspaper.

'Well, well,' said Neville, 'the wanderer returns.'

'Watchamate, Neville,' said the dejected Jim, 'and a pint of Large, please.'

'And where's your mate then?' Neville did the honours at the pump handle.

Pooley perused his unpolished toecaps. 'I have no idea,' he said softly. 'Hasn't he been in then?'

'No,' said Neville, 'he's done a bunk.' He placed the perfect pint before his patron. 'Jim, is everything all right?'

Pooley shook his head. 'Anything but. I don't know what's happened to John, the Professor says . . .'

'Three more pints over here.' The voice belonged to Norman.

'Excuse me, Jim, I'll be back in a minute.' Neville scooped

up the pennies Pooley had placed on the bar and went off to serve the shopkeeper.

'He's bunging money about like there's no tomorrow,' said Old Pete at Pooley's elbow. 'I'd dive in now if I was you.'

'Oh yes, and what's the celebration?' Jim asked, out of no particular interest.

'This Gravitite business. You know, that wondercrap that holds the stadium up. Norman's knocked up his own version and you'll never guess what?'

'He's won the Nobel prize.'

'Not yet. But he took his formula down to the patent's office and it turns out that there's no patent on it. The other geezer never got around to having his registered. Norman is sitting on a gold mine.'

'My old brown dog,' said Jim. 'Bravo the shopkeeper.'

'My thoughts entirely.'

'Watchamate, Norman,' called Jim along the bar. 'How's tricks then?'

'Never better,' crooned the half-drunken shopkeeper. 'One for my good friend Jim, please, Neville.'

'Cheers, Norman,' said Old Pete, 'nice one, old mate.'

'And another down that end for the fogey.'

'I've never cared for him, you know,' Old Pete confided in Pooley, 'gets right up my nose he does.'

Jim sipped thoughfully at his pint. 'He's all right, he's an individual.'

'He's a bloody nutcase! So where's your mate then? Work-shy as ever, it seems.'

'I don't know, I'm not sure.'

'Thought he'd be getting some mileage out of these.' Old Pete drew out his silver envelope. 'Did you get yours?'

'What are they?'

'Free tickets for the big match, everybody's got one.'

Pooley raised his eyebrows and his glass. 'Everyone in Brentford?'

'That's the size of it. A bit of good has come out of this fiasco.'

'I wouldn't go if I were you,' Jim advised. 'In fact, I'd give the whole thing a very wide berth.'

'My thoughts entirely, yet again. I'm advertising mine in *The Times*, there's a bungalow in Eastbourne in this for me. I'll give you a fiver for yours if you want.'

Pooley hunched low over his pint, which was shortly joined by Norman's freeman. 'Mine seems to have been delayed in the post. If you want to give me the five spot now, I'll drop it round when it arrives.'

'Do I look like a cabbage?' Old Pete asked. 'On your bike, Pooley. Good luck, Norman.' He raised his glass towards the inebriate shopkeeper. 'Here's health!'

'So, Jim,' said Neville, when he had done with his servings, 'what's to do then?'

Pooley shook his head. How could he possibly explain what was going on to Neville? In the cold light of day it all seemed so much nonsense. He was still not certain that he had actually seen what he thought he had seen. It was too grotesque. The more he thought about it the more convinced he became that it was some drug-induced fantasy, brought on by incense and whisky. But John, however, remained quite as dead. 'I'm not well,' Jim told Neville. 'Something I ate or something. As for John, I just don't know, truly.'

'I'm sorry you're not feeling up to much, Jim. You said something about the Professor before we were interrupted.'

'It was nothing.' Without Omally, Jim felt pitifully alone, somehow incomplete. 'Nothing at all, it doesn't matter.'

'As you please,' replied the barman. 'But listen, if John does show up, you can tell him he can have his job back here. He played straight with me. I owe him a lot.'

'We all do.' Pooley raised his glass. 'You are a good man, Neville. There's nothing the matter with mankind when there's blokes like you around.'

'Well, thank you, Jim, I appreciate that.'

'You're in a bloody wet mood,' said Old Pete. 'Seen the light, have you?'

'Something like that – belt up, you old bastard.'

'Thanks very much,' said Old Pete.

There was a sudden disruption in the middle of the bar. 'Watch this,' said Norman, clearing space in the crowd. 'Now just watch this.'

The onlookers and good-time-charlies, who had been accepting his free drinks, drew back to a respectful distance and egged him on. 'Watchagonnado?' they asked.

'A demonstration of the Norman Hartnell Mark One Flying Jacket, Wallah!' Norman opened his coat. Around his waist was a broad belt loaded with lead weights and general junk of the heavy variety. 'The miracle of Normanite.' Norman unbuckled the belt and it fell to the floor with a loud crash. 'Up and away.' To massed amazement, he rose from his feet and drifted towards the ceiling. 'He leaps tall buildings at a single bound!' the shopman called down to his speechless spectators.

'Bloody idiot,' muttered Old Pete. 'My glass is empty yet again.'

'Give the man his due,' said Neville. 'That is not the kind of thing one sees every day.'

Norman bobbed about on the ceiling, giggling foolishly. To Pooley's rear the shabby-looking man in the greasy brown trilby rolled his newspaper into a tight tube, inserted something dubious into the end and placed it to his lips.

'For he's a jolly good fellow,' sang the crowd, 'and so say all of us.'

'If he throws up on my carpet, he'll pay for the cleaning,' said Neville. 'Pooley, look out!' Jim ducked instinctively. Something whistled past his left ear and thudded into the haunches of a souvenir Spanish bull upon the bar shelf. 'Stop that man!' cried Neville, but the crowd was too entranced with Norman's antics. The shabby-looking man fled the Swan. 'It's a blowpipe dart,' said the part-time barman, examining the bull's punctured rump. 'By the gods!'

'That bastard Bob is not giving up.' Pooley climbed to his feet. 'Thanks very much, Neville.'

The barman sniffed at the end of the dart. 'Curare,' he

235

said. 'He was out to kill you, Jim, and in my pub, the bloody cheek.' Old Pete chuckled, Pooley had nothing to say. 'Curare,' said Neville, 'a distillation from the Amazon plant *Cameracio Apolidorus*. The natives boil up the tubers and the roots, you know. The poison maintains its potency for years, a single prick and you've less than a minute to say your prayers. Attacks the central nervous system, you see.'

'Thank you,' said Jim. 'I had no idea you harboured an interest in toxicology.'

'I did a night-school course at the Arts Centre,' said the barman, 'from their Poisoner in Residence. Funny what you remember.'

'Oh, dead amusing, yes. And how are you on anti-gravity? Your man Norman looks to be in some difficulty.'

Indeed the floating shopman was exhibiting signs of extreme discomfort. He was flattened against the ceiling and now very red in the face. 'Oh help!' wailed Norman. 'Get me down, for Godsake!'

Neville sighed deeply and climbed on to the bar counter, disciplinary knobkerry in hand. 'Take hold,' he called. Norman gripped the knobkerry, the onlookers gripped the barman's ankles. Amidst much puffing and blowing and with no small utterances of profanity, the zero-gravity shopkeeper was returned to terra firma and the weighted belt was hastily clamped once more about his waist.

'It's handy stuff though,' said Norman, breathlessly. 'Got it sewn into the jacket, you see.'

The onlookers saw. 'Clever,' they said, wondering if the source of the free drinks had now dried up. 'You are a genius, Norman.'

'A large brandy on me for Mr Einstein,' said Pooley, pressing his way through the crowd.

'My thanks, Jim.' Norman checked his belt. 'Perhaps in my zeal, I overdid it. I shall have to watch the walk home, or I could end up in orbit.'

'Norman,' said Jim, 'could I have a word or two with you in private?'

'As many words as you wish, Jim, what's on your mind?'

Pooley led the shopkeeper away to a quiet corner. The onlookers looked on in disgust and purchased their own drinks. 'A small word,' said Jim.

'And why not?' Norman tapped his nose. 'From one millionaire to another.'

'Ah, you heard about my bet.'

'There's not much stays quiet in Brentford. I do live next door to Bob after all.'

'Quite so, but listen, Norman. This Normanite of yours. A man wearing such a flying-jacket could, I suppose, drift up to the stadium, could he not?'

Norman looked doubtful. 'If the wind was favourable. I don't think I'd care to take my chances though. You could end up, well, up, indefinitely speaking.'

Jim nodded thoughtfully. 'Somewhat dangerous, yes I agree. It's a pity though.'

'What are you up to then, Jim?'

'Not me,' said Pooley, 'the Professor. He wants to get a look at the stadium before it opens, some matter of public safety, I believe.'

'He's got his free ticket, hasn't he?'

'I understand he'd like a private viewing.'

'He's a man of some influence, can't he swing it with the organizers?'

'I don't think they would approve, this is something of a secret operation.'

'Ooh.' Norman placed a finger to his lips. 'Mum's the word, eh? Well, I might be prevailed upon to . . .' He made thoughtful faces.

'To what, Norman?'

'To drive him up.'

'What?'

'A little top secret project of my own.' Norman spoke in the conspiratorial whisper much favoured by conspiratorial whisperers. 'I have done a bit of a conversion job on the old Morris Minor. The Hartnell Harrier is now the Hartnell Air Car.' Pooley shook his head, the man was a genius. 'A revolution in personal transportation with almost limitless potential in the fields of haulage, commuter-carriage, inter-city travel, et cetera, et cetera. Another first for Hartnell International.'

'Does it work?'

'Does it work? How dare you? It's a bit spartan at present, only a prototype, but when they start rolling off the production line. I've come up with some great little modifications,' Norman rattled on with boundless enthusiasm, 'a single tiny switch which cuts out those annoying red dashboard lights that always come on when you're half-way up a motorway. Rear headlights to revenge yourself on those blighters who come up behind you at night with their main beams on. A sweety dispenser, in-car commode, automatic pilot, self-contained . . .'

'You don't waste any time once you've an idea in your head,' Pooley put in hastily, to staunch the verbal flow which showed no immediate signs of abating.

'There's no time like the present, Jim. A lot of it is still in the ideas stage, but the car does work, I'm telling you.'

'And would you be prepared to take the Professor up to the stadium?'

'Why not? I'd like a sneak preview myself. There are also one or two matters I'd like his advice on. Tit for tat, eh, I'm sure he wouldn't mind.'

'I'm sure he wouldn't!'

'When does he want to go?' Norman asked.

'Tomorrow night, how does that sound?'

'The night before the games start.'

'What?' said Jim. 'They've brought them forward?'

'Yes, it was announced this morning, didn't you know?'

'No, I did not, oh dear.' Jim chewed upon his knuckles.

'There's no sweat, the car will be ready, sounds like a bit of an adventure. Yes, I shall look forward to it.' Norman raised his glass. It was empty. 'Want another, Jim?'

'I'll get them,' said Pooley. 'Another pint?'

'No. Just a light ale, don't want people thinking I'm a heavy drinker, light, heavy, get it, eh?' Norman tapped at his weighted belt and giggled foolishly. 'Can't keep a good man down, eh? Good man down? There I go again.' He creased up with mirth.

'Norman, you are a caution,' said Pooley, taking the glasses up to the bar. As he stood waiting to be served he pondered upon the rare coincidence that Norman had conceived and constructed the very means by which he and the Professor could enter the stadium, exactly when it was required, and that he should just happen to bump into him at the very moment. Many would argue that such a chance was one in a million, improbable to the point of near impossibility and they would no doubt be absolutely right.

42

By 'towels up', Pooley was what the English magician Crowley referred to as 'nice drunk'. He wandered off down the Ealing Road, hands in pockets, roll-up between his teeth. Jim paused a moment outside Bob the Bookie's, considering what form his retribution should take. It would have to keep for the present, Bob's security was of the Fort Knox persuasion and Jim did not possess the necessary military hardware to storm the premises. 'You will get yours,' he told the iron-bound doorway. Out of sheer badness, Jim ran his pocket-knife down the length of Bob's parked Rolls-Royce and signed his handiwork with a flourished JP.

Half-way down the Albany Road, he wondered if he should pop into the Police Station and report the shabby man's attempt on his life. Attempted murder was a punishable offence after all. But Jim's recent encounters with the law, particularly that personified by Inspectre Hovis, led him to consider this action pure folly. And of course the Professor had said that he preferred no police intervention in his schemes.

Jim steered his shabby shoe in the direction of the allotments. He hadn't been down that way for weeks and his own plot was in a sorry state. The rhubarb was running to seed, sending out its hideous tendrils towards the potato patch, and the runner beans were ripe for harvesting.

He unpadlocked the door of his hut, savouring that special aroma which is unique to the interiors of allotment sheds. He sought out a bottle of private stock from its secret hideaway and a folding garden-chair of uncertain security. Labouring bravely at its rusted springs, he set the thing up before his hut doorway, settled into it and uncorked the bottle. A sip or two told him that it was cabbage wine, one of Norman's specials, not a great vintage, but acceptable to his present condition. He picked a bit of stalk from his teeth and took another slug.

His thoughts turned almost at once to the comforts of the old barge which had been, until so recently, the headquarters of the P & O Line. That all seemed so long ago now. Another world. Jim became reflective in the way that only a drunken man can. He had not yet come to terms with the prospect of life without John. The future seemed an empty affair. Even if he got out of all this business with his life and copped the ten million smackers, the future looked far from rosy.

There was an ache in him that would not go away. It was the ache that he had felt when his father died. But then Omally had been there to comfort him in his time of loss. They had gone down to the undertakers together to say their farewells to the old man. Jim had placed a packet of fags in his pocket to send him on his way, John had shaken the dead man's hand and then the two of them had gone off on a week-long drunk. They had raised their glasses together, made many toasts and drunk away the sorrow. The ache had been soothed away, leaving nothing but the warmth of happy memories. But now Jim was truly alone and he sighed mournfully. He didn't even have a body to weep over or a grave to place flowers upon. He can't be dead, Jim told himself. He just can't be, I won't let him.

'You must let him go,' the Professor had said. 'A soul cannot be truly free until it is released by the bereaved. You must let him go.'

'Never.' Jim swigged greatly from the dusty bottle. 'Not until I know, not until I am really sure. But whatever . . .' He rose to his feet and shook his clenched fist towards the stadium. 'You will pay for this, you will pay and pay. Whoever you are, whatever you are, you will pay.' Jim sank once more into his knackered chair. 'But I just wish I knew how,' he muttered to himself.

* * *

'They're at it again,' Mrs Butcher informed her hen-pecked spouse. 'They're up to their old tricks again.' Mr Butcher cowered in the Parker Knoll and took shelter behind his *Angling Times*. 'Go out there, do something.'

Mr Butcher ventured a hopeful, 'They're not doing any harm, dear,' but his good lady wife knew it was coming and slapped away his paper with her polishing cloth. 'Get out there,' she cried.

'A fellow caught a twenty-seven pound pike down at the cut last week on a number nine hook, just fancy that.'

'I'll fancy something in a minute,' said his wife, in the way some wives are renowned for. 'Get out there, Reg, you tell them.'

'Tell them what, dear? They're only dancing, there's no harm in that.'

'No harm in that? It's heathen.' His wife crossed herself before the plastic Virgin on the mantelshelf. 'They are godless savages.'

'They're not savages, dear, they're on the town council.'

'Well, that's where you're wrong, they got the sack, them with their evil heathen ways.' She made threatening motions towards the instrument of many others' torture. 'I shall make a phone call.'

'No, don't do that.' Mr Butcher picked up his paper, folded it into the Peerage brass galleon rack and slipped his darned and stockinged feet into his Christmas slippers. 'Don't phone.' The phone bill nearly rivalled the national debt these days. 'I'll go out to them.'

'You just tell them to stop it. It's not decent, this is a respectable neighbourhood, or at least it was until . . .' With his wife's words coming hard upon his slippered heels, Mr Butcher hurried through the kitchen door and into the back-garden.

'Lads,' he called over the fence, 'lads, I say.'

Paul and Barry Geronimo ignored his calls. They wore the full tribal regalia of the Sioux Medicine Man, Buffalo Horns, beaded handings, buckskin loin-cloth, the whole bit. And they danced on regardless.

The dance was the Dance of Invocation to the Great Spirit. It would last for thirty-six hours, with only the occasional break for more Peyote or a trip to the toilet. During the latter stages of the dance Mrs Butcher would be carried, foaming at the mouth, into an ambulance and carted off for a period of intensive care at the 'special' hospital in Hanwell. Mr Butcher, for his part, would wave his wife the fondest of farewells, do a little dance of his own and take his *Angling Times* down to the Flying Swan, where he would do away with a month's housekeeping money with a reckless abandon unknown to him during the last twenty years.

But these things were for the future and so at present he leaned further over the fence and continued to call out imprecations to his dancing neighbours. It wasn't for himself, he told them, he had no objections. The sound of beating tom-toms was music to his ears. It was his wife, you see, she suffered with her nerves, she was not a well woman. 'Lads?' he called. 'Eh, lads?'

43

The evening turned into night and the night into the coming day. And it was another good one. The people of the borough prepared to go about their business without any particular interest. Tomorrow was coming, the great day of the games and they all had their free tickets. Well, almost all. Old Pete waved goodbye to a well-pleased punter and pecked his old lips at the bulging bundle of money-notes he now clutched in his grubby paw. 'Enjoy yourself,' he called. 'Come on the Bs!'

Norman had been up most of the night tinkering in his lock-up garage and the Hartnell Air Car was coming on a storm. He had definitely come up with a winner this time. As the dawn broke on the black horizon he yawned, scratched his bum, locked up the garage and trudged back to his shop for an hour or two's shut-eye.

Neville did not rise like a lark, more like a turkey on Chrismas Eve. He had a bad feeling that he could not put a name to. Something was very wrong in the borough, his nose told him so. But exactly what, that was anyone's guess. 'Probably nothing,' said the part-time barman as he lay in wait for Norman's paper-boy, pointed stick in hand.

Jim lay long in bed, nursing a hangover of extreme proportions. When the cabbage wine had gone he had done the unthinkable and broken into Omally's hut wherein lay a half-crate of five-year-old Scotch. 'If he is dead,' Pooley reasoned, 'he will forgive me, if alive then I can always apologize.' Such reasoning had got Pooley where he was today, wherever that might have been.

The Professor looked in at his door. 'Sleep on, sweet prince,' he said softly. 'You are going to need all the strength you have.'

Inspectre Hovis had had a rough night. It had all been in newspaper headlines again. Each announcing in big black letters the sacking in great disgrace of the great detective. His commander had given him twenty-four hours to wind up his investigations, arrest the master criminals and recover the gold. Hovis awoke in a cold sweat to the sound of his telephone ringing.

'It must be tonight,' said the voice of Hugo Rune. 'Be ready.'

Hovis replaced the receiver; his number was unlisted, he had not given it to Rune. 'Tonight,' said Inspectre Hovis, 'tonight.'

'And this is the London Olympics,' said the television set.

'And off you go,' said Neville, pulling the plug.

Young Master Robert danced before him in a youthful delirium. 'That is for the benefit of the punters,' he cried, 'switch it back on this minute.'

Neville gazed round at the deserted bar. 'Why don't you get stuffed?' he enquired under his breath.

'Your job's on the line here, pal,' bawled the bouncing boy. 'Get it back on, that's an order!'

'As you please.' Neville inserted the plug in its socket. He could have found a far better place to stick it. 'And to what do I owe this pleasure?' he asked.

'You useless skinny bastard,' said the Young Master. 'You and your paddy mate thought you'd got the better of me, didn't you? Thought you could wind me up, eh?'

'No offence meant,' said Neville, 'none taken, I hope.'

'Do you see this?' The boy waggled an official-looking document beneath the barman's nose. Neville did not like the smell of it. 'See it, do you?'

'I think I can just make it out.'

'Well, take a good long look.' He spread the paper out upon the bar-top. 'Peruse and inwardly digest.'

Neville cocked his good eye over it, firstly with disinterest, then with amazement, latterly with horror.

'You are selling the Swan?' he whispered in a creaking, breathless voice.

'Yes indeed. This dump never made a decent profit, most likely because your hand was always in the till.' Neville took the greatest exception to that remark, but he was dumb-struck. 'Well, now you can do the other thing. We're selling it off. The brewery is diversifying, expanding into other areas, leisure complexes, recreational facilities, the growth market of tomorrow. These old spit and sawdust pubs are a thing of the past. The Swan is finished, you are finished.'

Neville's brain swam in soup. 'I . . . you . . . what . . .'

'Watchamate, Neville,' said Jim Pooley who, upon rising from his pit, knew exactly where he should take his breakfast.

'Jim,' said Neville, 'Jim.'

Jim spied the barman's grave demeanour. 'Something up?' he asked, astute as ever.

'He's just about to get his coat on and go down to the Job Centre,' said Young Master Robert.

'He is what?' Jim looked at Neville. 'What is all this?'

'Not that it's any of your business,' said the boy, 'but this scrawny excuse for a barman is getting the elbow.'

'You are sacking Neville?' Pooley shook his head in order to wake up his brain. He surely hadn't had that much to drink last night. But perhaps he had, perhaps he was having the DTs. 'Sacking Neville?'

'He's out. The brewery is selling the Swan.'

'Selling it, for how much?'

The Young Master turned the property details, for such they were, about on the bar-top. 'Seventy-five-thousand pounds, more than it's worth.'

'And when does it go on the market?'

'End of the week. Interested, are you?' he asked sarcastically. 'You look like you could run to a sleeping-bag and a quart of cider.'

'There are no witnesses,' said Jim to Neville, 'shall I kill him now?'

Neville hung his drowning head. 'You know my feelings about murder in the bar.'

'This is a somewhat exceptional circumstance, we might waive the rule on this occasion.'

'You pair of no-marks, go screw yourselves.' With this parting shot, the Young Master stepped around the bar counter and drew himself a large Scotch. Grinning like a dead moggy, he took his drink off to a distant table.

Jim looked at the lost barman. 'Golly,' said he.

'The game would appear to be up,' the other replied. 'Have a pint on the house.' He took down a glass, stared through it wistfully and placed it beneath the beer spout.

'Seventy-five thousand,' said Jim. 'Not an unreasonable sum, all things considered.'

'Well beyond my means.' Neville pulled upon the pump handle and presented Jim with his pint. 'And yours also.'

Pooley smiled. 'Not necessarily. Have a little look at this, and take a large Scotch for yourself.' Jim dug out the now legendary betting slip and spread it before the barman.

Neville looked at the slip, he looked at Pooley, at the slip, at the Scotch optic, at Young Master Robert, at Pooley. Neville did a whole lot of looking. 'So it's true,' he said in a whisper, appropriate to the occasion. 'This is the genuine article. I heard talk, of course.'

Jim nodded. 'The real McCoy, as they say.'

'Congratulations.' Neville was unable to muster a lot of conviction. 'I mean, well done, I am happy for you.'

'Come on, Neville,' said Jim, 'it would be a great shame to see the Swan change hands or ever, God forbid, close down. It's kind of my past, I'd hate to see it go.'

'Then you . . .'

'Not me, Neville, you . . .'

'Me?'

'Of course.' Pooley grinned, a warm flush of pure pleasure crept all over his body. 'This is your pub, you should own it, it is your right.'

'My right?'

'I give it to you as a present,' said Jim, 'on the promise that you never change a thing, not a hair of the carpet, not a tatty old bar-stool, not a nothing. That you keep it as it always has been, for ever.'

'I promise.' Neville crossed his heart. 'You really mean it?'

Jim dug a leaky biro from his pocket and wrote upon a beer-mat, NEVILLE, IOU £75,000, signed Jim Pooley. 'I'll be around twelve tomorrow with the money, God willing.'

'God willing?'

'There are a few matters that the Professor and I have to sort out. Oh and Neville, you will take down that silly sign, won't you? I always liked The Flying Swan, just as it was.'

'Oh *yes*, Jim, oh yes indeed!' Neville clutched the beer-mat to his chest. 'Tell me once again that this is really true!'

'It is really true, and why shouldn't it be. Every man should be entitled to his "happy ever after", it's only fair.'

'Oh *yes*, Jim, yes, yes, *yes!*' Neville pulled the plug from the television set. 'Time, gentlemen, please,' he called. 'Come on now, gents, have you no homes to go to?'

The Young Master leapt up from his seat and stormed across the bar. 'Time, gentlemen, please? What's your game? Have you gone bloody mad?'

Neville took up the soda syphon and levelled it at the Young Tormentor. 'Should I, Jim? What do you think?'

'Oh. you should,' said Jim Pooley. 'You really should.'

The Brentford sun moved across the sky, became a projected image for the balance of the day, dipped towards the horizon and made off towards foreign parts. Night fell upon Brentford.

Neville sniffed at the air. It ponged like crazy, but a broad smile was on the face of the part-time barman as he tapped the top pocket which contained a certain signed beer-mat. 'We will ceremonially burn that,' he said, glancing at the ridiculous sign hanging outside the pub. 'Ye Flying Swan Inn, indeed!'

'I don't think I can go through with this,' said Neville's erstwhile saviour, 'I don't think my bottle is up to it.'

Professor Slocombe smiled. 'You will manage, Jim. My faith is in you.'

'But what exactly are you intending to do?'

'Well, I must confess that Kaleton has very much placed the cat amongst the pigeons by putting forward the start of the games. I am not as well prepared as I might like.'

'We are doomed,' said Jim.

'Nothing of the kind. The fact that he has done this suggests that he has doubts, fears that he will not succeed in his insane scheme.'

'But what of it all? You can't be certain he isn't telling the truth.'

'No, I cannot be certain, but the threat is palpable and we must make all efforts to confound his plans.'

'The Soul of the World,' said Pooley. 'Some adversary.'

'No, Jim, I will not have it. We now have the where-withal to enter the stadium, we shall see what we shall see.'

'Professor,' said Jim seriously, 'you have held your ceremonies here, upon home territory. I am not a fool, I know that here you are at your strongest, your most powerful. But up there, out in the open, on Kaleton's home pitch, we might not fare too well.'

'Jim, do you understand what is meant by the "balance of equipoise"?'

'Like Newton's third Law of Motion – every force has an equal and opposing force, that kind of thing?'

The Professor scratched at his chin. 'You are coming into your own, Jim.'

'I have no idea what you mean,' said Jim, although he knew that he did.

'Terrible forces rage and thrust, the universe is not a peaceful place, but the balance remains, one thing cancels out another. There is harmony. A universal plan exists.'

'God,' said Pooley, 'you are talking about God.'

'If you put it in those terms, then yes I am. Universal Spirit, call it what you will, for every yes there is a no, two sides to every question. Without an over-lying logic there would be just chaos.'

'I dare not think about the stars,' said Jim.

'That is one of the most profound statements I have ever heard.'

'It is?' Jim asked. 'I have others if you wish to compile a list.'

'Now is not the appropriate time, perhaps tomorrow.'

'If there is a tomorrow.'

'Aha!' said Professor Slocombe. 'Perk up, Jim, here comes Biggles.'

'What ho, chaps,' said Norman Hartnell, thrusting his head through the french windows.

'Watchamate, Norman, oh dear me.' Jim made a painful face as the scientific shopkeeper stepped into the study. He was clad in a leather helmet, replete with goggles. Little woolly explosions broke from his ancient RAF flying-jacket, a silk scarf hung about his neck.

'Wizard prang,' said Norman Hartnell.

Professor Slocombe glanced at Pooley. Jim made a brave face. In his left trouser pocket a nubbin of fluff resembled the ear-lobe of the legendary Jack Palance. 'Bear with him,' said Jim. 'He says it will work.'

'And so it will and does,' said Norman. 'Who's going up for a spin then?'

The Professor placed instruments of his enigmatic trade into a Gladstone bag and snapped it shut. 'If we are all ready,' said he.

Pooley took a deep breath. 'All right,' he said, 'let's go.'

The three men walked out into the night streets of Brentford. It seemed a clear night, peaceful, just like any other. But Jim and the Professor knew to the contrary. Something lurked, a big bad goblin, waiting to gobble them all up. Norman marched ahead with a jaunty step. He just doesn't know, thought Pooley, but what if he did? What if everyone knew? If things went badly tonight and all was as Kaleton had said, the world of men would soon be in for a dire shock. A rude awakening. All that was normal, all that was expected to be, all those plans and futures, gone up in a puff of smoke, or a bloody big bang. Or something. Jim had no idea what, but whatever it was was no laughing matter.

Norman led them to the row of lock-up garages, amidst many a furtive sideways glance to assure himself that they were not to be observed. Amidst many more furtive sideways glances, he took out his ring of keys and applied one to the lock. The up-and-over door did that very thing and Norman turned with a flurry of flapping arms. 'Your chariot awaits,' said he.

The Morris Minor stood, looking somewhat the worse for wear. Pooley and the Professor edged about it, peering and wondering. Strange metal carbuncles had been welded on to the bonnet and a battery of commandeered flue-pipes, vacuum cleaner nozzles and shower sprinklers projected from beneath the boot. Metal hawsers were strung across the car and secured to iron rings set into the concrete floor.

'Just to be on the safe side,' said Norman to the Professor, who was eyeing these with suspicion. 'Now if you two gentlemen would like to sit in the back? I need quite a bit of space in the cockpit.'

Pooley and the Professor climbed aboard and Norman swung back the driving seat after them. 'My, my,' said Jim, 'that looks quite busy.' The dashboard of the Morris now bore a distinct resemblance to that of Concorde, with rows of twinkling lights, gauges, dials, switches and the like.

'Mostly for show,' said Norman, 'for the Japanese market, they love all that kind of stuff.' He busied himself releasing the steel hawsers, then climbed into the pilot's seat and slammed the door. 'Safety belt on,' he said buckling himself up. 'Key ignition.' He did that very thing. 'Altitude check, zero, check, thrust plates activated, single interlock on, Normanite pods optimum factor six . . .'

'Norman,' said Professor Slocombe sternly, 'is all this pre-flight procedure actually necessary, or do I detect gamesmanship of the "bullshit-baffles-brains" variety at work here?'

'Safety first, Professor. As test pilot it is my responsibility . . .'

'Test pilot?' said Pooley. 'You mean that you haven't, er, actually flown this thing before?'

'There has to be a first time for everything.'

'Oh dear, oh dear, oh dear!' Pooley would have flapped his hands wildly and spun about in small circles, but he was firmly wedged in a very small space.

'Be quiet, Jim, have you no sense of adventure? Here we go, chocks away.' Norman revved the engine, engaged something which might have been a gear, but was probably far more complicated, and the car crept out of the lock-up and into the silent street. Norman placed his goggles over his eyes and leant back in his seat. 'Up and away.' The car bumped down the kerb and into the road, showing no immediate inclination towards taking flight. 'Up and away!' The Morris continued up the street, the only upping it seemed to have in mind. 'Bugger!' said Norman. 'There seems to be a slight technical hitch.'

Professor Slocombe examined his pocket watch. 'We do not have all night,' he said in a cold voice.

'We are a bit overloaded,' said the shopkeeper, 'but no problem, there's a couple of paving slabs in the boot for ballast, I'll just have them out.' He pulled the vehicle over to the side of the road, switched off the ignition, withdrew the key and climbed out of the car. Pooley noted that his safety belt had left with him, which was probably not an encouraging sign. The Professor was looking far from happy.

'Don't blame me,' said Jim, 'this is none of my doing.'

'Won't be a tick.' Norman threw open the boot and struggled with a paving slab. It tumbled into the road and fell with a loud crash. The mystery in that, thought Jim, is how it failed to do the obvious and land on his foot. 'Just one more and then we'll be off.'

Jim suddenly realized that he seemed to be sitting much further back in his seat than before and that the view through the windscreen seemed mostly sky. 'Norman!' he shouted, turning and tapping on the rear window, 'Norman!'

'Shan't be a tick, soon have it out.' This time the paving slab made a more muffled thump as it struck the ground.

'Oh, bloody hell,' wailed Norman hopping about on one foot, 'Oh, bloody . . .'

'Oh, no!' howled Jim. 'We're going up! Norman, do something!' The shopkeeper hopped and swore. All four wheels of the car were now floating free of the road. The Hartnell Air Car was taking to its avowed natural habitat. 'Norman!'

Suddenly realizing the gravity, or in this case non-gravity of the situation, Norman ceased his hopping and made a great leap at the rear bumper as it passed him by. He missed, floundered and toppled into the road where he lay drumming his fists and kicking his feet and crying 'Bugger,' over and over again.

The car began to gather speed and altitude in a direct mathematical ratio which was of interest to the Professor alone. 'I think you had better take over up front, Jim,' said the old man. 'I have never actually driven a car.'

'I have driven cars, but never one like this, and anyway . . .'

'Anyway, Jim?'

'Anyway, Norman has the ignition key.'

'Ah,' said Professor Slocombe. 'Now this presents us with certain unique difficulties. We would appear to be gathering momentum at a rate inversely proportionate to that of a falling object. Thus we are gaining mass. This is interesting, as Newtonic law would naturally presuppose an invalidation in the anti-gravitational properties of Normanite. One should cancel the other out.'

'Fascinating,' said Jim, growing sweaty about the brow.

'Yes,' said Professor Slocombe, 'but not good. If we continue to accelerate in this fashion, then I estimate we will strike the underside of the stadium,' he did a rapid mental calculation, 'in approximately fifty-five seconds, give or take. I would consider impact to be a somewhat messy affair doubtless culminating in our extinction.'

Pooley got the message without a further telling of it. He shinned over the driver's seat and began to tear at the dashboard. 'A bit of wire would be your man, Professor.'

'Ah yes, a "hot wire" I believe it's called, a sound idea.'

The Professor reached into a rip in the seat-back in front of him and with a display of remarkable strength, ripped out a length of rusty spring. 'Here you are, Jim, this should be the very thing.'

Pooley snatched the spring from the outstretched hand and delved into the dashboard. 'How much time?'

'Thirty seconds, probably less.'

Jim jiggled the spring and thrummed the accelerator pedal. And cursed a lot. Norman had done a thorough job in rewiring the car, he couldn't raise a spark. 'It doesn't work,' cried Jim, 'it doesn't work!'

'A pity,' said Professor Slocombe. 'It was a brave try though.'

The car sped upwards, gaining speed. Far below, Norman watched it receding into the sky. He counted down the seconds beneath his breath and closed his eyes. If it was of any interest to anyone, other than those personally involved in the impending disaster, his mental calculations tallied exactly with those of the Professor.

A small task-force of hand-picked officers crept along the Kew Road. Before them, two figures stalked from shadow to shadow, muttering to one another in urgent muted tones. One was lean and angular and had taken no sustenance whatever this day, the other was broad and bulbous and had only recently pushed his chopsticks aside after a twelve-course belly-buster.

'As Commanding Officer,' said Inspectre Hovis, 'I dictate the naming of names. This is Operation Sherringford and history will know us as Hovis's Heroes.'

'Phooey!' the other replied. 'As overall adviser on special attachment to the unit, I demand that this venture be called Operation Hugo, and we, Rune's Raiders.'

'I have no intention of arguing with you, Rune.'

'Nor, I, you. Rune's Raiders, or I go home.'

'All right, but it's Operation Sherringford.'

'Ludicrous! Must I forever pander to your inflated ego?'

The two continued their dispute as they neared the gasometer. Behind them the team of five officers slunk along. To them this was Operation Laurel and Hardy and they were the Lost Patrol.

'All right, Rune,' whispered Hovis, as the two of them skulked in the shadows. 'We're getting close now, what is the plan?'

'Plan?' asked Hugo Rune.

'*Plan*, man, you do have one, don't you?'

'Do you mean the plan for Operation Hugo, or that other one?'

Hovis muttered beneath his breath, no matter what the outcome of this operation was, he had determined that Rune's immediate future was going to be subject to the pleasure of Her Majesty. 'The plan.'

'Yes?'

'Operation Hugo,' spat Inspectre Hovis.

'Good,' said Rune. 'Now follow me.' He led Hovis on and the Inspectre beckoned the task-force to follow.

Rune's Raiders skirted the wire fence. It towered above them menacingly; tiny blue sparkles of electrical energy fizzed and popped about its upper regions saying, 'Just you try it.'

'I hope you know what you're doing,' Hovis growled as the field of static set the Inspectre's whitened pelt on end.

Rune strode forcefully on ahead in case Hovis spotted the hopeless look on his face. If he couldn't come up with a means of entry soon he was going to have to do a runner. The fence was endless, threatening. He plodded on, casting spells in every direction. Suddenly he halted in his tracks and a broad smile broke out upon his broad face. 'There,' said be, in a hushed voice.

Hovis collided with Rune's ample rear end. 'What?' he asked.

'There.'

Hovis followed the direction of the mystic's gaze. 'Well now, Rune, I underestimated you.' Not five yards ahead a ragged opening gaped in the wire. 'Congratulations,' said Inspectre Hovis. 'This way, men, and hurry.'

Rune smiled and shrugged modestly. 'I am a man of my word,' said he, 'I am Rune whose power is infinite, whose knowledge absolute.' I wonder how that got there, he wondered.

The Hartnell Air Car dipped away from the stadium with inches to spare and hurtled off into the night sky.

'Now *that* was close.' Jim Pooley gripped the wheel, knuckles suitably white, face a likewise hue.

The Professor's head appeared above the passenger seat. 'Exactly how did you do that?' he asked.

'There was a spare ignition key taped under the dash,' said Jim. 'That was handy, eh?'

'Handy is not the word I would use, Jim.'

'Do you ever feel, Professor . . .' Jim glanced back over his shoulder.

'That a power greater than ourselves is in control of our destinies?' the old man asked.

'Something like that.'

'It is a possibility the present circumstances might add weight to. You most definitely have a guardian angel, Jim.'

'That's a comforting thought.' Jim settled himself back behind the wheel.

The ancient scholar leant back in his seat. The teleportation of the key from Norman's ring to Pooley's hand had been a relatively simple matter, but it wouldn't do to tell the lad that. 'Drive on, Jim,' he told the pilot. 'Bring us about over the stadium.'

'I'll do my very best.' Jim had never been much of a driver, but whatever skills he might possess as a pilot were presently untried. 'Cor, look at that,' he said.

Beneath them the stadium spread, acre upon acre, huge beyond imagination. A thing to inspire wonder and awe, if not a good deal more. Enclosed by the concentric circles of the stands, seating for a million people, so it seemed, the arena lay beneath a vast dome which shimmered in the moonlight. Towards the five star-points, the Olympic villages rose like small towns. A futuristic sky-scape of tall towers, cylinders, domes and pyramids with raised walkways, practice-tracks, thoroughfares and stairways strung between them. The panorama was fantastic, beyond belief, beyond possibility. It beggared description.

'It's a corker!' said Pooley, very much impressed. 'Big Boda this one.'

'I have never seen the like,' said Professor Slocombe, staring with almost equal wonder, 'and I have been there and back again, as the saying goes.'

Pooley nodded thoughtfully, as was often his way when lost for words. At length he asked, 'What are those, Professor?'

The sage followed the direction of Pooley's pointing finger. 'Both hands on the wheel, please,' he said. 'What "those" do you mean?'

'Those thoses.' Jim's attention had become drawn to the ranks of tall pylons surmounted by silvered discs which sprouted variously about the star-points like fields of high-tech mushrooms.

'The solar cells I should suppose, Jim. They absorb the sunlight and project it from similar pads beneath the stadium, to simulate sky, provide light and create the visual camouflage.'

'Thank you,' said Pooley. 'And so where would you like me to park, as it were?' Professor Slocombe delved into his Gladstone bag and brought out a blueprint of the stadium. Jim glanced back over his shoulder. 'And how did you come by that, might I ask?'

'I stole it,' said the Professor in all candour. 'I was far from certain that the television images told the whole truth about the stadium. I had this lifted from the offices of a certain Covent Garden design studio.'

Pooley grinned and flew the car in sweeping circles above the stadium, humming gently to himself. His thoughts at present were unsettled as he had no idea what might lie ahead. That he was going to buy one of these cars when he came into the big money was a certainty. As for now, getting through the night was rather high on the list of priorities. Another confrontation with Kaleton was in the offing and Jim felt almost comforted by the prospect. That was, he supposed, because his life lacked direction. That he should become Kaleton's Nemesis, even if he pegged out in the process, lent a temporary purpose to an otherwise pointless existence. You will pay, said Jim to himself.

I do hope so, thought Professor Slocombe as he studied the blueprint without aid of a torch. 'We will go down,' he told Jim, 'at the southern tip, above the river, camp of the home team. I think we will avoid the Russian and American sectors, don't want an international incident now, do we?'

Jim took his bearings. 'Ah yes,' he said. 'The river, yes, I've got it, but where exactly – and how?' he added as an afterthought.

'Yes, how?' Professor Slocombe folded the blueprint and peered out of the rear window. 'There are heliports I see, but they have been constructed for vertical descent. There are no runways, and there is the matter of what will happen when you switch off the engine.'

'Oh yes?'

'Well, we'll float up into the air again, won't we?'

'Oh yes, I think the Hartnell Air Car is going to require a few more weeks on the drawing-board. So what are we going to do, Professor, bale out?'

'I'm not keen. Let us go down as slowly as we can, steer it around this way.'

Jim did as he was bid. They cruised down towards the camp of the home team, passing amongst the towers and pyramids, pinnacles and obelisks. At closer quarters it all became even more fantastic and unbelievable, a science-fiction landscape.

'How slowly can we go?' asked the Professor.

Pooley changed down and applied the brakes. 'Quite slowly, as it happens. It's quite clever this really, isn't it?'

'The shopkeeper certainly keeps us guessing. Take us in straight ahead.' The car dropped gently down from the sky and although it continued to wobble uncertainly, Jim did an admirable job in controlling it.

'I have an idea,' said the Professor. 'Can you take it in there?' He pointed to where a broad walkway disappeared into the entrance hall of one of the curious buildings.

'I'm not Luke Skywalker,' said Jim, 'but the force is with us, I suppose.'

'Oh yes, indubitably, Jim.'

'Right then.' Pooley eased back on the throttle and in fits and starts they approached the opening. 'Please extinguish your cigarettes and fasten your seat-belts.'

'Now is hardly the moment for levity. As soon as we are into the entrance hall, switch off the engine.'

Jim was suddenly more doubtful than ever. 'But we will float up again surely?'

'And lodge under the entrance arch.'

That, thought Jim, was as iffy a proposition as any he had yet known. 'In for a penny then.' The car bumped down on to the walkway with a squeal of tyres, bounced up again uncontrollably, the engine faltered and made coughing sounds. Jim gripped the wheel. 'We're going to crash.'

'Hold on tight, Jim. *Now!*' Pooley slammed on the brakes, tore the key from the ignition and made his personal recommendations to his Maker. The car ground along a side wall raising a stream of sparks and mangling metal, swerved, stopped dead and almost at once began to rise. There was a sickening crunch as it struck the top of the entrance hall. And then, a blessed silence. 'Bravo, Jim, you did it!'

'I did?' Pooley's face appeared over the wheel, nose crooked, a facsimile of the now legendary Chad. 'I did do it, I really did.'

'Right, now we have wasted more than enough time – to work.'

'Right,' said Inspectre Hovis, 'we have wasted more than enough time.' Rune's Raiders stood in a dubious huddle before the great gasometer, fingering an arsenal of weaponry they were certainly unqualified even to handle, let alone raise in anger. Hovis cocked his old service revolver. 'Now, Rune,' he said. 'Open it up, there's a good fellow.'

'Open it up,' Rune slowly remouthed the Inspectre's words, 'open it up.'

'We have the element of surprise to our favour.' Hovis turned to address the nervous constables. 'Now, gentlemen, I do not want a bloodbath on my hands. We do not know how many of them there are in there. No-one, and I mean no-one, shoots anyone until I give the order, do I make myself understood?' The boot-blackened faces bobbed up and down in the darkness. Constable Meek straightened his Rambo-style headband and wondered which end of his Kalashnikov was the killing end. 'OK, Rune, take us in.'

'Yes indeed,' said the Perfect Master, 'indeed yes. Take us in, now let me see . . .'

'Now let me see.' Professor Slocombe studied the blueprint. He and Pooley stood within the shadow of the entrance hall; above them the Hartnell Air Car roosted quietly. 'We go this way, Jim. Now try to keep your bearings, we may have to return at some speed.'

Pooley tucked the car's ignition key safely away in his top pocket. 'Exactly where are we going to?' he asked.

'To the very heart, Jim, the very hub. The core which

lies at the centre of the arena, this area.' He pointed to the blueprint.

'But there's nothing there but a black spot.'

'Indeed.' The Professor nodded gravely. 'This way now, follow me.'

The two men passed between the titanic structures. Their entire design and geometry was strange, unnatural, alien. Jim ran his hand along a handrail and speedily withdrew it. 'It hums,' he said, 'it vibrates.'

'It knows we are here.'

Jim shuddered. 'And what's it all made of, Professor? This isn't metal or glass, what is it?'

'Horn, bone, chitin, it is organic,' said the sage. 'I don't think this stadium was built, in the true sense of the word. I think it was grown.'

'Then it is . . .' the word did not come easily to Pooley's lips, ' . . . alive?'

'Not quite, it is dormant, moribund, if you like, it sleeps.'

'I do not like.' Jim tottered along behind the Professor, who moved with certain, long strides. 'What when it wakes?'

'That, my dear Jim, is what we are here to prevent. We must not allow Kaleton to activate it, animate it, whatever you will.'

'This big shot of his that will ring out across the universe?'

'The very same. A shot of energy, some activating chemical agent, or pre-programmed codification. Whatever it might be we must prevent it.'

'It's ever so quiet,' said Jim. 'There must be thousands of people up here, how come we haven't seen anybody?'

'I would suggest the use of a soporific gas, introduced into the air-conditioning at night to prevent any of the athletes wandering. We will not enter the dormitories to find out. Now wait.'

Jim looked up, somehow they had now entered the great arena. As usual Jim had been doing too much talking and not enough paying attention. He was lost, and now he was speechless. A low gasp arose simultaneously from two throats. They had entered a world of dream. Above them spread the weather-dome but from below it did not look like a glass canopy, more like a transparent membrane, breathing gently. And the arena itself, its scale was daunting, impossible to take in at a single viewing. The seating rose in great rings, rank upon rank, tier upon tier about a *circus maximus* built for Titans. The scope and symmetry was fearsome, yet it was fascinating.

'Oh indeed,' said Professor Slocombe. 'Oh yes, indeed.'

'Why?' Pooley asked. 'Why do all this if it is only meant to destroy?'

'It can destroy a million people here at a single go. But the whole point is that the entire world will be watching. More people watch the start of the games than any other single event, they would have to have something to look at.'

'It is inhuman, all too big, no human architect was a part of this.'

'No, Jim, it is as if all previous architecture was just a dry run for this. Baalbek, the pyramids, the temples of the Incas, the great cathedrals, all leading towards,' he gestured to include all that he could, 'a temple for the gods.'

Jim's head swam. 'You are talking about religion again.'

'Not religion. An ideology perhaps, a greater under-standing, a greater knowledge, but not one born of men. Worship of his gods has driven man to his most abomin-able of crimes, but also to his greatest of achievements. But this is not the work of man, but that of a higher order of being.'

'Esoterica was never my strong point, but this is the work of the devil.'

'It is all here, Jim, a masterplan, a great formula, the culmination of a hundred thousand years of accumulated thought and knowledge.'

'Then we are finished, Kaleton told the truth. Those that

would walk with the gods require somewhat superior footwear. Let's go out now, Professor, warn the army or something, take our chances on the ground.'

'No, Jim.' The Professor held up his hand. 'All this can act for good as well as for evil. We can save the games, save mankind. This is the product of High Magick. Knowledge is neither good nor evil, it is in how it is applied.'

'As ever you have grasped but a tiny morsel of reality,' came a voice from everywhere and nowhere. 'You think to construct a map of the universe, having nothing but the plan of your own backyard.' Pooley turned about in circles. The Professor stared into space. 'Proud little man,' the voice continued, 'puffed up with your own importance, creating God in your own image.'

'I am unable to see you,' said the Professor. 'Will you show yourself or must I call out to you in the darkness?' The air buzzed with an unnatural electricity.

'Proud little man,' said the voice.

'Do you fear me so much that you dare not show yourself?'

'Fear is a human concept, Professor.'

'As is love. But you would know nothing of that.'

'Love, fear, hatred, all masks and blinkers, walls of delusion hiding a higher reality.'

Pooley strained his eyes to see something, anything, but the stadium swept away in all directions, fading into hazy perspectives. The owner or owners of the voice remained hidden to view. Jim shivered. There was a terrible B-movie banality about Kaleton's conversation. One which, to Jim's extensive knowledge of the genre, generally terminated in such phrases as 'so die, puny earthling,' or something of a similarly unpleasant ilk.

'What do you want here, Professor? Have you come to plead for your precious humanity? Or perhaps for yourself alone?'

'On the contrary, I have come to issue you a challenge. There are old scores to be settled.'

'Old scores? I am intrigued.' The voice came close at

Pooley's elbow and the lad leapt back, keeping his failing bladder in check. Kaleton was sitting not two yards away in one of the rear stadium seats. Near enough to leap upon and kill, thought Jim, although he didn't feel personally up to the challenge. 'I thought perhaps you came in peace for all mankind.' The mocking tone in Kaleton's death-rattle voice grated on Jim's nerves, but the Professor seemed oblivious to it.

'Hardly that, Kaleton. I come to exact retribution. To punish you for your crimes and to finish a job which should have been finished a long time ago.'

Laughter exploded from Kaleton's hideous face and the stench of his breath reached Jim, curling his nostrils and crossing his eyes. 'And how do you mean to go about it? You are in my world now, I can smash you whenever I choose.'

'Perhaps and perhaps not, but hardly a victory upon a grand scale. I propose a far more noble scheme and one which I think might appeal to your sense of grandiosity as well as of justice.'

'Speak on.'

'I propose a battle of champions, to be held here and now.'

'Champions, battle, what is all this?'

'The protagonists are well known to each of us, light against darkness, good against evil, your man against mine.'

'Men? What men?'

'The sleeping Kings of Brentford!' said Professor Slocombe.

'What?' Kaleton's head shrank into his shoulders, his chest bulging out to receive it, then he sprang from his seat to land upon all-fours. 'You know of this?'

'Of the old battle, of the sanctuary, yes I know.'

Kaleton bounced and shook. Low howls and guttural sounds broke from his twisted mouth. Jim wondered where the lavs were. With a shudder, Kaleton rose once more upon two feet. He stared at the Professor, trembling and shaking. 'There was a battle once,' he whispered, 'long, long ago, when your people and mine fought, but then . . .'

'But then you were defeated.'

'Defeated, never! Look where you stand, Professor, does this look like defeat to you?'

'Then you have nothing to fear, you may enjoy your sweet revenge.' With that the Professor turned upon his heel and strode off down the long walkway towards the arena. 'This is my challenge, Kaleton. Take it if you dare.'

Jim watched Kaleton. He was perched upon his crooked heels, frozen as if lost in thought. In reminiscence, perhaps? The Professor strode on. Jim glanced down, the Gladstone bag was there at his feet. The old man had gone off without it. In his recklessness he had surely left himself undefended. Jim was moved to take action, but lacked the wherewithal. Should he open the bag? Chuck the whole lot at Kaleton? Or simply run like mad?

Without warning Kaleton shot past him, bowling him from his feet. Jim felt that hideous strength, the raw elemental power. It fairly put the wind up him. Climbing into the nearest seat Jim flopped, powerless to do bugger all except look on.

Moving with a fearsome energy Kaleton bounded down the walkway after the Professor. 'Raise your warriors!' he crowed. 'Raise your dead king, your champion! This time, the reckoning will be swift and bloody.'

Pooley sank into his seat and sought his hip-flask. And now Professor Slocombe was standing upon the artificial turf of the sports ground, arms raised towards the sky. Kaleton bounded about him like a monstrous hound, calling insults and provocations. And light was growing in the arena. A curious glow illuminated the two tiny figures, foreshortened to Jim's fearful gaze. Pooley popped the cork from the hip flask. 'I wonder what the poor people are doing tonight,' he wondered.

Professor Slocombe mouthed the syllables of an ancient spell:

> ' "And good King Bran had a battle axe
> King Balin a mighty sword
> And the warrior Kings rode out to war
> And they met at the river's ford." '

And there came, as sounds and as movements, a great restlessness within the very bowels of the earth, a rumbling beneath the streets of Brentford. Old Pete's dog Chips set up a plaintive howling which went unheard by his snoring master, the Hartnell Hear-it-all having been switched off for the night. At the pumping station, the mighty beam engine gasped in a lost Victorian voice. And beneath the water-tower something stirred. Beneath that tower of stone, forces long slumbering came into wakefulness. A sound, a call, an awakening.

Outside the teepee at the bottom of the garden, two braves ceased their dance and stood sweating beneath the stars. Their faces shone. 'And now it begins,' said Paul Geronimo, 'the dance is over, the great old ones return, now it begins.'

And so did it begin. From behind the yellow varnish of old portraits unviewed for a century in council cellars, faces gazed forth, eyes blinked open. Musty tomes and librams heaved, pages turned. From out the coffers of the museum, dust-dry hands reached up to take musty weapons, the rotting halberds, the lances and war-swords. Memories unstirred for a millennium, memories hidden in old walls and crumbling fallen waterfronts, in grassy mounds, in dolmens, long barrows, hill-forts, earthworks and holy groves. Memories. And the warriors beyond memory awakened, returned. The warriors arose from their unmarked graves.

And through the walls and floors, the stairwells and window casements from out of the worn flagstones and cobbled courts, the warriors breathed life. And up through the tarmac which smothered the old thoroughfares and swallowed up the ground of Brentford where once stretched dew-dappled hedgerows and corn-fields mellow with golden harvest reaching out to the gently flowing Thames, came Bran.

Bran. Bran the brave and just, the slayer of men. Bran with that great head of his, which still spoke on long years after it had been parted from his body. Bran with those great arms of his, which had broken men and cradled babies. Bran with his wild blue eyes, and even wilder hair-do. Bran the blessed. Bran of old England. King Bran of Brentford.

It was definitely him! King Bran's great hand closed upon the shaft of his battle-axe, drawing it from its museum case. He raised it to the heavens. Stretched up his arms, those arms of his with their steely thews, their cords of muscle, their knotted, tightened sinew. Raised up that great head of his, with its wild blue eyes, sweeping whiskers and quite improbable coiffure. And he called with a cry of triumph, 'To arms! To arms!'

Rune's Raiders bumbled about in the shadow of the gasometer as a seismic tremor rumbled beneath their feet.

'Something is occurring,' said Inspectre Hovis. 'Rune, open the door or I will not answer for my actions.' He turned his pistol upon the mystic. 'Make haste now or it will be the worst for you.'

Rune threw up his arms and in desperation addressed the gasometer. 'Open, Sesame!' he cried. 'Open . . . Sesame!'

Inspectre Hovis raised his pistol. 'You bloody pillock!' he swore.

'And good King Bran had a snow-white steed.' Now the warriors were mounting up their horses. Steeds reformed from the dust of ages, reanimated by the words of the Professor's calling. And the horsemen moved out towards the stadium, towards the new lair of their ancient enemy. A dusty legion passing through a dreamworld, at once foreign, yet oddly familiar. And they were of heroic stock, sprung from that mould long broken, long crumbled into nothingness. These Knights of old England, of that world of forests and dragons, of honour and of noble deeds. Holy quests. And the dust fell away from their armour, from the dry, leather harnessings, from those regal velvets. And the golden crown of kingship, with its broken emblem, rested upon the brow of Bran. The once and future King.

And the Kinsmen and the men-at-arms, the Knights Royal, breathed in the new air, the new unnatural air, laden with strange essences, flavours of this crude, uncertain century. And they rode on without fear. The boys were back in town!

High in the stadium, Pooley gulped Scotch and wondered what was on the go. The Professor stood alone at the very centre of the stadium, but Kaleton was nowhere to be seen. The stadium was silent as the very grave and had just about as much to recommend it. For in the stillness there was something very bad indeed.

'By the pricking of my thumbs something wicked this way comes,' said Jim. And he wasn't far wrong, for now came a chill wind and the sounds of distant thunder. Pooley gazed up towards the weatherdome, but it had completely dissolved away. The stadium was now open to the sky. Lightning troubled an ever-blackening firmament and the stars came and went as trailers of cloud drew across them like darting swords. 'Looks like rain,' said Jim 'which would just about be my luck at present.'

And then Jim saw it. The cruel dark shape cutting through the midnight sky. The great, crooked wings sweeping the air. The long narrow head, the trailing feet, eagle-taloned, lion-clawed. The thin, barbed tail streaming out behind. 'The Griffin!' Pooley ducked down into his seat. Further praying seemed out of the question, God was no doubt sick of the sound of Jim's voice. Pooley's nose came into close proximity with the Gladstone bag. *'The*

Professor!' Jim sprang up, scanned the arena, in search of the sage . . . the old man had vanished. 'Oh dear,' said Jim, 'oh dear, oh dear, *oh dear!'*

And now he could hear the sounds of the flapping wings and further shapes filled the sky. The legion of King Balin rode the sky above Brentford. The legion of the forever night, raised by the force-words of the arch-fiend Kaleton. And at the van upon that most terrible of beasts, rode Balin. 'Balin of the black hood. Balin whose eye was night.' Balin whose sword blade was the length of a man, although considerably narrower in width. King Balin of the iron tooth, the bronze cheek, the ferrous-metal jaw. Balin, the all-round bad lot. King Balin led his evil horde down towards the army of his enemy.

'I am going to count to five and then I am going to shoot your head off,' said Inspectre Hovis. 'I should like to say that there is nothing personal in this, but I would not lie to a condemned man.'

'Abracadabra Shillamalacca! Come out, come out, whoever you are!' cried Hugo Rune.

'One,' said Hovis, 'and I mean it.'

'Shazam!' cried Rune. 'Higgledy-piggledy, my fat hen . . .'

'Two, three . . .'

'I'll huff and I'll puff . . .'

'Four, fi . . .'

'Look there, sir!' shouted Constable Meek. 'Up there, up in the sky!'

'Birds?' said Hovis, squinting up. 'No, not birds, bats! No! *Bloody hell!'*

'And there, sir, who's that?'

Hovis peered about, following the constables wavering digit. On one of the high catwalks of the gasometer a solitary figure was edging along, carrying what looked to be a couple of heavy suitcases. 'What's going on here?' Hovis demanded. 'I demand an explanation!'

'What's he doing, sir?' The solitary figure was lowering

one of the suitcases down the side of the gasometer on a length of rope.

'Is this your doing, Rune? Rune, come back! Stop that man, Constable!'

'Blimey,' said Meek. 'And will you look at that lot!'

Along the Kew Road came the army of King Bran, riding now at the gallop. The war-horses heaved and snorted, their hooves raising sparks from the tarmac. The riders turned their noble faces towards the sky and raised their swords. King Bran ran a tail-comb through his gorgeous locks and urged on his charger. 'Giddy up, Dobbin!' he cried. 'Good boy there, gee up!'

Constable John Harney brought down Hugo Rune with a spectacular rugby tackle. 'Gotcha!' said he, quoting the now legendary headline from the *Sun*. It may not have been much, but considering it was all he was going to get to say in the entire book, at least it was something.

Hovis leapt up and down. 'Arrest everybody!' he cried. 'Get on the walkie-talkie, Meek. I want the SPG, the SAS, the reserves, the bloody Boys Brigade, get them all here!'

'Yes, sir.' Meek whipped out his walkie-talkie. 'Calling all cars,' he said in his finest Broderick Crawford, 'calling all cars.'

'Please, sir, about this suitcase?'

'What suitcase, what, Reekie?'

'This suitcase, sir.' Constable Reekie pointed to the thing which now dangled a few feet above his head.

'Arrest it, boy! Arrest that holidaymaker. That case is probably full of drugs.'

'It's ticking rather loudly, sir.'

'Ticking? Oh my God!'

'Duck, you suckers!' called a voice from above. 'Hit the deck!'

The army of King Bran reached the Arts Centre. From out the night sky their mortal enemies fell upon them. The dark creatures dropped down upon the horsemen, beaks snapping, claws crooked to kill. The legions of darkness led by their evil lord. Balin the bad. Balin with his brow of burnished copper. Balin with his nose of black lead, his navel of tungsten carbide and a rare alloy with a complicated chemical figure.

'No prisoners,' cried Balin. 'Spare not a filling, not a spectacle-frame, kill them all, kill, kill, kill!'

'Kill, kill, kill!' echoed his men, spurring down their nightmare steeds.

'God for Harry!' cried King Bran.

Tic-Toc-Tic-Toc went a certain suitcase.

Professor Slocombe laid a hand upon Pooley's shoulder. 'I think I have him distracted,' he told the flinching, cowering Jim. 'We must get to work.'

'All work and no play,' said Jim painfully. 'The hours in this job suck.'

'But the pay is good. Come, Jim, bring the bag, we must penetrate to the heart of the stadium.'

'What's going on downstairs?' Pooley asked, gesturing in a downwards direction. 'I saw all these flying things and now it sounds like a terrible punch-up.'

'It is only just the beginning, come on.'

'Not quite so fast.' Kaleton rose up before them. 'Don't take another step.'

'Help is on the way, sir.' Constable Meek crawled over to Inspectre Hovis. 'A Commander West is coming over in person. He's bringing a special task-force. He seemed terribly upset, sir, do you know him?'

Hovis buried his face in the ground and thrashed about with his legs. '*You're all under arrest!*' he foamed.

Tic-Toc-Tic-Toc-Tic-Toc went the suitcase.

'And now the end is near and you must face the final curtain,' said Kaleton. 'Tomorrow belongs to me, you are yesterday once more.'

'I'll name that tune,' said Jim.

'So die, puny earthlings!' Kaleton raised his crooked arms.

'Don't do it! Stay back!' shouted the Professor. 'Jim, the bag.'

Jim tossed the Gladstone to the old man. It sailed through the air and departed into the darkness. 'Sorry,' said Jim. 'I suppose that means we're in trouble.'

'You could say that.'

Tongues of fire grew from Kaleton's fingers, leapt into the sky, veered down towards the two men.

The armies of Bran and Balin locked in titanic conflict the length of the Ealing Road. Big and bad was the fighting, great and terrible the hewing, the war cries, the blood and the torment. There was cleaving and cutting, hacking and stabbing.

Old Pete turned in his sleep. 'Get down, Chips,' he muttered.

'And so die!' called Kaleton as he stood amidst the raining fire.

'I arrest myself in the name of the law,' said Inspectre Hovis.

Tic-Toc and finally Kaboom!!! said the dangling suitcase.

The gasometer erupted in a burst of crimson flame. The figure on the catwalk shinned up another staircase clutching his single suitcase. Torrents of debris filled the air and a cloud of golden dust.

In the stadium Kaleton shook and shivered, the flames about him guttered and died. 'You have done this, you have tricked me. The tower, the sanctuary!'

'I don't think I'll ever understand that man,' said Jim.

'Run for your life, Jim,' said the Professor.

'Now that I do understand.' Jim took to his heels.

Kaleton staggered down the walkway towards the gaming ground. 'The sanctuary, the wall is breached.'

'Blimey,' said Constable Meek emerging from a pile of golden debris. 'Look in there.'

Hovis raised his charred head and gazed at the gas-ometer. A great hole yawned in its side and from within glowed . . . 'Gold!' cried the Inspectre. 'It's full of gold!' Gold spilled from the ragged opening, but it was not just the gold from the robbery. This was a king's ransom, a god's ransom, the gold of centuries, the very gold of the gods, 'The Gryphon's golden hoard'.

'I get one per cent,' said Hugo Rune, 'and don't forget that.'

'God for Harry.' King Bran swung his mighty battle-axe taking several heads from as many shoulders. 'Forward men, the battle is ours!' The horsemen moved onward, carrying the fight to the very doorway of Ye Flying Swan Inn.

'Same old sign,' said Bran. 'A cup of mead later, I think.'

Upstairs Neville pulled a pillow over his head. 'Another bloody party,' he mumbled, snuggling down. 'Now where was I? Oh yes, Alison, the appliance.'

Kaleton bounded over the artificial turf. 'The sanctuary, the sanctuary.' Charles Laughton wasn't in it.

The figure on the high catwalk faced another stairway. Below him the battle raged, cruel and bloody. Other tiny figures danced before the torn opening, delving into the golden hoard.

From the direction of the Brentford Half Acre came the scream of police sirens as a convoy of armoured vehicles moved into view.

The solitary figure climbed up and up, labouring beneath the weight of his suitcase. The stairways led ever upwards, towards heaven – the gasometer was never this high – yet it was. Upwards and ever upwards.

'I think I'm lost,' said Jim Pooley, 'in fact I know I am.'

'Well done, Jim.'

'Now listen.' Pooley turned upon the Professor. 'None

of this is my doing, I don't see why I should carry the can.'

'Or the Gladstone?'

'You're the magician, wave the magic wand or something.'

'Really, Jim.'

'Well,' said Pooley, all sulks. 'I got us up here and a fine waste of time it's been. The least you can do is get us down.'

'There is a way, I think,' said the Professor, 'follow me.'

'My God!' said Commander West as the armoured convoy turned into the Ealing Road and slewed to a halt amidst the holocaust. 'Heavy riot gear, CS gas, shields, batons.'

'Rubber bullets,' the driver suggested.

'Rubber bullets.'

'Riot shields, sir?'

'I said that.'

'Helmets then.'

'Call for more reinforcements. Get on the blower, Briant. There's a full-scale war going on here. Good Godfrey, that's a head on the bonnet, isn't it?'

'Looks like a Viking head, sir.'

'No, more like a Saxon.'

'Or a Celt, sir.'

'Dammit, Briant! I don't give a shit about its nationality, get the bloody thing off my bonnet!'

Constable Briant stared out through the security grille at the carnage beyond. 'I'm a bit doubtful about going out there, sir.'

'You'll be on a bloody charge, constable.'

'Ten-four, sir.'

'Down this way,' said Professor Slocombe.

'It doesn't smell good,' said Jim.

'Just follow me.'

'Arrest all this gold. Meek, I saw you filling your pockets. Rune, put that back.'

'One per cent, Hovis, I'll take it now.'

274

'No you bloody won't. Meek, I'm warning you. Reekie, I don't know where you got that wheelbarrow but . . .'

The figure on the high catwalk gasped breathlessly; the stairways led up forever. But now he knew that at the top, at the top . . . he faced another stairway and prepared to climb. But his way was blocked.

'You,' said Kaleton. 'You did this? But you're . . .'

'Dead?' said John Omally, for it was no other man. 'I all but was. Your filthy creatures damn near had me in pieces. But I survived, I crawled away and I hid out. And I watched you and now I'm going to kill you. Where is my girl-friend, what have you done with her, you bastard?'

'You're a hard man to kill,' said Kaleton. 'However.'

Omally shifted his suitcase from hand to hand. 'Where is Jennifer?'

'She's nice and safe, would you like to join her? Shall I call Jennifer that you might see her one more time, kiss those soft red lips? She's so close you could reach out and touch her.'

'In here?' Omally's free hand reached to the gasometer, but an icy blast tore it away, numb and bleeding.

'No,' said Kaleton, 'she's in here,' he pointed to his mouth, 'and now you can come inside.'

'You've killed her, you . . . whatever you are.'

'Whatever I am. Who do you think I am?'

'You are Choronzon,' said Professor Slocombe, 'lord of all anarchy, destroyer. You are Choronzon.'

Kaleton spun about. Above him on a higher catwalk stood Pooley and the Professor. Jim's eyes bulged, filled with tears. 'John,' he gasped, 'John, is that you?'

'Watchamate, Jim,' said that very man.

'Blessed be,' said Jim Pooley.

'I am the Soul of the World,' cried Kaleton in many voices and many tongues, 'I am Choronzon, I am Baal, I am Kali, I am Shiva. I am all that has gone before and all that is yet to come. Ruination lies in my hands, ruination for you and your kind. You dirt, you worms. Your time is at hand.'

'Where's my girlfriend?'

'My future wife?' asked Jim. 'He's got her?'

'I am yesterday and tomorrow, Alpha and Omega. You are finished.' Kaleton twisted, distorted, the hideous mouth opened wider, swelled as if to encompass everything, the borough, the earth, the universe, the whole damn lot.

The earth trembled. The warriors beneath gazed up towards the iron tower. The riot police, prepared to batter skulls, halted in mid-swing. Rune made sacred signs. Meek continued to fill his pockets for the meek shall inherit the earth, after all. Hovis considered bee-keeping on the Sussex Downs. Behind Pooley's left ear a particle of dirt resembled the exact shape of the lost continent of Atlantis.

'I am Choronzon,' cried the voices of Kaleton, the voices of the millions gone forward into the oblivion of yesterday. 'We are the planet's revenge, we will have no more of you. All die.'

'But you first,' said Omally, priming the suitcase and thrusting it into the ghastly void which spread before him, the mouth of hell.

The façade of human resemblance fell away from Kaleton. He was an unearthly shape, an elemental, the bogey man, the nightmare of children, the dreams of the mad, the delirium of the dying. He was all that was opposite, life in reverse. 'You cannot stop us. You cannot reverse the process. A great shot will ring out across the universe. All will die, forever die, be gone. We are your Nemesis!'

Pooley swung down from the catwalk, struck the swelling creature from behind and catapulted it into space. Kaleton flew into the air, a whirling mass of neutrinos, primal flux, ancient evil made flesh, a formless horror that was many forms, many pasts and presents. And somewhere in that hinterland of time, lost between seconds, between yesterday, today and tomorrow, Omally's suitcase exploded. It might have been in Brentford or even anywhere in the unknown world or the partially explored cosmos. But it was within the universe that was Kaleton. Great streamers of trailing sparks spun across the sky, the gasometer rocked and shook, the stadium shuddered and trembled, the air swam with visions, dreams, memories.

Pooley clung to the rocking staircase and saw it all. The world as it was, torn by elemental forces, a battlefield of unreason. Man's ascent from the darkness, towards the glorious future. And he saw much more, the mistakes of generations who had lost their way. The terrible mistakes which had led to this. Pooley saw it all, and it was dead profound, I can tell you. All in the split second, or the lifetime or the eternity, it was all one and the same.

The streaming motes which were Kaleton, Beelzebub, the old serpent, the Grex, rained down upon Brentford. Flowed in a pure golden shower, dissolved and were gone. The stars returned, reason returned. Truth and tomorrow returned.

With a startled cry Jennifer Naylor returned from a deep, dark unknown place and fell into Omally's arms. There was a bit of a hush.

Commander West stood in the now empty Ealing Road wondering where Armageddon just went.

'Shall I cancel the reinforcements?' asked Constable Briant.

In the teepee at the bottom of the garden, Paul Geronimo said, 'It is done, the gods are happy, and now we smoke many pipes.'

'And possibly get some kip,' his brother suggested.

Neville turned once more in his sleep. 'Alison,' he said, 'you naughty girl.'

Inspectre Hovis struggled towards the hastily commandeered ice-cream van with an arm load of gold bars. 'Keep sticking them in,' he told Hugo Rune, 'there's plenty of room in the back.'

'Do I understand that you are taking an early retirement?' the mystic asked.

Professor Slocombe turned his face towards the heavens. 'It is done, I so believe,' said he, 'it is done.'

'Does this mean I am a millionaire?' asked Jim Pooley.

44

A beaming face beamed out across the world. 'This is the London Olympics.'

In the stadium flags flew, athletes marched and the cheering of a million voices rose towards the summer sky, like a prayer of thanks.

In the Professor's study Jim popped the cork from a bottle of champagne. 'Easy does it, Jim,' said the old man. 'That's a hundred-year-old vintage.'

'Put it on the slate,' the lad replied, distributing large libations. 'In five minutes the games begin, in six John and I take a stroll down to Bob's, in the company of the local constabulary. In an hour we shall be gloriously drunk.'

'I will drink to that,' said Omally. 'A toast to the Brentford Olympics.'

'To the games,' said Jim. 'Although not to their founder.'

'Hm.' John sipped champagne. 'That blaggard, what was he, Professor, was he a man or a devil or what?'

'I am not certain even Kaleton knew that. He loathed mankind because he was not of man, thus he had to prove he was greater than man. His character, if indeed he possessed one in the true sense of the word, was one of constant turmoil, a torment of raw conflicts. He was ego, power, good and evil by degree. He denied all human emotion but he was subject to it nevertheless. Egoism, pride, monomania, he craved recognition for his own mad genius.'

'The stadium,' said John.

'Indeed yes, the stadium was to be his apotheosis. I believe that had the stadium taken life it would have been literally unstoppable.'

'Then why didn't he set the thing off last night?'

'His super-ego would not allow it. He wanted the whole world watching when he demonstrated his power. I had to count on this "human" weakness, it was all I had.'

'You took a bit of a chance then,' said Omally.

'I took a good many chances – that Norman's car would work, that you would be in the right place at the right time with your suitcases.'

Pooley looked long and hard at the old man. 'There has been something of a run on happy coincidence lately,' he observed.

Professor Slocombe winked. 'I don't happen to believe in it myself. Drink up, Jim, I'll open another bottle.'

Pooley peered into his glass. 'So Kaleton was not the Soul of the World then?' he asked in a tone which almost amounted to disappointment. Omally gazed at him strangely.

'No, Jim,' said the Professor, dusting off another antique bottle, 'I refuse to believe that. Kaleton was composed of a chaos of organisms, you saw that for yourself. For him to maintain human form, or any other form for that matter, became more and more difficult for him. He knew his time was running out. I believe that Kaleton was somehow a product of the very pollution and decay he loathed so much. The product of many centuries' festering evil made flesh.'

'I hate to say anything in his favour,' Pooley replied, 'but there was a lot of truth in what he said. Great wrong has been done to the planet. Entropy is the order of the day. We've all been part of it, but we've never paid attention. Now no-one will know what he said, nor, I suspect, do anything about it if they did.'

'Good bloody riddance to him,' said Omally.

Pooley shook his head, 'But someone should do something, John, the world is going down the plug-hole, I realize that now. My eyes have been well and truly opened. What if Kaleton was the first of a coming race?

279

He's been a warning. Men must change their ways or pay a high price.'

Professor Slocombe nodded. 'A man of independent means might dedicate himself to such a cause,' he suggested.

'What do you say, Jim?'

Pooley smiled, patted his million-pound pocket and raised his glass for a refill. 'I say yes, Professor. I have much to be thankful for, I say yes.'

'You are a good man, Jim. Perhaps the future will find you to be a great one, although.'

'Although what, Professor?'

'Well,' said the old man, thoughtfully, 'I feel that somewhere there is a loose end. That somehow I have missed something obvious. There are still a lot of unanswered questions.'

'TEMPORA PATET OCCULTA VERITAS,' said John.

'Eh?'

'In time the hidden truth will out,' said Professor Slocombe.

'Perk up,' said Omally, sticking his head out through the french windows. 'Sounds like they're on the starting-blocks.'

High above Brentford the stadium was hushed, upon the rostrum the master of ceremonies raised his starting pistol to begin the first race. All over the world men drew closer to their television sets and held their breath.

'They're under starter's orders,' cried Jim. 'I am rich!'

Chapter the Last

There's never a policeman around when you need one. It's a tradition, or an old charter, or something. The sign on the door of the Brentford nick read 'GONE TO THE GAMES'. And that was that.

'Bloody typical.' Champagne Pooley levelled his boot at the constabulary door, setting off the alarm. But nobody came. The streets were deserted. Everybody had gone the the games.

'Come on,' said Omally. 'Let's get this done. If Bob gives you any trouble, he'll have me to settle with.'

'Well said, that man.'

The two turned away from the abandoned police station and made off up the abandoned Albany Road. They were just passing the abandoned recreation ground when a terrible thought struck them in anything but an abandoned manner.

'Could it just be possible?' asked this thought. 'That Bob the Bookie might choose, rather than pay Jim his winnings, to make away to distant parts, leaving naught behind him but an evil memory?'

Pooley and Omally stopped short in mid stride. John looked at Jim and Jim looked at John.

'Oh no,' gasped Jim. 'Say it isn't so.'

'It isn't so.' Omally broke into a run. Pooley was already way ahead of him.

As they neared Bob's shop on the corner of the Ealing Road, they saw to their shared horror that things were not as they should have been in that particular neck of the Brentford woods.

Several large vans were drawn up outside the bookies. Men in grey overalls were going in and coming out. They were going in empty-handed, but that wasn't the way they were coming out.

'Oh no!' A breathless Pooley skidded to a halt, Omally hard upon his Blakey-sparking heels. A surly-looking gent in a dapper business suit, armed with a clipboard and pen, was supervising the goings-in and comings-out. He offered Pooley a brief and disparaging glance. 'Do you work here?' he asked.

Jim shook his head.

'Then bugger off because *I* am.'

'You what?' Jim drew back his cuffs and knotted his fists. Omally held him back. 'Where is the proprietor?' he enquired.

'Inside.' The surly gent cast an eye over a rare potted lily that a grey-overalled minion was freighting from Bob's shop. He ticked it off on his clipboard. 'Rubber plant,' he said. 'Fiver.' He waved the minion away to the yawning rear door of one of the vans.

'What is going on here?' Omally demanded.

'Repossession. Oi, you!' the surly one yelled across the road to where Leo Felix was cranking Bob's latest Rolls-Royce up the back of his knackered tow truck. 'Careful with the chromework, Chalkie, that car's going to the auction.'

'Come on.' Omally thrust Jim through the open door and into the betting shop. Things didn't look too promising in there. The grey-overalled lads were setting about the premises with a will. Prising pictures from the walls. Rolling up the lino.

Omally grabbed the nearest by his collar and swung him aloft. 'Where is Bob the Bookie?' he spat through seriously gritted teeth.

'In there.' The minion offered shaky thumbings towards Bob's back office.

'Thank you.' Omally let him slide to the floor. 'Follow me, Jim.'

The Irishman took the shop in two long strides and the office door from its hinges with a single well-aimed boot.

And then he stopped. Pooley stumbled forwards and peeped over his friend's broad shoulder.

'Oh dear,' said he. 'Oh dear, oh dear.'

The office was empty of furniture, fixtures and fittings. On the bare boards, in a corner, huddled a cowering, cringing, quaking wreck of a man. It was Bob the Bookie.

Omally gazed down at the human disaster area. He noted well the dishevelled hair, the stubbled chin, the torn shirt collar and the broken finger-nails. 'Bob,' said John. 'Bob, what is happening here?'

The broken bookie turned up red-rimmed eyes to his uninvited guests. 'Oh no!' he wailed. 'No no no.'

'I like not the looks of this fellow,' Jim whispered. 'Let us collect the winnings and take our leave directly.'

'No no no.' The pitch of Bob's voice soared to new heights of tragedy.

'No?' Omally glared down upon him.

'No.' Bob shook his head furiously. 'All of the money. Gone. All gone.'

'*Gone?*'

Pooley tried to say 'gone' also, but the word would not come.

'Gone.' Bob began to gibber. 'All of it. I invested everything I had to cover your winnings. Put it all into The Kaleton Organization. Stocks and shares. A dead cert. Now this morning – gone. The Kaleton Organization has ceased to exist. I'm wiped out. Bankrupt.'

'*Bankrupt?*' Omally was across the room in a flash. And Bob was dragged from the floor and hoisted up the wall. 'All of the money? Jim's millions? You lost it all?'

'All.' Bob's head went bob bob bob.

'No.' Omally gave it a smack. 'Jim deserves his happy ever after. All he's been through. All he's suffered. You won't deny him it.'

'All gone,' Bob burbled. 'No money. All gone.'

'Then you are all gone too.' Omally's eyes narrowed and his hands closed upon the throat of the banjoed bookie.

'John, no.' Pooley found his voice. It was a still small

283

version of its normally robust self. But it was his none the less. 'Let him go, John. Leave him be.'

'Leave him be?' Omally shook Bob all about. 'But it's not fair, Jim. You should win out this time. You *should*.'

Jim shook his head. 'All that money. All those dreams. What can you say? Put him down, John. Put him down.'

'Jim.' Omally let the bookie sink back to the uncarpeted floor. 'Oh, Jim.'

'Let's go.' Pooley turned to take his leave. 'There's nothing for us here.'

'But, Jim . . .' Omally scowled down at the fallen bookie and prepared to put the boot in.

'Leave him alone, John,' said Jim, without looking back. 'Let's go.'

Omally threw up his hands. It was all too much.

'Hold on, Pooley, don't go.' Bob raised himself on a besmutted elbow. 'Wait. Don't go.'

Jim turned in the doorway.

'Pooley, I'm sorry. I'm truly sorry.'

'Forget it.' Jim turned away once more.

'No, wait.' Bob struggled to his knees. 'I want you to have something.'

Jim glanced over his shoulder. 'If it's a tip for the three-thirty, I'm no longer your man. I've given up betting.'

'No, it's this.' Bob fumbled in his jacket. He brought out something shiny and exquisite-looking. 'My new watch. It's not worth a great deal, but I'd like you to have it.'

'How much is it worth?' Omally tore the thing from the outstretched hand.

'A hundred at least.'

'A hundred pounds?'

'A hundred grand,' said Bob. 'I don't wear cheap tat.'

'A hundred thousand pounds?' Pooley sank in the doorway.

'Well, seventy-five at least.'

'We'll take it.' Omally held up the consolation prize.

'And call it all square?'

'All square?' Pooley found his feet.

'The betting slip?' Bob's voice quivered plaintively.

'Oh, that.' Jim took the passport to paradise from his pocket and gazed at it sadly. And then, without a second thought, he tore the thing to shreds.

* * *

'Seventy-five thousand pounds.' Omally admired the watch on his wrist.

'Hand it over.'

Omally grudgingly handed it over. 'I was only looking.'

'Indeed you were.' Pooley strapped his winnings to his own wrist.

They were strolling up the Ealing Road en route to the Flying Swan. They had a certain spring in their step.

'We've come out on top.' Omally thrust out his chest and drew in great draughts of healthy Brentford air. 'We have actually come out on top this time.'

'Perhaps by proxy. Sort of.'

'By proxy? What do you mean?'

'I mean it's owed.' Pooley took a nimble sidestep as Omally leapt at him.

'*Owed?*' Omally floundered in the gutter.

'Owed.' Pooley helped him up. 'To Neville. I said I'd give him seventy-five thousand. He needs it to buy the Swan. The brewery are selling it. Sacking him.'

'Sacking Neville?' Omally took in the enormity of Jim's words. 'Sacking Neville?'

'Kicking him out. Well, we can't have that, can we?' John shook his head freely. No, we certainly could not have *that*.

'So I gave him an IOU,' Pooley went on. 'For seventy-five thousand. Handy this, eh?' He tapped the wristlet watch. 'What a happy ever after.'

'A happy ever after?' Omally sighed. Then he put his arm about the shoulder of his dearest chum. 'You are a good man, Jim Pooley,' said he. 'And I'm proud to call you my friend.'

*   *   *

The two men approached the door of the Flying Swan.

Neither of them actually had the price of a pint in their pockets.

But for today at least, that was hardly going to matter.

And as to tomorrow?

Well, tomorrow's anyone's bet.

Isn't it?

THE END

A SELECTED LIST OF OTHER FANTASY TITLES
AVAILABLE FROM CORGI BOOKS

THE PRICES SHOWN BELOW WERE CORRECT AT THE TIME OF GOING
TO PRESS. HOWEVER TRANSWORLD PUBLISHERS RESERVE THE RIGHT
TO SHOW NEW RETAIL PRICES ON COVERS WHICH MAY DIFFER FROM
THOSE PREVIOUSLY ADVERTISED IN THE TEXT OR ELSEWHERE.

All Transworld titles are available by post from:

Book Service By Post, P.O. Box 29, Douglas, Isle of Man IM99 1BQ

Credit cards accepted. Please telephone 01624 675137,
fax 01624 670923, Internet http://www.bookpost.co.uk or
e-mail: bookshop@enterprise.net for details.

**Free postage and packing in the UK. Overseas customers allow
£1 per book (paperbacks) and £3 per book (hardbacks).**